THIS PLACE OF WONDER

"*This Place of Wonder* is a wonderfully moving tale about four women whose journeys are all connected by one shared love: some are romantic, some are familial, but all are deeply complicated. Dealing with loss, love, hidden secrets, and second chances, this stirring tale is utterly engaging and ultimately hopeful. Set along the rugged California coastline, *This Place of Wonder* will sweep you away with the intoxicating scents, bold flavors, and sweeping views of the region and transport you to a world you won't be in any hurry to leave."

—Colleen Hoover, #1 *New York Times* bestselling author

"Kristin Hannah readers will thoroughly enjoy the family dynamic, especially the mother-daughter relationships."

—*Booklist* (starred review)

"Barbara O'Neal's latest novel is simply delicious. Engrossing, empathetic, and profoundly moving, I savored every sentence of this story of several very different women who find solace and second chances in each other after tragedy (though not before facing some hard truths and, yes, a few rock bottoms). *This Place of Wonder* is one of the best books I've read in a long time."

—Camille Pagán, bestselling author of *Everything Must Go*

"I have never much moved in the elevated circles of California farm-to-table cuisine, but O'Neal makes me feel like I'm there. Rather than simply skewering the pretensions, *This Place of Wonder* pinpoints the passions. Some of these characters have been elevated to celebrity, some are newcomers to the scene, but all are drawn together by the sensuality, the excitement, and ultimately the care that food brings them. Elegiac but also forward-looking, this is a book about eating, but more than that, it's a book about hurt and healing and women finding their way together. I loved every moment of it."

—Julie Powell, author of *Julie & Julia* and *Cleaving*

WRITE MY NAME ACROSS THE SKY

"Barbara O'Neal weaves an irresistible tale of creativity, forgery, family, and the FBI in *Write My Name Across the Sky*. Willow and Sam are fascinating, and their aunt Gloria is my dream of an incorrigible, glamorous older woman."

—Nancy Thayer, bestselling author of *Family Reunion*

"*Write My Name Across the Sky* is an exquisitely crafted novel of three remarkable women from two generations grappling with decisions of the past and the consequences of where those young, impetuous choices have led. A heartfelt story of passion, devotion, and family told as only Barbara O'Neal can."

—Suzanne Redfearn, #1 Amazon bestselling author of *In an Instant*

"With its themes of creativity and art, *Write My Name Across the Sky* is itself like a masterfully executed painting. Using refined brushstrokes, O'Neal builds her vivid, complex characters: three independent women in one family who can't quite come to terms with their fierce feelings of love for one another. O'Neal deftly switches between three points of view, adding layers of family history into this intimate and satisfying study of how women make tough choices between love and creativity and family and freedom."

—Glendy Vanderah, *Washington Post* bestselling
author of *Where the Forest Meets the Stars*

THE LOST GIRLS OF DEVON

ONE OF *TRAVEL + LEISURE*'S MOST ANTICIPATED BOOKS OF SUMMER 2020

"A woman's strange disappearance brings together four strong women who struggle with their relationships, despite their need for one another. Fans of Sarah Addison Allen will appreciate the emphasis on nature and these women's unique gifts in this latest by the author of *When We Believed in Mermaids*."

—*Library Journal* (starred review)

"*The Lost Girls of Devon* draws us into the lives of four generations of women as they come to terms with their relationships and a mysterious tragedy that brings them together. Written in exquisite prose with the added bonus of the small Devon village as a setting, Barbara O'Neal's book will ensnare the reader from the first page, taking us on an emotional journey of love, loss, and betrayal."

—Rhys Bowen, *New York Times* and #1 Kindle bestselling author of
The Tuscan Child, In Farleigh Field, and the Royal Spyness series

"*The Lost Girls of Devon* is one of those novels that grabs you at the beginning with its imagery and rich language and won't let you go. Four generations of women deal with the pain and betrayal of the past, and Barbara O'Neal skillfully leads us to understand all their deepest needs and fears. To read a Barbara O'Neal novel is to fall into a different world—a world of beauty and suspense, of tragedy and redemption. This one, like her others, is spellbinding."

—Maddie Dawson, bestselling author of *A Happy Catastrophe*

WHEN WE BELIEVED IN MERMAIDS

"An emotional story about the relationship between two sisters and the difficulty of facing the truth head-on."

—*Today*

"There's a reason Barbara O'Neal is one of the most decorated authors in fiction. With her trademark lyrical style, she's written a page-turner of the first order. From the very first page, I was drawn into the drama and irresistibly teased along as layers of a family's complicated past were artfully peeled away. Don't miss this masterfully told story of sisters and secrets, damage and redemption, hope and healing."

—Susan Wiggs, #1 *New York Times* bestselling author

"More than a mystery, Barbara O'Neal's *When We Believed in Mermaids* is a story of childhood—and innocence—lost, and the long-hidden secrets, lies, and betrayals two sisters must face in order to make themselves whole as adults. Plunge in and enjoy the intriguing depths of this passionate, lustrous novel, and you just might find yourself believing in mermaids."

—Juliet Blackwell, *New York Times* bestselling author of *The Lost Carousel of Provence*, *Letters from Paris*, and *The Paris Key*

"In *When We Believed in Mermaids*, Barbara O'Neal draws us into the story with her crisp prose, well-drawn settings, and compelling characters, in whom we invest our hearts as we experience the full range of human emotion and, ultimately, celebrate their triumph over the past."
—Grace Greene, author of *The Memory of Butterflies* and the Wildflower House series

"*When We Believed in Mermaids* is a deftly woven tale of two sisters, separated by tragedy and reunited by fate, discovering that the past isn't always what it seems. By turns shattering and life affirming, as luminous and mesmerizing as the sea by which it unfolds, this is a book club essential—definitely one for the shelf!"
—Kerry Anne King, bestselling author of *Whisper Me This*

THE ART OF INHERITING SECRETS

"Great writing, terrific characters, food elements, romance, a touch of intrigue, and more than a few surprises to keep readers guessing."
—*Kirkus Reviews*

"Settle in with tea and biscuits for a charming adventure about inheriting an English manor and the means to restore it. Vivid descriptions and characters that read like best friends will stay with you long after this delightful story has ended."
—Cynthia Ellingsen, bestselling author of *The Lighthouse Keeper*

"*The Art of Inheriting Secrets* is the story of one woman's journey to uncovering her family's hidden past. Set against the backdrop of a sprawling English manor, this book is ripe with mystery. It will have you guessing until the end!"
—Nicole Meier, author of *The House of Bradbury* and *The Girl Made of Clay*

THE
STARFISH
SISTERS

ALSO BY BARBARA O'NEAL

THE
STARFISH
SISTERS

a novel

BARBARA
O'NEAL

LAKE UNION
PUBLISHING

Published by Lake Union Publishing, Seattle

www.apub.com

Amazon, the Amazon logo, and Lake Union Publishing are trademarks of Amazon.com, Inc., or its affiliates.

ISBN-13: 9781662513312 (hardcover)
ISBN-13: 9781542038096 (paperback)
ISBN-13: 9781542038089 (digital)

Cover design by Shasti O'Leary Soudant
Cover image: ©seksan wangkeeree / Shutterstock; ©Nikiparonak / Shutterstock; ©eddie linssen / Alamy Stock Photo / Alamy; ©Carrie Cole / Alamy Stock Photo / Alamy

Printed in the United States of America

First edition

For Amara and Arya and Séamus:
Be mighty.
Be brave.
Be anything you want to be.
Most of all, be yourself, because
you are amazing just as you are.

Prologue

Then

Joel hid in the woods until he saw them drive away in the preacher's white Chevrolet. Suze sat in the back seat, her shaved head so raw and painfully intimate. Her father drove, hands hard on the wheel. If Joel had believed for one second it would help her, he would have flung himself on the hood, holding on to halt them. A wild part of him wanted to do it anyway, give her a chance to run away.

But he'd tried that already. She would only be punished again.

So he waited in the cover of trees until the darkness was complete, then crept from his hiding place and took out the first can of lighter fluid. He squirted it methodically along the base of the church in a complete circle, then soaked the wooden steps.

Inside, he splashed pews randomly, and the aisle, and the window-sills beneath the indifferent geometric stained glass. He didn't hesitate to climb up to the altar, and he took his time, soaking every inch of the pulpit and the floor where the old man stood to preach his lies. His hands shook unexpectedly with a rage and sorrow he feared would devour him. He took a moment to steady himself, imagining the fire consuming the preacher alive. Calmly, he lit a match and flung it on the pulpit. When it caught, he moved without hurry down the center aisle, tossing matches on the pews. By the time he made it to the door, the pulpit was fully engulfed and fire raced along the floor. He took one moment to look back and then walked out, wiping away tears and snot from his face.

He disappeared into the night, hiding in the deep forest until fire leaped high into the sky, orange sparks against the night, taking pride that even though the volunteer fire department made it to the scene in less than ten minutes, it was far, far too late.

SIX MONTHS AGO

SUZE OGDEN TARGET OF BRUTAL ATTACK BY LNB

LOS ANGELES (AP)—Suze Ogden, the Oscar- and Emmy Award–winning actress, was severely beaten in front of her home in the Hollywood Hills early this morning. Camera footage showed two assailants, but no perpetrators have been apprehended. The Leviathan Nationalist Brotherhood, LNB, a hate group that has targeted a number of high-profile women in recent years, has claimed responsibility.

Ogden is best known for her role as Julia Brandeis in the historical drama *A Woman for the Ages*, a role that won worldwide acclaim, including an Oscar for best actress. She currently plays the steely and conflicted matriarch Alice Peterson in *Going Home Again*.

The LNB has targeted celebrities, media stars, and politicians they have declared enemies of the state. Last year they claimed responsibility for the death of first-year senator Nadine Truelove, one of the youngest politicians to ever serve as a California senator. Ogden has been outspoken in her criticism of the arm of evangelical Christianity in which she grew up, which has drawn the ire of more than the LNB.

A spokesperson for the trauma unit at Cedars-Sinai Medical Center said Ogden was rushed into surgery and her prognosis is unclear. At the moment, she remains in a medically induced coma, in critical condition.

CURRENT DAY

Chapter One
Phoebe

Suze arrives home in the middle of the night, when there is less chance of anyone noticing her arrival. I know she's coming because she texted me yesterday, one of the first communications we've had since I left her in the hospital after she was brutally attacked last spring. She's been my best friend since we were twelve, but a lot has happened over those years. Most recently, we had a massive fight at my grandmother's funeral last year, and both of us said things that should never have been spoken aloud. I wasn't sure I'd ever talk to her again.

And yet—

Six months ago, a radical group called the Leviathan Nationalist Brotherhood attacked her outside her home and nearly beat her to death. How could I abandon her to lie in a hospital with only hangers-on and people she pays? Since Dmitri died, she's been a hermit. I took the first flight to LA and sat by her side until she finally woke up. She squeezed my hand and thanked me and then told me it was okay if I went home.

So I did, swallowing the rejection I probably deserved.

And now she's home. Things are . . . complicated between us. I miss her. I resent her. She infuriates me. She needs me.

This morning, I'm up early to get some painting time in before life overtakes me. As I stand at my kitchen counter, waiting for the kettle to boil, I rest one foot over the other and nibble a slice of freshly baked cranberry bread. It's tender and dense, redolent with orange, one of the best batches I've made for a while. Maybe I'll take some up to Suze later.

The urge exasperates me. No matter what happens between us, I can't seem to shake this compulsion to take care of her. As my grandmother did before me.

To be fair, my grandmother also took care of me and everyone else. Shut-ins. Recovering addicts. The elderly in her church. Young mothers. She had a gift for it. Not the self-sacrificing, old-school kind of caretaking, but a matter-of-fact recognition that we all need love and tending. She didn't chop bits of herself off and give them up to others, as I've been known to do.

I peer out the window. From here, I can see the big house on top of the bluff. Lights are on, both in the foyer and the kitchen, which has wraparound windows that face south and west to display the best ocean views for thirty-seven miles, views of sea stacks and rocks and wild surf, the small coves hidden everywhere.

Our house. A song of the same name floats through my mind, delicate as mist. The house I discovered when we were kids, the house Suze bought out from under me, the house that has become her refuge, and how can I resent that?

Except sometimes I still do, even though I have my own refuge in this house and the studio I inherited from my grandmother.

The kettle whistles. I pour water over the Golden Eyebrow tea leaves in my cup, set the timer on my phone to let it brew. Break off another bite of cranberry bread.

She's home. I'm both longing to run up the hill to see her for myself and reluctant. Afraid of rejection, if I'm honest.

I also know she's a wreck, both physically and mentally, and needed to get out of the fishbowl she lives in.

What better spot to retreat to than the rare Frank Lloyd Wright masterpiece that sits empty almost all the time? It's kept shining and perfect by a crew of cleaners and gardeners and handymen I manage for her. When she first bought it, she begged me to do the job because she trusts me. Because of our history, because of all the things, I agreed. As with so much of my connection to Suze, I'm of two minds on the task. It gives me pleasure to be in the house I've loved since we were children, to run my hands over the gleaming wood (which, to be fair, she paid a fortune to have lovingly restored) and gaze out the windows at the glorious view of the rocky Oregon coast.

It also makes me feel like a servant in a way.

Suze. Suzanne. A thousand memories of her face move through my mind, at so many ages and stages—the girl with absurdly long braids who wandered onto the beach one day when we were twelve; the tortured teenager who was cloistered away by her terrible, terrible father; the struggling actress; the movie star. She's as fey as the Leonard Cohen song of the same name, as enchanting and elusive as sprites or faeries.

She's just so *beautiful*. Beautiful like a royal. Even that first summer we met, when she was skinny and ate every minute of the day, as if she were feeding a roaring furnace, and her hair was ridiculously, foolishly long, it was hard not to stare at her. Her face was strong, big nose and wide mouth and oversize eyes of a color I'd never seen before and haven't seen since, not quite blue, not quite green, like the curve of a wave rising to break—light-struck and impossible to ignore. When she turned those eyes on you, it was hypnotic. She hypnotized me, and all the guys, and then the world.

Never my grandmother, who said Suze was lost.

Now she's back, and again broken even though she says she's not. In my opinion, it started with the untimely death of her partner, Dmitri. He was an early victim of COVID, and died alone in his ICU room. It wrecked her. As it would anyone, but especially a woman who waited such a long time to find love.

I look up to the bluff. Lights have come on in the living room. I should go see her.

But rather than walking up the hill, I shrug into my rain jacket, pick up my oversize cup, and whistle for my dog, Maui. He's a big black shepherd mix with shaggy, soft fur and the joyful heart of a three-year-old boy. My granddaughter named him for the character in *Moana*, and it suits his goofy nature. "Let's go to the studio, buddy."

Chapter Two

Suze

The first time I ever earned any real money, I bought a house, because Beryl, Phoebe's grandmother, told me you can never go wrong with real estate.

Until that moment I'd lived a hardscrabble existence, first with my father, who never allowed me any money, then later trying to break into Broadway, waiting tables and scrambling for whatever parts I could get. But when I was twenty-one, I was cast as the lead in a very big film, *A Woman for the Ages*. Everything changed. I suddenly had so much money it seemed impossible to spend it all. Beryl advised me to buy a house, so I bought a cottage in Bel Air, and it started me off on the right foot. Two decades later, Phoebe was on a quest to save this place from ruin, and I bought it. To help her, honestly, though she didn't see it that way.

Still, it's one of my favorite investments and, at the moment, a refuge. The fact is, I had to get out of LA. I need to heal, and my therapist has been urging me to come here for several months. Last week, when I found myself rounding my house in Hollywood to check the windows for the fifth time, I realized I wasn't going to regain my sense of safety living where the attack took place. So I'm here.

From the window over my sink, I can see Phoebe moving around in the studio. It's such an open expanse of windows that anyone at the right angle could see in, but it's really only my house that faces that direction.

She's backlit by a floor lamp I can't see but know has a mica shade. She's wearing a long red sweater beneath her apron, taping paper to the battered, paint-stained table that takes up most of the middle of the room.

How many hours did we spend there, joyfully drawing and painting and talking? Beryl played music on a turntable in the corner, and wiggled her ample hips as she painted delicate feathers and trees and creatures of both land and sea. She always had paint in her hair, on her hands. Once she had a streak of turquoise above her elbow for a week, and laughed her head off when Phoebe finally asked, "Are you ever gonna wash that off?"

A pang twists my heart. I miss her so much. She's been gone only a little over a year, and it was hard on Phoebe. It was also hard on me, a fact that sparked the worst fight we ever had.

I met Beryl before I met Phoebe.

My dad was a preacher, a die-hard fire-and-brimstone type, who took over the Pentecostal church in Blue Cove, hoping to finally get the congregation he felt he deserved. It did finally come true for him here, but not for a while, not until Karen Armstrong got her hooks into him. It took her a couple of years.

My mama died when I was eight, of a virulent breast cancer that showed up and killed her over the course of six months. When she died she took all the softness and kindness of my world with her, leaving me with my father, harsh and dry as a moonscape, a man who only really cared about preaching.

He was an evangelical long before it was called that. He listened to Billy Graham and Oral Roberts and considered them a bit too soft. He called his churches the Blood of Christ, every single one of them, from Eden, Mississippi, to Rifle, Colorado, and Holder, Nevada, then finally Oregon. His specialty was reviving churches with declining membership, building them up, then being "called" to the next one. They were always small, off some big highway. The only difference in Blue Cove was the high tourist traffic, which he played to his advantage.

The church in Oregon came with a house, a sweet little two-story Victorian. It was plain, with a living room, dining room, and kitchen on the main floor and three bedrooms upstairs. My room had windows that looked out over the dunes to the ocean and the rocks, so I heard it crashing all day and all night, a steadiness that made me feel whole. In the spring, lilacs bloomed in clouds all over town and made the world smell like a department store.

The church itself was a white-framed building with a proper steeple and stained-glass windows all down each side. A steeple rose at the front, and he loved it as if it were his very own special signal tower to the heavens.

When we arrived I'd just turned twelve, and got my period three days later. There was no chance in hell I would tell him, so I stole a five-dollar bill out of his stash and took myself down to the local market, which was not a supermarket back then, not even close, but big enough I felt like I could buy pads without much notice.

But standing there, in front of all the options I froze. My underwear was stuffed with toilet paper and I was afraid it might soak through, but my face got hotter and hotter as I stood there, bewildered by the choices. So many different kinds! And tampons, too, but I didn't quite get how that all worked.

I missed my mother wildly, wishing ghost stories could be real so I could ask her this one thing.

A woman in a floaty blouse and jeans stopped beside me. Her hair was long, salt and pepper, tied back in a messy ponytail. There was paint on her hands. "You need some help, sweetheart?"

I looked at her, then away, petrified. My voice was gone, but I managed to jerk my head into a kind of nod.

"Let's see here." She chose a box. "These should do. They have adhesive so they stick to your underwear. I'm a long ways past my bleeding days, but I'm guessing this small size will work just fine."

I hugged the box to my chest and looked at her in gratitude. Her eyes were big and pale blue. Another streak of paint hung on her earlobe, and for some reason, it made it easier.

"You all right?" she asked.

15

I nodded.

"You just moved here with the preacher, right?"

Another nod.

"My name is Beryl Axford. I live in the house with the purple door down at the end of the road. You need anything, you come find me." She smiled. "I have a granddaughter your age. She'll be here in a couple of weeks. Maybe you'll be friends."

"Thank you."

"You have money to pay?"

"Yeah."

She patted my shoulder and left me.

Now, on a rainy day decades later, I press my forehead against the cold glass. Headaches have been my constant companion since the attack. The cold eases this one a little. I long for the studio space where Phoebe is moving around. It seems like I might be able to breathe there.

Across the span of dunes, Phoebe stands by the window of the studio in her red sweater, drinking coffee. I'm wearing a thick white sweater myself. It's cold and drizzly, the sea a restless dark gray. I watch for a long time, hoping Phoebe will send me a sign, but she never looks up.

Eventually, I move away from the window, into the kitchen. It's a Frank Lloyd Wright house, at least nominally, built by one of his assistants from plans FLW drew, and it is as extraordinary as that implies, with built-ins and acres of wood and glass meant to frame the views. When I bought it, it had been abandoned since the '60s, was rumored to be haunted, and was in danger of being torn down by the city. It had needed a lot of rehab—a long, expensive task—but I loved it madly. More to the point at the moment, I feel safe here, sequestered away from the world on the Oregon coast. It's my refuge.

I'm no purist, not like Phoebe would have been. She wouldn't have hung the paintings and drawings and photos of sea stars and anemones that I've been collecting all these years; instead she would have kept to the spirit of the house in some totally appropriate way. I don't even know what I mean by that, exactly. Maxfield Parrish prints? Architectural drawings?

But I love my choices. A watercolor of a tide pool hangs beside the window with fat pink and orange sea stars clinging to the rocks. The colors are soft, the lines easy, blurry, much like many others I've picked up at art shows here and there. I don't invest in art so much as collect the things I love, and in the process support struggling artists. Acting is not the easiest life, but it beats dragging around to parks and fairgrounds all spring and summer, hawking your wares.

Or maybe that's not fair. Maybe it just sounds like torture to me. For all the fame my work has brought, I don't love talking to strangers. My upbringing was so weird that I'm always sure I'm getting something wrong. It makes me reticent, if not exactly shy.

Which then is interpreted as my being stuck-up.

The drizzle is easing. A shimmer of light breaks through the clouds and fingers the tiny forest atop the trio of sea stacks called Starfish Sisters. I think of swimming between them as a girl, Phoebe diving to find treasures of all kinds and bring them up to show me, since I would not touch them with my own hands, then diving to put them back.

From the table I look down at the studio, but I can't see her now. The weight of things I need to tell her fills my gut with a mix of apprehension. I've kept so many secrets I should never have kept, and when I was lying in that hospital room after the beating, wondering if I might really die, I knew I had to confess them.

But how? How can I tell her the truth after decades of being silent?

This was always *her* house. She was the one who found it and dragged me back up the bluff to see it, standing empty and ghostly with the dusty furniture still in place and all the dishes, beautiful pieces made of pale-green glass. I didn't know then that they were Depression glass, but I do now, and I still have some of them. Back in the day Phoebe found a way in through a window in the back, and we took picnic lunches to eat on the vast, multilayered decks. We played house by the flagstone fireplace and imagined the guests we would host in the beautiful space. Here we envisioned the lives we wanted to build for ourselves, Phoebe a famous artist, me a famous actress.

I tuck my cardigan closer around me, feeling a pang.

The things you don't know when you're young could break you into a million pieces if you let them.

On the beach, birds are gathering meals, chattering to each other. I suddenly long for fresh air. An easy walk will do me some good, and while I was having trouble leaving the house in LA, here I can see for miles in either direction. No one can sneak up on me. No one even knows I'm here.

I take the stairs down to the beach and find I can take a deep breath for the first time in months. A couple with a dog walks far ahead in the distance, but mostly it's me and the birds. Phoebe could tell you every one of their names, taught by her grandmother, a great naturalist. I know seagulls and murres and some of the biggest prey birds, like eagles, but not all of them.

But I don't need to know their names to admire them. The gulls shine white in the patches of sunlight, bright against the muted blue water of the creek flowing out of the mountains. They ride the current down toward the sea, grooming their feathers and squawking, splashing in pleasure, then fly up and start over, like children going down a slide.

It gives me peace. My headache, almost constant since the attack, eases slightly. I breathe in the salt air.

~

I met Phoebe on this very beach. Early summer, right after my dad took over the church. The day was overcast, threatening rain, too cold for the Portland tourists who mobbed the place on summer weekends.

Phoebe was a scrawny girl, so skinny you could see the individual bones of her knees. Her dark hair was scraped back into a knot on the top of her head that dripped pieces of hair down her freckled face. A lot of freckles, actually—freckles across her nose and sprinkled down her arms and over her chest.

But all I cared about was that she looked like she was my age. She was the only person on the beach, bent over a tide pool, peering. "Hi," I said.

She looked up. "Hi."

"What's your name?" I asked.

"Phoebe. What's yours?"

"Suzanne. I'm twelve."

"Me too." Her eyes were a pretty color, green and gold, like the tide pool itself. "Where do you live?"

Reluctantly, I glanced toward the bluff that hid the town from us. "Behind the First Pentecostal Church."

"Oh." I couldn't tell if that meant she knew my dad was the preacher. "I'm here visiting my grandma," she said. "I come every summer."

"Does she live in a house with a purple door?"

She grinned. "You know her?"

"We met at the grocery store. She was really nice to me."

Phoebe nodded.

I peered into the water. "Whatcha looking at?"

"All kinds of things—anemones and sea stars and mussels. Oooh"—she pointed—"see the periwinkle?"

I hadn't lived by the ocean before, and all I saw were a bunch of things stuck to the rocks, but I didn't want to look stupid. "Cool." Something caught my eye in the water, a rippling movement. "Hey, what's that?"

"Wait!" She bent in close. "Holy cow! It's an octopus! Maybe it got stuck."

"Will it be okay?"

"I don't know." She looked toward the edge of the water, swirling against flat sand. "The tide is going out."

"But it comes back, right?"

She bit her lip. "Yeah, but maybe not for hours."

"My dad always says it's better to leave nature alone, let it do what it's supposed to do."

Phoebe straightened. "That's right." She reached a finger into the water and stroked the tiny octopus as if it were a cat. It moved, swayed, swirled, but didn't seem particularly alarmed. "Do you want to try?"

A primal shudder moved along my shoulders. I didn't like the idea of sticking my bare hand in the water at all. Who knew what lurked in there? "No, thanks."

She didn't seem to need me to talk, which was a relief. She pointed and squatted and peered, and I hung with her, trying to not look like a complete idiot.

After a while, she straightened and seemed to really see me. "You have the longest hair I've ever seen."

My braids nearly reached my knees. "I'm not allowed to cut it."

"Why?"

"If a woman have long hair," I quoted, "it is a glory to her, for her hair is given her for a covering." At her blank look, I added, "The Bible. My dad's a preacher."

"Oh. My grandma goes to the Methodist church. She makes me go to Sunday school sometimes. Is your dad Methodist?"

I shook my head. "Pentecostal."

She blinked. "You know, you could be Rapunzel."

"I like that."

She brushed her hands together, shedding dark sand. "You want to come to my grandma's house for lunch? Bologna, probably."

The closed doors of the world blew open. "Sure," I said, like it didn't matter much.

But oh, it did.

Did it ever.

Chapter Three
Phoebe

The morning is drizzly, but the path runs through a pine forest that offers some protection. Drops splat against the hood of my raincoat and against my nose, and I remember hurrying behind my grandmother on days like this, her galoshes sending out splashes of mud, my own smaller ones wading through the puddles on purpose. Now mine are the big feet, and my granddaughter, Jasmine, has the smaller ones.

Jasmine. She's ten and still mighty, a grasshopper of a girl with wild hair. Even this tiny thought of her lifts my spirits. She'll be here later this afternoon, to stay with me while her mother finds a place for them to live.

In London.

A pain stabs my lungs. So very far away. Portland is far enough. I don't know how I'll bear London. It isn't the distance, and of course I want her to have the experiences she'll have there—but how often will I see Jasmine? Will it fray our relationship? We've been as close as skin and bone since she was born, one of the great gifts of my life. Motherhood is a dangerous journey, full of pitfalls and terrors. Grandmotherhood is more a dance on a summer evening, full of love and hope. Or at least that's how it feels to me.

Water drips from tree branches onto my head as we wind around a small bluff and end at a square building tucked beneath a shelter of old trees. I unlock the blue-painted door, letting it swing open into the space I love more than any other on earth. The mingled scent of oil paint and damp wood strikes my sinuses, easing the muscles along my neck. I close the door behind me. Maui shakes the rain from his coat, then trots over to his bed in the corner and falls down with a huff.

This was my grandmother's studio before it was mine. Her second husband built it for her, a robust structure nestled for safety into the earthen side of the hill to protect it from the harsh elements. That wall against the mountain is solid wood covered with corkboard. Some of my grandmother's sketches still hang there, birds and trees, the detail of a butterfly wing, the branch of a long-needle pine. She was a naturalist and painted what she loved, all the things that sing and howl and sway in the wind.

My paintings and sketches and ideas, old and new, hang there, too. Snippets of a new fabric design, a contracted illustration for an article due next week, my starts and experiments. Jasmine has started adding her pieces as well—girls and cats with an anime feel, faces with giant eyes.

I've added a laptop for editing software, and a heavy-duty printer, which rests on a desk by the window, somewhat safe from water and paint.

In this room, I am fully myself. Here, I am a maker, an artist with a vision of the world that is entirely my own. Here, surrounded by color and memory and paper of a thousand sorts, and paintbrushes and pencils, and rolls of butcher paper to cover the solid walnut table in the middle of the room, I am me, Phoebe the Maker. I take a breath, let it go.

The view is centering. Spectacular. Opposite the corkboard is a wall of windows that overlook the sea, straight north along the rocky coast. Waves endlessly interact with rocks and cliff and shore. A cluster of three tall stacks, the Starfish Sisters, offers habitat for birds and seals, and along the top of the tallest is a patch of forest two feet wide, like hair. It's a tourist mecca in the summertime, but now, when the rains have arrived, we have it mostly to ourselves again.

Wrapping my body in an apron, I center myself with the scene, the one that inspired *The Starfish Sisters*, which is my picture book about two girls who love the tide pools, published six years ago. It hit the *New York Times* bestseller list for months and continues to do very well. At its heart, it is a love song to my friendship with Suze. With two fingers, I touch the cover of the book, standing on a shelf so I can have it close by. One of my biggest accomplishments, and a healing one.

But now, it's time for work. Pushing up my sleeves, I settle in.

For as long as I can remember, I've seen the world in terms of color: the sky—today cerulean, now light blue, now deepest gray—and flowers, peach and pale magenta and scarlet and that vivid, vibratory hot pink that almost buzzes under a cloudy sky. The gradations of rain clouds, the variations of tossing waves under many weathers. Color fills me, calms me, gives me an exit from this mundane world into one made of shimmer and blaze.

I'm lost in my painting when a knock sounds at the door. The work is shades of pink and magenta and green, branches and flowers and leaves winding their way across a background of jaune yellow, a very pale shade that makes me think of milky sunlight falling through a window to the floor. I love pink, every shade of it, from orangey hues like peach and coral to the vivid fluorescent hot pinks and into the purply orchids. Pink can be delicate or bold, sexy or innocent or happy. I've always loved it, much to my mother's despair. She hated that I loved pink and flowers and fairy tales and princesses. She wanted me to be tough, intellectual, sharp. Like her.

The dahlias my grandmother grew on the farm she left to me—that theoretically I now grow—are the model for my free-form design today.

I'm sitting at the table, intently and delicately layering dusky bluish pink into the throats of petals, so deeply focused that when the knock shatters my concentration, I literally jump.

Lifting my head in confusion, I peer toward the door, trying to come back from the place on the other side, wherever it is that my mind goes when I get into the flow. Music is playing softly from the speakers, Enya and Loreena McKennitt. Sunlight pokes through clouds in a couple of places.

The knock sounds again. Is it Suze? Maybe. If she comes to me, it will be easier somehow. I wipe my brush. "Come in."

The person who swings around the door is not Suze. It's Ben, the farm manager. He leans in, dark hair and a black beard streaked with white. "Is this a bad time?"

His face is always welcome. "Not at all."

He steps in and closes the door behind him. He's a solid man. Broad shoulders, strong thighs, a little belly beneath his shearling jacket. Big and sturdy.

I hired Ben last spring to manage the farm that my grandmother inherited from her father and ran brilliantly for decades. It's four acres of blossoms starting with daffodils in the spring, then lilies and dahlias in the summer. A manager had taken care of it for a long time, and when he died, I had to replace him ASAP. Ben applied. I'd known him distantly as a teen—he grew up here but spent his life in Africa and other far-flung locations helping build field systems for farmers in poverty-stricken places. He came back a year ago, after his wife died a couple of years before. Like me, he had inherited property in the area, in his case an alpaca farm he sold to a local family, keeping only the house and a few acres for himself.

He walks to the windows and runs a finger along a seam. "Any leaks?"

"No. It's at least twenty degrees warmer in here." One of his projects—there are many—was to install better windows in the studio before the rains come. "I can't imagine you ever do anything that isn't perfect."

He's still testing the seal with a thumb, tapping in a couple of places. "I've had my share of messes."

"Yeah?" I swirl my brush in mineral spirits, rub it again, distantly wondering if I should dive back in when he leaves or pause and get some lunch. In response, my ignored stomach growls. "What time is it?"

"Just after two."

"Ah. That explains my growling stomach." I toss the brush down on the battered wooden table, scarred and stained a multitude of colors. "What's up?"

He turns, and my artist self notices the way light falls on his face. Pale swaths gloss his straight nose, edge his lower lip, fuller than the top. His eyes are always a little twinkly, as if he's going to tell you a secret that will make you laugh. I have the feeling that he's mulling something over, and then he shakes his head. "Just checking on the windows. The rainy season is on us."

I nod, wipe the rest of my brushes clean, and toss them into a bucket. "You hungry? I'm going to make a BLT for lunch." We've become good friends over the past few months, unified by the weirdness of coming back after such a long time, and age and proximity.

"I could eat. Do you have any of those homemade pickles?"

"I do." Smiling, I scrub my hands at the sink, but even after a second round, orange stains my cuticles from the poppies I've been painting. "And the oolong tea you like."

"Excellent." His attention is captured by something outside. "Is that Suze? Is she back?"

I cross the room to stand beside him. She's on the beach, standing there with her hands in her pockets, her trademark hair flying in the breeze. Worry and hope mingle in my body. A lot of things in her life have tried to break her, but this last one seems to almost have succeeded.

I don't know what's happening between us, but seeing her sparks something in my chest. Hurt, resentment. Longing. "She is."

"She's had a pretty hard time."

"Yes." A flash of the news video about her beating rips through my gut. "It will help to be home. She's safe here."

"Doesn't the press follow her?"

I shrug. "They used to. Not so much anymore."

"Really?" He's frowning, watching her, his hands in his pockets, and I feel a tiny ripple of disappointment. Like everybody else, he's dazzled by her fame, even though we both knew her before. "Because . . . ?"

I give him a wry, slightly bitter smile. "She's not a sexy hot girl anymore."

"But isn't this the biggest show she's ever been on?"

"She plays a grandmother."

He looks at me, and the force of those pale-blue eyes strikes me. If I painted them, what color would I use? Phthalo blue mixed with flake white until it was very, very light. "So? Why would that matter?"

I laugh. Men are not touched by ageism the way women are, at least not until they're a lot older than he is. As someone said, "Men don't age better than women, they're just allowed to age."

We stand there a little longer and he starts to say something. "Phoebe . . ."

I wait, but he shakes his head. "Never mind."

"Sure? I'm in no hurry."

He smiles, maybe a little sadly, and I feel that thing happen, that soft puff of yearning that can still catch me at times.

But Ben is way out of my league. Once upon a time, for about twelve minutes, I had a body that could stop a clock, but these days I very much look like the grandmother I am, soft and hippy and so very ordinary. "Come on, let's go eat before I fall over in a dead faint."

We reach the back door of my house and slip out of our boots, padding inside in woolen socks. I reach for the kettle, but he says, "Let me. I'm working on my tea game."

"Be my guest."

I gather things for sandwiches, the fresh pickles, the bacon and tomatoes, bread. There's leftover bean soup from dinner last night. In the narrow space between counters and fridge and stove, Ben and I weave easily, used to the dance. He gets out a ceramic teapot and cups and the small teaspoons I like, a gift from Suze once upon a time, when she filmed a movie in England.

Ben is a widower, and an easy guy to be around because of it. There's no sex on the table, no unspoken dialogue to navigate. Every so often we bump, and we hardly even say sorry anymore. It's been so nice to have him around, all the companionship and ease of a long relationship with none of the tension.

"When does Jasmine arrive?" he asks, plucking a pickle from the bowl.

"Her mom worked today, so it won't be until late afternoon."

"Will Stephanie stay overnight here?"

"No, I think she has a flight in the morning from Portland." I slice the sandwiches in half and put each one on a plate, thinking I have plenty of time to go over and say hi to Suze before they arrive. Anxiety sparks along my neck. We have left things in such disarray.

The kettle clicks off. I watch as he measures the loose tea, his hands large and competent, tanned from being outside all the time. For the first time I notice that his ring finger is bare. It's been long enough that the stripe has disappeared. "I didn't realize you'd taken off your ring."

He spreads his fingers, looks at the empty spot. "It was time. She's been gone three years."

"Be careful," I tease. "Once the grapevine gets hold of that, you'll be inundated with casseroles and brownies."

He looks at me. "Is that what this is?" He points to the plates and bowls and pickles. "Seduction?"

"No!" A hot, hard blush rises up my neck. "We're friends."

A flicker of something dims the light in his eyes. "I know." He claps my arm, right above the elbow. "Sorry, I was teasing. I didn't mean to embarrass you."

"It's okay." I bow my head, willing the heat to leave my ears. "I've always hated this blush."

"It's charming."

"When you're twelve."

Thankfully, he lets it go and we carry everything to the table, covered by an ancient oilcloth left by my grandmother. As we sit down, he says, "For the record, I had a pretty bad crush on you back in the day."

I give him a skeptical glance. "No one had a crush on *me*. It was always Suze."

"Not me. I liked you."

"Really?" That soft, rustling awareness moves through me again. Maybe he's not completely out of my league, then?

"Really." He takes a hearty bite of his sandwich and chases it with tea. "You were stuck on Joel, that guy who burned the church down."

"I can't believe you remember that." My cheeks flame.

He nods.

"Pathetic." I shake my head. "God, I was so smitten! What happens to girls, I wonder? Up until I was about twelve, I was such a tomboy, and I didn't care what anybody thought of me. And then"—I sigh—"puberty turned me into a needy mess."

"It wasn't just you." His eyes are warm, resting on my face with something that looks like appreciation. "We all felt that way. For about five years, I thought about breasts pretty consistently every two or three seconds."

I burst out laughing. "That's a lot."

He nods. "Tell me about it."

"Kissing," I say. "That's what I thought about, a hundred times a day. I would sit in classes and imagine all kinds of ways I could kiss somebody." I take a bite, relishing the salt of bacon with tangy mayo, remembering.

"Hormones," he says with a sigh.

"Amen." I look up and there's something hot in the air that makes me think about how it would feel to *kiss* him, feel that beard against my chin. Would it be soft or springy? It looks soft.

"Are you thinking about kissing, Phoebe?" he says with a twinkle in his eye. "Because you've never been able to hide that blush."

I lift my chin. "I was remembering."

"Me too," he says. "You had a little blue halter top, with sparkly things on it."

It pops into my mind, a beautiful thing made of green and blue fabric with sequins laced on it in little patterns. Suze, with her clever fingers, made it for me, and I loved how I felt in it. "It wasn't that little."

He grins. "I wanted it to be littler."

"Tsk, tsk." A silence falls and I'm thinking about being fifteen and kissing and that top. "That was a hard summer." Especially for Suze, who was sent away to an unwed mothers' home, her head shaved, her life in tatters. I glance toward the window, up the hill. "I guess I should go see her."

Ben's eyes are calm. "You should."

THEN

You've Got a Friend

Phoebe

I spent summers in Blue Cove with my grandmother because my parents both had full-time jobs. My mom was a lawyer, hence our very nice house with a pool. My dad was a professor at a private university and often did research in the summer. He invited me to tag along, but I only wanted to go back to Amma's house.

At the end of every summer, I had to go home to Portland. I always hated leaving Amma, going back to the city, but the summer I met Suze, I was bereft. The world would be so lonely without her.

We spent the day before I left playing on the beach, having a picnic my grandmother packed for us. Sitting on a gingham tablecloth, wearing bathing suits—hers a one-piece my grandmother bought her because she didn't have one of her own, mine a blue bikini with little gold dolphins that was one of my favorite things in the world—we ate peanut butter and honey sandwiches and single boxes of raisins and tangerines. Between us were the hours and hours we'd spent together collecting shells, drawing in Amma's studio, eating, telling each other stories.

"This is the best summer I've ever had," Suze said, her knees up so she could rest her face on them. "I hate that you have to live in Portland."

I leaned into her shoulder, and our heads nested. "I never had a best friend before."

"Me either."

Waves crashed playfully on the row of low rocks. The day was warm and sunny, and the beach was full of people cramming one more weekend of happiness in before summer was over and the rains came. "Let's write letters every day."

She lifted her head. "That's a great idea! Except I don't know if I can get stamps."

"My grandma will help us." I warmed to the idea. "Let's go to Rexall and get stationery on the way home."

Two hours later, we wandered the old drugstore with its wooden floors, looking at boxes of stationery. "These are pretty," I said, pulling a box off the shelf. "Smell. Lilacs."

She frowned. "Too fancy." She liked some with piano keys on the bottom of each page. "We don't have to get the same ones."

"I only have five dollars." It was always me who paid for things—Suze never had any money.

"Oh yeah. Good point."

Right next to the stationery boxes was a row of diaries. I spied one with a blue plastic cover with a tiny key. "Hey!" I said, picking it up. "What if we share the diary? I'll write in it for a few days and then send it to you, and you can write in it and send it back."

Her face lit up. "I love this idea!"

So it began.

August 29, 19—

Dear Suze,

My mom told me I have to turn off the light in twenty minutes, so I'll write fast. She took me to the library today and I checked out ten books. It's been so rainy I will have time to read all of them even with homework.

I already started GO ASK ALICE, and it is really really good.

I hate being home! It's so noisy and I can't hear the ocean, only cars, and I miss you so so so so so so so so so so so so so much! My parents are fighting and they think I can't hear them, but I can. It makes me scared. I think they might get a divorce. If that happens, I will only live with my dad or my grandma. Maybe I could live with my grandma all the time and then we can go to school together in Blue Cove instead of me at Pine Hill, where nobody likes me and they all think I'm weird.

Anyway, I'm sad. I'm going to read a book.

Love,

Phoebe

August 31, 19—

Dear Suze,

I have to tell you about this book. GO ASK ALICE. It's so sad! About this girl who gets addicted to drugs and all the things she goes through. I read it in one day, and I cried and cried and cried. I wish you could read it, too. Maybe they have it at the Blue Cove library.

My mom left on a business trip for a week, so it's just me and my dad. I like it this way. We have TV dinners or sometimes we go out to eat. This morning, he took me to eat breakfast at this little café where they have jukeboxes on the table. I had elderberry pancakes and bacon, and my dad had blueberry pancakes, which are his favorite and my mom doesn't like him to eat them because she says he's getting fat. He was happy and talked to the waitress and made her laugh and told me about this time when he was a little boy and tried to catch a seagull and it pooped on his head.

I hope this isn't too boring, but I promised to write, so I am.

Write back!

Love,

Phoebe

Suze

It was a rainy, horrible day, but Beryl called to let me know the diary had come from Phoebe, so I huddled into my raincoat and my rubber boots and walked the half mile there after school.

Beryl flung open the door when I knocked. A cinnamon-scented cloud of steam escaped. "Come in, come in!" she cried.

I shook off my coat in the foyer and left my boots and followed her into the kitchen.

"I made cinnamon rolls," she said. "They're almost ready. Are you hungry?"

"Yes!" I climbed up on the stool at the kitchen counter, feeling all my troubles and tensions fall away to the floor, as they always did in this room.

Beryl wore a thick blue-and-white sweater, and her hair was tightly braided in a rope that fell over her shoulder. She poured milk into a red tin glass without my asking and set it down in front of me. "How's school going?"

I shrugged. "Everybody thinks I'm weird, so I don't really have any friends."

She leaned on the counter with one hand, the other propped on her hip. "Is that true? That everybody thinks you're weird?"

I gestured to my stupid dress that came to the middle of my shins. "Weird clothes. Weird hair. Preacher dad."

She stroked my face with both hands. "So pretty."

It warmed me. In truth, Beryl provided the warmth in my world. My father was hard and cold and punishing, a fact I tried to keep to myself. "Thanks." I lifted my head. "I do have one friend. His name is Joel. Nobody likes him, either, because he's new like me."

"Is that right? Tell me about him." She pulled the cinnamon rolls out of the oven, giant and fluffy, and while they were still hot, she spread thin orange-flavored frosting over the top.

My mouth watered, but I said, "Well, he's friendly and saves me a place at the lunch table, and never says a word about my weird clothes. He's really smart, I think, because the teachers all call on him and he always knows the answer."

"He sounds like a pretty good friend."

"The other kids are mean to him, too," I say, wiggling my fork in my hand. "He has really bad acne."

"That must be rough." She settles the pastry in front of me. "Bring him over sometime."

"Yeah! He likes to draw."

Beryl sat down next to me and bent in to smell the cinnamon roll. "That's a good scent, isn't it?"

"Yes," I said. It was the fragrance of love. After we finished, she brought me the diary and as always hugged me before I left. I swear, I lived for those hugs—her softness and the solidity of her arms, the smell of paint and spice and some layer of powder or something I couldn't name. She didn't rush. Her cheek rested on my head, and she rocked me ever so slightly back and forth, like I mattered.

September 8, 19—
Dear Phoebe,
    I picked up the diary today from your grandma's house. It was the first time I could go over there since you left, since my dad is getting ready for the anniversary week of the church, and I had to help the ladies of the church clean everything. We even washed under the pews! It was so gross. Mrs. Armstrong was there, bossing everybody around, and I know she likes my dad! She's gross. She wears a girdle!
    I asked your grandma to check if GO ASK ALICE is in the library, and she said she would. I found some books to read at the school library, and Beryl is keeping them in her house for me, and I snuck one into my room to read at night, THE TROUBLE-MAKER. Have you read it? It's so good, about this guy who is kind of an outcast and plays guitar.
    I miss you so much! School is awful. I wish I had something to wear that didn't make me look so stupid, but my dad says girls have to be modest. I'm sick of doing all the things his way. I don't think Jesus would care if I wore modern clothes!
    I'm taking home ec and maybe I can learn to sew good enough to make me something else. We looked at patterns today that the teacher has, and she told us to go to the fabric store and see what we like. I might walk over there after school tomorrow. My dad can't get mad if it's for school.
    When do you get to come back?

Love,
Suze

October 1, 19—

Dear Phoebe,

I FORGOT—don't ever say you're boring. I like how you think about things, like REALLY think about them, and you don't talk about shallow ordinary things, but always important stuff like books and ideas and art. I never read too much before I met you. Now, in less than one year, I've read 52 books! That's huge! I feel so much smarter.

I wish I didn't have to leave them at Grandma's house. (She told me to call her Grandma, because Beryl doesn't sound right coming from me.) At least I can have them there, though, and sometimes I sneak one home in the back of my underwear. You can't see it under my hair.

School here isn't great either. I'm friends with one person, Joel, who is weird, too. He's Coos Indian on his dad's side, but he lives with his mom here. She works as a receptionist at the Sleepy Cove motel, and I can tell she doesn't like me, and not even because my dad's a Pentecostal preacher, but because I'm me. Joel just moved here, too. He seems sad. We walk all over, talking and not talking. I think you would like him. He likes art, too.

I love the new books you sent. THANK YOU! I'm reading MISTRESS OF MELLYN.

Love,
Suze

October 2, 19—

Dear Phoebe,

I'm dedicated to writing here every single day if I can at all. I didn't know that writing would make me feel so calm, but it does, so thanks for that. It feels orderly to write down what I'm thinking.

Today I had to help cook for a church board meeting, and I burned the potatoes because I was daydreaming and my dad was *so mad*. He waited until everybody was gone, but then I had to cut a switch and he used it on me. My thighs hurt so bad I can't even sit down. I didn't cry, though. He can't make me cry even if he uses it a hundred times, but that would be hard. It was only twenty and I thought I would die by the end. Twenty stripes on my legs.

I used to love my dad.

Love,

Suze

October 3, 19—

I had to smear Vaseline all over the back of my legs to stop the stinging, and then my dress stuck to my legs and Nancy Gorton made fun of me at lunch. She really hates me for some reason. I was so embarrassed that I ran out of the lunchroom without eating, and Joel brought me some of his lunch, an apple and a milk and some cookies. I didn't tell him about my dad whipping me. It's too humiliating. Don't tell anyone and don't feel sorry for me. I'm going to grow up and get out of here and do SOMETHING IMPORTANT.

October 4, 19—

GO ASK ALICE is so sad! I cried so much my hair was wet. I wish I could save her, like I wanted to save Anne Frank.

I just realized both of those girls died. Let's not die! That would be terrible, for our diary to end like that.

Joel brought me some salve from his mom. He didn't say anything, just gave it to me. When I put it on the stripes, it really helped.

October 5, 19—

Dear Phoebe,

My dad took me to the mall in Seaside to buy some new shoes and then we went to Jo-Anns and I bought some pretty fabric, white with little blue dots on it, kinda airy and nice. The pattern is pretty boring, but I don't care. If I learn to sew, I can make my own stuff and my dad won't even know about it.

My dad has his men's prayer meeting tonight, so I'm taking the diary to Grandma to mail back to you. I can't wait to see you at Thanksgiving!

Love,

Suze

CURRENT DAY

Chapter Four
Suze

I walk the beach for an hour, turning around only when the rains return and start to pepper my raincoat. I'm still feeling shaky and tired, weirdly unable to find my footing after—

Oh, after everything.

When I was a kid, I always wondered what it meant to have a nervous breakdown—like, did you shake nervously? We have different words for it now, like "panic attacks." "PTSD." "Anxiety." "Depressive syndrome." So many diagnoses. My body was the part of me that was wounded, but my mind felt equally battered. Surprising after so many things could have wrecked me, but the attack in my own front yard was the trauma that broke the camel's back.

Breathing the beach air helps. I walk slowly, admiring the crash of waves into the rocks, the spray that spits high into the air. The water is turquoise in the shallows, dark gray out toward the horizon. Even noticing this tiny detail eases the muscles along the back of my neck. I think of Mary Oliver, exhorting us to go outside when we're in despair. Under my breath, I recite "Wild Geese," a poem I memorized to give myself comfort.

My energy is flagging and I head back up the bluff. The stairs are wood, seven flights broken by small landings. At each stop, I turn and look back over the ocean. In the distance, a trail of dolphins makes its leaping way along a cresting wave, and a peregrine falcon sails over the top of the stacks, seeking lunch among the murres, who fly away in terror at a gull's warning. It's cold and damp, but the air feels good in my lungs. Healing.

The stairs end between two houses, one a recent sleek glass design, the other a '70s build with the rafters and rectangular windows so prevalent in that period—a fact I would not know if Phoebe hadn't talked about architecture at least 40 percent of the time when we hiked up here to visit "our" house.

I let myself in and toss the keys on the table in the foyer.

Now what?

The silence that greets me is total. At my house in the Hollywood Hills, a small crew of people is often around—a housekeeper who comes five days a week and a chef who leaves prepared meals in my fridge, an assistant who handles everything from media requests to massage appointments, gardeners who tend the drought-friendly landscaping. There are others, specific to the season and task.

Here, the silence is deafening, the only sound the roar of the ocean. Cleaners do come twice a week, and I'm sure I'll find a meal service, but it will probably be delivery. In the absence of noise and bustle, I'm left with only myself and my thoughts, which seem chaotic and restless, bouncing from one thing to the next like a pinball.

My giant, long-haired Himalayan Ragdoll cat, Yul Brynner, wanders out and meows at me.

"I know. I've got you, babe." I stroke his silky head. "Let's get a snack."

I wander into the kitchen, think about a cup of tea, decide against it. Wander into the living room with its shelves and shelves of books and run my fingers over their spines. They're actual books I've actually read, not pretend titles lined up by color. Phoebe has always been a bookworm, and she got me started on the habit back in the day with stacks of Scholastic Book Club paperbacks she stored for me at Beryl's house.

Her house now, I guess. From my kitchen window, I peer out, but the studio looks empty.

Like me. Like my heart, which has no desires in it, no longings. I don't care if I ever act again. The character who has so revived my career in recent years is languishing in a hospital in a coma, and as far as I'm concerned, she can go ahead and die, and I'll be done with it, with the long hours and the constant pressure to look good, keep my weight down, be polite in interviews about things that don't matter at all.

This ennui has been brewing for a while, honestly. My longtime partner, Dmitri, a Greek director who swept into my world when I was long past expectations of a partnership, died of COVID. Like everyone else I was shaken by the pandemic, and then Beryl died a year later. Phoebe and I fought viciously at the funeral, leaving yet another hole.

The doorbell, sudden and unexpected, makes me jump a foot. I rush to the door, hoping, and when I see Phoebe standing there in a soft pink jacket, with a loaf of sweet bread in her hands, my heart starts to beat again. I want to hug her, hard, rock back and forth, but an invisible wall keeps me from doing it. Our friendship is not where it was. My trust is not where it was. Even after the attack, our connection has been quite tenuous, mostly texts with a phone call here and there.

Still. "Phoebe. Come in."

"I brought you some cranberry bread."

"Yum. Come in the kitchen. I'll make some tea."

"That sounds good." Her hair is cut in a straight line along her shoulder blades, dark brown still with only a few threads of white. She was always going to be thick in the hips and thighs, like Beryl, and time has proved that truth. This shadow shape makes me miss Beryl.

"I saw you walking on the beach," Phoebe says. "How was it? See anything good?"

"Yeah. The sea stars are coming back a little, aren't they? I saw a beautiful rose-colored one." As I enter the kitchen, I point. "And dolphins. They're still out there."

She sets the bread, still in a glass pan, on the counter. "I figured you can eat carbs for a while, right?"

I laugh without humor. "May as well. Pretty sure my career is dead."

"Eh, you don't know."

Silence falls between us, and I feel the awkwardness of knowing she's on a duty visit. Our friendship, once so deep and sustaining, has frayed so badly I barely recognize the garment.

That doesn't mean I don't miss her. "Look—" I say.

"Suze, I know—"

We both halt, wait. I fold my arms over my chest. "Thank you for coming to the hospital. It meant a lot to me."

She nods. "Of course. And"—she swallows—"I'm sorry about the fight."

"Me too."

"Truce?"

"Yes." It doesn't really solve the trouble between us and both of us know it, but it's something.

We settle at the built-in corner table, with its views of the wide, open sea. "How are things?" I ask, pushing the milk pitcher toward her. "The flower farm? Jasmine? I see that the book is still on the lists." I'm really proud of her work, although I was deeply wounded when she asked someone else to write the text, not me, as we always planned. "Quite an accomplishment."

"Thanks." She stirs cream into her mug, tilts her head, and looks at me. "Is that what you want to talk about?"

I shift my gaze to the view. "I don't know."

"How about we start with how *you're* doing?"

"I'm fine."

Phoebe smiles. "No, I don't think so."

"Okay, I mean, maybe not *fine* fine, but okay. Stable, I guess." A weight of discomfort presses on my chest. "You don't have to take care of me, if that's what you're wondering."

"I wasn't planning on it."

I feel the sting of that in my cheekbones. "Sorry."

"You don't have to apologize, Suze. Eat some bread." She cuts a slice and hands it to me on a paper towel. I see that same hand over the years—the girl, the teenager, the young mom—offering me cranberry bread, tuna sandwiches, books. "The flower farm is doing very well," she says, returning to my conversational gambit, "thanks to Ben Thomas. Remember him? He was a year younger than us."

I frown, trying to pull him up. "Dark hair, kinda chubby?"

She grins. "That's him. He's managing the farm. I hired him when Old Man Durgen dropped dead last spring."

"That's good." I bite into the bread, and an explosion of pleasure bursts in my mouth. "Jeez, Phoebe," I say with my mouth full. "This is ridiculously delicious."

"Amazing how good sugar tastes, huh?"

I nod fervently, shoving more in my mouth. Tart cranberries, sweet orange in the glaze. It's nirvana.

"Jasmine is coming today. It's her favorite."

Safe ground. "You must be so happy. Odd time of year for her to stay, though, isn't it?"

"I'm happy she's coming, but not for the reason." She takes a breath, and I feel the misery in her before she continues, "Stephanie has been offered a job in London." Her voice is calm, but her eyes fill with tears. She slaps them away with impatience. "She's going to find them a place to live."

"Oh, honey!" Jasmine is her *heart*. I reach for her hand and stop just in time. She still pulls her arm back, out of reach. "I'm sorry."

She shakes her head, folds her hands in her lap tightly. "This is harder than I thought. I'm sorry. Maybe I can't pretend things are normal. That *we* are normal."

"Seriously, Phoebe?" I narrow my eyes. "Why do you always do this? Give me love with one hand and take it back with the other?"

She stands, her mouth tight. "This was a mistake."

I feel winded. Unconsciously, I touch my chest, right in the middle, and to my horror, tears well up in my eyes and fall down my face as if I'm six. It's humiliating, but they don't stop. I expect her to roll her eyes and storm out.

Instead, she softens, then wraps herself around me, tugging me close, stroking my hair. "Oh, Suze, I'm so mean. You bring out the mean in me."

"I always have," I say, but her arms feel so good that I lean into her, taking comfort in the round of her shoulder, the faintly vanilla smell of her. She rocks me, just as I had hoped, and I wonder if I've manipulated her or if my emotion was real. Does it even matter?

I have no idea.

"Come to dinner tonight," she says, letting me go, but before she does, she strokes my hair in a familiar way. "Jasmine will keep us from getting too weird."

"Really?"

"Yes. I know you'll want to see her."

I nod. "Thank you."

A pause. In it, I feel our history—the diaries and promises, her art school days and my first movie. Joel, always.

"Okay." She lets me go. "I have to get down the hill. Come over around six, I guess."

"Do you want me to bring anything?"

She raises a brow. "Did you suddenly start cooking?"

When I left my father's house, I vowed never to cook again, and I haven't, aside from the wild spree during the pandemic.

"Ha." I wipe my face with the heel of my palm.

In that liminal moment, she touches my cheek. "You look like shit."

"Thank you."

"Are you sleeping?"

"No. Almost never."

She nods. Drops her hand. "Okay, I'll see you at six." Pointing to the bread, she adds, "Eat at least two slices."

Which means she's noticed my wristbones. "Promise."

She leaves, but a moment later, the doorbell rings. I open the door, and she looks sick to her stomach. "There's a dead squirrel out here. I don't know how I missed it before."

On my front porch step is a dead squirrel. It has been sliced from throat to tail. Entrails spill from its belly. Bile rises in my throat and I have to step urgently to the side of the poor squirrel to barf over the edge of the porch, which means I have to see it again as I turn back. "You couldn't have missed that." I look around. "Someone just put it there."

She bends over. "It's cold."

"It was probably killed somewhere else and brought here."

"Why do you say that?"

I point. "No blood." I press my hand over my belly. "You can go. I'll call the police."

"I'll stay until they get here. Let's go inside."

A fine trembling has started beneath my skin, and it infuriates me. "Let's look around, see if we see anything."

"Don't be ridiculous." She takes me by the arm and pushes me inside.

Chapter Five
Phoebe

The police think we're being alarmist, which infuriates me. "Look at the cut down the belly!"

The young deputy, blond hair cut into what we would have called a crew cut when I was a kid, shakes his head. "It could have been dropped by an animal. You said you found it when you came out? Maybe you scared it away."

"What animal?" I push. "What makes a cut that neat?"

He shrugs. "I don't know, ma'am. Any number of them, honestly."

Suze touches my elbow. "Thank you," she says to him.

"We'll make a note of it." He shifts his attention to Suze, who stands beside me. "I read about the attack in LA, Ms. Ogden, and I'm sure that's made you jumpy, but I reckon this is some critter who's lost his prize."

She nods.

"Nothing to be worried about." He tips his imaginary hat. "But you call us if you have any more trouble."

"Little lady," I mutter under my breath, but he's already on his way.

At least Suze snorts in appreciation. "Well, we couldn't possibly know anything, being so ancient and all."

I sigh. This makes me feel sick to my stomach. "Make sure you keep the doors locked."

"Thanks. I'll see you in a little while."

Stephanie and Jasmine arrive as I'm walking back down the driveway. Jasmine rolls down the window and cries out, "Nana!"

"Hey!" I wave as the car slowly moves by me and stops in the circular drive in front of the house. A cluster of Douglas firs drip water on the car, and Stephanie backs up to get away from them. The instant the engine clicks off, Jasmine is out of the car and flinging herself into my embrace, all grasshopper arms and legs. She closes her eyes and trusts me to catch her, because I always do, always will, and she melts into a boneless weight against my body. Her clouds of hair tickle my nose and she goes completely limp, her head on my chest. She smells of brown sugar. "Nana. I'm *so* glad I'm here."

I was just this way with my grandmother, and I'm filled with a purity of love and gratitude that's unlike any other emotion I've ever felt. "Me too." I kiss her head and she regains the shape of a girl. "I made some cranberry bread. It's on the counter."

"Not until you help us lug all this stuff upstairs," Stephanie says.

Jasmine huffs. "Fine."

My daughter, Stephanie, emerges with more dignity, pushing her glasses up on her head. She's what we once would have called statuesque, though I haven't heard anyone use that word in a long time—almost six feet tall, with a curvy figure, big breasts and broad hips, and thighs to carry her twenty miles a day if need be. Girls now own that body, wearing leggings to show off their curves, their tiny waists, but the body-positive movement came too late for Steph. Her wardrobe is unremarkable, very professional, suits and slacks and blouses designed to hide her bustiness. She keeps her blonde hair trimmed precisely to her shoulders and spends quite a lot of money on good cosmetics to enhance her gorgeous face—big eyes, wide mouth, great cheekbones. In many ways, she reminds me of my mother. Both lawyers. Both no-nonsense. Both too stubborn to do well in marriage. Stephanie has been divorced since Jasmine was in utero, and hasn't let anyone else close. Her ex was a football player who went pro, and she had no patience for the lifestyle.

"Hello, Mom," she says, bending to kiss my cheek, then unlocks the trunk. "She pretty much brought everything."

That arrow of dread goes through my lungs again. She brought everything because they'll be moving when Stephanie gets back. "I suppose that saves some time. Let's get it all inside."

Jasmine's room is the one I used to live in, a cozy pine-paneled space at the back of the second floor, overlooking a forest grove. A window seat with cushions occupies the dormer, and one entire wall is lined with bookshelves. I stack boxes in one corner while Stephanie clops up the stairs and deposits a suitcase in front of the chest of drawers that's been there as long as I can remember, sturdy wood painted a dozen times over the decades, and all the colors show in the chips and worn places. Jasmine drags two garbage bags into the room, opens one, and dumps the contents out on the bed. Her collection of stuffed animals tumbles out, approximately 750. I laugh. "Where will you sleep?"

She blinks. "With you. Obviously."

"No," Stephanie says. "We had that conversation. You're a big girl. You don't need to sleep with Nana anymore."

"But I like it." She dances over to me and slides her arms around my waist. Her head nearly reaches my chin. When did that happen?

"We'll work it out," I say. "Do you want to stay for dinner, Steph?"

She shakes her head. "No, I need to get back on the road. My flight leaves early tomorrow."

I study her, feeling her pushing me away. "Sure?"

"I'm sure, Mom." She shakes her head, like I'm a nag.

"Okay," I say as mildly as possible. She's stressed to the gills and I am almost sure to make it worse.

We all clatter back down the wooden stairs, Maui leading the way, pausing every few steps to look back over his shoulders. "We're coming," I say, exasperated. "Go."

He races the rest of the way down and whirls around, waiting for Jasmine, who falls to her knees and scrubs his chest. "Such a good dog, yes, you are."

Stephanie hesitates in the living room, her manicured hand tapping her smart watch. Her gaze is on Jasmine, and I glimpse a rare snippet of uncertainty.

In the pause, I offer, "Have a cup of coffee."

"Sure. I can do that."

I head into the big kitchen. It's dated, with '80s oak cupboards and a dropped ceiling I'd love to get rid of, but the light is good from a giant window that looks toward the forest. A big island makes the space usable. It's a homey room, meant for a serious cook. A couple of years ago, Stephanie gave me a Keurig for Christmas along with a bunch of compostable pods, and although I had resisted for ages, I have to admit I love the damned thing. I take her favorite mug, hefty with a seafoam glaze, from the shelf and start the machine. "Everything ready to go?"

She slides onto a chair at the island. "I hope so. The movers are coming to box it up next week and I won't be here, so—"

"I'm sure it's perfection," I say, and slide a saucer with cranberry bread toward her. She waves a hand in refusal, but I leave it there. "You must be so excited."

She glances at Jasmine, playing tug-of-war with Maui. "Yes. It's a really big opportunity and I've always wanted to live abroad." She pinches off a bit of sweet bread. Shrugs. "Just—I don't know."

I don't dare touch her hand and send her skittering off behind her walls. When she was a teen, I learned to talk about important things in the car or while I was doing some other task. This afternoon, I give her coffee, the packets of sweetener I keep for her, and the milk. "It's a big thing. You'd be inhuman if you didn't have a few nerves."

"I didn't say I was nervous," she snaps. "It's a lot."

I nod mildly, casting about for something safe that might also help her express her feelings. "Such an adventure! London!"

She prepares her coffee precisely and takes a sip. Then: "What if I hate it?" More quietly: "What if Jasmine hates it?"

"I don't think either of those things will happen," I say, "but if they do, you can make a different decision."

"I feel like I'm ripping her away from you."

I let go of a soft laugh. "Well, because you are. But we'll all be okay. I'll come visit. By then, you'll know where all the best pubs are."

"But I don't even drink! What am I going to do in pubs? In a culture that revolves around pubs?"

Finally, she's getting real. "You go to bars with your friends here. What do you do then?"

She sucks her upper lip into her mouth, a habit she's had since youngest childhood, and sighs. "I know. I'm worried that I'm being rash."

"You've never done a rash thing in your life." This time I do touch her hand. "What if you totally *love* it?"

Jasmine climbs into the chair beside her mother and leans on her arm. "I'm going to miss you," she says. "It's so far away."

"Aw. My girl." Stephanie lifts her arm so Jasmine can lean into her shoulder, and kisses her head. "You can call me anytime, okay? *Any*time. I will pick up."

"What if you're asleep?"

"Call back."

"Can we have a cat when we get there?"

Steph chuckles. "Maybe."

Jasmine smiles and lifts her face for a kiss, which Steph drops on her nose. In this, she is not like my mother at all. Sylvia was not affectionate. She wasn't hostile, but she didn't like to cuddle and I did. Luckily, my father and grandmother made up for it.

The doorbell rings, and Maui leaps to his feet, barking.

"Come in!" I call.

Stephanie says, "It's so weird that you live like that, never locking your door."

Suze peeks around the door. "Am I interrupting?"

"Auntie Suze!" Jasmine cries, and flies across the room. "You're home! Are you staying? Are you just visiting?"

"I'm staying for a little while." Suze scoops her up into a hug. "Oh, it's so good to see you, beautiful girl!"

"Want some coffee?" I ask.

"Sure." Tangled in Jasmine, she walks with the bouncing girl into the kitchen. "Hi, Steph," she says, and drops a kiss on her head. "You look fantastic, as ever."

"Thank you. So do you."

"Auntie Suze!" Jasmine says, leaning on the counter. "I saw you on TikTok!"

"What were you doing on TikTok?" Stephanie says. "I told you not to go there."

"It was at Ashley's house. Just for a minute, and we were practicing the TikTok dance, and then I saw Auntie Suze, and then I had to watch." She plants her palms on the counter and lifts herself up until her feet dangle. "Are you okay?"

"Yes." Suze tangles her hand in Jasmine's long, curly ponytail, touches her nape. "Thanks for worrying about me, but I'm good."

"And they said somebody beat you up—"

"Jasmine," Stephanie says, sharply.

In an echo of her mother, Jasmine sucks her top lip into her mouth. "Sorry."

Stephanie says, "Go get your iPad and bring it to me."

"It wasn't on my iPad! It was on Ashley's."

"Now."

She huffs. "Fine."

Stephanie waits until Jasmine is upstairs. "I am so sorry, Suze. She doesn't get it, but I'm sorry you—"

"It's really fine." Suze shakes her head.

Stephanie is blushing slightly. She's dazzled by Suze's celebrity even when she knows it's silly, that she's known her all her life. But she wants to do things right even more when Suze is around than she usually does, and that's a pretty tall order.

And it's not like it isn't easy to be dazzled by my old friend, even now, when she's wearing jeans and a long-sleeved Henley T-shirt and no makeup whatsoever. In the even northern light of the window, she's illuminated, the elegant swoop of cheekbones and jaw, those aqua eyes, her still-lush mouth. We're the same age, so I know she must have done a few things—eyelids, maybe, and her jaw, something to erase the lines on her décolletage. She's stunningly, staggeringly beautiful, as she always has been. There have been many times over the years that I envied the power that beauty commanded, but it never lingers. I've also seen the torture it has conjured in her life. People want to own beauty, make it their own, ruin it if they can't possess it.

In such simple clothing, her gauntness is accentuated. Her collarbones look ready to set sail. She's always been a person who lost weight under trying circumstances, something I try not to envy.

Instead, it triggers my wish to take care of her. "You're staying for dinner, right?" Maybe Stephanie will stay if she knows Suze will be here.

"Oh, yes, please. I haven't had a home-cooked meal in ages."

"I made chicken tortilla soup." Stephanie shakes her head, and I add, "I saved some of the base before I added chicken so Jasmine won't starve." The girl has gone vegetarian the past year, part of her transformation into an eco-warrior. "Sure you can't have a bowl of soup?"

She looks at her watch, then at the window, which is showing plenty of light. "I can have some."

Suze almost winks at me, and I'm grateful, at least in this moment, for her presence.

Jasmine absolutely loves setting the table—she loves eating at the dinner table, as a family, more than almost anything. We devour soup and freshly fried tortilla strips, Suze and I carefully skirting anything important. Stephanie asks what Suze knows about London, and she offers a few pointers along with her phone number.

Halfway through dinner, Jasmine says, "Did you know this is a tsunami zone? Where would we go if we heard the warning?"

"She's been deep into tsunamis the past few weeks," Steph says. "They had a section on them in school. Emergency preparedness week."

"Tsunamis wouldn't make it to Portland," I say. "There are mountains in between."

"Yes," Jasmine says, "that's correct. But it *is* a tsunami zone here. Where would we go?"

I crumble tortilla strips into my soup. "Where do you think we should go?"

"Straight out the front and up the hill."

"Very good."

"But it's really steep. How would we climb? Especially if, like, it's raining or something?"

"That's a good question," I say. "We can do a trial run if you want."

"Maybe I do," she says. "Did you know that a tsunami from Japan reached Oregon after the earthquake in 2011?"

"I didn't know that!" Suze exclaims. I suspect she does know, but this is why Jasmine loves her. Like my grandmother, and very unlike me, Suze has a gift for loving people as they are. "Did it do any damage?"

Jasmine is only too happy to fill her in, and then Suze brings out her jewel. "You know," she says, "I was in Sri Lanka when that really big tsunami hit."

"What? You were? Did you get hurt?"

"No, I was really lucky. I was filming a movie and we were high in the jungle when it happened. Our hotel was completely wiped out."

"I remember that!" I cry, and an echo of the painful worry I felt when the whole place went off the grid runs down my spine.

Steph scowls. "Maybe—uh—careful?"

"No!" Jasmine protests. "I'm not a baby, Mom."

"We can talk about it another time," Suze says, and she's instantly apologetic. There's something deferential in the angle of her head, and the way she crumbles a tortilla strip between two fingers. I haven't seen this in years, and it makes me furious with her brutal father, with the people who attacked her, the media who've made her life a misery at times.

"It's fine, Suze," I say, frowning a little at my daughter. "I'm sure Jasmine heard all about it at school."

"I did! Can I go get my notebook? I have all the details in there."

Her mother nods, wearily. "Sure." When Jasmine has bolted upstairs again, she says, "She's so full of everything right now. She carries this notebook with her everywhere—school, swimming lessons, the grocery store, everywhere."

"It's exhausting to be a working single parent," I say, but see immediately that it's exactly the wrong comment. She can be so prickly and defensive. I don't know where it came from. Then again, maybe that's me, too. Not that I like admitting it.

"Oh, yeah, Mom, as I was always very aware."

"Steph. That's not what—"

"Whatever. I really do need to go." She pushes back from the table.

Suze covers Steph's hand. "Finish your soup, darling girl. Your mom didn't mean anything."

Steph settles. Gives me an apologetic look. "Sorry, I'm just . . . freaked."

"I know."

Jasmine sails from the foot of the stairs to the table, notebook in hand. "Okay! This is about the tsunami in Japan." She regales us with a dozen bullet-point details.

"That's amazing," I say. "It reached all the way to Oregon!"

"But the big problem is, there's a really big fault off the coast of Oregon, and when it has its next earthquake—"

"Okay!" Steph says, raising both hands. "That's enough. I've got to get going, and I don't want to have earthquakes and tsunamis in my head while I drive."

Jasmine pouts. "I was just telling you. They taught us in *school.*"

"I know, baby," Steph says. "I have a lot to think about. Can you write it down and send me a letter?"

She shrugs. "I guess."

Steph blots her lips with a napkin, then pushes back her chair, and all at once my heart aches hard, in worry and loss and a million other mother things. She won't be gone that long this time, only a few weeks, but then she'll be gone for ages and very far away and I hate that idea so much, even as I know it's a great opportunity. Her expression is blank, which means she's feeling all kinds of things she doesn't want to feel. "I'm off, then," she says, standing.

"We'll walk you to your car." I hold out my hand to Jasmine, but she has tears in her eyes suddenly, and flings her skinny self into her mother's body.

"I don't want you to go!"

Steph breaks ever so slightly, tears welling in her eyes, too, before she can blink them away. She curls around her daughter, kissing her head and then just resting her cheek against her hair. "It won't be long, sweetheart. You love being at Nana's house."

"I want you to live here, too. I want us both to live here, not far away in London."

"I know," she says, not disputing it, or arguing, or presenting all the good reasons it will be great, just validating Jasmine's feelings. "I promise there will be things you love about our new house, too, okay?"

"Okay." Jasmine nods and pulls away.

Steph rubs her back and looks at me. "I'll walk myself out."

So they don't have to do it all again. I nod. "Give me a hug."

She wraps me up in a big hug, too, strong arms and soft shoulders and a fierce squeeze. "I'll call you when I land tomorrow."

"Text me tonight when you get home."

"Yes, that too."

She starts to pull away and I say quietly, "She'll be okay."

"I know."

And then she's gone. Standing in the doorway, I feel a hollowing out, a sadness that plagues me every time I have to part with her. Or Jasmine. It started when I was a child and forced to leave Amma every summer, and it got worse when I had to leave Suze. It always feels like some important thing is being ripped out of my body.

Chapter Six

Suze

The house scares me. It used to be completely by itself up here, empty and lonely. Now there are other houses, too, but I feel scared anyway. Vulnerable. Too many windows and doors, too many ways for someone to get in. Yul Brynner and I are curled in bed, and I've done all my nighttime rituals—no devices for an hour, washed my face, meditated—but I'm still lying here in the dark, hearing things.

The wind is blowing, so that's probably why I hear creaking and slamming and all the other terrifying noises I log in my book of terrors. Yul purrs beside me, low and soft and comforting, but if someone broke in, would they hurt him, too?

As happens so often, a visceral memory of the attack suddenly arrives and reels out in perfect detail.

Someone had thrown a bag of trash onto my sidewalk, and muttering under my breath, I padded outside to pick it up and dispose of it properly.

It was a beautiful morning, just after dawn, and I admired the way pinkish light brightened the cream walls of my neighbor's house across the street. Jacarandas bloomed on both sides of the street, soft purple, so pretty and strange, like Dr. Seuss had planted the trees in LA.

I felt good, thanks to a new yoga teacher, who was helping me work out the kinks in my aging back and hips, and a regimen of cannabis chocolate at bedtime. The world was quiet aside from a pair of finches chirping in the boxwood hedges that bounded the property, and I took a moment to stretch in gratitude, thankful for my soft pajamas and bright, fancy silk robe and the new haircut that had taken off so much extra weight.

Every detail is seared into my memory. Feeling so peaceful.

They must have been crouched behind the bushes, because I didn't even see anyone before the first blow landed, something hard across my upper back, knocking me to the ground. My palms dug into the earth, and another blow landed against my head. I cried out, covered my face and ears as feet slammed into me, into my ribs, into my skull. I scrambled to my feet, screaming at the top of my voice, but somebody yanked me by my hair and I hit the ground again. A fist or a foot or something landed in my belly, doubling me over, and another hit my head, and then—

Nothing.

Sweat soaks my back, and exasperated, I fling the covers off my body and turn on the lamp by my bed. It casts deep shadows in the corners, and I get up to turn the overhead light on, too. Compulsively—I know it's compulsive and yet I can't stop, which is I guess the definition—I round the entire house turning on lights and opening closet doors to make sure they're empty of malevolent humans. I check the doors. All locked and bolted. Yul Brynner tags along, curious, his tail in the air.

I thought it would be better here, but it appears my anxiety has followed me, fully clothed, after finding the squirrel.

Assured of momentary safety, I go to the kitchen and turn on the kettle. When Phoebe and I were in our early twenties, I lived in LA and she was going to art school in Seattle, so both of us were swamped and unsure of where our lives were going. We kept our connection by sharing books and ideas via letters and the rare, expensive phone call.

One of the books we read was about tea, the multitudes of styles and ceremonies, and we spent the entire year experimenting with various infusions, and black and green teas. Both of us now eschew coffee for the more nuanced (in our opinion) layers of tea.

My stock is a bit weary, but I find an herbal blend of chamomile and peach bits. The scent eases my tension, and I stand at the counter waiting for it, looking down the dark coast. A light is on in the studio, but I know Phoebe must have left it on. She wouldn't leave Jasmine alone.

The light serves to reveal the space, however: the big table in the middle of the room, the easels, the faded carpet. The windows must be new, because I don't remember them being so clear or solid.

On the table is artwork of some kind, but I can't see the details from here. The sight of it makes me ache, ache for the sense of belonging I found there, with Beryl and Phoebe, and sometimes Joel.

Joel. Being here makes me miss him, even if it's been decades since we were so forcibly parted. I wonder where he is, how his life has unfolded after he went to juvie for burning down my dad's church. It couldn't have been easy for him as a youth of color, in what basically amounted to prison for teens.

I move my head in a circle, loosening my neck. Joel. My father. That terrible—

No. There are enough issues I need to resolve without going back to all that.

But maybe I should go back to painting and drawing. Beryl taught both Phoebe and me, and while art became her career and I haven't picked up a pencil to draw in decades, I did always enjoy it. Not as a career—early on, I knew I wanted to act. We thought we would move to New York City and find an apartment and become famous and always stay best friends.

I did go to New York. Phoebe went to Seattle for art school, but never finished. By then, I'd spent years in school plays and had an eye toward Broadway.

Instead, a casting director for a new movie saw me in a waiting room and asked if I'd come to LA to test for a part. Which turned out to be the lead in a movie about a young woman striving against all odds to outwit her brutal father and live a bigger life in eighteenth-century England. It had been a wildly popular novel, and the search for the right person to play the part had been all over entertainment news. Phoebe and I had hotly discussed it several times ourselves, but neither of us dreamed it would be me.

But I brought everything I had to the role, and was uniquely prepared, after all. It was a hit. My career was made.

Just like that, people said. So lucky. Everybody loves a pretty girl.

Phoebe dropped out of art school in her third year to get married. We fought about it for months, with me pleading for her to at least finish and her insisting she really wasn't good enough to be a fine artist and retreating into the arms of the admittedly gorgeous but awful Derek, her husband and Stephanie's father. Everything I predicted about him and how he'd wreck her life turned out to be true, but I would never say that to her.

Although, really, I guess I had, in that last, spectacular fight.

Sipping my tea, cat winding around my feet, I'm okay. I'm back in my body, not my memories. When the phone buzzes on the counter, I jump three feet.

It can only be one person. No one else can get through.

"Phoebe," I say, answering with a sense of relief. "What are you doing awake at two a.m.?"

"I could ask you the same question."

"I don't really sleep anymore," I say. "What tea are you drinking?"

"Rose tulsi with honey. You?"

"Chamomile peach."

A little pool of quiet falls between us. "Are you okay?" she asks. "I see that every single light in the house is on."

"Uh." I glance over my shoulder, and it's true. "It makes me feel safer. It's really quiet up here."

"Do you want to come down here and spend the night?"

A swell of hope fills my body. "Really?"

"Yeah. Let me call Ben and he'll bring you down."

"Oh, no no no. I'll walk."

"Really?" Her voice is droll. "In the dark? Alone? In the middle of the night?"

"Okay, maybe not. It seems mean to wake him up."

"He's awake. We were texting. He doesn't sleep, either. Maybe nobody does over the age of fifty."

I take a breath. "Can I bring Yul Brynner? He has his own little carrier."

"How is he with dogs?"

"You mean Maui?" I laugh. "Fine."

"Oh, of course. They've met. Of course, bring him. I'll call Ben. Get ready."

"Thank you, Phoebe."

"No worries," she says, and hangs up.

~

I shove a pair of underwear and a brush in a bag and gather things Yul Brynner will need—food and a dish and a cellophane-wrapped litter box with litter, one of dozens I keep so he can be comfortable wherever we go. Phoebe's question about the dog makes me smile. Maui is a sweetheart, all size and fur and a big squishy heart. I found him in Mexico during a shoot for *Home*, back when I was still thrilled with the part and the cast and the surprising success of the series, before all the madness descended upon the world, before we were all locked up in our houses and I came here to at least be close to someone I loved, before Beryl died, before my fight with Phoebe. Just . . . before.

Maui was an adorable pup, all paws and ears. He wandered into the camp, clearly hungry, and everyone fell for him, feeding him tidbits of food that was much too rich for his young belly. He ended up with a nasty case of diarrhea, at which point no one wanted to look after him. I took him into my trailer and made him a bed beneath the table. Yul Brynner found him curious but also gross, so after the initial investigation, he left him alone.

The shoot was over a couple of days later, and I couldn't bear to leave the puppy behind. Phoebe had recently lost her old chow and I knew she was grieving, and although you're really never supposed to do this, I surprised her with the foundling. By the time I walked him up her driveway on a brand-new leash and harness, he'd been bathed and tended, and he was the most adorable thing on four legs. Phoebe narrowed her eyes when we appeared at her door, but within seconds, she was on her knees, letting him lick her face and cuddle up to her body. Jasmine, only six at the time, was there, and she went completely mad. Phoebe took him in, as I knew she would.

I tuck Yul into his carrier, and Ben is already knocking. I open the door. "Oh! Ben!" I say in surprise. "I remember you." It's funny how much a person can look like themselves over time. As a young teen, he'd been plump and awkward, with hair down to the middle of his back. He's grown into a solid and good-looking man with that aura of confidence that some people carry. It gives me space to take a breath. "Really nice of you to do this."

"No worries." He looks around the foyer. "This place is great."

I nod. "You should come back in the daytime. I'll show you around."

"Let's get you down the hill." He picks up the cat carrier. "Anything else you need?"

"No."

In his mud-splattered white truck, which I imagine hauling soil and wheelbarrows and such things, he doesn't chatter, and it's not awkward, just kind. "We went to school together, didn't we?" I ask.

"We did. You were a year ahead of me, so our circles didn't cross much."

"You hung out at the hippie house, though, right? That summer?"

"Yeah," he says quietly. "I still think about that place sometimes."

"Me too." It was the end of a lot of things for me, but people mostly don't know about much of it, except that my hair was shorn when I came back to school. Even now, the memory gives me a sad, dull ache in my chest.

Again, I think of the lie I must confess to Phoebe, the lie rooted in that summer. "Funny how things stick."

"I remember the church burning down," he says as we pass the lot where it stood, still empty after all these years.

"Yeah," I say. A knot of dark memory ties itself in my gut, a knot made up of so many threads—my father's rage and Joel's act of revenge and the loss of everything. Ripples of things I've never worked out, couldn't bear to. "Only pity is that my dad wasn't in it when it burned."

He glances at me. "He had a reputation as a miserable bastard."

"Understatement."

He nods. I'm grateful that he doesn't pursue it, and we don't say anything more until we pull into Phoebe's driveway. Lamplight glows in the living room and one other upstairs window, the room that was mine, after I survived all that happened. Phoebe is going to let me stay in my old room.

All the heat and loss and weight of time drop out of my body. If home is a person, mine has always been Phoebe. That lamplight gives me hope that we might resolve the still-simmering anger between us.

"Thanks, Ben."

"Anytime."

Chapter Seven
Phoebe

It was actually Ben's idea to pick up Suze. I'd been texting with him, as we often did in the middle of the night, talking about movies or books or politics or the world, whatever, and I mentioned that I was worried about Suze because all the lights were on. He suggested he could bring her down to me, and the way that landed in my gut, I knew he was right.

That's a big favor, I said.

Not really. Will you make me some of that rose petal tea?

Rose?

It smells like roses. You made it with honey.

I remember, and smiling, type, Rose tulsi. You got it. I'll call her right now.

They arrive less than a half hour after the phone call. The cat, in his enormous, padded, beautiful carrier, is a big Himalayan Ragdoll who seems perfectly calm. "He's gorgeous."

"He's a great cat," Suze says.

Ordinarily I would have met him by now, but her last cat, Melvin, died not long after Beryl did. It occurs to me for the first time that she lost her partner, Beryl, and Melvin within a couple of years.

And me, I realize. A river of mingled anger and guilt—*It's not my job to take care of her! But who else does she have?*—travels through my body.

Yul Brynner winds around my ankles. His fur is as soft as a breeze, thick and long. "Wow, he's so pretty!"

"Ragdolls always are," she says, stroking Yul Brynner's tail. "They're good travelers, too."

She's woven her long hair into a braid, and her face is devoid of makeup, revealing the circles below her eyes and the paleness of her lips. Ben comes in, carrying a bag. He's a little unkempt himself, his dark hair mussed, his shirt untucked. "Come in, both of you. Let's keep our voices down. Jasmine is sleeping."

Maui rounds us into the kitchen, and Yul Brynner crouches near the sink, wary. "Maui, give him some space," I say.

"You sit," Ben says. "I'll make the tea."

I smile. "You're the master now, are you?"

He winks at me. "Best teacher around."

I pat his back, taking comfort in his solidness, his reliability. It's been so long since there was anyone around for me to depend on. For all that Suze needs me, she's not the most consistently available presence. I know it's not her fault, but sometimes you want more than a voice on the phone. "Thank you."

A deck of cards sits on the counter, left over from the rummy I was playing with Jasmine. "Poker, anyone?"

Suze nods. "I'll play."

"Deal me in," Ben says.

I shuffle the cards, feeling something akin to peace. It's a single moment, but it's real—the camaraderie of my friends, Jasmine upstairs, tea and snacks at our elbows. I feel Amma there, too, approving. As she would have, I say, "Five-card stud, nothing wild."

Suze's eyes twinkle. "Not even tens?" It was always the card she wanted to be the wild card, one of the few things that irked Amma, who liked her poker straight up.

"Not even tens," I say, smiling, and deal.

~

When I get up in the morning, Suze is fast asleep in the bedroom that used to be hers, tucked under the eaves on the north end of the house. It's always too cold, but she loved the refuge it offered. Amma took her in after Joel burned the church down, and she lived here for the final two and a half years of high school. I was deeply resentful at first—or rather, jealous. My family was falling apart, and I wanted to live with Amma, who wouldn't let me. But she let Suze, saying she had nowhere else to go.

One of her posters, *The Rocky Horror Picture Show*, still adorns one wall, and she made the paisley quilt her final year of high school. Her braid peeks out from under the covers, and it pierces me. I was pretty evil for a while there. Not that Suze was exactly all sweetness and light. But probably no one would have been under the circumstances. Her father beat her nearly to death, she was sent away in disgrace, and her best friend—that would be me—kept a secret from her that I've still never shared.

It has come to me in the vacuum between us after the fight to wonder if my keeping this secret is partly what created so much distance between us.

A piercing sense of longing fills me. I miss our closeness. For all that is wrong between us, she is still like the other half of me, the missing half I found one day on a beach when we were twelve.

Yul Brynner sprawls over her legs. He meows at me. "I bet you're hungry," I say. "Come on."

He leaps down easily and follows me out. We trip downstairs, where Jasmine is eating oatmeal with berries while watching her iPad with headphones. She sees the cat and her mouth drops open. "Where did he come from?" She yanks off the earphones and drops to the floor, petting

Yul Brynner. "Oh my gosh, he's so soft!" He lifts his head and she bends to kiss him, giggling when he licks her nose. "What's his name?"

"Yul Brynner." At the weird look she gives me, I say, "It's a long story. He was an actor who was in a very famous movie Suze and I loved. *The King and I.*"

"Oh. Can I feed him?"

"Yes. She brought some food. It's in the cans over there. You can use a saucer." When Maui trots into the room, Yul Brynner holds his ground. Maui bends to sniff him, and they touch noses.

"How cute!" Jasmine cries. "Did Auntie Suze spend the night?"

"She did." I scrape food into the dish Suze left out and shoo Maui away so Yul Brynner can eat. Such an awkwardly long name, but she never just calls him Yul, so I won't, either. "Eat your breakfast, sweetheart. Let him eat."

She gets back up. "I wish I could have a cat."

I nod, washing my hands. "Maybe when you come back to the States."

"Why can't I have one in England? Maybe that would make me feel better."

"Maybe." I half smile—she's not above a little emotional manipulation. "Better to wait and see."

Her face falls, and this time it's not manipulation but genuine sadness. It creeps over her face like dusk. "I don't want to go so far away."

"I know, baby. But it's going to be an amazing adventure." To redirect, I add, "Suze always, always, always wanted a cat and her dad would never let her have one. My grandmother let her keep one here."

"Really? What kind of cat?"

"It was a tuxedo."

She wrinkles her nose. "What's that?"

"Black and white. A white ruff. Peter." I remember him as a kitten, one of a litter born at the hippie house, a place we all hung out the summer before Suze was sent away—a party house, really, but not in a bad way. Not like a party house would be now. The kittens lived in the barn, and we all adored them. Peter was the imp of the group, always getting into predicaments and causing trouble. Suze loved him from the very first time she saw him. He had a half mustache and a spot of white right on his forehead, like a horse, and socks on all four feet. Suze begged her father for weeks to keep that kitten, and finally she went to Beryl, who kept books and the diary and clothes for Suze.

We walked over from the hippie house, Peter in a box. He was only a couple of months old, but the kids who lived there wanted to get the kittens into good homes, and Suze begged them not to give him away yet.

"Do you think she'll say yes?" Suze asked.

I really didn't think she would. Even my grandmother had limits to the nice things she'd do for other people, and she already had a cat, a gray mouser who presented us with dead or half-living rodents weekly. "I don't know," I said.

Suze got tears in her eyes. "But he's so cute and he loves me!"

"He does."

We found Beryl in the studio, as ever, where she was bent over her table drawing the intricate details of a dragonfly wing. "Hello, girls," she said, straightening. "What have we here?"

Suze carried the box over. "This is Peter"—a name she took from Anne Frank's diary. "I love him so much and my dad won't let me keep any kind of animal, and maybe I wouldn't want a kitten around him anyway."

"Oh, baby." Beryl set aside her pencil and gave Peter her full attention. She lifted him from the box and settled him on her shoulder. "He's a cutie pie, isn't he?" Peter lifted a paw and gently touched her lips, purring. She stroked his tummy. "You want me to adopt him, is that it?"

"Not exactly," Suze said. "I want him to be my cat, but he has to live here. I'll buy his food and get him fixed and all that."

I leaned on the table, lacing Peter's tail through my fingers. It twitched in my hand. I wanted the cat to stay, but it felt like Suze always got the best of Beryl these days. If I'd asked her to keep a kitten for me, would she have done it? I didn't think she would have.

But then, my father wasn't whipping me with a belt for minor infractions, either. Or any infraction for that matter. Maybe, I thought, kissing Peter's tiny nose, I should get over myself.

Suze waited. You could see on her face that she didn't think it would work, but then Beryl said, "I don't mind. He can live here and be your cat."

Suze burst into tears, crying so hard she had to put her face down on her hands on the table. Beryl set Peter down and he frolicked right over and dived into Suze's hair. She picked him up, laughing and crying at once, and kissed him all over his face. He set his paws on either side of her chin and licked her tears.

Beryl came out from behind the table and nudged Suze into a hug. "It's all right, sweetie. Everything is going to be okay."

A swell of unspeakable jealousy rose in my chest, warring with my wish to be empathetic. I loved Suze, and I hated that her life was so hard, but Amma was *mine*, and now Suze was taking her. It wasn't fair.

But at that moment Peter leaped on my hand, wrapping his paws around my arm and digging his tiny sharp claws into my skin, then thumping his back feet against me. It made me laugh. I picked him up and cuddled him, kissing his soft kitten self, happy that he would live here now and be safe and I could see him all the time.

Suze lifted her head and wiped her face. Even then, I knew she wasn't crying over her cat.

In the modern day, Yul Brynner trills, and Jasmine laughs. I want to cry over both of those lonely girls, for everything they were about to lose.

THEN

Maybe I'm Amazed

October 12, 19—

Dear Suze,

The diary came today, so fast! I really liked reading your story, but I hate that your dad beat you with a switch. That's not okay! I think that qualifies as child abuse.

So is Joel cute? Is he like a boyfriend or just a friend who is a boy?

I started my comic book project. Ms. Alexander is helping me plan it and make a storyboard. I made two friends in art class, and they're coming over to swim on Friday night. My mom loves it when I have people over so she can do her big entertainment thing and make popcorn and buy root beer and play music over her precious sound system.

Honestly, I don't always know if people like me for me or if they think it's cool to swim inside. At least I know I can trust you. You like me for who I am.

That's all for today,

Love,

Phoebe

October 16, 19—

Dear Suze,

I hate everybody but you. My so-called friends came over on Friday night but they didn't talk to me the whole time. They only talked to each other. I didn't even know what to do. My mom thinks it's my fault, like I'm not being properly friendly, but what does that mean? I think they're bitches and I'm not going to have anyone over again.

Except you. I want you to come to Portland and swim in the pool and eat all my mom's snacks and wear a bikini.

I miss you so much.

Love,

Phoebe

October 28–30, 19—

Dear Phoebe,

I'm sorry about your party. I wish I could have been there. We would have had so much fun! But all those kids are stupid and I want to beat them up for you.

Just remember, you always have me.

I have so many things saved up to tell you I think it'll take up more than one page.

My friend Joel read GO ASK ALICE, too, and he said it's horseshit.

He's not a boyfriend. He's my friend. He has a lot of acne and he's self-conscious and so it's like me and my stupid clothes. We are the kids nobody else wants to hang out with. Or maybe that's how it started and now we are actual friends. Last night, we stole some of his mom's Kools and walked over to the house on the bluff (our house! Ha ha, like the song) and sat on the deck and looked at the stars for a long time, smoking. I like smoking, but I'm always afraid my dad will smell it, so I have to be outside.

Anyway, we were out there and he asked if he could brush my hair and I let him take out the braids. He's like, you could wear your hair like a coat. I laughed and said, Lady Godiva. He blushed the color of apples. It made me feel good.

I started cutting a little bit off the end of the braid all the time, a little at a time so my dad won't know.

But—ta-da! I made something in home ec that's so cute. Just a cute peasant top, but I can wear it with a skirt and my dad won't get mad. It has beautiful full sleeves and a tie at the neck. The fabric is paisleys in stripes of blue and white and yellow.

More tomorrow!

Love,

Suze

October 31, Halloween, 19—

Dear Phoebe,

I went to school as a Normal Girl today. Joel and your grandma helped me get my costume together, which was the shirt I made in home ec and some jeans I bought at Goodwill with the money I made helping the other girls in home ec finish their projects.

And a bunch of bracelets and some moccasins my dad let me buy when he felt bad about the whipping. I found this cool fringed vest in a box of donations some people sent to the church and snuck it out before anybody could see it. Since I couldn't do anything about the length of my hair, Joel talked me into wearing it down. I've never left it loose for school, ever.

I wish you could have been there to see their faces when I walked in! Nancy Gorton about blew a gasket—I thought her eyes would bug right out of her face. One of my teachers was all, this is a good look for you, Suzanne, and I rolled my eyes. It's a costume, I told her.

Joel went as a warrior, all painted with a leather vest over his chest. We ate lunch and people stared at us all day. We laughed so much.

Then I had to take it all off and go home like a good Christian girl, but for a little while I was free.

Love,
Suze

November 5, 19—

Dear Suze,

I wish I'd seen you in the "costume." That's how you should look every day. I bet everybody was amazed at how beautiful you are.

GO ASK ALICE isn't horseshit! I can't wait to talk about it in person. Will you introduce me to Joel? Maybe we can all go to a movie or skating or something. I'm looking forward to

Thanksgiving so so so much. I hate this school and my mom and everything about this city. I hate the rain and the clouds and not being by the ocean. Most of all, I hate that I can't hang out with you. Do you think your dad would let you come here and visit?

I keep worrying that you're going to make all kinds of friends at school and then I'll be the weird girl who lives in Portland and we will drift apart. My mom says that's what will happen. 😞

My dad says I can spend the whole Thanksgiving week there. He'll drive me down himself on Saturday morning, and I can stay the whole week until the next Sunday. I know you have to go to school and that's okay. Amma wants to do some painting things, too, and we're going to cook the whole dinner.

My comic book is so cool. I love it. It's the story of two girls by the sea, solving a mystery. Mrs. Gonzales said I can get it copied when I'm done.

Love,
Phoebe

November 6, 19—

Dear Suze,

Today was such a good day! We had a field trip to see a special showing of ROMEO AND JULIET. It's such a great movie! I cried my eyes out, and most of the girls did. The boys threw popcorn around, but I saw some of them crying, too. You HAVE to see it!

Juliet is so beautiful and I love her clothes. Maybe I should take home ec and learn to make velvet bodices. Wouldn't that be cool?

Gotta go. Mom's calling me for dinner.

Love,

Phoebe

November 7, 19—

Dear Suze,

I can't stop thinking about ROMEO AND JULIET. I asked my mom if she would take me to see it again and she said maybe, but she wasn't very enthusiastic. I have some allowance money and might buy the album of the music.

It's the saddest story of all time, and these two people died because they loved each other! The parents were fighting over stupid things like adults always do and even though the Prince ordered them not to fight, they kept doing it, and then Romeo and Juliet killed themselves. Romeo thought Juliet was dead and killed himself and then she woke up and saw he was dead and she killed herself, too. I can cry just thinking about it.

Grown-ups are so stupid sometimes. Like war. Like murders. Like all the things they do to wreck the world. We have to change the world. It's up to our generation to do it. I don't know what to do, but I'm thinking about it a lot.

Love,

Phoebe

November 10, 19—
Dear Suze,

I haven't had a chance to write and I'm going to put this back in the mail so you can have it for a while. My dad took me to see R&J a second time, and he said if I get an A in Geography, he'll take me again, so I'm studying really hard. I wish I could go to a movie whenever I want like a grown-up. I'd go every day.

Love,
Phoebe

November 17, 19—
Dear Phoebe,

The diary took a long time to come back. I thought you maybe stopped writing, and I was so happy when I went over to Amma's house and she had it waiting for me. She also made me hot chocolate and gave me some socks and I sat on the couch and read all the things you wrote. I wish I could see ROMEO AND JULIET! Maybe it will come here, but the only thing at the movie theater this week is THE FRENCH CONNECTION. Some kids at school are talking about BILLY JACK, and I really want to see that. They went down to Seaside to watch it, but Joel said it'll show here, too, because his mom says the theater here shows all the movies.

Here is something else: *YOU* ARE MY BEST FRIEND OF ALL TIME! I mean it, Phoebe. I feel like when we met, it was like finding my long-lost sister. Never think I will ever have a friend like you, ever ever ever. Joel is my school friend, and we get along really well, but it's not like you and me.

I can't wait to see your comic! Two girls on the beach! Does one have blonde hair and one have brown hair? ☺

Thanksgiving is next week! I'll write every day and give it to you when you get here.

November 18, 19—

This is one of the BEST DAYS OF MY LIFE!!!! I GOT A PART IN A PLAY! And not just any play— *ANNE FRANK*, and you will not believe this, Phoebe, but I got the part of Anne!!!!!!!!!!!!!!!!!! I am going to play the most wonderful character in the history of the world in a play! Me, the weirdest girl in school!! I can't even believe it. I don't know what made me do it, but they had tryouts last week and I loved the book so much and felt so connected to Anne that I decided it would be cool. I didn't think I did very well because after I read, the whole room was quiet and then they just said, "thank you, Suzanne," all polite and stuff. I was blushing when I walked out, I know it, but Joel said later that I did really good, like good enough he almost cried, so I thought maybe it wasn't so bad.

But ANNE FRANK! The lead!! I am so happy I could cry. In fact, I did cry.

Love and rainbows and sparkles and diamonds and dancing,

Suze

November 19, 19—

I don't have much time, because I have to
bake a bunch of cupcakes for the bake sale on
Sunday and I had a meeting for the play so I had
to tell my dad it was a home ec club thing. He saw
that I was making money helping other girls make
clothes and thought that was a fine thing for a girl
to do (a fine thing, oh brother) and now I can use
that as my excuse whenever. He likes that I'm
earning some money, too, though he takes some
of it. Anyway, I made the cupcakes, three dozen
white cake and three dozen chocolate along with Mrs.
Armstrong. She wears so much perfume it chokes
me, and although she's supposed to be modest in
dress, she really likes sweaters that show off her
gigantic boobs! Yuck! My dad always makes excuses
to come talk to us in the kitchen when she's around.
It's embarrassing.

November 20, 19—

You will be here today! I can't wait to see you!
Hug you tight!

CURRENT DAY

Chapter Eight
Suze

I surface from sleep to discover the bedroom is flooded with light, and for long moments I simply lie there, feeling safe and secure, the way I always have in this place. Here I was safe from my father, from the cruelty of the world, tucked into Beryl's care.

I came back here to live after my father sent me away to an unwed mothers' home. He had always planned that I'd return to his care, in his new church in Texas, but I flat out refused. I asked Beryl to help me make a case for emancipation, and she gladly dived in and offered me shelter.

So I spent the final two and a half years of high school in this bedroom. The first year was painful and full of grief, but the second I began to really heal. Beryl and Phoebe loved me back to life, along with a series of parts in the school theater department.

Where would my life have ended up if not for Beryl? I can't even imagine.

A familiar sense of well-being fills me now. I can't remember the last time I felt so safe, at peace. The house is silent, and Yul Brynner is nowhere in sight. I slide a hand out of the covers, but he's not on the bed. Phoebe must have let him out of the room. I can tell I've had a good sleep when I stand and stretch. How long has it been since I slept like that?

Years. Literally. The attack made it worse, but I haven't been able to sleep in ages. It started after Dmitri died. We never lived together, although we often slept at each other's houses, but we'd been together almost two decades by the time he fell ill. The world lost its sheen, and the hours of night were extra dark, and even when the most acute stage of my grieving was over, I couldn't find a way back to effortless sleep. As soon as I slid into bed, my brain would start throwing out all kinds of things—memories and problems and what I should eat for lunch the next day. Important things and stupid ones. After the beating, I found myself waking up with panic attacks, gasping and sweating, which made even the *prospect* of sleep terrifying.

It's been slowly improving, and I hope that being in Blue Cove will settle my nerves, help me heal.

What a way to start! Of course I slept with the safety of Phoebe close by, and the comfort of knowing I wasn't alone. The realization makes me a little misty.

Downstairs, Yul Brynner sits on the dining room windowsill, his tail swishing as he squeaks at a bird outside. He doesn't even look at me. He's happy here, too.

Phoebe left me a note on the counter. For a moment, I'm afraid to pick it up, afraid she's left so she doesn't have to tell me in person to go home.

But when I pick it up, it says only, *Went to the studio. Eat something, then join us.*

Some of the cranberry bread from yesterday and a bowl of apples sit beside the kettle, and she's left out an array of teas. Peach oolong. Green Dragon black tea. Earl Grey, never my favorite. I don't love that smoky flavor. I choose the peach and turn on the kettle.

It's only then that I realize it's ten thirty. Holy cow. How could I have slept so long? I'm a morning person!

I guess I've been more exhausted than I thought.

Anxious to get to the studio before they come back and I lose my chance, I make a cup of tea in a go-cup, then grab an apple and a slice of bread and hurry out the back door, on the path beneath the dripping pines. The sun makes everything glitter, and I find myself slowing to look at it, noticing the birds trading notes in the tree branches, and the rich, earthy scent of the forest floor. A sudden memory of Joel bolts through me—the bend of his neck smelled just like this, hummus and needles and pines.

Have I ever loved anyone like that, fully and without reservation? I loved Dmitri, deeply, and we had a strong, sexy, tender relationship, but I'm not sure I ever dropped my guard completely. Maybe it isn't even possible to feel the power of a first love ever again. Maybe nobody would even enjoy it.

I knock at the door and Phoebe yells, "Come in, you dork!"

Laughing, I push open the hobbit door in time to hear Jasmine say, "Nana! That's not very nice."

Phoebe is wrapped in her paint-spattered red sweater and a bibbed apron. A thin streak of yellow marks her left cheek, and I can see she's been painting with her fingers, once her favorite thing. "She knows better than to knock."

The smell of paint and time and lingering hints of the Nag Champa incense Beryl burned adds a layer of almost instinctive calm to the sense of well-being from the long sleep. I feel her presence, almost hear the songs she would sing under her breath, the easy way she talked about life and nature and human traits and God and prayer and faith, the latter three in ways that my father might have called heretical.

She came to his church a few times. It surprised and thrilled me to see her there. She didn't dress up as much as some of the women, but she wore a skirt and blouse, and wove her hair into a tidy braid. It didn't change the tan she always sported, especially rare in coastal Oregon, but she spent so much time outside, studying nature, seeing to her flower farm, communing with the hawks and finches and starfish that she was always deeply tan. The memory of her in the pew, giving me a wink, reminds me how much I was loved.

Maui leaps up from his corner and comes over to offer his greeting, back end wiggling his whole body. I bend to kiss his nose and he slurps a kiss over my chin.

"Okay, Maui, that's enough, baby," Phoebe says. "God, he loves you."

"That's because she saved his life!" Jasmine says. She's wrapped in an apron, too, and she's painting something.

I amble over. "What are you guys working on?"

"Mine is a girl!" Jasmine says. "With a cat like you had once. A tuxedo."

The drawing is quite good, with an anime feel. The cat is black with a white ruff, his green eyes tilted. I look at Phoebe. "You told her about Peter?"

"I thought of him this morning for some reason."

I measure her, and she doesn't meet my eye. What I remember about the day I asked Beryl to let him live here was that she was so jealous. Unreasonably jealous. Was that when the trouble started between us?

But I'm not going to stir the waters here. Mildly, I say, "He was a great cat. I don't know what I would have done without him."

Jasmine asks, "Did he die?"

"He did," I say, "but not until he was a very, very, very old man."

"How old?"

"Twenty, which is something like a hundred and two in human years." I point to her drawing. "You did a great job. Is the girl from a game?"

"Kinda. I mean, she was, and then I drew her my way." She pats the empty stool next to her. "Do you want to draw, too?"

I glance at Phoebe for permission and she gestures like a game show host—*it's all yours.*

First I wander to her side of the enormous table to see what she's working on. It's an elaborate, detailed design, yellow and white vines against a forest-green background. I can see where she's used her fingers to make round spots of yellow along the edge of each big leaf. "Very William Morris," I say. "Fabric?"

"Wallpaper, actually. It's become very popular the past couple of years."

"I love it."

"Thanks." She dips a thin brush into a pool of paint and draws a tiny line along a petal. "You sleep well?" Her tone is impersonal, as if she's talking to a shop clerk. Beneath it, I feel the swirling of all that's unresolved between us.

I answer in the same tone. "Understatement."

"Good." She examines my face. "You look a lot better."

"I guess Yul Brynner and I will have to move in with you."

She snorts, and although I was kidding, it stings. I sip my tea.

"Jasmine wants to go to the Pig 'N Pancake for lunch in an hour or so," Phoebe says. "Want to come?"

I can't read in her eyes whether she really wants me to, but I'm desperate not to be alone. "That sounds *so* good."

"Come draw with me," Jasmine says. "There's paper over there, and"—she gestures her hand in a swirl, just like her nana—"all those things. Crayons, pencils, whatever." She pulls a black metal tin, long and narrow, from the jumble. "Watercolor if you want."

I settle my tea on the lower table so that it won't spill on the art, as Beryl taught us, and peel off my sweater and sit down with a fresh piece of paper, feeling the old lure of calm. In those days, I never lacked for ideas and would be drawing before I fully sat, but now I look at the paper and feel frozen by all the years I haven't done this, by all the bad drawings I will do again until I get the hang of it.

"Just paint color," Phoebe says, picking up on my discomfort.

I glance at her. As if she feels it, she looks up. "Purple," she says, her mouth lifting on one side.

"Purple," I echo, smiling. It was Beryl's favorite. "The color of morning glories."

"And pansies!" Phoebe cries.

I raise my hands, spreading them across the horizon. "Sunrises and clouds!"

Phoebe lifts her hands, palms to the sky, and imitates Beryl's voice exactly: "Sea stars, the beauties of the tide pool."

I crack up, and so does she, and for a long moment Beryl is in the room with us, and nothing has ever gone wrong.

"Purple," Phoebe says, and bends over her vines to trace a dark line with a brush no wider than a single hair.

I nod, and begin. But it's not purple that calls me. Instead, I choose billows of phthalo blue, so bright and water-struck, then some orange, some Mars black. Dots of magenta, too light, so I let the water saturate the cake of watercolor more completely and try again. Better.

Time moves around me in eddies and waves. It's both now and many other times. Beryl and Phoebe and I painting woodland creatures, learning to draw feathers, playing with patterns. She directed us loosely, gave us little lessons in all kinds of things, offered encouragement and praise. When Joel joined our little crew, his work was head and shoulders above ours. Phoebe was always the better of the two of us, but Joel was in a class apart and Beryl treated him accordingly. A memory of the pair of them bent over one of his nature scenes comes back to me. His black hair loose on his shoulders, Beryl standing next to him, one hand on her hip as she points to something. I wonder if he became a fine artist. His mother left town shortly after—

Well, after everything. After I was sent away. After he burned the church down.

In the today studio, music is playing, something with flutes, and Jasmine swings her foot, tilting her head this way and that. I dip my brush and let go of the outside world. I splash color on the paper and splash some more. I think of Peter, who traveled with me all over the world, and how he comforted me, sleeping on my pillow with me when I wanted to die of sorrow, right upstairs in the room where I slept last night. Beryl gave me refuge in a world that had been extremely harsh.

What a blessing she was in my life. I suddenly wonder if I could write about her. Lately I've been feeling the call to write, more than the journals I still keep.

But what? An essay, maybe? My gut resists. A short story. No, not that either. A letter? Yes, maybe. A letter of gratitude to Beryl.

We're all startled when the door opens and Ben comes in. His hair is wet, springing up in curls. "You guys about ready to take a break?" He asks all of us, but Phoebe is where his eyes fall. I noticed last night that his eyes are all for Phoebe, just as they were that long-ago summer when everything went so horribly wrong. He was on the periphery, a little younger than us, and his crush on her was like a clutch of flowers he carried around for all to see.

"Sure." Phoebe starts to wipe her hands and realizes she has many colors layered on her fingers, her palm. "Let me wash up."

"Yeah, do that," he says, pausing to look at Jasmine's work. He taps the edge of the page. "Dude, this is really good."

"Thank you. I messed up her eyelashes on this one a little bit."

"They look great to me."

Jasmine sucks her cheeks in, giving her a fish mouth, and I grin. Phoebe used to do the same thing when she was concentrating. "Time for the Pig 'N Pancake?"

Phoebe nods. "Sure."

Pig 'N Pancake is an Oregon institution, known in part for their pancakes, served with buckets of whipped cream. I haven't eaten there in ages, and while I don't know that I want to wander out in public, I also don't want to be alone. I want to be with Phoebe and Jasmine and Ben more than I want to hide. I wash my brush and wipe paint from my fingers.

"You're coming, right?" Jasmine asks, taking my hand. I love how physical she is. Always hugging, touching, leaning.

I glance at Phoebe with a raised brow. *Still okay?* She nods.

"Yes," I say. "And I am going to totally *pig* out." I made a fake laughing sound.

Phoebe rolls her eyes. "Oh brother."

It isn't until we pile into Ben's truck, Phoebe in front, me and Jasmine in back, that I realize I haven't been in public in months. It's not like I have a full-blown case of agoraphobia, but between the pandemic and Dmitri's death and the loss of Phoebe's support, I feel shaky in the world, without a spine. A ripple of anxiety threads upward through my chest. "Uh, maybe," I say, "I should go home. Do . . . something."

"Something?" Phoebe says, raising a brow. "You might want to come up with a better excuse than that." But she's smiling over her shoulder. "It's only lunch."

I focus on her clear eyes, the shape of her eyebrows. Nod.

Chapter Nine
Phoebe

When Suze hesitates outside the Pig 'N Pancake, I stand behind her and put my hands on her shoulders. "I'm right here with you." Because even if we haven't been communicating recently, of course I know she's been having panic attacks. She's prone to them, and considering everything that's happened to her, it's not surprising.

For a long time after her first movie came out and through the years of her very visible fame, walking out in public would cause such a stir that it wasn't worth it. In Blue Cove, the locals have always given her space, and we'd often done little jaunts like this. The worry now is the lingering fear of strangers, of some random human trying to smash your head in.

A visual of her on a network of machines in the hospital flashes in front of my eyes, and with it comes the sense of terror and despair that lived in my body while I waited for her to wake up. I promised the heavens a million things: that I would forgive all the things she said to me, take back all the things I said to her, if they would let her live.

Let her live, let her live, let her live.

We haven't yet had that talk. Maybe we never will. Maybe the damage will live in both of us for the rest of our lives, stamping on our attempts to forget, to heal the rift. I feel like a married couple who was all set to divorce when one of them got cancer.

But this—today, last night, the studio—is easy. How many rounds of cards did we play with Amma? How many times did we sit in the studio and silently heal the usual rifts and pains and furies of friendship? So many.

The Pig 'N Pancake was a place we always came when my grandmother was feeling the yen for a good, big breakfast. She loved eating, and especially loved breakfast with all the trimmings. I feel the same love for the place. A waitress with a bouncy red ponytail leads us through the restaurant, which is fairly quiet this time of day. Suze is wearing big sunglasses and a hat, but a couple of people do a double take anyway. "Can we have that booth in the back?" I ask.

The girl nods. We all shimmy in, Suze against the wall, her back to the room. "Thanks," she says.

I nod.

Jasmine sits next to her, swinging her feet. "I'm having blueberry pancakes," she says. "With all the whipped cream."

"And milk," I add, thinking a little protein might help offset the sugar.

"Hot chocolate!" Jasmine says.

"Save that for later," I say. "You don't want to get too hyped on sugar."

I turn my attention to the menu. My stomach growls, and a yawn overtakes me. "I'm going to need a nap when I get back."

A man a few booths down is glowering our direction, and I glare back: *What's your problem?* Then turn my attention to the menu.

"Not me," Jasmine says. "Naps are for babies."

"You can have quiet time, then," I say. "In your nest of animals."

She giggles.

The waitress returns with coffee for all the adults and milk for Jasmine. We order full breakfasts, even Suze. "The fresh air," she says to me with a half grin.

I return it, warmed. It was shorthand during the pandemic times, when we ate ourselves silly—pancakes and steaks and cakes, experimenting like we were teenagers again. I invented a white cake with raspberry filling that is still in rotation, and she focused on savory pies. "Good food," I say. She was grieving Dmitri, and the cooking was a way to give her something to do, the first cooking she'd done in decades. It had been good for all of us to have her here, for me, for Jasmine, for Beryl. We had our own little family of women. "That cheese leek pie you made is still one of my favorite foods of all time."

She closes her eyes, making a soft sound. "So good." Discarding her hat, she says, "Did you keep all those recipes?"

"Of course." To Ben, I explain, "We were here during the pandemic and cooked a ton."

"Sounds good."

"Where did you spend quarantine, Ben?" Suze asks before I can shake my head.

"Africa," he answers, erecting a wall of protection. What I know is that his wife died during that time. I don't think it was COVID, but I haven't asked. It's clear he doesn't want to talk about it.

Suze nods. "I kinda miss some of those days. It was so much less pressure."

"Well, people died," Ben says.

"Yes," she says, looking at him directly.

I touch his hand. "Her partner was one of the early casualties."

"I'm sorry," he says. "I didn't mean—"

"It's all right." She shakes her hair from her face. "I also liked some parts of the quarantine."

"I liked it, too," Jasmine says. "I got to come here and Nana took care of me because my mom had to work from home and I got on her nerves."

Suze leans against Jasmine for a moment. "It was great to all be together, wasn't it?"

"Yes. Remember that pie we made with potato chips on top?"

"I do!"

"Amma loved that one," I say, pierced suddenly with missing her. Those last few years she was frail and needed help moving around, but she was still mostly herself and mostly loved to eat. We were very careful to be sure she wasn't infected with the virus, and she never was.

"Like anything else," I say, "it was a mixed bag. Bad for some people, good for others."

A shine brightens Suze's aqua eyes. "Yeah." She brushes hair from her face, and I'm glad to see her relaxing in a public place. It's her hometown and with her oldest friend, but it's progress.

Jasmine says, "Why can't I come back now?"

"You're here now," I say.

"No, when my mom goes to London. Why can't I stay here with you like I did then?"

"Your mom would miss you too much."

She bows her head, sucks in her cheeks. "I don't want to move so far away."

Suze leans into her, whispers, "I've been there. It's really cool. You might see castles."

"I know." She shrugs. "I like Blue Cove the best."

"You can come back," I say. "And I'll come see you, too." My stomach is aching a little, both for her worries and my sense of loss. But as a grandmother, my job is always to facilitate the best thing for her. To that end, I say, "What if we go to the library and get some books about England?"

She considers. "Okay. That might be good."

"I think you're going to love it," Suze says.

Jasmine nods, drinks milk through her paper straw.

"To change the subject completely," Suze says, "can one of you recommend an electrician? I'm having trouble with a fuse knocking things off."

"You still haven't fixed that?" I ask.

"Not urgent if I'm not there."

"I've been pretty happy with Blue River," Ben says. "They did some work on the greenhouses a couple of months ago."

"Cool. Thanks."

"I'll give them a call for you."

Suze simply accepts the help. "Thanks."

Two waitresses bring out our food, pancakes and bowls of whipped cream and piles of bacon and scrambled eggs. We dig in happily. Jasmine gives us some more facts on tsunamis, and Ben gleefully joins in, impressing her.

It isn't until after the meal, when we are stuffed to the gills and leaning back happily, that the whole thing goes south. Suze glances over her shoulder, sees the restaurant is thinly populated, and asks Jasmine to let her out. Her mouth lifts on one side and she says to me quietly, "I'm going to the bathroom *all by myself*."

I chuckle. "You want me to come with you?"

"I can do it."

Jasmine takes her hand. "I want to go, too," she says, and some part of me knows she's being protective, as she's seen me do.

"That would be great."

They saunter toward the ladies' room.

Ben says, "Hey, Phoebe."

I look at him. "Hey, Ben."

"I was wondering if you might—"

Yelling breaks out at the front of the restaurant, and I'm on my feet before I register that it's the man who was glaring at us, furiously screaming at Suze, who's trying to push Jasmine behind her, but Jasmine isn't that compliant. I hear the man say, *Elites . . . ruining the country . . . God will punish*, and then I see Jasmine pull away from Suze and kick the man in the shin.

"Shut up!" she cries. "You're a bully!"

The man raises his hand as if to strike Jasmine, but Suze shoves him with both hands. "Don't you dare."

By then I've reached them, and so has the store manager, who sticks her hand between them. "Get out," she says to the man. "Or I *will* call the police."

He starts to rant, and she pulls the phone from her pocket. "I mean it. And you'd better not ever show your face in here again."

"I'm a regular customer!" he protests. "She's a Hollywood elite who—"

"Is safe here. You get out."

He whirls around and storms out, muttering. I drop to my knees and grab Jasmine. "What were you thinking?"

"He was being mean!"

"I know, but you just can't do stuff like that." Tears well in the back of my throat. What if he'd had a gun? What if he'd hit her? "Let adults manage things, will you?"

Suze is standing there, frozen. Her hands are shaking, and Ben comes up beside her. "Let's get you home."

"We should report it to the sheriff," I say, standing. "Considering the squirrel."

"Squirrel?" Ben echoes.

I cover Jasmine's ears. "A dead squirrel on her doorstep."

Suze's face goes pale. "Do you think he was the one who did it?"

"I don't know. If it was, I would feel better because he's clearly not part of an organized group like the LNB."

"How could you possibly know?" Ben asks.

I raise my eyebrows. "He seems incompetent, more like the guy who yells at you for crossing his lawn than part of something so organized."

Ben scowls. "Don't underestimate people like him. There's a lot of anger and frustration in the world."

Suze is visibly shaking. "Let's get you home and call the police," I say.

She nods jerkily, and I feel a wild sense of the unfairness in the world and the weight of my own guilt. Suze has suffered plenty, mostly thanks to her father, but I've played a role, too. I have secrets I've kept too long.

Is it too late to put them right? I think of Blue River Electric. That might be a way to begin.

THEN

I Think I Love You

Phoebe

The Saturday before Thanksgiving, I was up before the sun, and by the time my dad had his first cigarette and cup of coffee, my suitcase was in the car. "Anxious to get to Amma's?" he asked with a wink.

"Yes. My friend Suze and I have a lot of plans."

He stroked his thick mustache, eyeing me over the curling blue smoke of his L&M cigarette.

"You need to make friends here," my mom said, bustling into the kitchen. She wore her silky robe, belted tight around her middle, and a pair of mules with feathers on the top. Her toenails and fingernails were red. She poured a cup of coffee. "What about the girls you had over to swim?"

I rolled my eyes to cover the intense embarrassment that still burned in me over that night. If she thought I was contemptuous, it was better than if she felt sorry for me. "Not everyone needs a million friends," I said.

"Not a million," my mother said in her direct way. "A couple would be fine."

"Mom!"

"I'm saying that maybe if you reached out and tried to be friendlier, you'd have more friends, more of a social life."

"Like you?" I shot back, because really all she did was work and have cocktails with her lawyer friends.

It was impossible to get her mad, though, and she raised an eyebrow. "I'm allowing the Thanksgiving week trip, but you are not going to spend the entire Christmas break in the back of beyond, hiding from your life."

"Lilly," my dad said mildly, lifting a hand. "Leave her alone."

"Maybe Suze can come here," I said.

"But—" My mother shook her head. "Phoebe, I hate to say it, but that girl is strange. All that hair, her weird clothes."

"Oh, I'm sure! Don't be so judgmental, Mom!" Heat pulsed in the hollow of my throat. "That's not her, it's her dad. He won't let her cut her hair and makes her wear those clothes so that boys don't look at her."

"I'm sure it works," my mother muttered.

I shoved my chair back with a loud scrape and said to my dad, "I'll be in the car."

With every mile between us and Portland, tension slid away from my neck and shoulders. It wasn't just Suze. It was going toward my grandmother and the studio where we would spend our time painting, and the beach and tide pools and the taste of the air. My parents fought all the time lately, and not hearing their furious, low voices would be a relief all by itself.

Watching fog-draped pine trees swish by the car windows, I asked my dad, "Why did you leave Blue Cove? It's so much better than Portland."

He took a breath. "Well, kiddo, it doesn't have a lot of opportunities for a guy like me. I was never going to be a fisherman or a hotel manager. I wanted to read books for a living." He winked at me. "Now I do."

"Couldn't you have taught high school English?"

"I could have," he said, "but to tell you the truth, I didn't want to. From the first time I found out you could live at college as a professor, there wasn't another damned thing I wanted." He reached for my hand on the seat. "They call that a vocation. And knowing what you're supposed to do for work is one of the best things that can happen to a person."

It was the first time I'd ever heard this idea. "When did you figure it out?"

"Pretty much the day I walked onto the campus, freshman year."

I nodded. Looked back to the trees, trying to imagine what my vocation would be. "I used to think I wanted to be a marine biologist," I said. "I like tide pools and the ocean, but that's a lot of science."

"Mmm."

"And then I thought it might be that I wanted to be an architect, because houses are so cool."

"They are," he agreed.

"I'm drawing a comic book in art class," I told him. "Maybe I could be an artist?"

"That's not surprising. You are so good at drawing and painting."

I tried to imagine what it would be like to spend my days in a studio, painting all the time. "Maybe a comic book writer," I added.

"Cool."

This was what I loved about my dad. My mother would start arguing for architecture, for being sensible, even though it was years and years until I had to decide. My dad let me be . . . me.

As we descended from the mountains, following switchbacks through the forest, my heart felt as light as it ever did. I could breathe. "I hate my school," I said.

"I've been kind of getting that." He paused, looking in the rearview mirror, then at me. "Do you think it's the school or the stage of your life you're in? Junior high is always pretty cutthroat."

"No one likes me."

"I don't believe that's true at all. Why do you think that, sweetheart?"

"Because I don't have any friends?" I retorted. "They think I'm weird. The only class I like is art." I glowered. "I wish I could come here and go to school."

"Mmm. Well, maybe that's not the best idea, either. What if we found some art classes after school or something? Maybe that would be a good carrot. Cuz you have to go to school, and you have to do well. Otherwise—"

"I'm cutting off my nose to spite my face," I finished.

"Right."

We arrived as the skies opened up and poured down rain. We had to dash into Amma's house, dripping all over the floor. Just the smell of the house made me feel better. My dad and his mom chatted about Thanksgiving Day and the plan for him and my mom to come back, and I tolerated it, wanting to get out of there and over to Suze, the one friend in my world who really got me. "Can I go now?" I said finally.

"Give me a hug," Dad said, and pulled back to hold my arms in an earnest way. "Think about what you want, honey."

I nodded. Kissed Amma and bolted out the door.

Suze

Phoebe ran all the way to our house in the rain, a big black umbrella over her head. She shook it off on the porch, so she didn't see me at first. It gave me a chance to fill myself up with her actual presence. Her dark, curly hair, her skinny arms. Her sweater was soft pink, something I wanted to touch. She was the first friend who really saw me, saw past the clothes and the hair, and liked me for me. She listened to me in a way that made me feel heard.

I was watching her shake off the rain, and smooth her curly hair, and then turn toward the door, where I was waiting. When she saw me, she gave a little screech. I laughed and pushed open the screen door. We hugged. Hugged hard. I smelled Herbal Essence shampoo, and the sweater was soft as could be. She pulled back and looked at my chest. "Are you wearing a bra?"

I grinned and pulled my shoulders back. "Yes!" I glanced over my shoulder to be sure my dad was nowhere in sight. "My dad is writing his sermon. Let's go." I grabbed her hand and pulled her upstairs. In my bedroom, I closed the door and unbuttoned my shirt and showed off the white bra Grandma had taken me to buy. "Now you're not the only one."

"They're getting big fast!" She looked down at her own chest. Beneath the pink sweater, small breasts pushed up, but she honestly didn't even really need a bra yet.

"Can I try on the sweater?" I said, and felt stupid. "I mean, you don't have to let me."

"No, it's okay." She peeled it off, revealing her ribs and Young Miss bra. "It's cashmere."

"It's so soft," I cried, pulling it over my head. The fabric brushed my skin like breath.

She eyed me. "That looks way better on you than it does on me. I would send it to you, but my mom would kill me."

"No, that's why I brought you up here. I have to show you something!"

I gave her back the sweater and, moving a chair against the door, opened my closet. From a box in the back, I took out a peasant blouse made of lightweight cotton, the fabric printed with paisleys. I'd laced the sleeves and neckline with red velvet ribbon, and it was beautiful. I pulled it on over my head. "I have really learned a lot about sewing."

"Oh my gosh!"

I held out my arms and felt the power of the transformation. "I feel like a hippie when I wear this."

"Where can you wear it? Your dad can't have changed his mind that much."

"He doesn't mind the peasant blouses." I glance at the door as if he might burst through. "The jeans I keep at school and change when I get there."

Phoebe laughs. "You're so smart."

I pulled jeans on and pulled my shapeless dress over all of it, hiding the peasant blouse. My dad didn't care if I wore pants under my dresses.

I just couldn't wear them alone. "C'mon," I said, and tugged her down the stairs. "Let's go meet Joel."

~

He was waiting for us by the movie theater, as we'd arranged. I saw him leaning against the wall, smoking, and suddenly got worried that my only two friends in the world wouldn't like each other. Joel looked hard with his long hair and jean jacket and the cigarette. His acne made his face red, and today it looked aggravated, which made me feel protective. "He is a really good person," I said. "He's such a good artist. You guys will like each other a lot."

Phoebe said in a funny voice, "That's him?"

"Yeah. Joel!" I called. I'd shed my dress and hidden it in my backpack. I'd taken out the braids and shaken my hair out, and it flowed like a cloak around me, heavy and too much, but I had discovered people noticed me when it was loose like this. "This is Phoebe."

He eyed her, lifting his chin her direction while he took another drag off his cigarette. He tossed it aside and held out his hand. Phoebe held hers out and they shook, and it seemed like there was a strange little space between them when he didn't let go that fast, and she was very quiet. "Hi" was all she said.

A ping of jealousy rippled through me, but I wasn't sure who I wanted to keep to myself. I plunged between them, taking each one by the arm. "Movie is going to start! Let's go!" But I really wanted to get off the street in case my dad was finished with his sermon or somebody from church saw me.

"What are we seeing? I didn't bring any money."

I point at the marquee. "*Billy Jack*! It came!"

"What?" Phoebe's mouth opened. "Cool. But I still didn't bring any money."

"I got it. I've made some money babysitting and sewing."

"I'll pay you back," she said.

"My treat," I said. "Both of you."

Phoebe

Joel had the shiniest, longest hair I'd ever seen on a boy. It fell like a satin curtain over his shoulders. Light sank into it and glowed outward. My fingers itched to feel it. He did have acne, like Suze told me, but it didn't take away from him much. His dark eyes rested on my face easily, as if he liked it, and I felt something in me open, expand. His hand gave me a zing, and when I would have let go, he hung on.

Then Suze was between us and we were in the movie with popcorn and root beer and the movie was starting. It was so intense and made me cry hard, and when we stumbled out into the dark, rainy afternoon, I felt hollowed out. "That was rough."

All three of us were quiet, walking side by side. We stopped in the candy store and got a bunch of penny candies, and then without even talking about it, we took the trail to our house on the hill. I let us in by the lower window, and we carried our stash upstairs to the kitchen, which looked out over the water. Joel sat beside me. "Did you ever live on a reservation?" I asked. "Like the kids in the movie?"

He shook his head, lips downturned. "We lived in Seattle and Portland before here," he said.

"I live in Portland."

He gives me a half grin. "I heard that."

Blushing, I bowed my head, wanting to sink through the floor.

"Sorry, I didn't mean to make you blush," he said, and I blushed even worse.

"I hate this!" I said, pressing my hands over my face to hide it.

Suze said, "Phoebe, it's okay. You look cute when you blush." She peeled a red licorice string out of the package and gave me one. "You can't blush and eat at the same time."

With her hair loose, so long it piled on the floor next to her, and the soft peasant blouse that was ever so faintly see-through, and her jeans, she didn't look like my Suze. She was beautiful, almost too beautiful, like a model or something. It made me feel weird and I didn't know if I liked it.

Which gave me a sense of shame. Did I want her to have to wear horrible clothes and keep her silly braids in all the time? No.

Except—maybe one of the things that united us was the way we were both misfits. If she wasn't a misfit, would she even like me anymore?

We talked about the movie. "It was supposed to be about peace, but it was really violent," Joel said, lighting a cigarette. He stood up to open a window and sat on the sill, letting the smoke get sucked out.

"You're right," Suze said. "But how can you be peaceful if everybody else is violent?"

I was haunted by a scene of the kids in the diner getting flour poured on their heads. It was so humiliating.

"Gandhi did it," Joel said.

"But this is America," I said, lured by argument. My dad loved to debate, and so did my mother, and they loved getting into these deep back-and-forthings. Not their fighting, but the way they talked about ideas. "America, my dad says, takes revolution and sells it back to you for a dollar ninety-nine."

Joel cracked up. "That's good."

"He's a professor," I said, proud.

"Fancy," Joel commented.

"Not really."

"Phoebe likes to pretend she's not rich," Suze said, something pointed in her tone, "but she is."

I looked at her with a frown. "That was a mean thing to say."

"I didn't mean it like that," she said nonchalantly. "It's just a fact."

It still stung. She was making us different. "We aren't rich."

"You have a swimming pool," Suze said. "You're wearing a cashmere sweater."

Again my ears burned. She was right. "You should see what some of the girls in my school wear. Where they live."

"It's okay," Joel said. "We don't choose where we're born."

"I know." I shot Suze a look. "You didn't choose to be a preacher's daughter."

"That is true." Her face changed, and she suddenly jumped up. "What time is it?"

I had a tiny watch my mother had given me. "Four forty-five. Are you in trouble?"

"Dang it! I gotta go. I have to be in church at five." She hugged me. "Be good," she said in a singsong, and rushed out.

Joel and I sat there. I couldn't think of anything to say, and he was quiet, too. Why did I always have to be so awkward?

I was about to make an excuse and go home when he said, "It stopped raining. Want to walk on the beach?"

A swell rose in my heart. I hoped it didn't show. "Sure."

Suze

I ran down the hill, trying to avoid splashing mud on my legs, and managed to get into the kitchen through the back door five minutes before services started. Two of the church ladies were making coffee in a giant percolator, talking in quiet voices. On the counter were trays of simple treats, brownies and oranges, like we were all in kindergarten, but my father's edict was that fellowship made a stronger church, and it seemed like he was right, because the congregation had been growing these past few months.

"Hello, Suzanne," said Mrs. Henry, a plump older woman who often did this work. She nodded toward the ladies' room. "You have time to clean up before they start."

I washed the splatters of mud from my shins and calves and splashed water on my face. My hair was damp, but it looked nice the way little bits curled around my face, and my cheeks were red from exercise, which even I could see made my eyes look super, super bright. For a minute, I got stuck in looking at my face, at the end of my nose and the shape of my mouth, and wondered if I could be in the movies. Be Juliet, be Anne Frank, be anyone but me, honestly. It seemed like it would be so much fun. How did a person even do it?

I heard the choir start to sing and raced out to the sanctuary. It was packed tonight for the Saturday evening prayer service. I took my place on the second pew from the front, on the outside. Tonight, I sat next to Mr. and Mrs. Nesbit, who ran the hardware store. She was one of the women who wanted to mother me, and patted my knee when I sat down. I gave her a distracted smile, grabbing the hymnal and flipping to the page shown on the bulletin board on the wall by the pulpit. It was my job to change the numbers before every service, standing on a stepladder to slide the black digits in and out of the rows.

The singing ended and my father took the pulpit. He was a tall man, blond and broad shouldered, and I knew women liked his face, which was handsome unless you'd seen him so furious that he switched you. Once I saw a picture of a Nazi in the encyclopedia at school, and he reminded me of my dad. Handsome, but cruel.

My dad didn't do long sermons on Saturday prayer meetings ordinarily, but he had a pet peeve about people overeating on holidays. "Friends, as we enter this traditional week of celebration, let us be mindful of our habits. In Proverbs 23:20, the Bible says, 'Be not among winebibbers; among riotous eaters of flesh: For the drunkard and the glutton shall come to poverty: and drowsiness shall clothe a man with rags.'"

I pulled my sweater around me in the chilly sanctuary and tuned him out, thinking instead about *Billy Jack* and rescue, and getting jealous knowing that Phoebe and Joel were probably hanging out while I was stuck here. It made my stomach twist with jealousy: over Phoebe, over Joel, over my friends being friends without me. I thought Phoebe had a crush on Joel, too, and that was a weird feeling. It wasn't that I liked him, but I didn't want her to like somebody more than she liked me. I hated that I had to be here, instead of with them.

If God was so great, why did he drop me into such an awful situation? It was a thought that came to me a lot lately.

Phoebe

Joel and I had to walk all the way round the bluff, which took us by the lit-up church where Suze no doubt sat. We could hear Reverend Ogden preaching, his deep, booming voice traveling easily through the windows. "Do you go to church?" Joel asked.

"My mom is an atheist, but sometimes I go with my grandma. Do you?"

He gave me a little sideways grin. "I'm Indian. We have other kinds of church."

"Like what?"

"I'm teasing you. I don't know. We never do anything, either."

I eyed the brightly lit windows, with their colorful designs. "I wonder if it would be good. To like, believe in something."

"Nah." His face looked hard. "Her dad beats her, you know."

I nodded, blinking back sudden tears. "I wish I could save her."

"Me too. My ma says you have to be wary of men in power."

I blinked. He'd used "wary" in a sentence! I didn't know any other guy who would do that, and an electric sensation ran through my body. We kept walking, taking the cut between the dunes that led to the ocean. The sky was thick and heavy. I pulled up the hood on my raincoat in preparation for the rain that would almost certainly fall any second. "Do you have a hat or something?"

"No. I'm used to rain."

"Sometimes I wonder what it would be like to live somewhere the sun shines all the time. Like Arizona or California."

"I like the rain. It gives me room to think."

We made it to the beach and the crispy sand that was washed hard and flat. I'd been to other beaches, but none of them had this walkable, hard sand I loved. The waves were soft and ruffly, flowing flat and friendly this side of the stacks. "What do you think about when you think?" I asked, and was embarrassed instantly over how stupid it sounded.

But he didn't react badly. "Lots of things." He tucked his hands in his jeans pockets. "Space travel lately. I've been reading this cool science fiction book about other planets, and now every time I look up at the stars, I think about what planets might be around them."

"Cool. What's the book?"

"*A Wrinkle in Time*." He looked at me. "Have you read it?"

I stopped in my tracks. "I *love* that book!"

His grin this time was big, making his eyes tilt. In the dark, you couldn't really see his acne at all. "Right on. That's right, Suze said you love to read."

"I do. You can pick up a book and go somewhere else."

"Yeah. I gotta say I didn't really like *Go Ask Alice*, though. It seemed kinda fake. Like she gets addicted to drugs in five seconds and she's peddling to elementary school kids? Who does that?"

I frowned. "I hadn't thought of that."

"No big thing. Just didn't make sense."

"You're right, though," I exclaimed, retracing the narrative in my mind. "I mean, that's hard core, right? Dealing to little kids."

"Yeah."

We drew up to the Starfish Sisters. The trees on top of the biggest sister were outlined against the clouds. I stopped to breathe it in, the moment, the sky, the trees, and the smell of the ocean. "When I'm in Portland, this is what I think about. This spot, right here."

He stood next to me. "What about it?"

"The trees," I said, pointing. "The tide pools. I love those tide pools with my whole heart. I'd like to *be* a starfish in a tide pool."

He laughed. "Kinda boring, though."

I laughed, too.

The rains suddenly started again, not drizzle, but solid rain. "Shit!" Joel said. "Run!"

We did, dashing over the hard sand toward the dunes and leaping over the stream. We didn't stop until we smeared ourselves against the wall of a garage, sheltered by the roof and a tree. I laughed, wiping rain off my face. "Whew!"

He leaned on the wall beside me. "I had fun with you today," he said.

My stomach flipped. I looked at him, standing a lot closer than any boy had ever stood. "Me too."

"Would it be okay if I called you?"

"Yes!"

Right then, in the rain and the soft shadows, he leaned closer. It took me a second to realize he was going to kiss me, so our lips didn't fit quite right at first, and then he cupped his palm around my cheek and gently turned my face toward him, and we connected.

It was the first time I ever kissed a boy. His lips were slightly chapped but firm. Sensations, heat and something buzzy, moved through my body like lava, through the hollow of my throat and the inside of my elbows and all through my stomach.

He lifted his head. "Is that okay?"

"Yes," I whispered, and he moved around in front of me until our bodies were touching tightly, chests and thighs, and kissed me again.

It was heaven on earth.

He walked me home when the rain lightened up, holding hands. It was the most romantic day of my life. I ran inside, floating. It wasn't until I got all the way in that I wondered how Suze would feel about those kisses. He was her friend, after all. Would she get mad? She did say that she didn't like him as a boyfriend, though, so it was probably okay.

Suze

Sunday morning after church, I was washing dishes with two of the church ladies when my father stormed into the room. He never came in there, and I was suddenly on high alert. Did someone see me at the movies yesterday?

"Thank you, ladies," he said to the women. "I need to speak with my daughter alone if you wouldn't mind."

"Of course, Reverend." One touched my shoulder as she passed, so I wasn't the only one who'd picked up on that mood.

I reached for a dish towel to dry my hands, but before I could do it, he slapped me so hard I staggered to the right and lost my grip on the towel. Stunned, I raised my hand to the burning spot. He'd never slapped me before. "What did I do?"

In his hand was a printed piece of paper, which he shoved in my face. "Are you in a play?"

Cold washed through me. *Not the play. Please not the play.* "It's about Anne Frank, Daddy. It's not a bad play or anything. She was a girl who hid from the Nazis—"

He swung his hand again, slapping me from the other side, and I gasped at the pain. "I know who she is! Why did you think you could prance around onstage parading your vanity in front of the whole world?"

I straightened up. "I got the *lead*, Daddy! I'm really good at this!" When he started to slap me again, I ducked away and ran across the room. "I deserve a life of my own!"

"Oh, you do, do you?" His hands were in fists. "You deserve the life I tell you you'll have. Get yourself home right now."

My hands were shaking. Keeping the table between me and his hands, I ran out the back door and into the house. I could feel him following me with deliberate steps, and I sank onto the couch, trying to come up with defenses, but there weren't any. I started to cry, imagining another girl in the role of Anne Frank. It was the first thing I'd wanted for myself like this, wanted so badly I couldn't stand to lose it.

When he came through the door, I said, "Daddy, I'll do anything you want, serve extra, take care of the children in the nursery, whatever you want, but please let me do this! Please!"

"Oh, you'll do anything, will you?" He slipped his belt from the loops at his waist. "You want to be a Jezebel like all those women out there, strutting their bodies in the street and tempting men to sin? You want to show off? You want to be admired?"

I sobbed. "No! I just want to act. I'm *good*—"

"Stand up!"

"No, Daddy. Not the belt, please!"

"Stand up!" he roared. And when I did: "Turn around and grab on to the back of that chair."

I obeyed because it would be worse if I didn't. Closing my eyes tight, I gripped the chair and braced myself, but I still couldn't help crying out when the belt landed across the backs of my thighs. Again. And again. I don't know how many times. I wanted not to cry, but the tears poured out of me and I fell down to my knees, sobbing. Blubbering. "You're grounded for the week," he said, putting his belt back on.

"No! Daddy, please! Phoebe is here!"

He didn't even bother to answer.

Phoebe

The next morning I was tortured with guilt over the kiss with Joel, and terrified that Suze would hate me. She said he wasn't her boyfriend, but maybe she'd be upset anyway. I mean, what were the rules? I wanted to talk to her about it before he did.

Twice I went to the house, but nobody answered, and when I peeked into the kitchen windows at the church, nobody was there.

Amma and I were sitting down to dinner when a boy about ten delivered an envelope to the door. I recognized Suze's handwriting and tore it open. A single piece of notebook paper was inside.

Dear Phoebe,
My dad found out about the play and he gave me the belt, and I'm grounded for the rest of the week. I am so sad! I'm going to miss your entire visit and I won't be able to do the play, and I HATE HIM SO MUCH!
One of these days, I'll get away from him, I swear.
I am so so so so so so sad about the play.
Love,
Suze

PS Write everything down for the whole week and leave it with Amma so I can read it when I'm free. Love you. Have fun with Joel. He's such a nice guy. (I think you like him, and that's okay.)

"What is it?" Amma asked.

I raised my head. "Suze landed the lead in a play, *Anne Frank*, and her dad found out and gave her the belt and grounded her." Tears welled up in my eyes. "This is so unfair! She never gets to do anything. Her dad is so mean!"

She reached out and took my hand. "He is mean. He is a terrible man, Phoebe, and there are a lot like him in the world. There is nothing you can do for Suze right now except be there for her when you can."

"Can *you* do something?"

She took a breath. "I do what I can, honey. I'll keep doing that, I promise."

CURRENT DAY

Chapter Ten

Suze

I remember a Sunday school class in some church or another. The details of the place are murky. All the churches blurred together after a while, sanctuaries and basements and pulpits and kitchens melding in a single memory file. Sunday school rooms boasted kid-size chairs and scarred tables and coloring pages of Jesus and the disciples. We sang songs and memorized Bible verses, and it was a happy place, cutting things out to glue on paper, using crayons to explore the lesson of the day. Bible verses still float through my mind at the oddest of times: *"But the fruit of the Spirit is love, joy, peace, patience, kindness, goodness."* *"Love one another."* *"The greatest of these is love."* And one that singsongs through with power, though I would almost swear my dad never uttered it because it was too positive: *"Our God is able to do exceedingly abundantly above all we ask or think."*

Those were never the verses my father focused on in his sermons, which I assumed was a function of adults versus children. The grown-ups got the serious stuff, the harsh judgments and fiery admonitions, while the children learned about Jesus and love and kindness.

In this particular Sunday school class, my young, pretty teacher showed us a photo of Jesus as a brown man. He gazed kindly from a painting I now realize was a version of the Catholic *Sacred Heart of*

Jesus. But for me, in that moment, it was the friendliest version I'd ever seen. I couldn't have been more than eight or nine, and right then, Jesus became my friend.

All at once, I understood that this kindly God could keep me company and listen to my worries and prayers and even sleep next to me at night when I was afraid. My mother must have already died, because I missed her the most at night, when I felt the emptiness of her death pressing into my room, ready to smother me. I asked the teacher if Jesus could stay with you while you fell asleep, and she said, "Oh, of course, Suzanne! What a wonderful idea, to talk to Jesus while you fall asleep."

That was it for me. Jesus of the big brown eyes and happy smile was my constant companion. I imagined that he strolled along beside me to school, double-checking when I crossed the street to make sure I didn't get hit by a car (which had happened to a girl in our class—she had not returned to school, though she hadn't died). He sat with me during lonely sandwich suppers while my dad worked on his latest sermon, and when I fell asleep, I imagined Jesus held me, stroking my hair the way my mother had, once upon a time. Sometimes, Jesus sang to me.

Unfortunately, he couldn't protect me from my father, and in my fury, I turned my back on that comforting prophet. Even Beryl's gentle religion couldn't penetrate when I returned to Blue Cove.

As I sit in my kitchen looking out to a restless gray ocean, I can press my fingers into the ache the loss of my religion left behind. An REM song rolls through my memory, a song that wrecked me the first time I heard it.

Now I think about the man at the restaurant. The men who attacked me.

Was I too outspoken, too harsh, when I spoke out against the LNB? Maybe. I knew they'd killed Nadine Truelove, a freshman senator from California who had vowed to stand up to them.

But when I was a broken teenager, shamed and hidden away, I'd vowed to stand up for other girls. I promised myself that I'd never stand by in silence.

So I speak up. Against the Taliban, against Tea Party radicals, and yes, against the LNB, a radical white-supremacist sect out of the mountains of Colorado.

The day of the interview when I got myself in such hot water, we had pulled out of Afghanistan, and the country was falling to the Taliban in record time. Days. I kept thinking about all those girls, *all those girls*, six-year-olds and teenagers and earnest writers and budding scientists, girls who'd been happy about school and learning things and getting ready to take their places in the world—all sidelined, swept out of schools, suddenly forced to stay at home.

Every last one of them wore Jasmine's face in my mind. Jasmine, who carried around a little notebook to write things down, who wrote geography reports just for herself, who loved to read.

Jasmine. What a fierce little being she is! I don't remember where I was when Stephanie was born. Traveling somewhere with some movie. Those were the years when I worked pretty much all the time, going from filming to promotion to pre-production on one movie after another, twelve in fourteen years.

But I was home visiting Beryl when Jasmine was born in Portland. By then, my career had settled into a good rhythm. Not easy, because it's not an easy world, but because by then I worked in television, I could mostly live at home. Dmitri still filmed a movie every year, so he was on location four or five months, and we both enjoyed the fact that this allowed us to live our own lives and still have the relationship.

We knew Steph was due, so I headed up to Oregon a week or so ahead of time. Steph had asked Phoebe to be her coach because she'd already left her husband, so Phoebe was in the room when Jasmine arrived in the world.

Beryl and I drove up two days later. By then, Beryl was in her late eighties and not as comfortable driving as she had been. Although her eyesight was good, her reaction times were not, a confession she made herself when she gave up her keys. Phoebe and I both suspected there'd been some sort of a minor incident, but Beryl never shared.

We listened to CDs of folk songs and belted the words out at the tops of our voices, and I remembered a time Beryl drove me to Phoebe's house for a long weekend. I wonder now why my dad let me go, but he did. I was so intimidated by the big house, the swimming pool in the basement, Phoebe's much more comfortable world. "Remember when you drove me to Phoebe's house?"

"Yes. She looked forward to that for months."

"Me too." I shook my head slightly. "And then I was so intimidated by seeing the world she lived in. It was so different than mine." I remembered the tidy row of clothes in her closet, so many beautiful things. Her bathroom—her own bathroom, which she didn't share with anyone else—was filled with fancy cosmetics, and she had shelf after shelf of records by a turntable in her room. "I was so jealous."

"You girls were always jealous of each other. Like sisters, sure the other one had the extra helping."

"She did have a better helping in a lot of ways. Parents, grandmother, money."

"And she would have said that you had the beauty and the boys."

"I would have traded in a hot minute."

Beryl looked at me. Light caught the deep furrows in her cheeks. "Would you?"

I raised my eyebrows. "Then, maybe. Now, no way."

At the hospital, we found Stephanie sound asleep, Phoebe in a chair by the window, a tiny being in her arms, wrapped in a burrito of blankets, only a headful of hair showing. Phoebe beamed when she saw us. "Look, Jasmine," she said in a sweet voice. "Here's your Amma and auntie come to see you."

Jasmine was wide awake, trying to gnaw on her tiny fingers, and it felt like she locked eyes with me, eyes the smoky blue-gray of newborns everywhere. I fell instantly, completely in love, and my heart exploded with sorrow. Both were true: that I missed a baby who'd be grown by now, and that I would adore this girl forever.

"Hi, Jasmine," I said, touching her finger. "I'm so glad to meet you."

We were fast friends from that moment on. So when the reporter asked me about the shooting of Nadine Truelove by the LNB, I lost it. She'd been the youngest female senator to ever serve in California, a woman of color, and they had killed her. Killed her. I ranted for three solid minutes about religious oppression and the rise of overt white supremacy, about the terrified little boys running around trying to control the world with their violence and attempts to corral and kill women.

It was only at the end, when I realized that the entire set was quiet, that I knew I'd gone too far.

I thought they'd trim it, cut it, shape it up.

After four decades in the entertainment industry, I should have known better. They knew they had a click-generator. The interview went live two days later and was viral in fifteen minutes. I made every hit list for every nutty right-wing organization in the country. Maybe the world, because I didn't spare any of them.

After we left the Pig 'N Pancake, I was shaking so hard I couldn't get my shoulder bag over my head. Phoebe had to help me loop the strap over my body. I was so unsteady that she sat me down in the booth and brought me a glass of water.

"Can you take me home?"

"What about Yul Brynner?" Jasmine asked.

"I'll come get him later," I said. "You'll look out for him until then, right?"

"Of course. Can he come sleep with me when I take a rest?"

"That's up to your nana."

Phoebe said, "Are you sure you want to be alone? I don't mind if you come to the house."

"I need to talk to my therapist," I lied. "I'll come down later, if that's okay."

"That's fine. I have some more work to do, so I'll be in the studio later. Join me whenever you're ready."

The healing atmosphere of the studio brushed over my mind, but at the moment I couldn't contemplate being even that far away from the locked and bolted rooms of my house. When they dropped me off, I unlocked the door, slammed it behind me, and made a beeline for the kettle. I'm still shaking, but less violently. It's turned into a fine trembling that runs below my skin, through my veins. I plant my palms against the counter and try to breathe, all the way in, all the way out, but my body remembers—*a blast of something solid coming out of nowhere, slamming into the back of my head—*

—A boot blasting into my left ribs—

—Yanking on my hair, pulling up up backward—

—My father's belt making a sound as it swung through the air, the slap as it connected—

—A knee pinning me down as a razor ran over my scalp—

—A baby's cry—

I press my fingers to my temples.

One of the things my therapist has been working on with me is my wrecked nervous system. Right now it feels shattered, maybe broken beyond repair. All these years I've turned the traumas of my life into bricks I could use to climb up and out, but now all those steps are crumbling and—

A bright knock lands against my kitchen window. I yelp, crossing my arms defensively as I stagger backward.

But it's a seagull. He's landed on the railing around the deck, and the noise is him rapping his big yellow beak against the glass.

He's a big bird. A factoid I know from Phoebe, the bird fanatic, is that some of the largest seagulls in the world live around here. This one is bright white with black wing feathers and banded stripes on his tail. He's fully two feet tall, and when he cocks his head sideways, looking at me, some of the wild terror in my body eases. "Hello. Has someone been feeding you?"

He taps his beak against the window again, as if he's answering me, and it surprises a laugh from me. "You're used to getting your way, aren't you?" Phoebe would kill me if I fed him, but I'm sorely tempted. I mean, I perform for my supper. Why can't seagulls?

But I don't feed him. Phoebe has impressed upon me the importance of letting wild animals be wild. Instead, I brew my tea and watch the waves, trying to anchor myself in their rhythmic movements. A low bank of clouds rolls in, heavy and purple, and beneath them the sea starts to toss. I wonder what storm is out there on the feral ocean, and something in me eases as I think of it, the water and the beings beneath it, and the clouds and the rain. A hardness in my chest slips away. The gull sits with me, just on the other side of the glass, until rain starts pattering against the window and his feathers. As if it annoys him, he flaps his big wings and flies down to join his cronies at the shoreline, where the rough surf has left a thick row of debris. Good eating for birds.

My phone rings with a number I don't recognize, but it's a local area code. I pick it up and cautiously say, "Hello?"

"Hello, ma'am," says a woman. "This is Blue River Electric. We had a cancellation and can fit you in today if you want us to take a look at that breaker box."

"Oh!" Ben must have called them already. Since the alarm system is connected to that box, I'm grateful. "Yes, please. When?"

"Like now-ish? He can be there in about ten minutes, if that's okay."

My immediate reaction is to put it off, but why? It needs to get done, and what else am I doing? "Okay. That's great."

"He'll be right there."

I hang up and call Phoebe. "The electrician is already on the way. Thanks."

"You're welcome. I thought it would be better to get it taken care of. We probably don't want that house to burn down."

"No, that would be sad."

"Jasmine and I are taking our rest, but we'll go down to the studio after. See you there, okay?"

"Yes. Thanks, Phoebe." I almost add, "I don't deserve you," but she'd just agree.

Before I've fully hung up, the doorbell rings. Smoothing my hair, which is a fool's errand since I know I'm a mess, I call out, "Coming!" and open the door.

A man stands on the porch, sheltered from the rain. His long, salt-and-pepper hair is pulled back into a braid. His brows are heavier than I remember, and the jawline is going a little soft, but he's still himself, tall and lean, wearing jeans and a good jacket.

All the air leaves my lungs and I stare at him for a long moment. A million memories roll through me, glazed with grief and incandescent love and a longing so sharp and pure that I feel it still in the depths of my gut. "Joel," I say in an airless voice.

His expression is unreadable, but he stares right back at me. In my peripheral vision, I see his hand clench. "Suze," he says.

It's madness, because I haven't seen him since we were fifteen years old, but there's no resisting it—I step forward and hug him. Hard. It's completely impulsive and probably really weird considering how many decades it's been since I've seen him, but his arms come around me, too, tight, and we press together in wordless memory, things too hard to speak, things too big. Into his neck, which smells exactly the same, of rain and earth and hope, I say fervently, "It is so good to see you."

He stands there, quiet, hugging me back. Our bodies are tight together, as if it were just the other day we did this, instead of years and years and years. Enough years to fill a whole life.

And it doesn't matter. He feels right. He says, "Jesus, you smell exactly the same."

It goes on a long time, until I feel like I might dissolve entirely.

"Sorry," I whisper, but I can't quite let go. So many things rise through my body, dark and bright, side by side. My shaved head. His fury. The endless days we spent here and in his mother's house when she was at work. The days I spent wondering why he deserted me. Learning he'd been sent away.

The baby. That little girl I was forced to give away.

Something deep within cracks open.

So intense. So long ago.

I'm embarrassed to realize there are tears leaking out of my eyes, and I force myself to step back. He reaches out and is about to brush them away, but I step back at the same instant, mortified. "Come inside."

His face is entirely expressionless as he follows my lead. I can't help wondering if Phoebe knew he would be the one to show up.

THEN

I Don't Know How to Love Him

Monday, Thanksgiving Week

Dear Suze,

I got your letter last night. I'm so PISSED OFF at your dad, and I wish I could help you somehow, but my grandmother said there's nothing we can really do. So I'm writing every day.

Joel and I walked on the beach last night and talked about A WRINKLE IN TIME. He's a really nice person and I am glad he's your friend. I invited him over to do some art in Amma's studio today and it was really fun. He's a good artist! He drew a picture of you and both of us miss you so much.

Truth—I do *like* him, like him, and I think he likes me, too. He asked for my phone number and I thought it was probably okay since I asked you if he was your boyfriend but you said no way, that he was just your friend. I wish we could talk about this on the phone or face-to-face because I don't want to get it wrong.

But now that you're on restriction, there's nothing to do. I feel so lonely without you.

I drew some comics for you. Suze and Phoebe go to NYC.

Love,
Phoebe

Phoebe

Joel came over for dinner with me and Amma. I could tell she liked him. She leaned in to listen when he talked, and filled up his plate three times. Unobtrusively, asking questions to keep him chatting.

After dinner, we walked down to the arcade, a building in the main part of town that's old and musty but still kind of fun. "Want to play pinball?" he asked, and I was glad to do whatever, but it turned out I was pretty good at this machine called Eight Ball. When Joel ran out of quarters, I cashed in another three dollars and we played for ages, winning replays until finally those quarters were done, too.

"You want something to eat?" Joel asked, pointing to a snack bar. "Candy bar or some fries or something?"

"No, thanks," I said, thinking I didn't want anything on my teeth in case he kissed me again.

"How about we split a Coke?"

"Okay."

He ordered it and I looked around the room, wondering what it would be like if this was where I lived and I got to hang out here. Kids were playing air hockey and foosball, which I was good at because we had one in the game room at home and I'd been practicing. "You play?" I asked, pointing.

"Yeah." He offered me the Coke and I took a sip, thinking that his lips had been right on that straw a second ago. His expression was quizzical when he tilted his head. "You do?"

"Yes. My dad taught me. He's into all kinds of games."

"Cool." He eyed the table, where a row of quarters waited. "It looks like a lot of people are in line to play. Let's go outside. If you won't be too cold."

"Nope." I had my rain jacket over a sweater. Even if it poured, I'd be fine. Joel, on the other hand, only had a jean jacket. "You're the one."

He took my hand, right in front of everybody in the room, and led me toward the door. "I'll be fine."

I wondered if everyone saw it, that a boy liked me, that he was holding my hand. I felt every inch of it acutely, the flatness of his palm, his long fingers. We walked without speaking down the covered pavement by the shops. Rain poured overhead, and I could hear the ocean.

My blood seemed hot, and under my hair, my neck was burning up. I wondered if we would kiss again, if he wanted to. And just then, he looked over his shoulder and drew me into an alcove that led to the stormy beach. It was empty.

He tucked me up against the wall and, with his eyes dark and liquid, asked, "Can I kiss you again?"

I nodded, and he lowered his head and our lips locked. We kissed for a long time, just our lips, and then sometimes Joel kissed my neck, which turned me on so much that I even made a sound. When he was doing that, he slid his hand under my sweater until he touched bare skin and kept kissing my neck. Everything in my body felt alive, wild, free, and I put my hands under his shirt, too, opening my palms to feel his waist. It was hot and silky.

He found my lips again and pressed our bodies together. "You okay?"

I swallowed, already missing the taste of his mouth. "Yeah."

He smiled. "Me too. You taste good."

"So do you."

I lifted up on my toes and kissed him again, pressing our chests together. He held his hands on my waist. "I think I need to walk you back home."

"Okay."

We held hands all the way, talking about color and light and things I never dreamed I'd talk about with a boy. At my grandma's driveway, he kissed me again, lightly. "See you soon, Phoebe."

I nodded, and watched him walk away, lean and loose limbed, and I thought I would never feel so alight again in my life.

In fact, it was a very long time.

Wednesday before Thanksgiving

Dear Suze,

Sorry I didn't write yesterday. It was a busy day! I went to Seaside with my grandmother to get groceries and when we got back, I helped her cook. She says cooking is really important and that I need to learn to be good at it. Good food is important for your body, and serving it beautifully makes an ordinary day festive. That's nice, right? My mom doesn't care about dinner. We usually only all sit down together once in a while, and my dad doesn't really cook, so he makes TV dinners when he's the one who is home. I love it when I'm here and we eat together every night, even if it's just soup and bread, which it is a lot.

Joel came over when we got back and stayed for dinner, which was Amma's mac and cheese, which he ate so much of that he had to lean back and burp at one point, which made us all laugh. Amma says he's a growing boy and is going to shoot up.

After dinner, we walked downtown and played pinball at the arcade and talked about art stuff, like how to do shading on living things, and what our favorite paint colors are (mine is alizarin crimson, his was a color I think is so ugly, yellow ocher).

I wish you'd been with us. I could feel you like a ghost all night. I wish I knew how you were doing.
Love,
Phoebe

Sunday after Thanksgiving
Dear Suze,

I am so sorry I haven't had time to write!!!! My mom and dad came on Wednesday and we've been doing family things, even my mom, who seems weirdly happy. She got a promotion at work, with a lot more money, and she always likes making more money. We ate like pigs and played a million games (I won Scrabble three times!) and hung out. Joel went somewhere with his mom, so I talked to him on the phone, but we didn't get to go anywhere again.

I'm leaving the diary so you can read it and write in it, but PLEASE call me as soon as you can. Amma said you can use her phone and she'll pay, no problem.

I MISS YOU SO MUCH! The good thing is, it's only a month till Christmas vacation and I'll see you then.
Love,
Phoebe

November 29, 19—
Dear Phoebe,

Joel told me he kissed you. I can't believe you guys did that! Like I didn't even exist. Like it didn't matter that I was imprisoned in my room for the entire Thanksgiving vacation and no one even cares. You hung out with each other like I don't even matter. I'm so so so so mad at you!!!!!

I'm not going to be in the play. My dad forced me to quit. I couldn't stop crying when I told my teacher.

I'M SO MAD AT YOU!

Suze

[PAGE TORN OUT]

Dear Phoebe,

My dad imprisoned me for the whole week. It killed me that you and Joel hung out the whole time and painted and went to the beach and had fun and I was STUCK IN MY ROOM. I wanted to cut my hair but I was too scared, so I cut some ribbons in my skin, on my thigh, where my dad will never see them.

I hate my life. I hate my dad. I hate that I'm stuck here in this house for five more years until I'm 18. I wish I could run away like GO ASK ALICE, but I don't know where I'd find some older guy to let me live with him.

I wanted to be in the play so bad, and now I can't do it. I wanted to BE WITH YOU during Thanksgiving and now you're back home and that makes my heart hurt SO BAD. I miss you. I wish you lived here.

[PAGE TORN OUT]

December 1, 19—
    Dear Phoebe,
        I am fine. Don't worry. I'm glad you and Joel had fun. He told me he kissed you, which you might have said. I don't know about this diary right now. I'll try to call you, but I don't know when.
        Love,
        Suze

CURRENT DAY

Chapter Eleven
Phoebe

After we drop Suze off at her house, Jasmine and I have rest time. Not that she likes it that much, but I'm attached to my naps. When I'm refreshed, we head down to the studio. I can tell she's restless. Art is great for a couple of hours, but she and Maui are bouncing off the walls. Looking through the windows, I see that the rain has stopped. "Why don't you go play outside?" I suggest, swishing a paintbrush in water.

"Finally!" She pulls on her hoodie and Maui jumps up, grabbing a stick he dragged inside earlier. Jasmine takes it. "Let's play fetch," she says and leans in. "That means I throw it, you bring it back, okay?"

I chuckle. "Don't go too far."

When they leave, I think about those words. If I yelled for her and she didn't arrive within a minute or two, I'd be in a panic. So unlike the days when Suze and I tumbled through the forests and beaches all day without anyone worrying. We had bikes and rode them for miles on trails and beaches, around town and to explore places we would surely have been forbidden to visit, like the junkyard and a strip club down on the county road. A hole in one of the walls let us peek inside to the tired, dark interior, where women gyrated in a bored way. Still, it gave us a thrill to see naked breasts.

We also collected everything from shells to pine cones to snakeskins, and took them to the studio to paint and draw. Suze loved feathers, loved trying to capture the iridescence of the vanes, and she liked collecting rocks, too. My tastes ran to flowers, dandelions and roses, the dahlias in my grandmother's farm fields—such a glory when they bloomed in July and August!—anything with petals.

It took me literally a decade to recognize that my love of flowers and the sea has always been the direction I wanted to take with my art. This direction, illustration and flowers. Color. Bold, bright color.

All the things they looked down on in art school.

The plan had always been for Suze and me to go to New York City after high school, and room together in a garret we imagined would be romantic. Instead, when it came time to apply to schools in the city, I was afraid. Afraid to be rejected, afraid I would never measure up, afraid to be so far away from my father and my grandmother and all the things I understood in Oregon. I did want to go to art school, but in the end, I only applied to schools in the Northwest. I got in to both Seattle and Portland, and chose Seattle only because my grandmother told me I needed to at least get that far away from home.

Embarrassed at my small ambition, I lied to Suze and told her I didn't get into anything in New York. I asked her to come to Seattle with me, but she was dead focused on making a name for herself on Broadway. Like millions of girls before her, she headed for the bright lights.

I headed up I-5 and dived into art school. It was fantastic from the start. I loved my classes and made friends. My teachers encouraged me and pushed me. It was the most I'd ever liked school.

Sometimes it scared me. I didn't always want to push the envelope, or make ugly paintings to get oohs and aahs. Not that everyone did that, and it's not that fine art is all strange or ugly. It's not. But when I was in art school, the things I loved were beautiful paintings of giant flowers and pensive women looking out windows. They were very much not in fashion.

I met Derek my second year. He was in my studio class, and was generally acknowledged to be the most promising artist in our year. His work was bold and harsh, with lots of nudity rendered in thick lines, and he had a confidence that was rare for a nineteen-year-old.

The first time I saw him in class, I was absolutely smitten. His hair, so thick and black and shiny, falling around a face as beautiful as a dark angel's. He was the kind of guy who should have been with the pretty girl from Omaha in figure drawing, but for some reason, he liked me back. He liked my paintings, the size of them, the colors I used. He loved my breasts and painted them—both painted on them and painted renditions of them on canvas. It was embarrassing to have him show that work in class, and I always blushed when I saw someone look at me, measuring.

It was a hot, hot love affair. We had sex everywhere, in a thousand ways, as horny as only nineteen-year-olds can be. My passion for art was subsumed by my lust for Derek, and he used that to his advantage. He often dropped comments that only one artist could be primary in a relationship. It terrified me. Would he leave me for a non-artist?

God, the things we do for sex and love! I want to go back in time and shake that smitten child. Suze tried. My grandmother mounted an entire campaign that included a trip to Paris on my winter break junior year.

They failed.

For two reasons, really. The first was that I landed with an instructor that fall who loathed my work. Loathed. He loathed women, but I didn't get that then. I just thought there was something wrong with me, with my grasp of the finer ideas of art. Derek landed a modest show, and the instructor loved him.

And only two years after she arrived in New York, Suze was invited to come to Hollywood for a screen test. For the lead role in a book we'd both adored, a historical about a beleaguered and fierce woman who makes her way triumphantly through the world.

When she landed it, so easily, I was both desperately proud and wildly jealous. She was always going to be the star in the world, and I was always going to be the mouse.

Derek and I started living together at the end of my sophomore year. We'd been dating the whole year, spending nights at his crowded, shared apartment, where no one ever did the dishes and the air smelled of dirty shoes and beer. At the start of the summer, both of us had good jobs waiting tables, so we found a tiny cottage, just a bedroom and kitchen, a postage stamp of a bathroom, and a living room barely large enough for a couch and a single chair. I filled the windows with houseplants and bought used pans and dishes at Goodwill that I used to make dinners and bake the treats we loved to eat when we were stoned. I developed a little fame over my muffins and scones and quick breads, thanks to Amma's instruction.

The reason we chose the cottage was the big shed in the backyard. It was unheated and not really big enough for the canvases Derek was painting, so he continued to use the space he'd rented in downtown Seattle, while I set up in the shed, sweeping out the spiders and dirt. It had two big windows that faced north, and enough room for an easel and two long tables against the far wall. A rolling cupboard held my supplies.

The year in that house, June to June, was one of the happiest times of my life, despite the fact that art school was kicking my butt. I loved the people, loved being around other artists and the wild, far-reaching imaginations that made conversations so much fun. At parties, someone always had a guitar or a banjo or a recorder to play music, and someone else would read poetry they'd written, and we'd have loud debates about the palette of Kahlo or the technique of Matisse or the differences between Impressionism and Fauvism. I loved only thinking about the work and what was emerging, and having paint under my fingernails like Amma.

But the truth was, that summer between sophomore and junior year, painting on my own in that studio of my own, I had to face the reality that I didn't love postmodernist styles, or abstract anything. I loved representational work, and things that Derek and most of the rest of my peers and teachers rolled their eyes over. I loved paintings that were too girly for words—flowers and cats and windows and interiors. I loved Matisse's cats and William Morris patterns and *New Yorker* cover illustrations—oh, to have a cover on the *New Yorker*!—and saturated pinks and oranges and blues that everyone thought too overt. Too much.

I struggled in classes with criticism of paintings I didn't even love myself. Abstract work felt cold and distant to me, like planets in some faraway galaxy. I wanted warmth and love and coziness.

That summer in my studio, I painted interiors, rooms with overstuffed couches and cats lounging on the cushions. I did watercolor gardens and pen-and-ink renditions of my grandmother's flower farm. I didn't show any of it to anyone, but I felt like me for the first time since starting school.

I felt like myself when I baked cranberry orange bread and learned to roast vegetables on rainy days. I loved being in my body when Derek and I made love in our tiny bedroom on our mattress on the floor, reveling in each other's flesh, giving and receiving endless pleasure. Sex made us artistic, and art made us horny, and we reveled in all of it.

That was the summer Suze was working in France, filming her first movie, and her letters were filled with wonders—the cobbled streets and old houses and the grueling days. Because I was happy in my own skin, I was happy for her. Because I was in love, I could imagine her falling in love, too. In the spring, I went to the premiere and realized that she was going to be very, very famous, and I didn't even mind that, because

I knew the secret I carried in my belly, the baby who would become Stephanie, my girl.

~

Decades later, in my grandmother's studio, I lift my brush and tilt my head. The dahlia wallpaper is nearly finished, but there's something a little bit off. To help me see it more clearly, I upload it to my computer and open the design in Adobe. In a new layer, I manipulate the darks along the leaves and the stems. Better, but not there yet.

Another layer.

A knock sounds at the door, and I'm relieved. Suze has finally come down the hill. I've been fretting about her, about the encounter in the diner. "Come in!"

An enormous bouquet of dahlias, some a little worse for the wear, parades itself into the room. "The last of the blooms," Ben says, settling the flowers on the table where I'm working. "It's going to freeze tonight, so I thought you might like them."

Looking at the real-life flowers, I see instantly that what I'm missing is another round of subtle color, deep in the throats of the petals. "I've been struggling all morning with a problem and now I see exactly what it is." Sliding a particularly pretty one from the vase, I hold it toward the window, narrowing my eyes to pick out the peach, the pink, the touches of magenta at the base of the petals. "Thank you!"

He stands there a moment.

I look up. "Everything okay?"

"Yeah," he says, and the shine of his eyes lands on my face. He clears his throat. "I was actually wondering, Phoebe, if you'd go to dinner with me."

At first it doesn't sink in. "Like tonight? It's going to be busy."

"Not tonight, and not in town. I thought we could get dressed up and drive up to Poseidon and have some surf and turf or something."

Now I look up. A heady mix of intense yearning stirred with extreme embarrassment washes through me. "What? I mean . . . yes? But are you—"

He steps closer and covers my fingers where they lie on the table. "Asking you on a date? Yes."

I gape, feeling as if a giant hand has shaken my world. A sensation I nearly do not recognize wakes up and rolls through my gut, my thighs.

I hesitate for so long that he looks embarrassed, and he steps back. "I'm sorry. I got it wrong. I thought it was mutual. It's okay."

"Wait!" I grab his arm as he's about to turn away. "You just . . . I didn't . . . uh . . . I'm surprised, that's all. I forgot how to like someone that way."

A slow smile lifts one side of his mouth. "Like how?"

"*Like* like," I say, and realize I do, that I have been *liking* him for quite some time. All those days when he made tea in my kitchen, when he fixed the windows in my studio. When I noticed his mouth and then insisted to myself that I did not out of embarrassment over my wish to have something like that in my life again.

I take a breath. "Ben, I would love to get dressed up and go to Poseidon and get a margarita with you. When?"

"How about Friday night?"

"Yes. I'll ask Suze if she can babysit."

Is it my imagination or does he look at my mouth? I look at his, neatly framed with his thick black-and-silver beard. I've never kissed anyone with a beard before. His lower lip is full, red. I realize I'm staring and, predictably, blush.

"Okay." He grins. "Okay!"

And then he's off and I'm standing in my studio, flush with pleasure and anticipation and things I had completely forgotten.

A date. With Ben.

Chapter Twelve
Suze

It's awkward in my house after Joel comes in. I have no idea what to do with my hands or where to look or if I should talk or not talk. My body is noisy with reaction, blood racing through my veins, thoughts and memories chasing each other through my brain, my mouth dry as a bone, my limbs shaky.

Joel simply goes about the business of the electrical problem. I watch him open the fuse box, and he moves differently, like a man, like the grown-up man he is. Silver threads through his long hair, but it's still beautiful hair. His jaw is softer. His hands look like they've been used hard, with scars and marks and calluses, but they're still beautiful, long fingers and wide palms. His frame is still lean, almost ropy. Beryl used to say we either get too lean or too fat as we age, and it proves true.

He mutters about the electrical problem, something to do with frayed wires in the main breaker box, and takes the plates off several light switches and outlets, muttering some more. I follow him, standing in doorways as he tracks the trouble.

Finally, he heads back to the fuse box and closes it. He turns, not quite meeting my eyes. "I have to get some parts, but this is a pretty serious issue. The kitchen looks good, but don't use anything in the bedroom and living room area until I get back."

"I had the kitchen updated three or four years ago," I say, crossing my arms. "I thought the rest had been done when I first bought the house in 2012."

"Doesn't look like it." He shrugs back into his performance raincoat. Expensive. His boots, too, are high-end waterproof hiking gear. It's hard to look directly at him, so I can only gather these details. He's wearing old-school Levi's with copper rivets. "Won't take me long."

"Okay." I feel like there is something else I should say, something to fix the moment I pulled away, but I can't think what that would be, and he simply goes out the same door he came in. Winded, oddly on the edge of tears, I sink down on the banquette and pick up my phone to text Phoebe:

Did you know Joel was back in town??????????

Yes. I thought I told you. He's been back a few years now. Longer than me.

What???? Was he here during the pandemic?

No, I think he was in Salem taking care of his mother. I don't really talk to him. We're not friends or anything.

Why not?

No reason, really. Our paths don't cross.

I hold the phone in my hand, a thousand memories tumbling through my mind. Joel and I met the first day of seventh grade, both outcasts and outsiders. I think of that boy, with his brutal acne and hunched shoulders, hiding his face behind a fall of thick black hair. I think of the Joel he grew into by the time we started high school, tall and lean and way too good-looking, still my main person after Phoebe, or maybe equal to her.

I text: Did you know he would be the electrician who showed up?

No! OMG!

I told Phoebe everything back then, but she doesn't know the truth about Joel, that he and I were deeply in love for over two years. We kept it to ourselves, all through ninth and tenth grades, even though it irked Joel a lot.

But she struggled with friends and boyfriends. I didn't want to hurt her feelings. She had a gigantic crush on him for literally *years*. He was safe, the boy who lived in Blue Cove. She'd kissed him a few times, even though he was my friend first.

The first betrayal, hers.

The second was mine, because I kept the truth from her: that I loved him, and he loved me back, and we have some pretty heavy history. She knows that he burned the church down, and I always thought she'd put the rest of the pieces together, but somehow she never has.

Even I can see it's stupid to keep this secret after so long. I saw the mistake by the time she and I were twenty, but by then, I'd hidden some of the most important parts of my pain from her, and she was struggling enough in art school and with her longing to be an artist, and then I landed the part and my life took off and it was all unequal, and she married Derek and—

The time was never right.

The facts are so simple. I could blurt them out in a single paragraph. I could say, *Phoebe, Joel and I fell in love at the start of ninth grade and we had a serious relationship and the baby you think was Victor's belonged to Joel. I didn't tell you because I was afraid you'd be mad and you were so lost yourself.*

A pain that never really goes away has risen in my gut, where it mixes with other traumas, other times, other things. *I feel the blow to the back of my head, hitting the earth, tasting dirt—*

My father grabs my hair, roaring—

I stand up, open the patio door to let in the cool air, take in deep lungfuls. I told Phoebe I was going to call my therapist, and it's important, but I hold the phone in my palm, feeling texts buzz and buzz and buzz again.

From Phoebe:
Suze? Was it weird?
Suze, you okay?
Are you all right?

The air fills my head, my lungs, settles me. On top of the Starfish Queen, which is what we always called the regal middle rock, birds touch down and take flight, bringing food to others, keeping watch for hawks.

I text: I'm okay. Sorry. Got distracted. My nerves are pretty raw.

I bet. You want us to bring Yul Brynner back?

Some small part of me had been maybe hoping to go back down there tonight, but that's foolish. I live here. I can't go live at my friend's house, even if I did when I was a teenager, though it wasn't her house then. It was Beryl's.

Sure. Joel had to go get some parts, so I have to stay here.

Jasmine wants to come over anyway. She loves that house as much as we did.

She sounds so friendly. It breaks my heart, because the whole reason I came back is to work out all the things between us, to finally tell her the truth. But instinctively, I know that the fight that ostensibly wounded our trust in each other was nothing compared to this secret, the secret I've kept for decades.

What would Beryl do? I wonder.

I'll put the kettle on.

Chapter Thirteen
Phoebe

Jasmine and I load Yul Brynner into his carrier and drive him up the hill. Maui insists he needs to be included, which makes for a crowded cab. I feel weirdly happy and keep forgetting why, and then I hear Ben's voice again, asking me out.

On a date.

I'm excited to tell Suze. She knows how long it has been since I've had a date or the possibility of a relationship, or even a good roll in the hay. Between caring for Amma in her last two years and the pandemic, I didn't have many opportunities. Or desire, honestly, though I thought I'd get over missing sex with another person and I haven't.

Jasmine chatters about the history of Ragdoll cats, about which she has written an entire page in her little notebook. I'm murmuring in response, but honestly, my mind keeps returning to Ben's warm eyes, his big, solid body—

Oh, don't do this!

The warning sounds in a nasty voice in my head. *Don't get your hopes up, who do you think you are, you're too old for this nonsense, men have never really liked you, why do you think this would be any different?*

A big blue truck with BLUE RIVER ELECTRIC painted on the side is parked in the circular driveway. I did know that Joel lived in town—I've seen him sometimes in the store or at a restaurant, always by himself, wrapped in a weary sort of sadness that comes from life losses. His mother died during the pandemic, which I saw in the *Blue Cove Crier*, a weekly newspaper that comes out every Wednesday, but I don't know anything more. I had such a wretched crush on him when we were teenagers, a crush that ended only when he was sent away for burning down the church.

Why did I always yearn for a boy, anyway? After Joel was sent away and I was in high school, I transferred the longing to Billy Mascarenes, a dark-haired charmer who had more girls than he knew what to do with, and pined for him for a full year. Finally, I had an actual relationship in my senior year, with a fellow artist named Andy who'd been in classes with me for years. We connected over an assignment to imitate our favorite artists and both of us chose comic books. We learned about each other's minds and bodies and hearts, and broke up only when his family moved away after graduation.

But as I hold the door for Jasmine and Maui to jump down, Joel comes out the front door, a thick utility belt around his waist. He's still good-looking in a haunted sort of way. I wonder what has left those lines around his mouth.

Seeing me, he lifts his chin my direction. "Hey, Phoebe! How are you? You guys are still friends, huh?"

I've been keeping her at such a distance that this is a loaded question, but honestly, how do you stop being someone's sister? Suze is my family. There's unresolved stuff between us, but . . . "Yep. How's it going back in Blue Cove?"

A nod. "Good enough. I was sorry to hear about your grandmother. She was one of the best people I've ever known."

"She was. I still miss her."

He gives Jasmine a kind smile. "Hello, young lady. Is this your grandmother?"

"She's my nana," Jasmine says. "We brought Yul Brynner back to Suze."

He gives me a quizzical look. "Like *The King and I*?"

"Yep." I touch my girl's head. "This is Jasmine."

"Like *Aladdin*," she pipes up.

It makes him laugh. "Smart, too, I think. She's inside."

Maui bounds up the steps, Jasmine right behind him with the cat carrier in hand, leaning sideways to balance the weight of it.

"How are you, Phoebe?" Joel opens a toolbox on the side of the truck and reaches inside. "I see the flower farm every morning on my way down the mountain. It's a splendor."

"A splendor," I repeat, smiling. "You always had the most surprising vocabulary for a guy."

"Yeah?" He glances at me over his shoulder, and I remember how bad my crush was, a living thing that was born of a single week of kisses followed by nothing at all. "Thanks," he says as he straightens. He's gathered a handful of bits and pieces. Waits for me, and we walk up the steps. "You were the only person I ever met who read more than I did."

"Suze was pretty close."

"Nah. You always outread us both." He gestures, and I step inside ahead of him. Maui bounds toward me, slurps my hand, runs back toward the kitchen, his nails clattering on the floor. I'm here all the time in my capacity as caretaker, for which Suze pays me too much money. I've repeatedly told her I'd do it for free, for the love of the place, but she continues to deposit a ridiculous sum in my account every month.

The thing is, I do love the pleasure of the quiet rooms when I'm here by myself, disturbed by nothing but my ghostly presence. I love the space and have since I climbed in a window when I was ten and found the abandoned rooms still perfectly furnished, as if someone ran away in the middle of the night. The truth was much sadder—an old man died here and had no heirs, so the place fell into probate and was somehow forgotten.

Filled now with animals and a little girl and Suze and Joel, it's an entirely different place. The kettle has made the window behind it steamy. A seagull is sitting on the railing outside. Jasmine and Maui have landed in the living room, near the bookcases, and Joel walks toward the back of the kitchen. "Don't turn anything on," Suze says, poking her head into the living room from the kitchen. "The electricity is off."

"Okay."

Suze stands by the counter, one foot over the other—it's a tic we both have, one among many. In the soft, stormy light, she looks haggard. Older than I could ever have imagined back in the day.

As if to mock us, behind her on the shelf is a photo of the two of us when we were three weeks past our twenty-first birthdays, at the premiere of *A Woman for the Ages*.

She invited Amma, too, but Amma didn't want to bother with all the folderol and dressing up. I was a nervous wreck on the inside, but my entire job for the night was to be support for Suze, who pretended she wasn't nervous, but I knew she was by the torn thumbnail on her left hand, which a nail tech fixed with some glue and fresh polish and then painted with a bitter something to keep her from doing it again.

We got ready at her new house in Bel Air. It wasn't huge, only three bedrooms, but it boasted a courtyard with a swimming pool under palm trees, floor-to-ceiling windows in all the interior rooms, and an elegance of line my years of architecture drooling could appreciate. "Did you ever think you'd really have a house like this?" I asked the day I arrived.

She snorted. "No way! I'm still pinching myself. Beryl told me to buy real estate, so I did." She squeezed my hand. "A swimming pool! Just like yours."

"It's gorgeous," I said, squeezing back.

By the time the makeup people and stylists were finished with us, we both looked fantastic. I was at my slimmest, thanks to an art school schedule that left little time to eat, and lots of sweaty, hot sex with Derek. They dressed me in a shimmery sheath that displayed a lot of cleavage, and swept my hair into an updo, and made up my face so that

I looked like a model. I barely recognized myself and couldn't wait for the photos.

But Suze. "Oh my God," I breathed when she came out. Tears sprang to my eyes. "Suze!"

The gown was a tip of the hat to a flapper dress in a shade of aquamarine that matched her eyes exactly. It was beaded over net, barely there over the shoulders with a plunging back. The iridescence caught her curves and displayed her slenderness. Her hair was simply caught back in a sort of french twist that made her look glamourous, and her face was all eyes and lips. "Good, right?" she said with a crooked smile. "Properly Cinderella."

"I'm so proud of you."

She hugged me. Our sequins and slipperiness made a swishing sound. The stylist shrieked. "Your makeup!"

Suze whispered, "Thank you for being here to share this."

It was a dazzling night. The press went wild for her. At the parties, everyone crowded in to talk to her, and she managed it all as if she'd been in the business for decades. She was confident and smiled easily but not too much, and listened carefully when people asked questions, then answered exactly right, every time. I'd always known she could act, but this was a whole extra talent.

Or maybe it was all the same. Maybe she was acting now, acting the part of a successful actress.

Which she was, overnight. By morning, the reviews were pouring in, and the critics adored her. By the end of two months, the movie had outearned all its competitors and was on track to being one of the highest-grossing films in history. By the end of the year, Suze had made another movie and signed to do two more. Her life grew so hectic that I wasn't able to see her very often, and I understood.

In the photo on the shelf behind exhausted modern-day Suze, a match to one on my bedroom bureau, we are both young and beautiful, on the brink of the next chapter of our lives. Our hands are clutched so tightly you can see the white on Suze's knuckles, and our bodies are very close together.

The woman before me in her kitchen is world weary and vulnerable. I haven't seen her this way since we were teenagers. I think of her lying in the hospital bed after her father beat her so badly for being pregnant, utterly still, attached to all the wires and tubes. I think of the second hospital bed, after another beating, and my stomach squeezes hard.

Impulsively, I cross the room and hug her. She's taller than me, but skinnier, and I feel her limbs like twigs and branches, not flesh. Even so, she melts into me, her face against my shoulder, her long arms around me. She sighs and tucks her nose into my neck.

We don't say anything. I know this is what she needs, what she longs for. Why do I find it so hard to be generous? I sometimes think this is the legacy of my cold mother, who pushed and prodded and loved me but mostly did withhold affection, both toward me and toward my father.

I run a hand up and down her spine. "Everything's going to be all right."

"Is it?"

"Yes," I say, emphatically. "Yes."

I feel her take a breath, fortifying herself, and she straightens, tucking a lock of hair behind her ear as she glances over her shoulder to where Joel is working on the breaker box. There's something in her expression that looks stricken, and I wonder if they've ever talked since he burned down her father's church. So furious. We'd all been so furious with her dad, and Joel was the one who expressed it for all of us.

A long time ago.

I say, "Joel, will you walk me through what you've done once you finish?"

"Sure thing. Nothing too complicated."

"Walk us both through," Suze says, and looks at me. "I'm going to be here awhile this time."

"That's good," I say. "You need some time to heal."

"Maybe I need to be home for good." She looks out the window toward the Starfish Sisters. As if to illustrate how perfect the view is, a bald eagle sails between us and the rocks. A squawking madness goes off, seagulls yelling, smaller birds swirling up in crowds. The eagle snatches one and flies away, chased by three others and a pair of seagulls squalling punitive curses after him.

"Wow," I say, awed.

"Yeah," she whispers. "How do I forget how fantastic this place is?"

"Well, it's an outdoor kind of fantastic. A *wet* outdoor fantastic." I pause. "Um, I need a favor?"

She inclines her head. "Anything."

I look to see where Jasmine is, and she's in the other room, dragging around a mouse on a string for Yul Brynner to chase. In a quiet voice, I say, "Ben asked me out. Wants to go up to Poseidon on Friday night."

"What?" she squeaks. "Phoebe!" Her face lights up. "That's great."

"Could Jasmine spend the night? We might be up late."

"Oh my God, yes. We will have a blast!"

"Who will?" Jasmine asks, ambling into the room.

"Me and you. Want to spend the night with me on Friday?"

Jasmine opens her mouth wide. Her gray eyes are so bright it almost stings. "Here?"

"Where else?"

"Will I have to sleep by myself?" She gives me a side-eye, like I will complain, but what do I care? It's kind of sweet that she still wants to sleep with an adult.

"No! You can sleep with me if you want." Suze tilts her head. "I might *cuddle* you, though."

"I don't mind."

"Cool, then." She winks at me. "It's a *date*."

"Yay!" Jasmine leaps over to hug Suze. A mean little part of me twinges with jealousy—as with my grandmother, I sometimes want to be the One.

Even I know it's petty. I should be grateful that she has so much love in her life.

"All right, then."

"Who wants lunch?" Suze says, picking up her phone. "My treat. Sub sandwiches? Salads? Tacos?"

"Sushi," Jasmine cries.

"Guess again," I say. "No sushi around here."

"There's a whole ocean right there!" Jasmine gestures to the water.

I shrug. "Still no sushi." Joel has wandered into the room. "Let's let Joel choose."

"Choose?" he echoes. He looks at Suze, and I see that he's as dazzled by her as he ever was. She swore they were friends, but he was madly in love. I tried so hard not to see it, but it was plain.

"Lunch," she says, and there's something in her face, too, when she looks at him. Something lost, something confident, something full of—what? Love, heat, lostness.

Which would be weird, since they were never together. Suze returned to live with Amma after the baby was born, but Joel never came back after his stint in juvie.

But that looks like more than old friends. *Maybe*, I think, looking from one to the other, *I got it wrong*. Did Suze lie to me? A whisper of heat licks along my lungs, breathes on the lingering rift between us. Has she been lying to me all this time?

I think of the letter in my drawer, lying unopened for decades. I'm also guilty.

"Subs, tacos, salads?" Suze repeats. Her voice is silky and warm. Calm.

Joel shakes himself ever so slightly, as if he's been off in another world. "Nah, that's all right. I want to see if I can dig up some diagrams from this era, and I can do that best from the office."

"I have a computer," she says, and points to a room down the hall.

The air fills with a musky blue atmosphere, so thick I could move it around with my hands. "No. Thanks, though. I'll be back later," he says.

I look at Suze, who is watching him go. She closes her eyes, steels herself. I realize I've seen her do this a thousand times—shake it off, like a dog coming out of a river.

She picks up her phone. "If no one else chooses, I'm going with pizza again. Better pick."

"Subs!" Jasmine cries. "I want egg salad."

"Yum." Something compels me to reach for Suze. I wrap my fingers around her wrist for just a moment, thinking of all the questions I should have asked long before now. She allows it for a minute, then gives me a false little smile and moves away.

I suddenly remember Suze from the summer between tenth and eleventh grade. That terrible, wonderful summer.

In those days, she wore this expression for all kinds of reasons I didn't understand until later.

THEN

Nights in White Satin

SUZE

We were all three freshman in high school. Phoebe and Joel never had any kind of girlfriend-boyfriend connection, or if so, it was only in Phoebe's mind. It was sometimes annoying how she mooned around about him, but I didn't want to hurt her feelings.

By then, Joel and I been best friends at school for nearly three years. We'd both made some other friends, but we mainly hung out with each other, stained early by the outsider label.

That day, it was raining when school let out. All the other kids had rides or got on the bus, but Joel and I were stuck walking. It was pouring, like twenty garden hoses were going overhead all at once. No umbrella would stand up to that.

So we tucked ourselves into an alcove in the library to wait it out. Carrels lined the space and a trio of hard chairs rested against the wall. We claimed them, facing the windows, and pulled out our books. He was a good student, really good in math, but mainly he loved to draw. Like Phoebe, which made me like him more. He drew wolves and whales, dolphins and starfish, all kinds of animals, all in pencil with intricate, layered detail. I had one of a cat on my wall, which he drew just for me, since I wanted a cat so bad and wasn't allowed to have one.

The night before, my dad had whipped me again with a belt because I forgot to bring in the laundry off the line and it got wet. It wasn't a long whipping, but it was hard core, and I had bruises on my lower back and thighs that meant I couldn't change for gym. The chairs were too hard and I folded up my sweater to sit on, but I still couldn't get comfortable. Tears stung my eyes, and I felt so angry that I thought I could literally blow up.

"You okay?" Joel asked.

I bowed my head. "You know how you hear those stories about people combusting, like burning down to absolutely nothing for no reason?"

"Yeah."

"I get so mad sometimes that I feel like I could combust like that."

No alarm crossed his face. "Don't." He moved closer and reached for the end of one of my braids. "I would miss you."

He smelled like the forest floor, fragrant and earthy, and I bent my head until my forehead touched his shoulder. "I hate him so much."

"Me too. He hurts you." He rubbed my upper back gently.

Something in me stirred, and I raised my head. Our eyes met. His were big and dark, with thick lashes—intense eyes, eyes that saw everything. What I saw in them right then was something I hadn't suspected before, like maybe he was seeing me in a new way.

Just like I was seeing him in a new way, or maybe I was recognizing it, a thing I'd buried because Phoebe had such a bad crush on him. And now I felt bad, but what was rising in my body was much bigger than that old crush from two years ago.

Two years ago.

Still. A friend didn't make out with the object of her best friend's crush. Maybe this was a bad idea. Maybe she would get mad at me.

Except that the smell of him filled my head, swept downward through my body. His gaze fell to my mouth, up to my eyes again, and a feeling like static electricity buzzed through me.

"Suze?" he said quietly.

Acting on some impulse I'd never felt in my entire life, I leaned in and touched my lips to his, very lightly. Then, appalled, I started to pull back, but Joel caught the back of my neck. "More," he said in a gruff voice. His mouth was soft and pillowy and still kind of firm, and the sensation sent rockets through my body, down to the tips of my fingers, between my legs, and most embarrassing of all, the tips of my breasts.

But I didn't want to stop. He didn't either. He scooted closer until our thighs were touching, and my left breast was pressed into his chest. Like it was a movie or he'd practiced, he cupped my jaw and tilted my head so that we could fit together even more tightly, and then—oh, Lord—he nudged open my mouth with his tongue and we kissed deep. I thought my entire body would melt into a puddle. I yanked away, afraid suddenly. We stared at each other. His hand was on my ribs, and I ached for him to move it higher.

"Was that okay?" I asked.

He smiled, very slowly, and brushed hair over my shoulder. "Very okay."

After that, we were both all in. Joel and I would go to his house, which was empty because his mom was at work, and watch TV, the after-school specials or *Dark Shadows*, and have a snack, like apples or cookies, and then we'd make out. Sometimes we stayed on the couch and sometimes we went to his room and lay down on his bed, spreading our bodies against each other, ribs to ribs, lips to lips. He loved to take my hair down and stroke his fingers through it, and I loved for him to take off his shirt so I could feel his skin.

I tried not to think of Christmas and Phoebe arriving and having to tell her what had happened.

September 23, 19—

Dear Phoebe,

I love high school! Even the first week feels like a completely different place. Mr. Otis, the drama teacher, asked me to stay after class today and said he'd been talking to Miss Peach at the middle school about me, and she thinks I'm one of the best acting students she's ever had. Imagine that!

I have something else to tell you, though, and I just don't know how you're going to take it.

[PAGE TORN OUT]

September 23, 19—

Dear Phoebe,

I love high school so far! I have really cool teachers and it's fun to pick all my classes. I have Joel in two of them, and mostly none of the bullies in any of them. Mr. Otis, the drama teacher, asked me to stay after class today and said he'd been talking to Miss Peach at the middle school about me, and she thinks I'm one of the best acting students she's ever had. Imagine that! The first production of the year will be *Our Town* and he wants me to try out, and I need to figure out how to get my dad to let me do it. It doesn't work to do it behind his back—he just kicks my ass and I hate that. Lately, he's really spending a lot of time with Karen, Mrs. Armstrong, and I think they might actually get married. She's pretty nice to me, and maybe I'll see if she can help me talk to my dad. I'll offer to do extra Sunday school classes or use

Murphy's oil soap on all the pews or whatever he wants.
If he sees the play, he'll see it's not anything bad.

Or maybe I should offer to do a play with all the
kids in the church! That's a good idea, too.

Anyway. I'm excited for the new year. Hope you
are, too.

Love,

Suze

PS Joel says you should read DANDELION
WINE. You would like it. I thought it was kind of
boring, honestly, but you might like it.

October 1, 19—
Dear Phoebe,

I never knew kissing could feel so good. Kissing
and kissing and kissing, until my lips are sore and
every part of me is buzzing. I never knew that

[PAGE TORN OUT]

October 2, 19—
Dear Phoebe,

I tried out for the play, and Mr. Otis said he would
talk to my dad if I get a part. Which I will. I know I will.
They are going away (!) to a conference for two weeks
and they said I could stay with Beryl. I'm so excited. I
wish you could be here, but it will be way more fun to
stay with her than in my own house. You are so lucky to
have such good parents and a great grandmother. I want
to be like her when I'm old, kind of eccentric (which I
mean in a good way) and full of good ideas and wise

and not all shriveled up like so many old women get. Why does that happen? The old ladies in the church are either so tiny a good wind would blow them away or they can't walk very well and are bent over or they're bitter. Beryl isn't any of those things—she even has a boyfriend she says she'll never marry. Do you think it's because she's an artist? Will it keep us young to be artists?

I'll put this in the mail today.

Love,

Suze

October 8, 19—

Dear Suze,

Did you tear out some pages? It kinda looks like it. You can scribble things out if you want. I don't really like it to have pages torn out. I think it might not be very good for the spine and other pages.

High school here is pretty much the same as junior high. I like my art class (painting) and English. We're going to read OLD MAN AND THE SEA, by Ernest Hemingway, which looked boring but I read a couple of pages and it's good. In art, I'm working with oils and Mr. Jain said I can come up with my own project because I've been taking all the art classes on the side. I don't know what I'm going to do yet. Anthony is in my class and we have lunch together, and also science, so at least I have a partner. It's funny that both of us have a good friend who is a boy. I think Anthony likes me, but I don't like him in that way. He did say that we should go to the homecoming dance together, just to mess around, so I'm going.

Amma is the best person in the world and I'm jealous that you can see her whenever you want and that you are staying with her for 2 weeks without me!

So happy for you and the play. Tell me what part you get.

Love,

Phoebe

October 15, 19—

I'm sorry I haven't written very much. I'm just depressed. My parents had a gigantic fight and my dad left for a few days, and I was stuck with my mother who wanted to try to make everything good, but I hate her. She always nags my dad to be somebody he's not, and she nags me, too, and not everything is supposed to be all perfect like she wants it. I'm even more sad now that I think of you with Amma, living the life I want to live, while I'm stuck here with two parents who hate each other.

October 17, 19—

Sorry. That was kind of a mean entry. I'm just sad. My dad is really sad, too, I can tell. I don't know why they are fighting so much. I mean, they've always fought, but they make up and it's okay, but lately, they have these big stupid fights and then they don't talk to each other for days.

My mom left for a business trip yesterday, so my dad and I had pancakes at the pancake house, and my dad had four blueberry pancakes with syrup and bacon. He says he's getting fat, and he shouldn't eat them, but I like it when he's happier. The pancakes made him smile for a few minutes, anyway.

So then he said, What would you think about living in Los Angeles? And of course I said no way. I can't be that far from you and Amma and Joel and Blue Cove. Blue Cove is my place.

He nodded and said he thinks my mom might be happier in a bigger city, so she could grow her career. I asked about his career, and he didn't really say anything. Where would he work in LA?

I will be so mad if we have to move. I'm so tired of being a kid! Life will be so much better when we grow up. We'll have our apartment in New York City and I'll be an artist and you'll be a famous actress and we never have to deal with our parents again. Just Amma. And my dad.

Tell Joel I read DANDELION WINE and I loved it so much! Such a magical story. Maybe I could write to him, if you give me his address.

Love,
Phoebe

Suze's Private Journal

November 9, 19—

Dear Diary,

I had to buy a new journal to write in, because this is just to you, not to Phoebe, because I want to keep this for myself, or maybe I'm worried about what she'll think or . . . I don't know. I don't want to write this in the journal we trade back and forth. Too many chances that somebody will read it and I'll get in trouble. So much trouble.

I am no longer a virgin. (!!!)

Today, Joel and I walked up to the house and took our blankets and picnic and spread everything out on the bedroom floor, which looks right out at the ocean, and finally, we took off all of our clothes and were completely naked with each other, looking and touching and kissing and, oh, doing all the things we've learned about each other's bodies until now. I thought I would be scared, but his body, all long and lean and smooth skin, his thighs and belly, his hair falling around me like a black curtain, him wrapping up in my hair, tying us together like my hair was a cloak, all of it made me feel like I was melting, melting into him, him melting into me, like we were becoming a new creature. We did become a new creature, something made of love and kisses and hope and possibility.

Love,
Suze

PS We used a condom, but I'm going to ask Beryl to help me get some birth control pills.

Suze

All through the winter and spring, Joel and I learned each other's bodies. Every second we could, we stole away to touch and kiss and look and try things—everything. It was thrilling and dangerous and fun and we were so much in love we lit the skies. I was incandescent, and Joel walked like he knew his worth.

Most of the time, we were in his bedroom while his mother worked. One late May day was hot and he took off his shirt and I took off mine and we took our time, kissing and touching, and laughing.

I will never know how long Joel's mother stood there. Probably not long, considering, but we didn't realize we were being observed until she clapped her hands hard and cried out his name. "Joel Minough, are you out of your mind?"

We broke apart, pulling the covers over us, backing away from her rage. At first that was all I could think of, getting away from her, but then she cried, "Her father will *kill* you. Not threaten, actually kill you."

"Mom!" he began. "We've been careful, just like—"

"I didn't mean with the daughter of the craziest man in the entire town."

"Please don't tell my dad!" I cried. "Please. I'll do whatever you want."

She yanked the sheet, exposing us both, and I clapped my hands over my breasts, pulling my hair around for modesty. "Get up and get dressed now. You"—she pointed her finger—"go home right now." Her angry gaze turned to Joel. "And you are going to your father's house the second this semester is done. And if I catch the two of you within a half mile of each other in the meantime, I'll do the beating myself."

"Mom!" he protested.

She slammed out of the room, and we stared at each other for a long moment, both of us sensing that everything was lost. I flew to him and kissed him, and he held me hard. "Get dressed."

So I did. And I walked home with the greatest sense of disaster I'd ever known. Even then I knew something worse was coming.

CURRENT DAY

Chapter Fourteen
Suze

Phoebe brings Jasmine over in the late afternoon on Friday. The weather is surprisingly mild, sunny and not at all windy. "Let's go have a picnic at the beach," I suggest.

"Cool."

We don layers in case a squall moves in, then head the back way through town so we can stop by the little grocery that's been on Main Street ever since I can remember. We pass the lot where the church once stood. Wild gooseberry and kinnikinnick and wildflowers have covered every inch of the burned shell. The house still stands, abandoned. I wonder why no one has ever bought this lot and built some holiday homes, but I feel the hauntedness.

"This place is creepy," Jasmine says, taking my hand.

"It is. My dad had a church here," I say, surprising myself. A knot of unresolved anger twists through my diaphragm. "It burned down."

"Did he die?"

"No. Nobody died."

She looks at me for a moment, but honestly there's not a single thing I can offer a ten-year-old about a monster like my father, who moved away to some other poor town. The less said the better.

"I like that bus," she says finally.

Across the alley from our old abandoned house is a Victorian in considerably better shape than it was the summer I was fifteen. The clapboard is painted bright white, with trim in several shades of blue and yellow. The porch is hung with a swing, and I remember weaving macramé plant hangers there.

An abandoned bus is still parked on the back of the lot. It's painted cheerfully, and seems to have been done over into a she-shed sort of thing, with curtains at the windows and a flower garden planted around the door. I offer Jasmine a tidbit of history. "Can you see the murals on that bus?"

She squints. "Kinda. Flowers."

"Your nana painted them when she was a little older than you are now." I love that someone has taken the time to refresh them, and it occurs to me that, even then, Phoebe loved painting flowers.

Jasmine is underwhelmed. "Oh."

The grocery has wooden floors and the kind of food tourists might pick up for a couple of nights in—a little fruit, lots of wine, bread and milk and cereal. "Let's eat junk food," I declare.

"Yes!" Jasmine pumps the air. "You should know that Nana doesn't approve."

"Oh, we all get to let go of the rules sometimes. She gets that."

"What're your favorites?"

We choose thin, salty potato chips and a bag of frosted circus animal cookies, a jar of whole dill pickles, Hershey's Kisses, big red grapes, cans of root beer, and string cheese, then carry the bag down the path to the beach. A few people are walking at the other end, but here by the Starfish Sisters, we only have to share the space with seagulls and a power walker in red shoes. I spread out a blanket I brought with me, and we use rocks to hold the corners down. It's so much like the days with Phoebe that I feel some mending going on in my soul.

"Which seagull comes to see you?" Jasmine asks, peeling a stick of string cheese. "Do you think it's one of those guys?"

A crowd of them mills around the creek, some poking through the sand, others grooming and bathing, a sight that never tires. Is there anything more exuberant than a bird splashing water on its feathers? "Maybe. We should really notice his markings and see if we can spot him in the crowd next time."

"Why are some of them brown?"

"They're young. Your nana would know when they start to be all white, but I don't."

"She knows a lot," Jasmine says.

I nod, watching a pair of murres super-pedal their arms, looking like little flying footballs. I pop grapes into my mouth, and catch sight of movement in the water. "Hey, I think that might be a whale out there!"

She jumps to her feet and shades her eyes. "It *is* a whale!" She watches, rapt, as it breaches, magnificently, and dives back into the water, leaving a sudsy wake. "Wow," she sighs. When it is no longer visible, she plops down beside me and digs her feet into the sand. "I might want to be a marine scientist," she says.

"Yeah? Do you want to study tsunamis?"

"Well, that's one thing. They cause a lot of damage, you know, and if people could be warned faster, it would help."

"Definitely."

"But really," she says, gazing at the horizon, "I just like the ocean. I would like to be a fish, and swim around down there and learn new things." She peels string from her cheese. "Maybe I would find treasure."

"Oooh, I like that idea. Pirate treasure!"

"Yeah. There were a lot of ships that sank out there, did you know that?"

I did know it, but it's more fun to hear what she has to say. "No."

"It's one of the most dangerous coasts in the world," she says with pride.

"Ah. What kind of cargo did they carry?"

"All kinds of things. Gold, of course."

"Of course."

"And sometimes jewels or stuff like that, and all kinds of things, really. Sometimes they were on their way to China or Japan."

"Is there still a lot of lost treasure?"

"Maybe. People still look for stuff."

"Mmm." I open the cookies and grab a handful of pink and white frosted elephants. "If I found treasure, I would like to find a crown. With rubies."

"I would like to find a diamond necklace."

"I would like to find emeralds."

"You already have an emerald ring."

"Yes." I hold out my left hand, where the square-cut emerald Dmitri gave me lives on my ring finger. We never married because I didn't want to, but I wore the ring to please him. Looking at the deep translucent color, I think of him, his big way of laughing, of living, a big drinker, a big eater, a big chance-taker. It still seems impossible that a virus could have felled him. It was a brutal way for such a social man to have died, and it still hollows me out to imagine him alone in that hospital room, forbidden any visitors at all, myself included.

"Was he your husband?"

"No." From the bag, I choose a Hershey's Kiss and peel the foil away. "But we were together a long time. Almost twenty years."

"Didn't you want to get married?"

"No," I tell her honestly. "I liked my own way of doing things."

"Hmm." She pulls hair out of her face and takes a bite of a cookie, studying my face. "Do you miss him?"

"Dmitri?" She met him a couple of times, though not here. He didn't care for the cold Oregon coast, but when Jasmine and Phoebe and Stephanie came to visit, they stayed with me. Dmitri went to Disneyland with us, and enjoyed it as much as Jasmine did. She adored him from the first moment. "Yeah, sometimes. It's easier now than it was at first, which is how life goes."

"He was really nice."

"He was."

"Was he old when he died?"

I take a breath. "Kind of. But he probably would still be around if not for COVID."

"COVID," she says with a weariness far beyond her years.

"Exactly."

We're quiet for a little while, eating our feast and watching waves rise and fall and ripple toward shore.

"I want my nana to be a hundred before she dies," Jasmine says into the space.

I nod, listening, feeling there's more.

"If she's a hundred, then I'll be grown up and maybe married and have some kids and it won't be so horrible that she has to die."

My heart folds completely in half, squeezes itself until I nearly can't breathe. "That's really sweet, Jasmine."

"Do you think she will? Live to be a hundred?"

"Why not?" I say. "She's healthy and artists are known to live a really long time because they love their work."

"Is that true?"

I chuckle, hold up my hands. "I swear."

She nods.

"Amma was ninety-four. That's almost a hundred."

"Amma? Yeah. I went to her funeral."

"I remember. It helped your nana to have you there to hold her hand." I think of the house afterward, the parade of people; then finally, it was only Phoebe and me, left behind in the yawning emptiness of Beryl's house.

She nods, sucking the frosting from a cookie. "I remember things from when I was two. We had this house with a window seat and my mom said I couldn't remember that but I do. It had purple flowered cushions."

"That's impressive. Most people don't have memories that early."

"Do you?"

"Maybe not from being two, but I remember a lot. My mom died when I was eight, and I was so sad that I made myself think about everything I could remember, over and over."

"Your mom died when you were a little girl?"

"Yeah." A wisp of memory comes to me, her blonde hair, the way she sang to me, and I feel a pain so old it's polished to a patina.

"I can't even stand to *think* about my mom or Nana dying." She stares at the horizon, and I wonder if I shouldn't have said that. Then she asks, "How did she die?"

"Breast cancer. There were not many treatments in those days."

"Do you still miss her?"

"Not really." I give her a chocolate Kiss. "Let's talk about happier things."

"I don't really feel that happy. I don't want to move to London and no one is listening to me."

This is above my pay grade, but it feels like she's really confiding in me, and I can't let her down. "It can really be hard to make a big change like that," I say.

"I liked our house in Portland. I like being close to Nana, and I have all these friends at school who are going to miss me, and I'll miss them, and what if nobody likes me in England?"

I take that all in. "Well, first of all, people will definitely like you in London. I've been there. I've met the people and they are really nice. And you are an extremely likable person."

"Did you meet any kids, though? And also, you're a movie star, so everybody is nice to you."

I laugh. "That is kind of true, although I hate to admit it, and no, I've never met any English kids, but I have met you."

"I think I'm kind of weird."

"That's fine," I say, shrugging. "Normal is kind of boring, don't you think?"

"Nana is normal."

"Not even."

"Yes, she is!" Jasmine cries. "She has a normal house and a normal car and she eats normal food and she does normal things."

"Does that mean you think she's boring?"

She smacks me and makes a groaning noise. "No way! She's really fun. She loves to play games and she teaches me all kinds of things—"

"She is all that. And she's not normal because she's like . . . one of the best people in the world." A surprising sting of emotion rises in my throat. "Right?"

Jasmine pulls her knees to her chest and rocks a little. "Yes."

I toss an arm around her and pull her close to me, wrapping my big sweater around us.

She wails, "I don't want to go to London! It's too far away!"

I lean my cheek against her hair. She smells of sunshine and wind and the untainted sweat of children. "She will come see you and you will come see her. And I promise, one hundred percent, that you will find magical things in London. So many magical things."

"Like what?"

"Candy that's not like the candy you get here, for one thing."

"Really?"

"Yes. And there are castles you can visit, like so many of them." I pause, trying to think what would appeal to a ten-year-old. "Oh! You might be able to have high tea, which is a bunch of tiny sandwiches and tiny desserts and tea served in beautiful tea sets, like the prettiest tea sets I've ever seen."

"That sounds kind of good."

"Maybe your mom will let you get a cat."

"She won't," Jasmine says sadly. "She doesn't like cat hair on things. She's only telling me that she might let me have one so I won't feel so bad about leaving Nana."

"That's a pretty dark thought from a kid."

"Everyone tells me I'm old for my age."

"You are that, kiddo. For sure." On the horizon, a bank of clouds is gathering. We watch it for a few minutes. I wonder if I should tell Stephanie what Jasmine said, how much she's dreading the move. But is that my business?

"Come on," I say. "Let's go check out the tide pools before the rain comes."

When we walk back up the hill, Maui is agitated and runs to the front of the house as we let ourselves in the back. "Stay here," I say to Jasmine.

"What? Did something happen?"

"Stay here. I'll be right back."

Outside on the deck, I feel a sudden clutch of fear, and pause, listening. I can hear only the sound of the surf and a loud seagull. Maui has not come back, and I can't leave him out here, so I round the deck and go down to the path to the front yard. My heart is pounding, my ears straining to hear anything out of the ordinary.

Nothing. Maybe he's just being a silly dog.

When I emerge from the path to the front of the house, he's sniffing the gravel of the driveway intently. No one is around. "Maui!" I cry. "Why did you run off like that?"

He looks up, tongue lolling, but abruptly, he turns toward the forest and lets go of a long howl. It's a loud, eerie, protesting sound, and every hair on my body stands on end. I peer into the trees, but nothing looks strange. Frozen in place, I hold my arms and try to penetrate the darkness.

Nothing.

Maui returns his attention to sniffing the dirt, following some invisible trail, and I wonder if he's smelling the squirrel that was left. Maybe it *was* killed by another animal.

Jasmine suddenly pops out the front door. "What are you guys doing?"

"Jasmine! I told you to stay put."

"I was just curious," she says.

Maui romps up the steps and slams into her legs as if he hasn't seen her in forty-seven years. I pause for a moment and look around carefully. No footsteps I can discern in the gravel, but there wouldn't be, would there? I turn in a circle, looking carefully, but I can't see anything out of place.

I let go of my breath. "Inside, everybody," I say with a confidence I don't feel. When we're safely inside, I lock the door and make sure the back is locked, too, and pull the shades. I wonder briefly if I should call the police, but what would I say? *The dog was acting weird and howled at the trees?* No. I'd feel obligated to call Phoebe, too.

She needs to enjoy her date night. It's a little thing to give her.

"How about spaghetti?" I ask Jasmine.

"Yes! Can I help?"

"Of course."

Chapter Fifteen
Phoebe

Getting ready for my date with Ben, I have to face my feelings of insecurity with my body. My too-big hips and breasts that don't sit anywhere close to where they once did and the wrinkles at my throat. How much do I hate those wrinkles?

"Stop it," I say. I'd never want Jasmine or Stephanie to talk to themselves like this. Instead, I run a hot shower and step under the spray. I touch my arms, my throat, my breasts, my thighs and thank each one. I think of Ben's face, his glittering eyes. A swell of hope makes the world feel light and shiny.

In a special bag in one of my bathroom drawers is a collection of exquisite makeup brushes Suze brought me from Paris a few years ago, along with high-end cosmetics that, while they can't make me into a star, can definitely make the best of what I've got. At first, I was reluctant to use them, but she encouraged me to think of my face as one of my canvases, which turned makeup into something fun.

The year she came to Portland at spring break, the year we were thirteen, we'd had makeovers at the mall.

The whole week was one of the most fun times I ever had. My dad took us to the movies, twice, and to the zoo, and on Thursday, he dropped us off at the mall so we could get ready for the party on

Friday. My mother had insisted and we were having some kids over for a pool party.

Suze was like a kid at the circus when we got to the mall, wide eyed and so full of longing.

One of the cool things we'd discovered early on was that our birthdays were five days apart—mine on May 20 and hers on the twenty-fifth, which made me a Taurus, her a Gemini. School wasn't out until June 6, so I wouldn't see her during "our" week, and we decided to celebrate each other now. We wandered the entire mall, looking at earrings and books and trying on eye shadow at the cosmetic counter. One lady was so taken with Suze's eyes that she made her up all the way, with foundation and blush and this subtle aqua eyeshadow and dark-blue eyeliner and thick mascara. "There you go, sweetie," she said. "You look like a model. Maybe you should go to New York. Those girls make a lot of money."

Suze gave me an amused glance. She squeezed my hand. "Now do Phoebe."

"Sure," she said, but I could tell she was not enthusiastic. As my grandma always said—not about me, obviously, because she thought I was gorgeous—you couldn't make a silk purse from a sow's ear.

"That's okay," I said. "We want to keep shopping."

"No!" Suze protested. "I want to see."

So I reluctantly submitted to the same full makeup treatments, and when she spun me around—surprise!—I didn't look like a model.

"I love how that makes your mouth look so sexy," Suze said.

The makeup had made my freckles disappear, and my eyelashes looked great, but I was still just me, not a presto chango version like Suze. "It's nice," I agreed. "Can I buy the mascara?"

"Of course," the woman answered. "Anything else?"

"No."

We cruised through the fashion shops, trying things on, low-rise jeans in saturated shades of red and purple and green, some so low I was afraid my butt crack would show if I bent over. We tried on bodysuits to go with the jeans, and I was pretty happy with the way my shape was displayed with those low jeans and clingy sweaters. Like my grandma, like my mother, I was curvy. Suze looked like a stick in those clothes, but when she tried on a silky blouse in blues and greens, she looked like a future version of herself, some person she'd have to grow into, and it was amazing.

We passed a jewelry store and stopped to admire the diamonds. "What kind of engagement ring would you want?" I asked.

"Not a diamond," she said. "Maybe a ruby."

"I think that might be bad luck."

"Superstition." She waved her hand dismissively. "Emerald would be fine, too. How about you?"

"Something super simple, but very sparkly." I pointed to a pear-cut solitaire. "That one is pretty."

But Suze had moved on to the bracelets. "Wow," she cried. "Look at this one!"

It was a delicate tennis bracelet, set with small, square-cut jewels in the colors of the rainbow, red, orange, yellow, green, blue, purple. It was set in silver or maybe white gold, and it shot fire from every stone.

"That is the most beautiful thing I've ever seen," she breathed. "What kind of wife would be lucky enough to have a bracelet like that?"

"It's beautiful. Maybe it wouldn't be a wife, but a mistress."

"Imagine having something that was so beautiful. For no reason except beauty." She touched the glass, and I could feel her yearning like a fire. It made me wish I could buy it for her myself.

After that, we spent ages wandering the record store and the bookstore, and then split up for one hour. We would shop for each other and then meet at Walgreens for lunch and eat strawberry shortcake and exchange presents.

I headed for the makeup counter and bought the eyeshadow and liner, then rushed to Foxmoor for the silky shirt, and then popped into the bookstore and bought a copy of *Green Darkness*, a time-travel novel by Anya Seton, which my grandma told me we'd both like. I'd give it to her, then borrow it back.

I barely made it back to Walgreens in time, but Suze wasn't there. I popped into the store side and bought a funny birthday card with a kitten on the front. She wanted a cat so badly.

Her beauty always made it so much easier for her, I think now, feeling anxious about my body as I flip through the clothes in my closet.

The thought lands with a thud in my gut, full of the weight of the lies I tell myself about her. Easy? No. Life was never easy for Suze.

When Ben comes to the door at last, he's carrying a bouquet of pink and white carnations. "I actually bought these," he says with a wink. "They didn't have anything as pretty as the farm, but pretty enough."

I laugh and bend my head to smell their pepperminty freshness. "One of my favorites to paint, honestly. Thank you. Let me put them in water and we can go."

He follows me to the kitchen, watches as I pour water into a vase and cut the packaging from the stems. I'd settled on a simple wrap dress. I'm suddenly conscious of the plunging V-neck, the way it hugs my gigantic butt. In contrast, he's brushed and polished, wearing a softly elegant blue suit coat over a pale-pink shirt and jeans. Dressed up but not too much.

And so gorgeous. His bright eyes, his beard, his wavy, dark hair. Every woman over forty on the entire Oregon coast would be more than happy to invite him into her bed. What in the world is he doing with me?

Stop that. Again, I would hate it if Stephanie or Jasmine thought that way about themselves. I meet his eyes. "You look wonderful. Every woman in the county will be jealous of me."

"Not as jealous as the men will be of me." He admires the display of cleavage with a smile. "That dress suits you."

"Thank you."

He holds out his arm. "Shall we?"

We drive up the coast to a restaurant that's locally famous for its setting, Poseidon. It sits by itself on a promontory overlooking a stretch of ocean littered with sea stacks and crashing waves. With very little beach for humans, it attracts seals and sea lions, and at certain times of year, whale sightings are not uncommon.

"I love this place," I say as we pull into the parking lot. I'm feeling as giddy as a teenager, full of anticipation and possibility and nerves, but I'm also steadied by the recognition that this is Ben beside me. Ben, who's been in my kitchen and my studio a hundred times the past few months. Ben, who makes tea the way I like it. Ben, who is as steady as anyone I've ever met. "My grandma and dad and I used to come here."

"It's an institution, for sure, but they say it holds up pretty well."

"I'm sure it does."

The building itself is a '60s beauty made of timber and glass. The host leads us to a corner table, with views for miles outward to the horizon. Beneath us, high tide is rolling in under the blue dusk, and for a moment, all I can do is admire it. This. The view, the low murmur of voices and clink of dishes, the smell of garlic wafting through the air. How long since I've been out? Ages. Years.

When I look up, Ben is watching me, his eyes bright as morning.

"What?" I ask.

"I just like your face," he says, and I feel a slight blush.

"I like yours, too," I say, but it sounds stupid and I feel awkward again.

But we are just ourselves. Ben and Phoebe. We've been hanging out as friends for months, and I enjoy him so very much, I'm not going to make this weird. "This was such a great idea," I say.

"Let's pig out," Ben says. "Appetizers, salads, mains, all of it. What do you say?"

"I'm in."

He grins.

We order crab cakes and prawns, beet salad and Caesar salad, halibut and duck, and share all of it. He tells me about the food in a village in Sudan and waking up to the sound of roosters on a trip to Spain.

Images of a soft gray dawn fill my head as I peel the shell from a shrimp so fresh it was swimming this morning. "That sounds incredible. I haven't traveled much, honestly."

"Any particular reason?"

"Not really. When I first married, I was pregnant, and then we had Stephanie so fast, and both of us were artists, so we weren't exactly rolling in money. Then I was a single mother and working freelance as an illustrator. Haven't had a lot of space."

"When Stephanie left home?"

I poke a crab cake with my fork, mulling that over. With anyone else, I would make some excuse, blow it off, but with Ben I feel the yearning to be real. My actual self, not some vague, idealized version of me. "I came back to Blue Cove to help my grandmother. Maybe I was afraid of going out on my own. I was comfortable here. Then she got sick and I took care of her."

His expression is kind. "It's not too late, you know."

I lift a shoulder. "I guess."

"Where would you go? If you could go anywhere."

I taste the crab cake, and it's so good I close my eyes—salt and seasoning and a perfect amount of breading all arranged to showcase the tender, sweet crab. "Oh my God, this is good." I point with my fork and he obliges. Nods his approval. Waits for my answer.

"I know I should say someplace far away and very different, but I'd really love to go to England and see castles. Is that embarrassingly twee?"

"Not at all. The UK is beautiful." He eats with gusto for a few minutes. I find myself watching him tear a roll with strong, tanned fingers. Everything about him is sure, clear, easy, and I wonder what that would be like—to be at home in yourself so completely. I don't think I ever have been.

But in that moment, I want to try. I sink into my body, wearing a dress that makes me feel pretty, and the delight of the food, and the pleasure of the falling light on the ocean. Even more, the deliciousness of Ben—*Ben*—sitting here with me. How did I bury my desire for him all this time?

Moments flash through me. The day in my studio when he ran his fingers over the old windows and suggested they should be replaced before winter. The light haloed his thick hair and the shape of his shoulders and I'd felt a quick, hot awakening. One that I quashed as fast as it came, fearful of looking foolish, or maybe of claiming my own longing.

He looks up and catches me studying him. His expression softens. "Thank you for coming tonight. I've been trying to ask you out for about a month."

"What? Why didn't you?"

"You're a little intimidating. A successful artist. So competent."

"Is that how you see me?"

"Some of it." Against my knee, I feel his thigh, and the air between us is charged, electric, as if we are magnets pulling together and pushing apart. I want very badly to kiss him. The waiter appears, and we both look up.

"Ready for salads?"

We nod.

Ben says, "You'll get a chance to travel to England now, won't you? With Stephanie moving to London?"

I nod, but my stomach flips. "It makes me nervous."

"What parts?"

"The plane. Getting off in a different country."

He nods, listening without judgment, which feels surprisingly good. "I get that. Not dismissing your fears, but England is not a big jump."

"I keep telling Jasmine that."

"Is she still worried about it?"

"Yes." I pause, and pieces fall into place. "Maybe I'm not really making it much better. If I'm conflicted or afraid, she probably picks up on that."

"Good insight." He swirls a shrimp in cocktail sauce, squeezes lemon over it. "Have you heard from Steph?"

"Not a lot, but she seems to be getting her bearings. She emails, and I know she's had a FaceTime with Jasmine." The waiter collects our plates. "I was thinking the other day about how much she adored me when she was little. It's nice to get some of that back with Jasmine, but it also kills me to know she'll grow out of it."

"All the more reason to have things in your life that matter to you. Like your art." He touches his lips with a napkin. "You'll tell me if I drop something in my beard, won't you?"

I grin. "Of course."

"Are you going to write another book, do you think?"

"That's a question I've been getting a lot, actually. My publisher would like me to, but I really wrote that one because I wanted to have something appropriate for Jasmine."

"Ah, that's nice. But isn't it you and Suze?"

I take a breath. "It is. I'd been working on a comic book about us for years, and it just emerged like this."

"Well, I think it's quite a beautiful book. I'd love to see you do more."

"Thank you. It has been remarkably lucrative, actually."

"I'd think so."

"When I was in art school, I thought I had to do everything the way the other artists were doing it, but I love illustration."

"Isn't illustration art?" He shifts, and I feel his warm body along the side of my hip. I want to press closer, but allow it to just be for now.

"Technically, yes, but in the kind of art school I attended, there's a lot of emphasis on fine art, and the only true mark of success is showing in big galleries, becoming an artist people want to collect."

"Did any of the people you went to school with get famous?"

"One of them, a woman from Omaha nobody really took seriously because she was so pretty and blonde and earnest. She does these gorgeous portraits."

"And you," he says. "*New York Times* bestseller."

His voice is deep and warm, his body so near. "Yes," I say, claiming it aloud. "Me too." I take a sip of water, shift the conversation his direction. "Is it okay to ask about the fact that you don't have kids?"

"I think we're moving into that level of intimacy," he says, and I can tell by his tone that it's slightly tongue in cheek. We've been pretty intimate conversationally for a while. "I did want kids. Never occurred to me that I wouldn't have any. But my wife didn't, and she would have had to carry a lot more of the burden of care. Her career was very important to her."

"Like Suze."

"A bit, I guess, but Suze had a baby, right? Gave it up for adoption?"

It's not something we ever talk about, not Suze and I, and certainly not Ben and I. It startles me a little. "How do you know that?"

"Small town. Everybody knew."

"I guess they probably would have."

"Well, and her shaved head. It had to have been hell to come back to school with her short hair and that label hung around her neck." He puts the words in air quotes: "Unwed mother."

I nod, a wash of remembered shame moving through me. I wasn't the friend to her then that I should have been, but I also didn't really know what to do. My own life was a mess with my parents getting divorced, selling the Portland house, feeling so bereft at the loss of the life I was comfortable with. In my fifteen-year-old self-centeredness, I'd believed our pain to be equal.

How could I have ever believed that?

The waiter brings our salads and the conversation lightens, turns to the flower plans for next year, some new cultivars he wants to try at the farm, and the series of paintings I'm working on, and how much fun it is to have Jasmine with me. As we're winding down, ordering coffees and one slice of their famed blueberry cobbler to share, he mentions that it was one of his wife's specialties. "She grew up in Michigan," he says, "and they have great blueberries there, but nothing like ours."

I smile. "Oregon: everything is better."

"Agreed." He touches my hand lightly, lifts it away.

When the cobbler comes, I ask about his wife. "You met her in . . . was it Cairo?"

"In a hotel restaurant, actually. She was on a break from an archaeology dig, and I wanted to see the Nile."

I want to ask if it was amazing, but I don't want him to get distracted, and of course the Nile was amazing. I mean, what an absurd thing to even ask. I lean on my hand, watching his face as he remembers. "Why did you like her?"

He meets my eyes. "She was pretty. She had really nice hair and . . . well, tits."

If it were a first date of an ordinary sort, the comment would be out of place, but we've been talking about everything under the sun for the past six months, since he came to work for me, and I know he has this earthy side.

I laugh, and straighten a little because this is one of my attributes, too, even if they're not exactly what they once were.

He tilts his head, meets my eyes for a long moment, and something new rises, knitting a bubble around us, creating a world that is only ours. The potential leaves me a little breathless, and more than a little terrified. If I give in to all these . . . desires, will it undo me?

And yet, there he is, the Ben I've come to know so well, smelling of something delectable I once understood and haven't forgotten. It draws me closer. He takes my hand.

"And? What else?" I prompt.

"Do we want to talk about her?"

"Why not? I want to know about you."

"Fair enough." He moves his thumb over my knuckles. "She was really smart, and independent, and she made me work pretty hard to get her attention." It's his turn to edge closer. His thigh and mine are touching, the skin heating between us. "What about you? How did you meet your husband?"

"Oh my God, it was such a long time ago." I take a breath and let it go. "We met in art school." I turn my hand and Ben moves the pad of his thumb over the center of my palm. It's heady, such a light whisper, and I feel the pulse moving down my wrist, up to my elbow, beyond. "He was a junior when I was a freshman, and he was kind of the *it* guy, you know? Everybody thought he was going to be a really big star." Ben moves his index finger along the back of my hand. It sends tiny stars through my body. "I had a big, big crush on him. That was my style in those days, you know, crushing from afar."

He laughs a little. "Don't we all?"

"Maybe." I nod. "For a year, he didn't even know I existed, and then we were in a class when I was a sophomore and he noticed me."

"Why did you like him?"

"He had great hair, very thick, very dark"—I realize that Ben, too, has that same thick, wavy hair, so dark, and I suddenly wonder if I will have the chance to plunge my fingers into it—"and he was good-looking, and he was kind of the king of the school." I lift a shoulder. "Sex was really the main thing if I'm honest."

"The things that lead us when we're young, huh?"

A richness has risen between us, shimmering and full of promise, and I look at his mouth. "Only when we're young?"

The lights are low, and the sun has set, and in our quiet little corner, Ben raises a hand and cups my jaw. His eyes touch my lips, then my gaze, and then he leans in and presses his lips to mine. It's deliberate and direct, just like him, and I lift my chin to meet it. His beard is silky soft against my chin, and his lower lip is plump, and he smells like dawn, like earth, like all things that grow. I make a soft sound and pull him closer, opening my mouth to his tongue, to this splendid new thing.

To Ben.

He raises his head, smooths hair from my face. "Shall we get out of here?"

In the car, I feel nerves rising. I haven't had sex with another person in . . . so long. I try to think back, and it must have been a guy I dated in the 2010s before I came back to Blue Cove to care for Amma. I'd not really had a serious relationship since long before that, busy as I was with my child and building my career and all the things it takes to be alive in the world. Men distracted me, knocked me off track. I'd date someone, get too invested, feel devastated when it didn't work out, blame myself. It was a terrible merry-go-round, and I eventually stepped off, choosing to simply find short-term "sex affairs" with men who also wanted to get laid without a lot of strings attached. Most human adults need sex and the touching that goes with it.

But then Amma took a turn and I came back to Blue Cove and there hasn't been an opportunity until now. As we get closer to my house, I feel my nerves rising, my thoughts tangling over what my expectations are, what this might be, if we are going to ruin this good friendship if we find out we can't make a sexual relationship work.

We don't talk a lot, and at my house, I get out. "Are you coming in?"

"Am I still invited?"

"Yes." At least that much I know.

He follows me into the quiet house. Only the light over the kitchen counter is on, and I grasp for something to hang my nerves on. "Do you want some tea?"

"Not really," he says in a low rumble. He drops his keys on the side table and takes off his jacket, tosses it over a chair.

"That's going to get dog and cat hair all over it."

"I don't care." He steps up to me, takes my hand, and positions it on his waist. Our chests brush. I smell his skin, slightly hot, and it makes me literally dizzy, so I grasp him more closely and lean in with a kind of delirium that feels utterly unlike me and impossible to resist. "I just want to kiss you."

He envelops me, taller and bigger in a way that's primal and satisfying. I feel the whole of him. He bends in and kisses me with the same command he brings to everything else, a confidence of movement and knowledge, his hands on my back, my waist, then down to my butt, so happily. He makes a low sound and bends into my neck. "If you knew how many times I've thought of this. You have the most luscious body." He kisses my neck, my throat, opens my wrap dress and kisses my breasts.

"Let's go upstairs," I say, and lead him. And there in my long-empty bed, we have very physical, very noisy, very satisfying sex. He knows his way around a woman's body, and his vigor gives me permission to let down my guard, and it is good.

It is very, very good.

Lying curled in his arms, listening to his sleep breathing, fear clutches me again. How can I trust this? How can I allow myself to be vulnerable again? It feels like I've been keeping the world at arm's length forever.

I roll ever so slightly closer, burying my face into his skin. In his sleep, he rumbles slightly and tucks me into his chest, and it's all I've really ever wanted, right here. Love. Connection. Peace.

This, please.

THEN

I Can Hear You Calling

May 30, 19—

Dear Suze,

I found out my parents are taking us to Italy this summer, for two whole weeks. I'm so sad! I mean, I should be glad, I guess, but I don't want to miss the summer with you and Joel. Last summer was so much fun and I have been looking forward to this one so so so much!

Also, they fight all the time. Like, alllllll the time. About everything. Which plates to put on the table, how to stop at a stop sign (how hard can it be? Just stop!!!), where I should go to college (like it's any of their business). I don't think my dad is sleeping in their bedroom anymore. I found him on the couch a couple of times, all settled in like he's used to it.

So I don't get why they want to take a vacation together. I hope they don't fight the whole time. I think they should go by themselves, have a second honeymoon, and leave me here. Amma says I should adjust my attitude and try to get something out of it. Italy is a place where a lot of great artists developed their skills.

It's just not going to be as much fun as hanging out with you and Joel.
Love,
Phoebe

June 4, 19—
Dear Phoebe,
Are you kidding me? Italy???? And you're mad about it?
You are spoiled.
The End.
Love,
Suze

June 4, 19— #2
Just kidding. I'm super super jealous, though. I wish I could go someplace like that, even with fighting parents.
Not that my dad is fighting. I think he's going to marry Mrs. Armstrong. They've been all moony lately and I wouldn't be surprised to see a ring on her finger sometime soon.
Also, you won't be seeing Joel this summer anyway. I thought I told you that he's going to Seattle to stay with his dad this summer. He really doesn't want to but his mom insists, so he has to. He left already, the last day of school.
So it'll just be me and you, like old times. But there's something fun going on—I made friends with these hippies in the house behind the church. There's

five people who actually live there, but a lot of others who come over. I really like a girl named Mary, and her boyfriend. They're so nice, and Mary is teaching me to macramé. They also have KITTENS! Five of them. One is the sweetest little baby you ever saw, black with a half-white mustache. He gets into things so bad. Mary's brother is so sweet and nice, named Victor. He has blond hair that he wears in a braid and he knows how to do this very intricate beading. He taught me to make earrings, which of course I have to hide.

I miss you. Can't wait for you to get here. Two weeks isn't that long. We still have the whole rest of the summer.

From Joel

June 3, 19—

Dear Suze,

This is my new address, so you can write me whenever you want. All the time. I'll write you, too.

My dad wants me to get a job, so I've been applying at all kinds of restaurants. I think I might have a job as a dishwasher at a fish house, which wouldn't be so bad.

This is short because I feel so bad about this, about us getting caught and it was totally my fault, and now you're stuck in Blue Cove without me and I hate that. Don't let your dad hurt you.

Write soon,

Love,

Joel

June 10, 19—

Dear Joel,

It was my fault as much as yours. I hate this, too, but everything will be okay. We'll write letters all the time and I'll try to call you from Beryl's house. It will be okay, truly. I'm so glad your mom didn't tell my dad. He would LITERALLY have killed me.

Phoebe will be coming in a couple of days and that always makes me so happy. If you're not here, I also don't have to feel so worried about how she'll take it that we're together now. She's had a crush on you forever. Which you know, but I don't think you're as worried about hurting her feelings as I am. It's going to break her heart and that makes me feel like a rotten friend, but I also don't know how me & you could have not fallen in love. We are SOUL MATES. I really believe that. I could look all over the world and not find anybody who was as right for me as you are.

Do you want to read the same books, maybe? That's how me and Phoebe keep talking sometimes. I'll read whatever you want. Also, you can tell me whatever you're thinking and I'll do the same. Or tell me about your day, from getting up to going to bed.

A dishwashing job sounds like fun. You'll make some money, and I know you like to be with your dad sometimes, so you don't have to act like it's all terrible. I know it isn't. ☺ My dad wants me to get a job, too, but I'm not cleaning hotel rooms. I mean, how gross! Maybe I'll see if I can find somebody who will hire me to wait tables. That wouldn't be so bad. I'd rather work in one of the boutiques and sell tourist stuff, but I can't wear my normal clothes all the time downtown or my dad will see me. And who would hire the yokel girl with her stupid dresses hanging down below her knees?

A bunch of hippies moved in behind us. They're going to fix up a school bus and go on the road, drive down the coast to Baja, maybe all the way down to Patagonia (which I thought was someplace else entirely, but is at the southern tip of South America). That would be fun, wouldn't it? Maybe we can travel like that when we get out of school. Hitchhike in Europe.

Speaking of which, Phoebe is going to Italy with her parents. I'm SO jealous! I'm trying not to be, but I would kill or die to go to Europe, and she's whining about it. She just doesn't get how lucky she is, I swear.

Anyway, everything is really going to be okay. Trust me.

Love you lots and lots and lots and lots and lots and lots and lots. Write back RIGHT AWAY.

Suze

June 16, 19—

Dear Suze,

My dad got me up early to help him in his garden, at 6 am because he says that's when the best garden things happen. I don't like getting up early but it was nice out there, for sure. Lotta birds singing and tweeting and all that. Worms and slugs all over (worms good, slugs bad). My dad puts out little dishes of beer for the slugs and one of the things I do is empty the ones from the day before and add new beer. He buys beer just for this, since he doesn't drink and sometimes I want to steal a beer for myself, but he'd notice.

After the garden, we eat breakfast. Toast and eggs and coffee, which I like. He goes to work and then I have time to myself. I walk around the neighborhood or read or sometimes do push-ups and sit-ups because it's kind of boring. All that time and nothing to do. There's a bookstore a few blocks away—it's a big place, with two floors and a bunch of used books in the basement. I found a paper-back of THE DRIFTERS by James Michener for a quarter and I really like it—a bunch of people traveling around Europe and Morocco. I'd love to do that—like you said. Hitchhike around Europe with our backpacks. Let's plan that for after we graduate.

Anyway, that's enough of my boring day. I applied for a job at the bookstore, and at first I don't think the lady thought I'd be good at it, but the application said to list your five favorite books and I couldn't stop at five, I had to write down ten, and she was like, you read all these books? And I said, and a lot more. She said, these are kind of old for you, aren't they? I shrugged and told her nobody cares what I read, so I read everything, but my favorites are history and science fiction. She smiled then, and said ah, past and future. Which I never thought about before but is kind of true.

So maybe she'll hire me. I'd like it better than washing dishes.

Did I give you THE FORGOTTEN DOOR? Maybe
it's in my mom's house. I kinda want to read it again.
Love love love love love
Joel

PS This is the list. What are yours?
1. SLAUGHTERHOUSE-FIVE
2. BURY MY HEART AT WOUNDED KNEE
3. 1984
4. STRANGER IN A STRANGE LAND
5. OLD YELLER
6. THE MARTIAN CHRONICLES
7. THE FORGOTTEN DOOR
8. BLACK ELK SPEAKS
9. BRAVE NEW WORLD
10. CUSTER DIED FOR YOUR SINS

Phoebe

When I got to Amma's house, I gave her a hug and then ran all the way to Suze's. I banged on the door, but she wasn't there, and I poked my head inside the church, but there was only a woman sweeping in the kitchen. "Have you seen Suze?" I asked.

"She's made friends with the young lady over there," she said. "Mary. Sweet girl, comes over to help with the food sometimes at church. Makes macramé."

"Thanks."

I followed the sidewalk around the side of the church, down the side of the house, across the alley lined with tall lilac bushes. Beneath three towering alder trees, the house sat in a wide pool of shade. On the generous front porch, a pretty girl with hair the color of pale sunlight sat in front of an enormous jute creation of knots. Next to her was Suze, her own hair shortened to the same length as Mary's, to her hips. She'd claimed her hair was so heavy it was giving her headaches, and the school nurse agreed, so her dad let her cut it. She was wearing a halter top made of what looked like scarves, her shoulders bare and tan. I'd never seen her look like this, and it gave me an odd feeling. When had she changed so much?

She caught sight of me and leaped to her feet. "Phoebe!" she cried, and ran down the steps and over the sidewalk in bare feet to hug me so tight I almost couldn't breathe. Happiness burst through me as I hugged her back. She was much taller than me now, and her arms and legs felt strong and ropy. Her hair fell in my face. I smelled Herbal Essence shampoo and sunshine, and I thought life could not be much better than this.

"Oh my God," she said. "I'm so happy to see you! I missed you with my own entire heart."

"Me too, me too, me too." I rocked her back and forth, and she laughed, then took my hand.

"Come meet Mary."

"Where's your dad?" I asked, alarmed on her behalf if he saw her in this outfit.

"Karen's holding down the fort. He's at a conference. She doesn't care about what I do."

"That's pretty good."

"Tell me about it."

I allowed myself to be led, but it was like being a mortal entering the land of fairies. Mary and Suze were so slim and tall and ethereally beautiful that I felt like a troll with my curly hair and big boobs and big butt. All the things my mother said came back, that I needed to be more fashionable, that I needed to diet, that I should get a different haircut, that I just needed to be friendly. I felt my blush rise.

Mary stood, smiling, and came over to me, taking both my hands in hers. "Phoebe! I'm so happy to meet you at last. Suze has been talking about you nonstop."

A puff of ease blew through my dark thoughts. "Thanks. I mean, I'm glad to meet you, too."

"Do you want some lemonade?" she asked. "Suze will get it for you."

"Um, sure."

"Come sit by me." Mary patted a paisley-printed cushion. A nice breeze blew through the area, and from inside came the sound of music I didn't know. "Mary," called a voice. "Maybe some Rolling Stones, huh?"

"You're in charge, Victor." She grinned at me. "My brother. He doesn't like the music I pick."

Suze came out of the house with a big purple aluminum glass, already sweating. "It's the best lemonade I've ever tasted," she said, and another tiny thread of jealousy or something wound through me. It used to just be us. I didn't mind Joel, although he was in Seattle for the summer, but I didn't want to share this short, precious time with Suze. I took a sip to be polite.

The lemonade hit the back of my throat with a shock of sugar and lemon, sour and sweet, and a smoothness I'd never tasted in lemonade in my life. "That's so good!" I gasped, and took another drink.

Suze sank down beside me. "Told you."

Right then, a guy came out, clearly Mary's brother. They could almost have been twins. He was lean and tall, with long limbs and long blond hair tumbling down his back and the slightest goatee around his mouth, so pale you had to look close to see it. His eyes were light blue, and the only word I could think of was "kind." He sat beside Suze, and I tried not to stare, but it was impossible.

He was beautiful. Every single thing about him. His cheekbones and his eyebrows and his ripe red mouth that made me think of kissing, and his long hands and even his bare feet, which were tan and high arched and perfect. He tugged her hair, and I could tell he liked her. She smiled up at him, and I could tell she liked him, too.

Of course he already liked her. I tried to quell my jealousy, but once in a while it would be nice to be the one noticed.

~

The weeks before my trip to Italy were some of the best times Suze and I ever had. Something was different about her, something easier, softer. She was very affectionate with me, looping her arm through my elbow, brushing my hair after we swam in the ocean. We walked everywhere, miles and miles—up to the house, which still stood empty and (to my mind) lonely on the top of the bluff. No other houses had been built up there, so we were always alone and safe. We hiked in the hills around Blue Cove, taking picnics to the top of the outlook reached only by a challenging hike through the steep pine forests, and ambled through the clearings alongside the Blue River, careful to keep an eye out for bears, rattling the walking stick Joel had made for Suze last Christmas, a hand-carved and painted length of pine hung with sleigh bells, a gift I still coveted.

The only thing missing, really, was Joel. I longed for his presence and asked Suze over and over when he'd be back. She said she didn't know. She missed him, too, but whenever I brought him up, she changed the subject. Maybe she was tired of my crush on him. It wasn't like there was anything between us after that Thanksgiving two years ago. We were friends. Just friends.

And I mean, I guessed I wouldn't have blamed her.

The most fun we had was at the hippie house. Music was always on the stereo, and a handful of people were always sitting on the porch or on the couches that lined the living room, or working on the bus. People smoked cigarettes and bongs and drank beer, which freaked me out at first, but I got used to it. No one pressured us, and in fact, the whole group looked after us, aware that we were quite a lot younger. They called us baby hippies, a label both of us loved.

We spent time with the kittens and helped paint the bus. Victor was in charge of the painting on the outside, and when he found out I could paint flowers and vines as easily as write my name, he put me to work. I drew an entire garden with grass and flowers and butterflies as a mural on both sides, and Victor came behind with black paint to trace my lines very carefully.

He was the most amazing person I'd ever met. He was a vegetarian, like Mary, who cooked all the meals and made all the bread they ate, sprouting grains and buying lentils in bulk when she went to Portland every few weeks. They had a garden we all helped to weed, rows of corn and vast expanses of squash and melons and beans climbing up the fences. I liked weeding in the hot sun, feeling the heat beat deep into my spine and the top of my head, but mainly I liked it because Victor would sing while he worked. His voice was lyrical and hypnotic, and he sang all kinds of old folk songs about fairies and princes. "You look like a fairy," I said one day as we painted a stretch of the bus. I was carefully filling in the detailed petals of a red dahlia.

He smiled. "Do I? That's a nice thing to say."

I realized too late that he might take it another way. "I'm sorry. I didn't mean—"

"That I was another kind of fairy?"

I blushed, hard. "Yeah. Sorry."

He touched my cheek. "But I am a fairy, Phoebe. You know that."

I didn't actually know what he meant, but I played along. "Can you enchant people?"

"Sometimes," he said, and dipped his paintbrush into the green we'd mixed for the grass, growing like swords from the bottom of the bus.

I was happy.

And then I had to go to Italy.

CURRENT DAY

Chapter Sixteen
Suze

After a dinner of spaghetti, Jasmine and I are reading together silently in the living room while the rain falls, a dog and a cat keeping us company. I've lit a fire and it's cozy and comfortable and I feel more at peace than I have in months. Maybe years.

Jasmine is half sprawled on the couch, her paperback propped on her knees. It's a mystery of some kind, which Phoebe says is the only thing she's reading at the moment. I get the comfort of reading mysteries. It's reassuring when things are wrapped up. Unlike life.

I haven't been able to settle into any books for a while now. All I can manage are shorter pieces—essays and long-form articles. I wandered through a collection of short stories. Tonight my mind jumps from one thing to the next. To the surprise of seeing Joel, so surprising that I don't even know how to think about it yet. To Phoebe and our friendship, which seems to be healing, although it's even more important now to tell her the secrets I've kept for so long. That I loved Joel. That he loved me.

That the baby I was forced to give up for adoption was his.

My heart skitters away from that hard truth. Instead, I twist a lock of hair around my finger and think about my career, which is in total crisis mode. It was all I ever wanted, and now I don't know how I feel about it. I'm not sure if it was the attack, or the pandemic showing me what life could be like if I didn't work all the time, or the grief of Dmitri's and Beryl's deaths. Maybe all the above.

I just find myself longing for something else. Not more. Less.

From the time I was asked to come to LA for a screen test for *A Woman for the Ages* to the premiere of the film was barely under a year. My life changed so much that I felt like the frog in Neil Diamond's song "I Am . . . I Said," a frog with dreams of royalty who became a king.

Beryl loaned me the money for the coast-to-coast flight. The director, Jonathan Best, who was the man who saw me in the waiting room off Broadway, arranged for me to have a hotel room, something I didn't realize was unusual until much later.

Everyone gossiped that he wanted to seduce me, but it was never like that. In some ways, he actually reminded me of Phoebe's dad—excited about my talent, protective of my naivete, encouraging, and never, ever inappropriate. I was lucky.

After the screen test, he let a day go by and then called me to say they were going to offer me the part, but he wanted me to have an agent, and he'd taken the liberty of phoning three of them on my behalf. His advice was to go with a woman, which I did. Edwina was young then, too, barely twenty-five, but she was connected to one of the best agencies in the business, and she showed herself to have barracuda instincts when it came to negotiating terms. Thanks to Edwina, I escaped some of the traps that befall young actors, and started making real money with that first movie.

Everything about my life took on a Cinderella glitter. The work was extremely difficult, and I was in nearly every frame of the film. My inexperience showed, which caused delays and trouble on set, but mostly everyone was patient with me, and I had great chemistry with my costar, Jason Tremaine, who'd been a child star and knew a lot about that world.

We filmed for five months, on location in a Provençal town, another staggering delight to me, who'd never traveled anywhere. It thrilled me to be on an airplane, to hear people speaking another language, to eat new and unusual food. I was game for everything, anything, and drank it all in so that if it all dried up the next year, I'd at least have had this experience. I sent Phoebe letters, trying to write in ways that would give her the experience.

Dear Phoebe,

The days are long on set. We have to be in place at 5 am, which means I get up at 3 in order to have time to eat and get to the set. Whoever is in charge sends croissants and coffee and fruit to my room, and someone else calls, always twice, to make sure I'm actually up and moving. They do my hair and face when I get to the chateau so all I really have to do is take a shower and pour myself in the car that takes a crowd of us to the set. Jason and Annalise are almost always in the car with me, since we're in so many scenes together, and we don't talk very much. Honestly, Annalise seems hungover most of the time, and she has cold compresses over her eyes. (Just between us, obviously.)

We work on scenes at the chateau and in the local village we've taken over. It's so beautiful, Pheebs, seriously. It's exactly like the book, the little alleyways and the old gray stone, and the smell of bread baking and horses clattering on the cobblestone streets. It's magical.

And honestly, even though I am dead tired every night when we get back to the hotel, I *am so happy. This is the happiest I have ever been in my life. I love acting, love inhabiting this character, imagining myself in the time. Most days, I start working without a solid sense of connection and then there's a click, almost audible, and I'm not me anymore. I'm not pretending to be Sarah, I am her. It's like reading in a way, except with more props. I know you get what I mean.*

The only thing that would make it better is if you were here. Xoxoxoxox
Suze

She wrote me back with just as much energy, telling me about art school and the projects she was trying to birth, and Derek.

Right at the start, Edwina said, "It might be difficult, but try not to get involved with anyone while you make this picture. It will distract you." And I saw how true it could be in Phoebe's focus on Derek. I got it, totally. He had that lost bad-boy vibe and a way of walking that made you think he'd know what he was doing in bed, and they shared the art thing, a passion and love of it that bonded them.

But I also noticed that more of her energy was going to the boy than to the work. I didn't say anything because—

—because I was afraid I might lose her through all this. It was a lot, this big dream falling in my lap, not just a part, but the part of the year. It was always going to go to an ingenue, and I happened to be her.

I also wrote letters to Beryl, full of the details of nature and the environment I knew she'd like.

The chateau is over 400 years old, and it sits next to a thick forest that's almost like something out of Hansel and Gretel, a place where you'd find the witch's cottage if you went far enough down the path. I've noticed some birds I've never seen, one that is like a robin and close to it in size, but has muted blue feathers on its chest instead of red. Lavender grows wild, and I've sent you some to smell. It's kind of amazing to walk along and suddenly smell perfume.

I'm very tired today. We worked five 16-hour days in a row to get "the emotional intensity" Jonathan wanted, and it was effective. When I had to cry over the loss of my friend, I was able to get going very easily! Everyone said I did a great job. I hope they didn't know I was actually crying (if I think about that awful time in Portland I can cry like nobody's business). But maybe it doesn't matter.

When we wrap, I'll be back in Oregon for a couple of weeks, to rest. I already have two more movies lined up. My agent said I need to buy a house in LA, and I might ask your advice about that. I have no idea what to do, but I see that she's right. I think there's going to be a lot I have to learn about the business side of my life and how to manage money and what to do. You're a businesswoman, and I hope you can guide me.

I found some feathers and leaves I thought you'd like. Write soon!

Love you so so so so much!

Suze

When the movie wrapped and all the plans were made for releasing it, appearances at talk shows and media training sessions and how to conduct myself on the red carpet and how to answer hard questions from an interviewer and a million other things that seemed slightly ridiculous but proved themselves necessary, I called her to express some of my terror. "What if I'm terrible?" I cried.

"You will not be terrible," she said with a cluck. "You know that. Say it out loud."

I took a breath. "I will not be terrible. In fact, I'm going to be very, very good."

She laughed. "There's my girl." I heard clanking in the background, the faint sound of the Rolling Stones. "You are about to lose something you don't even know you have, however, and you should spend a little time appreciating it."

"What do you mean?"

"The minute that movie comes out, you're going to be famous. Very famous. Everyone will know your face, and it's going to change your life in ways that you can't imagine right now."

My stomach flipped, both in anticipation and fear. I wanted to dissemble, protest, be modest, but I also knew it was true. The production company and everyone around me were counting on it. The picture was slated to be the biggest movie of the year. "Yeah," I said, quietly.

"Take some time, sweetheart, to be anonymous. Walk around busy places. Go to the grocery store. Go see Phoebe and eat out."

Standing in the kitchen of my new house with the phone pressed to my ear, the turquoise line curling away to the wall, I looked out at my swimming pool and thought of how lonely I was, all the time. If I got famous, maybe I wouldn't be so lonely anymore. "I will." I closed my eyes. "Thank you. I love you so much, Beryl. I don't know what I would have done without you."

"You're a great light, sweetie. I love you."

Sitting with Jasmine so many years later, I realize that she will carry Beryl's memory forward in time. It comforts me to think of her going to the end of her long life (may she live to 150, never mind one hundred), carrying the face of a woman who has shaped all of us so much.

She will carry memories of me, too, and Phoebe. All of us a background swirl to Jasmine's life, which will hold big loves and hates and broken hearts and dreams and losses and all the other things. For a moment, I try to imagine her at forty, a marine biologist professor with oversize glasses, maybe, or an athletic treasure hunter with a gorgeous partner who loves her. Or maybe she'll be an artist like her grandmother, and her grandmother before her, and living at the flower farm with a tumble of children.

All good possibilities.

When Phoebe and I tried to imagine our lives, we found it hard to imagine that we'd ever be thirty, much less forty, but we did conjure great futures for ourselves—she living in a funky old brownstone in Manhattan, showing her canvases at high-end galleries. There would be articles in glossy magazines about her and photos of her ever-so-hip self in her loft studio. I would be an actress, and we would go to each other's openings, and toast with champagne and tell each other everything. We pinkie swore to never give up our careers for a guy.

But Phoebe did. I was so upset that she'd let Derek talk her out of finishing art school, that she'd drop out to be a wife and mother instead of sticking to the path she'd imagined for herself, that I couldn't leave it alone, even when she asked me to respect her wishes. Beryl, too, was distraught, but even both of us talking ourselves blue didn't make any difference. Phoebe insisted she knew what she was doing. Looking at Jasmine, reading her book in the soft yellow light cast by a lamp, I think maybe she did.

If I'd been able to keep my daughter, I wouldn't have gone to New York. I wouldn't have been auditioning. I wouldn't have had the life I've had.

If Phoebe had come to New York with me, she would never have met Derek, never had Stephanie, and the wonder who is Jasmine would not exist. The thought gives me an actual, physical pang.

Maybe it's impossible to play the what-ifs backward. Life takes the path it takes.

～

Jasmine and I are making toast when Phoebe knocks. "That must be Nana," I say, licking jam from the tip of my finger.

"Yay! She can eat breakfast with us!"

I open the door to Phoebe, and it's obvious something is wrong. "What is it?"

She glances at Jasmine, who is giggling at the seagull cocking his head and trying to coax her to come outside and give him food. "Close the door. I want to show you something."

"Jasmine," I call over my shoulder, "stay put. We'll be right back."

Maui jumps up to go with us, but Phoebe says, "Stay," and points to the floor. Alerted by something in her voice, he sinks to the ground, but his ears and shoulders are alert.

"What's wrong?" I ask. I lower my voice. "Did something happen with Ben? I mean, he seems—"

"It's not that." She walks down the driveway, gesturing for me to follow, and then stops. Points back to the house.

There, on the side of the house in bright-red paint, is the word WHORE in letters two feet high. My gut drops, and I think of Maui, warning me. "Damn."

"We need to call the police."

A sense of creeping dread crawls up my spine, the backs of my arms, raising gooseflesh. "When we got back from the beach last night, Maui was acting really weird."

"What do you mean?"

"He ran out here, and sniffed around, and then howled"—I gesture at the trees—"but I couldn't see anything amiss. So we went inside and locked everything up."

"Holy shit," she says. I'm braced for her to yell at me over not keeping Jasmine safe, but instead she says, "They must have come back. Did Maui give any other warning?"

I have to think about it. "No, not that I can think of. We were just reading and listening to music."

She touches my arm. "I'll call the police."

A fine trembling has started in my veins, and before it can turn to visible tremors, I go back inside and sit down at the table with Jasmine, forcing myself to only look at the seagull. He has a striped tail, not quite black but darkest gray. Yul Brynner has hopped up on a stool inches away from the bird and is making hiccupy hunting sounds that make Jasmine laugh even more. "What is he doing?"

Focus on the now.

"He is under the mistaken impression that he could take that gull down."

"Like kill him?" Jasmine asks, eyes wide.

"He can't," I say as reassuringly as possible. "That gull is bigger than he is, but cats like hunting."

"Does he ever catch other birds?"

"No." I pick up my toast and think about taking a bite, but the bright-red paint floats across my vision and I set it back down. "He's an indoor cat. He does sometimes catch mice or bugs."

"Aw! Poor mice."

"I try to get them outside."

Phoebe comes back into the room and nods. Something about the angle of her head is softer, and I remember that she had a date with a hot guy last night. It gives me something else to fill the place where my worry wants to ramp itself up. "Want some tea?"

She lets go of a breath, kisses Jasmine's head, and says, "Sure."

"Can I play on my iPad?"

"Yes, just for an hour." Phoebe slides into the vacated chair. I click the button on the kettle and it's nearly hot already so I prepare a cup for her, a hearty English breakfast single source I discovered in London. As I settle the cup in front of her, along with milk and sugar and a small spoon, I say, "So . . . how was your night?"

Everything about her softens, all the angles of elbow and neck and jaw, and she looks out toward the sea. "Really good."

I wait, but she gazes toward the waves with a cat-that-swallowed-the-canary look. "That's it? That's all you're going to say?" I lean in, whisper, "Did you sleep with him?"

She blushes, neck to hairline, and says, "I don't kiss and tell."

I laugh. "You don't have to."

In a gesture I remember from our youth, she covers her cheeks with her hands, presses her lips together. Her eyes shine over the top of her fingers. She nods, slowly.

I reach over and squeeze her forearm. "Good."

A knock sounds at the door, and Jasmine dashes into the foyer. "Wait, baby," I cry. I leap up. "I've got it!"

I run to the door and haul it open, but it's not the police. It's Joel, and I feel myself getting shaky again. I forgot he was coming to bring a new part for the breaker box.

He scowls as he points to the scrawled word on my house. "What the hell?"

"We called the police." I shake my head, but the trembling starts again in my body, and this time I get flutters of the baseball bat against my head—*flash*—a razor buzzing away my hair—*flash*—

I squeeze my eyes tight, shake my head, trying to fling the memories away. Joel takes my arm. Maui noses my leg.

Jasmine. She's inside.

I suck in a breath, center myself in my gut, blow out the breath, open my eyes. Joel is close, and I see a circular scar beside his mouth that I remember. Focus. Breathe in. His lips are thinner than they once were—he had such full lips for a boy—but still beautiful, his mouth wide and, just now, stern.

"Okay?" he asks.

I look up, meet his velvet, dark gaze, nod. "I'm good. Thanks." It feels weird to speak in such ordinary ways, and I feel our old selves, hungry and lost, behind all the polite moves of our reacquainted selves.

It happens, I tell myself. People meet again. What was is just what was.

A car pulls up outside, and it's the sheriff. A middle-aged man, tanned and ropy like a runner, steps out. "Hey, Bryce," Joel says.

He comes up the walk. "How you doing, Joel," he says and shakes his hand, like he's the one who made the phone call.

"I'm fine," he says. "She's the one who has a problem."

Bryce nods. He has close-cut blond hair and a face carved of sharp angles. His last name will be Larsen or something spelled with an *e* instead of *o* to designate his Norwegian roots. A village of former Norwegians settled here long ago, and their roots go deep.

Until he looks up, he doesn't register who I am, and then he does. "Ms. Ogden. Pleasure."

I reach out a hand to greet him, and give him my solid shake. He returns it respectfully.

"This is the issue?" he says, pointing.

"Yes. Someone left it overnight at some point."

Phoebe comes out on the porch, closing the door behind her. "It was here when I came to pick up my granddaughter."

"Have you had any trouble? Any threats?"

I give him the rundown. The dead squirrel, the guy at the Pig 'N Pancake, now this. "I'm on the target list for the LNB. They put me in the hospital six months ago."

"I heard about that. I'm sorry." He purses his lips. "I wouldn't be surprised to hear there was a chapter in the mountains around here. Lotta crazies up there in their compounds. I'll dig around."

"The guy who verbally attacked her at the Pig 'N Pancake earlier this week seemed like a regular," Phoebe says. "It seemed like the waitress knew him."

He writes something on the pad in his hand, then lifts his sunglasses to see the paint more clearly.

Jasmine pokes her head out. "Hey, what—"

I block her view with my body and hustle her back inside. "None of your business, kiddo," I say, closing the door with my back. "Go wait in the living room, please."

She cocks her head. Considers. "Okay."

"I'll make sure she stays inside. Bryce has some more questions."

The sheriff has taken some photos. "I'll ask the lab about the squirrel, see if they got anything. Don't hold your breath—things take a while here. Not like LA."

I nod. "I grew up here, you know."

"In the meantime, I assume you have an alarm system?"

"I've had a problem with it, I think. But—"

Joel raises a hand with a plastic bag of various parts. "That's what I'm here for."

"I'd suggest making sure it's on all the time."

This does not make me feel better, but I remember Maui barking wildly when Joel arrived yesterday. Maybe Phoebe would let me borrow him until they figure out who is targeting me.

Again. As if it's happening right now, I see the trash on my sidewalk, feel the sun on my face as I walk toward it—

Sweat breaks across my brow and down my neck, and I force myself to take in a long, slow breath. Hold it for a count of four. Breathe out slowly. Joel walks Bryce to his car, and they exchange a few words. I continue the breathing until he comes back up the steps. "Did the men get things all straightened out?" I say with an edge of annoyance.

To my surprise, he smiles ever so slightly, and claps me on the shoulder. "Don't you worry your pretty little head, girlie." His tone is sardonic. "The boys got you covered."

My nerves are shaking but calmer now. "Come on in. Want some tea?"

"Coffee?"

His request kindles the softest puff of . . . yearning? Peace? "I might have some."

Jasmine dances out into the kitchen, a drawing in her hand. "Look! Maui and Yul Brynner."

The cat is especially good, with an exaggerated mask and anime eyes, and she's captured something goofy about Maui. "Sweetheart, this is amazing!" I curl a hand around her neck, feeling her thick hair, and suddenly feel Beryl all around me, the sense of her bosomy body, the softness of leaning into her. I can almost smell her, fog and ocean and hints of oil paint.

Time, I think. *Rivers of time we can only ride forward.* I kiss Jasmine's head.

Phoebe says, "We should probably get back. I have to finish some work."

"Can I stay here with Maui?"

"No, Suze has things to do, too." She gives me a look over Jasmine's head that I can't quite interpret. I know enough to back her up. "But Maui can stay." She looks at me. "If you want him to."

"Oh, yes, please."

"Come on!" Jasmine says. "Why can't I stay, too?"

"Joel and I have some things to do here," I say. "I'll come find you guys later. They said it might be sunny this afternoon. Maybe we can all walk on the beach? Have your nana show off her tide pool knowledge."

"Okay." She leans close and hugs me with her whole body, unself-conscious, her head against my meager chest. Beryl was probably much nicer to sink into.

"You okay?" Phoebe asks.

I nod.

"Come find us later." She hugs me, too. I smell hints of Beryl, but also the fullness of Phoebe herself, intensified as if her body temperature is higher. I think of Ben holding her and something in me lightens.

"I will."

They leave me and Joel standing in the kitchen, alone. I stick my hands in my back pockets, not quite able to look away from his sober, kind face. A thousand tiny moments and dozens of big ones wash around my brain, making my heart flutter wildly. I swallow. "I'm glad you're here."

"Me too." His eyes soften. I notice his throat, and he swallows. His tone is gruff when he says, "How about that coffee?"

It takes a few minutes to locate the coffeemaker, and another couple to dig coffee out of the freezer. It's good to have something to do with my hands. "I hope this is still good," I comment, examining it. "I bought it over the summer."

"It'll be fine. I'm not that picky."

"You don't like tea."

"Nope." He gives me a half smile. "But if it's trouble, you don't have to bother."

"Well, I'm all in now," I say, pointing to the coffee grinder I've also pulled out.

"I see that." He dips his head toward the utility room. "I'm going to take a look at that alarm while you're doing that."

"Thank you." Pale light casts gloss over the part of his hair, throws into relief the crow's-feet around his eyes. "It really will make me feel better to have it working."

He nods. I step sideways to let him by, and as he passes, I take a breath to inhale his scent, startled that it's exactly the same.

Before he entirely passes me, he stops. "Sorry about being so aloof all day yesterday. It's a little weird to see you."

"It is weird. I mean—" I shake my head. There's so much between us, so many things we never had the chance to sort out that there's almost no way to approach them. And yet I'm hungry to hear about him. His life. His thoughts. "How *are* you, Joel?"

He looks out the window, and I see a dozen things cross his face. "Good and bad. How about you?"

I spread my hands. "Same."

He moves into the utility room, and I grind beans, wash the pot, fill it up with water. The smell of coffee must be one of the headiest in the world, but it transports me, always, to the fellowship hall at my father's church. I was often the one making it, serving it, cleaning it up. Maybe that's the reason I still don't drink it. Like cooking, it reminds me of things I don't ever want to think about again.

Some of Phoebe's cranberry bread is wrapped up on the counter. When I start slicing it, Maui trots into the kitchen, his tags jingling. Hope gives him a big toothy grin. "Dogs don't need bread," I say, but look in the fridge for something more appropriate. "They can have turkey, though."

He slurps it up. Waits for more. Yul Brynner leaps lightly onto the counter for his share, and I give him some tidbits, too. They both stare at me, and I laugh. "It's not time."

Joel returns. "The alarm is very outdated. I don't think the software is supported any longer."

"That explains a lot," I say, leaning on the counter. I almost cross my arms and stop in time. I don't want to appear to be defensive, and the actor side of me knows that I need to keep my body open and relaxed if I want him to feel that way. Or maybe all this is silly. It's been decades. We've both had lives.

Be normal, I say to myself. *Treat him like any old friend.* "What do you want in your coffee?"

"Just black."

I pour a cup and offer the plate of sliced bread, picking a piece up as I curl into the banquette, my feet under me. Yul Brynner trots over, tail high, and settles behind me, smelling my ear. Maui huffs and lies down on the floor. I feel like I have a team.

Joel gingerly perches on the other side of the table, and studies me as he sips the coffee. "It's strange to see you in person after seeing you on screens."

"Did you see my movies?"

He nods. "A few." Inclines his head. "All."

I grin. "Really?"

"Of course. You're the only famous person I know, and I liked watching you grow up and become this . . . powerful person."

It feels impersonal, but what did I expect? "Thank you for that."

"But you don't actually look the same in person. I mean, I guess nobody does."

"Right. There's a lot of artifice in the screen version."

He meets my eyes. "The real-life version is a little less intimidating."

That's a lot closer to what I might be seeking. My heart is racing a little, and when I reach for a napkin, my hands are shaking. Pulling back into my body, I take a breath.

"Are you okay?"

I'm about to lie, to blow it all off, but instead I tell the truth. "Not really. Not for a while. I'm rattled by . . . everything. The attacks. The sneakiness of someone on my property." I lift my shoulders. "You."

"Yeah. Me too, honestly." I see him swallow. He takes another sip of coffee. "I read about the attack. Are you recovered?"

"Physically." Saying it aloud settles my body a little. "I don't really want to talk about that, though, if that's okay."

"I get it. No worries."

The music has settled into a soft bit, swirling around us like this is a movie. I smile as I say, "So, you have the advantage. You know a lot more about my life than I know about yours."

He leans back. "Uh. Okay. Where to start?"

"Tell me everything."

For a long minute, he's quiet, just looking at me. Then he takes a breath. "Let's see . . . everything since I last saw you . . ." He ticks off items on his fingers. "Juvie, Seattle with my dad, community college, lost years, married, settled down, got divorced, moved back to Seattle to take care of my mom, watched my old girlfriend become a big star, got married again, divorced again, came back to Blue Cove about seven years ago."

So much pain in those simple sentences. For me, for him. "I never thanked you for burning down the church."

It surprises him into a laugh. His eyes crinkle and I can see the crooked eyetooth on the right, and the sound is exactly the same, slightly hoarse and comically high pitched. "My pleasure, ma'am," he says with a salute. "Where'd you go when you—"

"Got out of the home? Yeah." That's tender territory. "Beryl helped me emancipate myself. I lived with her through the rest of high school. How long were you in juvie?"

"Eighteen months. I got lucky. No criminal history, and extenuating circumstances."

I think of him then, a smart, fierce young man of color. "Juvie had to have been hell for you."

He looks away, shrugs, but I can see the sorrow around his mouth. He clears his throat. "They showed pictures of you after your dad—"

"Tried to kill me?" I fill in with a humorless laugh.

"Yeah." His jaw goes hard, and there's a suspicious sheen over his eyes. "God, I felt so helpless."

Now there's a river of dark emotion rising, and I can't avoid the tears in my own eyes. "You set me free, Joel. You totally did."

He bows his head, and I can feel the weight of our losses, but the silence gives me space to calm myself down. We sit in the quiet for a time. The music lilts around us. Outside, clouds chug across the sky. The ocean washes to shore.

I've forgotten how still he can be, his limbs quiet when other people would be wiggling or tapping or restless. I forgot how much I liked it, how much space it gives me to breathe.

After a time he says, "Now you. Tell me everything."

"Me? Um . . . let's see." I lift my hand and count on my fingers to mirror him. "Got sent away to Portland, came back and lived with Beryl, went to New York after high school, got discovered"—I spread my hands, like *ta-da*—"made a bunch of movies, bought a big house in Hollywood, and made some more movies."

"Fell in love with a big director."

Dmitri. My soul gives a little wail. "Yeah. We were together nearly twenty years. Until he died."

"I'm sorry," he said. "COVID, right?"

I nod. "The worst was that he was alone in the hospital. I hated that so much."

"Same with my mom."

"I'm sorry. I hadn't heard."

"Thanks."

"No kids?" I ask, and then wish I hadn't.

"Only the one," he says. "You?"

"Same." An old pain rustles. I see her dark hair, her newborn blue eyes.

"Did you"—he leans on the table, hands steepled tightly—"see him? Her?"

"Her." I swallow hard. "Yeah. For a very short while. She had a lot of hair, and a beautiful little mouth." A lot of memories are blurry, but not that one. After so long, the memory no longer brings tears, but thinking of how Joel never even had that glimpse of her brings a fresh swell of sorrow. I bow my head, touch Yul Brynner's long tail.

Joel closes his eyes. Breathes. Then: "I am sorry you had to go through all of that alone, Suze. I really am."

"It wasn't your fault."

"Still." He straightens, picks up his cup, and it's empty. "Mind if I help myself?"

"Not at all."

We can't stay in that place of darkness. *I* can't. When he comes back, I ask, "What were the lost years?"

"Ah." He wipes his clean-shaven cheeks. "Just . . . the usual bullshit. Fights, bad jobs, bad relationships. Looking for something I didn't know how to find."

"What pulled you out of it?"

"My first wife, Ella. I met her in Seattle. Solid as granite and didn't put up with nonsense and self-destruction."

"Good for her."

He nods, looks toward the sea. "I broke her heart, though—I couldn't be the guy she wanted."

"We all do that when we're young, don't you think?"

"I wasn't that young by then. Almost forty."

"Oh." I allow myself a smile. "That's a few lost years."

"Mmm. Did you?"

"Have lost years?"

"Break hearts."

"Of course." I'd had my share of tempestuous relationships. "The difference is, my peccadilloes were fully documented by the paparazzi and the tabloids."

"Well, that would suck."

"It's a weird world."

A beat between us. "I'm glad you're here," he says.

"Me too."

For a minute, maybe two, we're simply silent, looking at each other. It feels like a million years have passed and no time at all. It feels like he's always lived in some secret part of my body and now I've opened the door. It feels like oxygen. It feels like a prayer.

He picks up his cup and drains it. "I'm going to see about getting you an alarm system that works. Is that okay with you?"

"Very."

He stands. "I'll get to it, then." On the way by, he touches my shoulder for longer than a casual moment. I close my eyes.

"Thank you," I whisper, and then he's gone.

~

Right after he leaves, my agent calls.

"Hey, Edwina. What's up?" She never calls, only emails, so something is up.

"Not the best news of all time," she says.

I've been expecting something like this. The new season is set to start filming in a month and some decisions need to be made about what to do with my character, who has been languishing in a coma for quite some time to give me space to heal. But I've pushed the time a little too long, I guess. "They're going to kill Alice on *Going Home Again*."

"Not exactly."

"They're not going to leave her in a coma, are they?"

"No. They're replacing you with Morgan Millstone."

"What? Viewers hate that!"

"Viewers are clamoring to have her back, and they don't want to go through another season waiting for you. The network is gambling that they'd hate the end of the show more."

"But she looks nothing like me!" Morgan is an actor about my age but she has a completely different look—like a cat standing in for a dog. "How will they explain it?"

"I don't know, Suze. I'm so sorry. It'll be some idiot thing about plastic surgery or something. You know the things they do."

A hollow feeling pours through my gut. I thought I was ready to get out of Hollywood, but this is all I've known my entire adult life. "Wow," I manage.

Edwina says, "Are you ready to come back? I could probably get them to hold off for a couple of months if that's what you want."

I'm shaking my head even though she can't see me. "No, I'm not ready. I . . . I can't right now. I don't know when I will be, not for television. I need to work through some things."

"Totally. I get it, and I'll let them know. How about I send you some scripts I've collected for you? Maybe a movie in a few months would be a welcome change?"

"Okay." I am not sure that will be the answer, either, but I have nothing to put in the yawning space where my career has been all this time. "Thanks, Edwina. I know you're just the messenger."

"I hope you get to feeling better, Suze. The world misses you."

I doubt that very much, but I say dutifully, "Thanks. Send me the scripts. I'll take a look."

Yul Brynner senses my mood and jumps into my lap, his tail waving beneath my nose, tickling me. "Silly cat," I say, laughing, but that's why I have him. A dog will only build your ego, but cats have a sense of humor. At my feet, Maui barks. "Sorry, I didn't mean you."

On the beach below, the sun is breaking through. I impulsively text Phoebe. Headed to the beach with Maui if you want to meet me there.

See you in 15 minutes!

Another ding lets me know I have an important email. Edwina has already sent the material. Six scripts. Some of them will be terrible and one or two might be interesting. I'll give them a look.

Later.

"C'mon, Maui. Let's go for a walk."

Chapter Seventeen
Phoebe

Suze and Maui are already on the beach when we arrive. Jasmine runs toward her like she hasn't seen her in a year, arms out, palms high. Her body makes a joyful X against the landscape, and the artist part of my brain files away the contrasts—sea and sky and rock, flesh and bones and hair. I wish I could bottle her essence right now, bottle all the essences of the girls and women she will be through her life. I wish I could witness all of them, participate.

I'm sloshing with happiness today. At odd moments, I flash on the feeling of Ben's naked body against mine, the gusto he brought to bed, to kissing, to pure, animal enjoyment. It freed something in me, something careful and withholding. I could be myself with him, utterly and completely, because over the months our friendship grew, I learned to trust him. I still do.

It's the strangest feeling.

And today, I'm wide open. Open to the sunlight, to the almost painfully huge love I feel for this child in this moment, to the startling sensation of Suze, walking there in her long white sweater, her hair in a messy bun that leaves artful tendrils falling around her face. Again I notice that she looks a couple of decades older than she did the last time I saw her.

As she bends to admire the shell Jasmine is showing her, I see the slight stiffness of her hips, the fact of age lying on her, and I wonder why I got so very angry with her at my grandmother's funeral.

The fight had been building for ages, probably decades, built block by block, a resentment here, a slight there, some mortar of jealousy (both directions), pebbles of misunderstandings. It killed me when she got to live with Beryl, when all I'd ever wanted was to come to Blue Cove and stay here with the woman I loved most in the world. I knew why Amma offered shelter to my best friend, and I also knew it was a saving grace for her, but that didn't halt my jealousy.

Suze had been mad at me—ever so slightly, but definitely—ever since I dropped out of school to marry Derek. I was envious of her big life, and she envied my child, a fact I understood. Thinking of the baby she gave away gives me shame and sorrow in equal measures, but in those days, I envied her freedom and she envied my connections.

We loved each other, too, of course. It was a rare month that we didn't have at least an email exchange, and every few months, there was a long phone call. A few times, we traveled together—I met her in Paris a couple of times, and I visited her in LA, and she came home to Blue Cove often, especially after she bought the Wright house. A house she bought when I was trying to save it from developers.

Before that she'd often stayed with me, in her old bedroom. It was comforting, and safe, and nobody bothered her here because the town didn't suffer paparazzi.

I was utterly furious when she bought the house. Our house. She swooped in and dropped more money than it was worth, paying off developers and pouring a ton of cash into the restoration. Which it needed, absolutely, but I'd already figured out a path for that—*my* plan had been to turn it into a museum/gallery, restoring the Wright-school details and then housing a collection I planned to build from local artists.

But why was that better than what happened? I can build a museum elsewhere if I want to, and it really wasn't a great location, out of the way, up the hill. My grandmother pointed that out at the time, but I didn't want to listen.

It felt like she'd usurped me. It bewildered her, and she offered to involve me in the restoration and then seeing after the house itself when it was restored. I swallowed my anger, where it joined a million other things, large and small, and lived there until that fight at my grandmother's funeral.

It feels, suddenly, like a long time ago.

In this soft mood, washed by the clean ocean air, watching her with my beloved granddaughter, I can see the pair of us as children, not much older than Jasmine. Her hair sweeping the sand, her awful dresses. She swept into my lonely, friendless life like a princess in a movie, and no matter what I did, she loved me. Still loves me, although I've given her a lot of reasons to walk away.

On this beach where we met, where we spent endless hours talking and walking and lying side by side in the sand, dreaming about the future, I feel my love for her as the power it is. I've loved her all my life and I love her now. It's oddly piercing, and I don't know why.

"What have you found?" I ask, joining them.

"Shells," Jasmine says, holding out broken bits. "And look how many sea stars there are!"

She points to a shallow tide pool around the base of the rocks. A half dozen purple and pink stars cling to the rocks, looking plump and cheerful. "That's great." I knew they were still suffering from a wasting disease that had attacked them from Baja to British Columbia in the 2010s. This is a good sign. Maybe the plague would move on.

As all plagues eventually do.

We peer into the tide pools for a while, and then Suze suggests we walk. Jasmine runs ahead, stopping like a puppy to check something out, then trotting along ahead of us.

"My agent called this morning," Suze says, conversationally. "They're going to replace me with Morgan Millstone on the show."

"What? She doesn't even look like you!"

"That's what I said."

"Are you furious?"

She takes a breath, lets it go. "Honestly, I should be, but I don't care." She looks at me. "Is that weird?"

"Do you think you might just need more time to heal?"

"Maybe, but they're starting the new season and they want to get things moving. I'm not ready to go back."

"You shouldn't." Water ripples over my bare toes, and it's shockingly cold. "I worry that you're still in danger."

"I can hire people if it comes to that, but I just want to be here for a while."

Something in her voice makes me look at her. "What's on your mind?"

"Sometimes I feel like I've been carrying around this giant bag of shit for most of my life. Dragging it behind me when I was tired, sitting on it when I was wiped out, asking porters to carry it when I was busy, but always keeping it."

I laugh. "Good visual!"

"I want to let it go. And I don't really know how."

"You could walk away."

She gives me a side-eye. "Yeah, gosh, why didn't I think of that?"

"Touché. Sorry."

Her sweater ripples in the wind. "I think I have to be here to work it all out. My dad, that summer." A pause. "The baby."

The baby she gave up for adoption. My heart squeezes with painful memory. I nod slowly. "Do you want to talk it out?"

"Not right now."

"Is your dad even still alive?"

"I don't know. Even though they didn't charge him with child abuse—"

"Assholes."

"The good thing is, I don't think he'd get away with it now." She shrugs. "Different times."

"Sorry, I interrupted. You don't know where he is?"

"Nope. And do not care. People hated him even if he didn't get charged. And thanks to Joel there was no church left."

I press my lips together, thinking of his hectic appearance when he brought a letter for me to give Suze. Which I truly intended to do.

And never did.

It was the letter, his distraught appearance at my grandmother's door, that confirmed what I'd suspected all along. He was in love with her. My guilt is as heavy as an anchor, and I shut the door on it quickly. It can't help right now.

"He was one cruel motherfucker," I say with feeling.

Suze laughs, and I feel justified in keeping my secrets for another day. "Those words out of your mouth! Oh my God."

I glance at her, the wind catching her hair and tossing it in her eyes. The face that is as familiar to me as my own, and in that moment, I'm so glad she's back. When she's with me, I am freer to be myself.

The recognition blooms, a truth hidden beneath so many layers of time and resentment. Attempting lightness, I shrug. "You're not the only one who can turn a phrase." I call out, "Jasmine! Want to get ice cream?"

She whirls around and runs back to us like a platypus, hands flapping, knees kicking, a goofy expression on her face. I wish for her this perfect unselfconsciousness forever, but I know it won't last. Instead, I wish for her to have people in her life with whom she can be her entire, whole self, like I was with Amma, the way I was sometimes with Suze.

A whisper creeps in. *The way I am with Ben.*

Too soon!

Jasmine runs in front of us, Maui chasing her, playfully trying to grab her ankles. I slow, my hands in my pockets, and confess, "This whole thing with Ben is scary."

"Scary how?"

"He's such a good friend, and I don't want to mess that up, but oh, Lord." I widen my eyes. "Last night was . . ." I shake my head, tell the truth. "The best sex I've ever had in my life."

Suze laughs. Her eyes crinkle at the corners. "This is bad how?"

"I haven't let myself feel so much in a long time. Like, what if it all falls apart and he breaks my heart and then I lose my friend as well as my lover and then I'm all alone again?" Tears fill my eyes, tears of wonder and fear and overwhelm.

She loops her arm through my elbow. "Listen, I mean this in the best possible way, Phoebe."

I look at her.

"So what? So what if it ends? What if he dies? What if the world ends? What if? Would you really trade having this . . . joy . . . right now for some awful thing that might not even happen?"

"I know what you're saying, but it's not really that easy, is it?"

"It's only harder if you insist. Don't take things away from yourself before you even get to enjoy them."

"I don't do that."

She raises her eyebrows. "Good. Then don't." She squeezes my arm. "Enjoy it! Jeez, Phoebe, you should see the way he looks at you."

"Really?"

"Like he wants to lick you from head to toe and then start over."

A heat of memory runs below my skin, head to toe. "Well . . ."

She laughs, full throated, and I can't remember the last time I heard it. Maybe she's finally starting to heal. "There you go."

I try to trust it, I really do. But life has a habit of pulling the rug out from under you.

THEN

WHAT IF WE WENT TO ITALY?

Phoebe

Italy

My parents didn't fight. Not on the way to the airport, which usually caused all kinds of conflict, not on the long flight over when both of them drank a lot of wine and even let me have a little. I started to feel pretty great, honestly, like maybe things were going to be okay.

We stayed in Rome for four days, and on the final day, my parents went out to dinner, leaving me to myself in the room. I was strictly forbidden to leave, and they'd called for a meal to be delivered to me at six. I truly didn't mind, because I liked how they were being with each other. I sat by the open window with a notebook in my lap and wrote to Suze.

June 22, 19—

Hi, Suze.

I promised I would send you postcards, and I did send two already, but a letter is better. Italy is beautiful! It's really, really hot, too, which I don't like, but my mom keeps telling me to enjoy the sunshine, and I guess I do like that part. I'm getting really tan, and she bought me a pretty blue dress that kinda hides my big butt and I feel pretty when I wear it, though I'm sure you'd look 10 times better in it.

We went to the Colosseum and the ruins of the city today. It was kinda sad, to think of all those people there so long ago and they're all just dead along with their city. I felt the same way at Pompeii, which I wanted to see so bad so we went there. It was super sad. Everybody frozen in place, their lives done, right there, while they were eating dinner. It makes my heart hurt. I filled up half my sketchbook, though, and Naples was a cool town, kinda shady and all the boys whistled at me, which I both like and don't like. Somebody pinched my butt on the tram and I was so mad but when I turned around, everybody played dumb. A boy flirted with me on the Spanish Steps, and he was really cute! Something about Italy makes me feel more grown up.

My parents haven't been fighting at all. It's nice. I wonder if they just needed a break from their ordinary lives. When they're like this with each other, I can see why they fell in love.

I hope you're having fun with Mary and Victor and everybody and that you don't miss me too much. If you talk to Joel, tell him I said hi.

Tomorrow, we go to Florence.

Love,

Phoebe

July 2, 19—

Dear Suze,

I love Florence! We have to come here someday. I want to paint everything I see and have filled up two sketchbooks. Everything about it is beautiful—the buildings, the river, the sky, the trees, everything. I wonder if you can study art here? I've been thinking a lot about that since we've been here, what I want to do when we get out of school. We've talked a lot about New York City, but I don't know if that's THE perfect place. We should consider all of our options, as my dad always says. I do know I want to be an artist. There's really no other career that would make me happy, period. You're going to be an actress.

Oops, my parents are back! It's our last night, and we're going to dinner.

Love,

Phoebe

Later—

I am crying so hard I can hardly see to write this, and I want to call you, but my parents won't let me. THEY ARE GETTING DIVORCED!!! My mom is moving to LA and wants me to live there with her, but I won't move. I swear I will not move. My dad is staying in Portland because he has a job there, but he won't keep the house because it's too expensive for one person to pay for.

I feel so mad! So betrayed! Why did we have to have this big fun trip if it was only going to end like this? They've been getting along so well,

251

so why not give it another try? They said they've been trying and it's not working, and they will give me the summer with my grandmother to figure things out.

But I don't want to figure things out! I want them to stay together and live in Portland and keep my beautiful bedroom. I don't want things to change like this. I'm SO SO SO SO SO MAD! I wish you were here.

Love,

Phoebe

CURRENT DAY

Chapter Eighteen

Suze

When I return home, it's only Maui and me. Walking up to the house I've previously loved, I try to talk myself into feeling safe. It's the scorpion problem. When we filmed in Mexico, I loved the landscape, the villa, but once I found a scorpion in the bathroom, and forever after, that room was ruined.

The squirrel, the raving guy at the Pig 'N Pancake, and the paint on my house are like the scorpion. They've ruined my fragile peace of mind. With Maui at my side, we round the exterior of the house, and then, inside, we make a map of the rooms, looking in closets and under beds, checking locks. Yul Brynner joins us, tail high and fluffy.

When it is established that the house is secure, I give both animals a treat, then wash my sandy feet and brush my hair. It's still very long, longer than is fashionable for sure, but I've let it start to gray and I love the way the blonde and gray weave together. I rummage around the cupboards and fridge for something I can eat, and there's little. At home in LA, I order food most of the time, but there's also a woman who comes to cook for me three times a week, leaving healthy, prepared meals in the fridge.

Here, there's less. A few slices of pizza are left over, but their cold, congealed tops are not in the slightest bit appealing. There's a half gallon of milk, some boxes of pasta, three chunks of cheese in various states of decay. One is pretty solid—I only have to slice mold off the very edges, skim a slice on the top and bottom, and it's good as new. Cheese is meant to mold, after all.

I never cook because I grew so tired of it when I was the main food preparer in my father's house, but every so often I do get a yen. Right now, rather than call for another pizza, I can make one of my cornerstone favorites, baked macaroni and cheese. It will make me feel loved.

It was a specialty of mine, once upon a time. Baked mac and cheese is a great potluck favorite, and I made mine with a recipe Beryl showed me. It freezes well, so I make the full casserole and stick it in the oven. Outside, the sun has been overtaken by heavy clouds, and it's raining hard, sideways rain driven by a wind that whips up the waves, tossing spray high into the air. Birds huddle together in the shelter of various rocks.

On the speakers is a playlist made of my favorite soundtracks. One is from my fourth movie, a romantic spy thriller set during the Cold War, in which I played an American in love with a suspected double agent. Another is from my first picture, *A Woman for the Ages*, and both suit the mood of the night, moody and quietly dramatic. I sip tonic water over ice and think about that girl, the one who made the movie.

It was such an exciting period, the excitement of being plucked out of a crowd in a waiting area in New York, the nausea of getting myself to LA for a screen test all on my own. I was terrified it was all a big lie, that I'd get to Hollywood and find a weaselly guy waiting, no movie.

Instead I auditioned in front of a big director and one of the stars who'd already been cast, and the woman who'd written the screenplay. Auditioning was the easy part—stepping into the role, donning it like a cloak. I knew the story inside out because Phoebe and I had read it with zeal only two years before, and discussed it half to death. Wildly romantic, with forbidden love and sex and all kinds of tortures and setbacks. We adored it, and especially loved the happy ending.

They loved me, and I was cast the next day, which led to phone calls to Phoebe and Beryl and the people I knew in NYC. I found an agent who negotiated a dazzling amount of money, and I was launched into the madness of Hollywood. When the movie was critically acclaimed, especially for my portrayal of Sarah, my career was made.

That started the whirl. For a solid two decades, I mostly worked. I made movies and promoted them. I lived in hotel rooms and on planes and in cars sent to pick me up early in the morning in strange locations. I suffered food poisoning and smoked heavily and dabbled with addictions to various substances and had too many lovers, which was a favored tabloid subject.

I fervently hoped my father saw all of it. Every single bit.

Phoebe and I drifted apart somewhat during those years. How could we not? She was raising Stephanie, supporting Derek as he tried to make a name for himself in the art world. She wasn't painting much, and I know it bothered her, but I was careful never to say anything.

But when I could, I included her in things that would be fun— once she and Stephanie came to an awards show with me, and another time I flew Beryl, Phoebe, and Steph to Paris for a whirlwind trip. It made a big impression on Steph, who was born big boned and suffered in the throwaway fashions of her childhood. In Paris, she learned the elements of classic dress and has never wavered from them.

In my early forties, I met Dmitri. On set, of course. He'd recently divorced wife number three, and was nearly fifteen years my senior, but the first time I met him, I knew we'd be a thing. It took a while, nearly a year, for me to let him into my bed, perhaps because I sensed it might be very serious, but once I did, we were together until his death.

How can I leave all that behind? The glamour is fun. The fame. The money. I'm too young to retire and do nothing. That sounds awful.

And yet, how can I stay? I'm tired to my very bones.

With a cup of oolong tea at my elbow, I open my laptop and download the scripts my agent has sent. Six of them, and she's starred two. I save them for last, and open the others one by one, read the treatment and the opening pages. No. No, no, and no. The ones my agent starred are slightly better, but the part I would play in each one is a woman who exists only in her relationship to other people. None of them have agency. They're on screen to prop up a husband (or be killed by him) or be a mother who is annoying or "bossy" (much like the part in *Going Home Again*) or—in the case of the last one—provide comic relief when she falls in love with a con man.

How is that funny? A lonely woman reaching out and getting taken?

Old men are not cast as props for their families. Why is it so impossible for Hollywood to even *see* a woman over fifty? What happened to wisewomen and elders? It's a pet peeve lately. Georgia O'Keeffe was over sixty when she finally started traveling the world. Ruth Bader Ginsburg was on the court into her late eighties. She wasn't propping up a bunch of men. She placed her body squarely in front of them.

I peer through the deepening gloom to the shimmers on the ocean beyond the window, tapping my front tooth with a thumbnail. Where are all the good parts?

A knock at my door startles me. It's nearly dark, with the softest spill of bluish light holding out against the storm over the sea. My heart races as I stand up and go to the door, listening. "Who's there?" I call.

"Joel."

I swallow, feeling threads of yearning and nerves and terror as I open the door. He's standing on the porch, one foot out, his hands on his hips like an old-time sheriff, a peculiarly singular tic that he had even when we were young that somehow makes me lower my guard. The stance makes me notice that his shoulders are still straight and square, his posture good. Instinctively, I pull my shoulder blades down my back, trying to stand up. "Hey. I didn't expect you back today."

"I wanted to make sure you were all right." He cocks his head. "After everything."

"I'm good, thanks. I walked on the beach with Phoebe and Jasmine and it settled me."

"Good. I won't keep you, then. Lock your doors."

A shimmer of twilight catches on his cheekbone, his lower lip, and a wave of yearning washes over me, pure and direct. "Joel, will you stay? I made macaroni and cheese."

"You cooked?"

"I cooked everything in my father's house," I protest. "You know that."

"But I've read about you," he says in his low voice, "and you stopped cooking when you left home."

It thrills me that he's been following my life. "Sometimes there's no other choice."

"I don't know about that," he says. "I manage pretty well with a microwave and my friend Marie Callender."

I'm glad he's lightened the mood. He had a knack for that, easing my heaviness. "Stop. You don't really eat frozen meals all the time?"

He shrugs, and I realize he's still outside the threshold, rain pouring down hard just beyond the shelter of the porch roof. "Come in. You'll be soaked."

Maui comes running, barking three minutes too late. "Some guard dog!" I say. He wags his tail cheerfully.

Joel comes in and takes off his coat. "Can I hang this up?"

I point to the hooks behind the door. Inside, the air is warm and humid and smells of toasting cheese. Joel is tall, taller than me, which is always a nice surprise. Dmitri wasn't, but I didn't mind. It's just nice when a man is. Like now.

Okay, stop.

But I think he might be as nervous as I am, because as I turn to close the door properly, he turns from hanging his coat and we bump into each other, my left shoulder against his middle chest and belly. A

259

puff of scent comes off his shirt, the faintest tinge of cologne mixed with soap and fresh shaving. It nearly buckles my knees.

He catches my elbow, as if I might fall. "You smell amazing," he says, and the timbre of his voice is ever so slightly rough.

"So do you."

For a beat, we don't move, as if noticing these things is something that should be acted upon. And I'd like to act. All I can think about is acting. Reaching for him, kissing him, pressing our bodies together. It both feels like a million years ago and like last week that we knew each other so intimately, learning every corner of each other's bodies, the sounds we made and the things that—

I swallow, so awash with desire that I feel I might evaporate. "Um"—I gesture—"let's go to the kitchen."

He drops his hand and we move as one being toward the kitchen and a pool of light waiting there. Maybe it's safer, in the light, in the ordinariness of counters and a table and the scent of macaroni and cheese, but I don't think so.

I pick up my tea and take a long swallow as if fortifying myself. For what? I feel him standing beside me. An atmospheric pressure rises in the air, born of love and loss and longing and the purest desire I have felt in a very long time.

I'm trying to think of something to say, and then he's standing behind me, sweeping the hair off my neck before he bends to place a kiss at my nape. I close my eyes, flooded with a thousand memories and emotions and hungers, the ache of missing him when I was in the unwed mothers' home, the hundreds of times I thought I'd glimpsed him in a street, the dreams that woke me up for years. They all fill me. A very small sound escapes my lips.

"Is this okay?" he whispers, fingers light against my skin. I feel the vibrations of his touch through my hair, and his mouth is dry and warm.

"Yes," I whisper, and lean backward into him, feeling him along my back, my legs. My heart is beating too fast and a tremble moves below my skin, setting it alight. His hands move on my belly, his lips along my skin.

I turn.

He looks at me, hands on my waist. His eyes are dark and liquid, the same eyes I remember, and I reach up to pull the tie he has used to contain his hair. It spills free, thick and cool. It smells the same, of forest and pine and his own notes of health, a fragrance that belongs entirely to him.

When he bends in to kiss me, that hair falls around us, brushes my cheek, and even before our lips meet, I feel grounded, as if I've been flying out in the ethos somewhere and my feet have come to land on the earth. Here. With Joel. We kiss and disappear into each other, kiss lightly and deeply, and with great care.

"Oh my God," I whisper, my hands on his face, my index fingers on cheekbones, pinkie along the edge of his jaw. In the middle, the long-ago acne scars left on his cheeks.

His precious, precious face. He looks at me, brushes hair from my brow, touches my mouth, the corner of my eye. "I can't believe you're here," he says softly.

We stand there, swept into our own weather system, pulsing with time and loss and desire. Memories wash through me, wave after wave of them—meeting the boy who had the locker beside mine, also a newcomer to the school, dressing up for Halloween. Going to movies, watching TV in his basement, playing kickball on the hard sand of the beach, the heat of his hands on my body, the way we cried out in sorrow when we were torn apart.

We rest our foreheads together. I breathe him in. My hands are on his neck and his have stayed on my waist, and I both want to kiss him until we're both oblivious to anything else, and don't. "It doesn't feel like it's been so many years," I say quietly.

"I know." He lifts his head. The long weight of time and knowledge shows in his eyes. "We probably shouldn't do this."

"Do what? Have sex?"

He nods.

"I guess it would be the prudent thing," I say, and stand on my tiptoes to press my lips into his. "To wait." I kiss him again. And again. Until he kisses me back, and we're both ravenous. I take his hand and lead him into my bedroom. Skylights provide even, pale light as I take off my shirt. He takes off his. His skin is the color of pine bark, and he's never had any chest hair. I press a hand to his heart. "I'm a little afraid," I say. "I'm not as well preserved as you are."

"I'm a grown man," he says, reaching for the front clasp of my bra. "I know how grown women look."

Then my breasts are bare, and in his hands, and he doesn't seem to mind at all, because he bends his head and kisses them, and then we're falling together to my bed. The pale light burnishes his body, a body I make my way around, remembering, discovering new valleys and marks and scars with my fingers, with my mouth. He traces my waist and my arms and the hollow of my throat and the scar low on my belly.

We move together, within and without, and some wild thing, pressed down for such a long, long, long time rises up in me, expands through my heart and my mouth as he fills my body with himself, as we move and murmur and kiss and twine together. I find myself weeping as he moves within me, and I taste my tears on his lips, or perhaps they're his tears, I don't know.

~

Hours later, we get up and go to the kitchen, both of us ravenous. The macaroni and cheese is on the counter, cold, so we dish up big bowls and microwave them and I pour us big glasses of sparkling water over ice.

We curl up on the banquette looking toward the ocean. It's completely black outside, but the sound rises up to us, steady and roaring.

The rain has slowed, but it still patters on the windows and the skylight. "This is so good," I say, taking a breath.

"You've always been a good cook."

"Mmm. Thanks." Our toes are side by side and I reach for his, wiggling. He wiggles back. "It's really pathetic that you never learned."

He grins, and it's wolfish, and I think it's really quite unfair how gorgeously he's aged. "Mostly somebody is always willing to do it for me."

"Huh. I'm so thrilled to join the crowd."

He leans into me, rests his hand on my thigh beneath the kimono I've tossed on. He's wearing his T-shirt and jeans. His feet are bare. "You could never be one of the crowd."

"That's what you have to say, isn't it?"

He leans against me, rubs his cheek on my shoulder. "Not in this case."

I let it go. I'm going to enjoy right now, whatever this is. The rest can work itself out later.

He raises his head and starts to eat again. "It's a little weird that you're so famous and you're also this person in my heart." He presses his fingertips to the middle of his chest. "Like, always."

"Me too," I say quietly. "Do you still draw, Joel?"

"I do," he says. "More painting now. Just had a show at a gallery in Astoria."

"Really. I wish I'd known."

"Good way to get girls," he jokes.

"No doubt." I shift so that I can look at him more easily. "Can I see them?"

"Sure." He picks up his phone and opens his photos, then an album, and hands it over.

The paintings are abstract landscapes and animals, rendered in vivid colors. "How big are they? They look huge."

"Some of them are. The biggest are six feet by seven."

"Wow. You need a lot of wall space for that."

He nods, raises an eyebrow. "You'd be in my target demographic, actually."

"How much does this one cost?" I show him one of a swirl of feathers and leaves, like an autumn wind sweeping everything ahead of itself.

"It's sold, but it went for twenty-four thousand."

I blink. "That's substantial."

"Not bad."

"If you command that kind of money for a painting, why are you working as an electrician?"

He takes the phone and scrolls through the paintings, and for a moment I think he won't answer. "It's not that reliable," he says. "Sometimes I'll do a series that sells out in five minutes, and sometimes they'll just sit there." He shrugs. "I don't like to put too much weight on the creative work, you know?"

"That makes sense. Phoebe goes the other way, I think. She likes to know she can make money with the art, so she keeps her focus there. Have you read her book?"

"Of course. Everyone in Blue Cove has read it." His fingers smooth a lock of hair from my face. "Interesting that both of you have done so well in professions that are so often discouraged."

"And so have you." I touch his oval fingernails, testing the smooth texture, imagining his knuckles splattered with paint. "Maybe it was Beryl."

"She was so good to all of us." He turns his hand over and I trace his long lifeline. "Is it weird to be famous?"

"Yes." I frown. "Don't get weird about the fame. It ruins things if you let it."

"Does it?"

I take a breath. "It has. You get used to it yourself, but when somebody else comes in, it's totally weird and hard to navigate."

"Like what parts?"

"Mmm. Just attention. People recognizing me, talking to me like they know me, photographers, all the selfie stuff now." I shake my head. "That's a lot more prevalent and people are bold. I don't go out to dinner in major cities anymore for that reason. You can't really enjoy it."

"I can see that." He places his empty bowl on the table and takes a long swallow of water. "It's a little weird to me, not gonna lie." He gestures to everything around us. "You're also beyond a little bit wealthy."

I nod. "Also true."

"It must be fun, though."

"Money is more fun than fame, but honestly, after a certain point, you've kind of bought anything you want. When you're dreaming about money when you're young, it's because you don't have things, and money offers a sense of freedom. Like to buy that car you think you want, or a trip somewhere, or—"

"Like this?" He taps the bracelet on my arm. "When did you buy it?"

It's a tennis bracelet set with topazes in a rainbow hue. "After my first movie. I saw one like it at a mall in Portland when I was about fourteen."

"I remember." He moves it back and forth on my wrist, setting the red, the purple, the orange and yellow on fire in turn. "You told me about it and I always wanted to buy it for you." He raises my hand, kisses the knuckles. "Better that you were the person who bought it for you."

I smile at him. "Yeah, exactly. At the time I first saw it, I wondered who I'd be married to if I ever had a bracelet like this. Instead, I married myself."

He touches the tips of my fingers, one at a time. "Was it lonely?"

"Sometimes. But not really. I could have married any number of times."

"I'm sure."

I can't resist stroking the smooth skin of his inner arm. "Were you? Lonely?"

Something heavy crosses his face. "I would have been better off not getting married, honestly."

"So why did you?"

"I thought I should."

"But neither of us has had another child," I say quietly. "That breaks my heart."

"Mine too. Who did she look like?"

"You. She looked just like you. Such dark hair."

He raises his eyes, showing a deep expression of grief. "I wish I could have held her."

"Me too," I whisper, and lean into him, hiding my face in his shoulder. "I bet she's tall."

"I wonder if she draws or paints or acts." He strokes my hair. "I wonder if she's ever seen you on TV or something and wondered if you seemed familiar."

A pain stabs my gut. "Oh, that's a terrible thought."

"I'm sorry."

We sit in the quiet, and it feels exactly right, that we should be here so many years later, in this very space where we made love so long ago. Impulsively, I say, "I missed you, Joel. Like, always. Is that weird?"

"Same." I feel him take a lock of hair into his fingers and thread it around his knuckles. "I tried to see you once."

I lift my head. "When?"

"I don't know exactly. I knew you were going to be onstage with a movie premiere in Seattle."

"Because you stalked me?"

His grin is swift and sexy. "Yes. I did."

"So what happened?"

"I mean, I went to the premiere and I was in the audience, like right up front. I kept hoping you'd see me and then we'd have this big reunion and"—a shrug—"I don't know. You didn't. And your life was clearly so good."

A little shattering sensation moves across my heart. "You were in the audience? I hate that I didn't see you. It's so bright that it's hard to see anything. I wish you would have sent me a note."

"I didn't think you wanted to talk to me."

"I called your mom once," I say, running my hand over his chest. "She told me you were married and I should leave you alone."

"So many missed chances," he says.

"Not this one."

He brings my hand up and takes my index finger into his mouth. I've never thought I would like this, but heat rushes through me. His eyes are molten dark and I can feel the wet give of his inner lip. I bend in and kiss him, and this time we take each other with a kind of starved brutality, leaving bruises and banging teeth, joining in a kind of frenzy. I collapse on his chest, his hands on my bare back and think, *How will I ever survive this?*

Chapter Nineteen
Phoebe

"Nana," Jasmine says as I'm getting supper ready. "I need to talk to you."

"Of course." I slide a cookie sheet of soy "fish" sticks and Tater Tots into the oven. It's a horrible meal, but I have to admit I like it, too. I sit down across from her. "What's up, darling girl?"

"I don't want to move to England." She pulls out her notebook. "I made a list of my reasons. I want to read them to you."

She's so young and so old in the same body. Her hair is pulled back into a ponytail that puffs out like the head of a dandelion, and her big gray eyes are serious. There is no face on this planet that I love better. Tears prick the back of my eyes, and I have to blink to keep them where they belong. "Of course. I'm glad to listen."

"Number one—I don't want to be so far away from my nana." She looks at me, raises her second finger. "Two, I like living by the ocean, not in the city. Three, my mom can fly back and forth a lot easier than you can. Four, it's healthier for kids to live in nature. Five, I can have pets here and my mom won't have to deal with them." She moves to her left hand. "Six, London has a lot of crime. Seven, England has a monarch and I don't agree with that. Eight, they won't like my American accent and might make fun of me, and that would really hurt my feelings. Nine—well, that's all." She closes the notebook. "I am still working on it." As if she's the CEO of a small corporation, she folds her hands on top of the notebook. "But you and my mom need to listen to me. I'm not just being a kid. This affects my life, too, and I should have a say."

I nod, folding my own hands over hers, and let my gut settle. Of course she's right about a lot, but she's also wrong, and she doesn't know the good things. Also, it's nonnegotiable, no matter what she thinks or how persuasive her arguments are. I remember wanting so desperately to live with Beryl instead of my parents, and it would have broken my father's heart. And it would break Stephanie right in two. "That is a great list. I'm proud of you for being so logical."

She yanks her hands from beneath mine. "But you're still not going to listen, are you?"

"Jasmine, you know I love you and I want you to be happy. But this is not my decision. It's your mother's. And you know what else?"

"What?"

"I know you love her and want to be with her."

She blinks away tears. "I do love her. I *miss* her." She steadies herself. "But I still don't want to go."

"It's going to be okay, Jazzie. I promise."

Her face says she doesn't believe me. I reach for the checkerboard on the side of the table. "Let's play while we wait for dinner. We can talk more about this, okay?"

"Fine."

We set up the board and she takes red, as always. "Last night, I read that once London was bombed for nine months in a row, every single night."

"Ah."

"Is that true?"

I pause. It's not exactly correct, but the facts will not help. "The Blitz," I say. "It was a long time ago, during World War II." I move my piece.

She frowns at the move, takes a minute to evaluate her choices. "What's World War II?"

How to sum up such a conflagration in a sentence or two without being too reductive or simplistic? "It was a terrible war. A very bad leader came to power in Germany in the 1930s, and he tried to take over Europe, but he was defeated."

"And he bombed London?"

"Yes. And many other places. Your move."

She jumps my piece and takes it, and I take hers, leaving her to study the board a second. "But how was there anything left after all those bombs? That's like a whole school year!"

"It was. But the English refused to give up. Maybe you can explore some of it when you're there."

"I don't want to go to a place that gets bombed!"

"That was over eighty years ago," I say.

"I don't care. I don't want to go there in case it happens again." She leaps two of my pieces and gets crowned. "America doesn't get bombed."

"Well, it has been sometimes, actually, but I don't think that's what you're going for here."

"I just want to be safe. How can you be safe if there's tsunamis and bombs and pandemics and school shootings? And *wars*?"

For a moment, I say nothing, trying to gather my thoughts. When I was ten, I wanted to create a campaign to pick up all the litter in the world. I was worried about birds getting slimed by oil spills and about nuclear bombs destroying the world. I decide to go with the truth. "Unfortunately, my sweet, terrible things can happen. Here or England or anywhere. But mostly they don't. Mostly we're okay."

She looks unconvinced. The buzzer goes off on the stove. I stand and kiss her springy hair. "You'll be safe in England. Please set the table."

She jumps off the chair and opens a drawer with place mats and cloth napkins, taking a moment to mull over the color she wants for today. I love that she chooses a cheery sunflower pattern, one of my designs, and lays out the flatware.

I bring the tray of fish sticks and Tater Tots over, serving us both before taking the pan back to the counter. She's poured herself a glass of milk and me a glass of bubbly water over ice. We have our rituals, especially after she stayed with me for over a year during the pandemic.

We sit down. She squirts ketchup on her plate and dips a fish stick in. Without speaking, she eats three fish sticks and a half dozen Tater Tots and then washes it down with milk. "*How* can we be safe, Nana? That's what I want to know."

"Well," I say, and call up my own grandmother. What would Amma have said under these circumstances? It wasn't as dangerous for kids when I was a child, honestly. Or maybe it was. Either way, I know what she would say. "The truth is, baby, that you can't stop bad things from happening. All these things you've been worrying about—tsunamis and pandemics—those are not predictable."

"My friend Bennie's grandma died from COVID and so did Uncle Dmitri. I couldn't stand it if that happened to you."

"It didn't," I say, and pick up a fish stick. "And most people didn't die. Almost no people will ever see a tsunami in their lifetimes. Epidemics happen, but only once in a while, and we have all kinds of tools now. Getting bombed, here or in England, is probably something you don't have to worry about. You can take that off your worry list."

"What about school shootings? We have drills all the time. You can't say that won't happen because it does."

One of my most painful fears, a thing I'm not sure I could survive. Looking at her serious gray eyes, I see both her resignation and disbelief, and I can't say it won't, and it kills me. I hate it that I can't stand guard over her twenty-four hours a day with a sword drawn. "I can't. But guess where they *don't* have them? London."

"What? Why not?"

"That is a very complicated question, my dear, but I can tell you that I've never heard of one."

She leans her head on her hand, musing. "That's good, I guess."

I wonder if I've taken the wrong tack. Will she be more worried than ever? I take a breath and reach for her hand. "You know, Jasmine, good things happen all the time, too. You just have to focus as much as you can on the good things."

"But I worry!"

I grin. "That's because you have an amazing imagination. Maybe try to direct it toward good things more."

"Maybe," she says with a shrug.

"You could also stay off the internet and stop looking for disasters."

"But Suze said today you were all into Pompeii. I'm going to look that up."

"Try looking up good things instead."

"Like what?"

"Varieties of cats? What kind of flowers to grow?" I raise a finger. "How about, 'What are the best ten things about living in London?'"

"That's a good idea, actually." She pops another Tater Tot in her mouth, glugs the rest of the milk. "Can I be excused?"

"Sure."

Ben texts me in the middle of the night. You awake?
Am I ever asleep?
  ◠ Want some company?

This has been our pattern for quite some time, months. We text back and forth, and then he comes over for tea and company. We play poker or rummy or some other card game, and then he goes home and we go to sleep. Now, an anticipatory shiver runs through me. Now, things are different.

I think of Jasmine asleep in the other room. Jasmine is sleeping. 😴
We can be quiet.

It's not that. It feels weird.

Ah. We don't have to do anything. Just hang out.

I'm not sure I can now, though. I'll want my hands on him. I'll want to bring him to my bedroom and have sex. The craving for it scares me a little. It's not particularly controlled and I like being in control.

I think it's better if we just text this time.

The dots appear. Disappear. Appear. Disappear. Finally: Okay. I'll see you in the morning, then.

We can text if you want

That's okay. I'll just read. Xox

A hollow ache settles right below my breastbone. Maybe I should tell him to come over anyway. We had such a great time the other night, and I think I really like him, and I know he really likes me.

But I'm worried about what Jasmine will think, if it's really okay to have a man over to sleep with me. A thousand things like that. And also my own terrors. But this is how to chase somebody away, isn't it?

How do I let myself take a risk?

I write a text. Sorry, I'm feeling a little awkward about Jasmine being here.

Erase it.

Try again. Having boundary worries about Jasmine. You ok with that?

Erase it.

It's not you or us or anything. I'm just feeling weird about Jasmine.

Erase it.

Leave it alone, I think. *Just leave it all alone.* Except, as I fall asleep, I think about how he felt around me, how it felt to be held and touched and kissed. How we talked into the early-morning hours.

Why did I tell him not to come over? I fling back the covers and pick up my phone. Four a.m. What if he hasn't turned off his notifications?

Still. I don't want him to get the wrong idea. I open our text string and type: Sorry. I'm probably worrying too much what Jasmine will think. See you tomorrow?

There's no reply. But I can at least get back to sleep for a little while.

~

In the morning, Jasmine and I walk over to the studio. It's cold and overcast, not a great day for being outside, but great for artwork. She needs to stay off the iPad. Her obsession with tsunamis and bombs and natural disasters is simply a focus point.

My creative brain is itchy, and I set aside the wallpaper painting and pull out some gessoed boards, smaller, twelve by twelve. I let my hand hover over the rolling container of acrylics, and feel turquoise and yellow calling me. I squirt some of each on the board and tilt my head. What do I want? A triangle. A square.

Jasmine is worried about change. Stephanie is making a good move for her life. It's a great opportunity, and it's good for Jasmine to see her mother choosing big steps, being brave. London will be an amazing adventure, even if it's challenging at times. I want Jasmine to be able to enjoy it—and maybe even anticipate it. So often I've taken the safe path. I want more for Jasmine.

While I was sleepless last night, I tried to think of ways to help her, and I came up with a couple of projects we can do together.

In a vase on the main table, the dahlias Ben brought last week are starting to fade, dropping petals in pink and peach and white, and it gives me a little pang. He hasn't texted me today. Have I messed things up?

But if a simple no to an invitation messed it up, what kind of connection would it be? I sweep the petals into the trash, irritated with myself. I've always been terrible at relationships, loving too much, loving the wrong people. It's like I'm tone deaf in that arena, but I really don't want to be that person now. Haven't I grown up after all this time? Learned my own value?

I like him, and I'm mad at myself for that, even. Why should I expect it to be a big thing?

Except that it seemed important the other night. It felt like something real. It felt like I could trust him.

Focus. Jasmine needs me.

I move the board to a drying area. "So," I say, spreading out a big piece of white butcher paper, "let's do something."

"Okay." She leans on the table. Her hair is pulled back into a scrunchie, the curls boiling out in a puff at the back and escaping in tendrils by her ears and nape. Baby hair lines the edges of her hairline, pale against her warm golden skin. "What is it?"

"Did you look for the best things about London on your iPad last night?"

A shrug. "Yeah."

I give her a pink Sharpie. "Write one of them down."

She chews on her lip. "I know what you're doing."

"Yeah? What am I doing?"

"Trying to change my mind."

"I am. Because I really, truly, in my heart of hearts, think you are going to love it."

"Really?"

"Really." I smile and pick up a red Sharpie. "They have double-decker buses. You could ride on top." I draw one, with a girl waving from a window.

She giggles. "They have a big old castle," she says, and draws a square building with turrets.

"Ah, yes. There's more than one. The king lives in one, and one is an old, old thing from ages ago, and it has a dungeon."

"There's a king?"

"Yep." I draw a face with a crown.

"Is he handsome?"

"Not especially." I draw a teapot and a tray with little cakes. "You can have afternoon tea, with little sandwiches and cakes. I will make sure we do that when I come visit."

Jasmine stares at the paper. "I miss my mom," she says. "I don't like thinking of her so far away."

"Aw, sweetie," I say and gather her into my arms, kissing her head. "Shall we call her? I'm sure we can reach her right now."

"Okay."

I pull out my phone and dial Stephanie's number from the video app. It rings on the other end, and I pull Jasmine close, turning us to face the window so the light will be good.

Stephanie appears on the screen, and she looks beautiful—rested and clear eyed. "Hi!" she says. "What are you two up to?"

"I miss you, Mommy!" Jasmine cries.

"I miss you, too, but guess what? I found us an apartment today, which they call a flat, and I think you're really, really going to love it."

"Can I see it?"

"I'm not there right now, but I can go there tomorrow and show it to you. It's on a high floor, so you can see the river and a big park, and there's a little garden on the roof."

Jasmine nods.

"Steph, you look great," I say, hand on Jasmine's back. "London agrees with you." My heart settles to see her looking like this, as if she's looking forward with pleasure instead of dread.

"I love it here," she says. "I feel like I fit in. In so many ways."

"I'm glad. We're doing fine here."

"What have you been doing, Jasmine?"

"I stayed overnight with Suze and she taught me to play blackgammon."

"Backgammon maybe?" Steph smiles, but she narrows her eyes. "What was Nana doing?"

"I was—"

"She had a date!" Jasmine cries. "With Ben."

Stephanie's eyebrows rise, but her smile is genuine. "Really, Mom? I love it."

I try to shrug it off. "It was nice."

"Hmm. You'll have to tell me more. I like Ben. He's a good guy."

"He is."

A cluster of noises arise on the other end, and Stephanie looks over her shoulder. "Sorry, I have to go. My partners are here to pick me up for dinner."

"Dinner in the morning?" Jasmine asks.

"No, sweetie. It's six in the evening here." She smiles. "Blow me a kiss."

Jasmine complies, sending handfuls of kisses toward her mom, one after another. "Love you!"

"Love you more," Stephanie says, blowing kisses back. "Bye, Mom. Love you, too."

The phone goes dark. I feel enlivened but also slightly depressed by her glow. Her clear happiness. She isn't coming back, ever.

And I want that for her. I want what makes her happy. I deeply, truly do.

But where does that leave me?

"Do you feel better, sweetheart?" I ask.

"I guess." She heads for the wide, low desk where she's been working and settles in. For a minute, I watch her, and I think she's trying not to cry, but I won't go and try to insert myself into that personal grappling with pain. It's good for her.

And yet. God, I'm going to miss them! Both of them!

I wander to the window and look out at the sea, trying to identify the strange feeling in my heart. Am I sad that Stephanie is settling in so easily? Why would that bother me?

The waves are high today under a low, dark sky. They roll in as if on a highway, and crash with dramatic violence against the rocks. I raise my eyes to Suze's house and see her on the balcony with another person. They're just standing there, drinking coffee, but there's an air of intimacy about them that makes me think—

And then I realize who it is.

Joel.

A strange, ancient thing twists my heart. Joel. All this time, Joel. I think of the way they looked at each other in the kitchen that first day.

I think of him burning down the church.

It was always Joel.

I say aloud to myself what I've always known. "They were in love. The baby was his. Suze has been lying to me for a long, long, long time."

And I let her because I didn't want to know. A crumpling pain crackles through my lungs. What have we done to each other all these years? What have we done to ourselves?

THEN

Hello, Darkness

Suze

I knew I was pregnant by the time school started, but I lived in such a state of terror that I ignored it, and I didn't get to see Joel until the first day. We saw each other in the hall, and walked straight toward each other, like we were magnets. His face made everything in my soul feel better. All the worry and danger and grief drained away at last for a second, and I saw the same thing on his face. A little smile, his eyes shining. He grabbed my hand and looked over his shoulder and then dragged me outside into an alcove and kissed me like he was drowning and I was air. I kissed him back like I was a plant and he was the sun. We connected our souls and our hearts, and life suddenly felt like it might be okay.

Until he lifted his head and looked down. "Suze?"

No one had been close to me at all, and I'd been doing pretty well with my clothes, but I was definitely starting to show. I couldn't close my jeans, so I turned them under and wore big peasant blouses. At home, I still wore the giant horrible dresses my dad insisted upon, and nothing showed beneath them.

Joel moved his hand to my belly. "Are you pregnant?"

To him, I couldn't tell a lie. I nodded.

He closed his eyes, rested his forehead against mine. "Oh my God. I'm so sorry. Why didn't you tell me sooner?"

"I don't know." I hung my head. "I was scared."

Joel pulled me into him, into a fierce hug. "I'm so sorry, Suze. I'm sorry I wasn't here. I'm sorry—you must have been so worried."

We both cried. Cried because we were sad and mad and had no power. And then we walked away from school and up to the house on the hill, where we stayed all day, eating snacks we picked up at the market and drinking soda and trying to figure out what to do. We tried to come up with a plan ourselves, but it was hard to know who would help and who would separate us again.

Of course the person who came to mind for both of us was Beryl. She would not betray us. She would help us figure out a plan. Tomorrow, we would go see her.

Then, both exhausted, we stretched out on the floor and turned to each other and made love gently. It was so holy I wept again, feeling something in me heal and unfurl. With Joel, I was safe and loved and whole.

It was the last time we were together. That very evening, my father saw me silhouetted against the light coming through the window in the church kitchen. He beat me so fiercely I thought I might die, and if I did the baby would die. When he'd worn himself out with the belt and his fists, he made me kneel and shaved my head.

I waited until he was in bed and walked my bruised and battered self to Amma's house. Choking, knowing I didn't have much time until my dad came for me, I asked to use the phone, and called Joel.

His mom answered. "You need to stay away from him," she said, and hung up.

I would have respected it, but this was urgent. I called back, and before she could say anything, I said, "Please, my dad is going to send me away. I just want to talk to him one time."

"He's not here," she said, and hung up.

That's when I threw up blood and Beryl took me to the hospital.

Phoebe

I was swimming in our pool (maybe for the last time, because my dad said there was a buyer very interested) when my dad came to get me. "Phoebe, it's Amma on the phone."

"Can I just call her back?"

"No, honey, you need to take it."

So I climbed out of the pool and wrapped myself in a beach towel and sat down with the phone by the back door. "Hello?"

"Phoebe, I have some bad news."

"Did somebody die? Not Suze?" I covered my mouth, shaking before she even said the rest.

"No, she's not dead, but her dad beat her up pretty bad. She's in the hospital."

Tears leaked out of my eyes. In a whisper, I asked, "Is she going to be okay?"

"That's a hard question to answer. She's in pretty bad shape both physically and emotionally, and she could probably use a good friend in her corner."

"Can I come down there?"

"Her father isn't letting anyone in to see her, and unfortunately he has a lot of people on his side."

"How can he be in charge? Why didn't they arrest him? That's child abuse!"

"It absolutely is. But—" She struggled for control. I heard her clear her throat. "He isn't going to be charged."

Fiercely I said, "I hate him so much. It's not fair."

"It isn't." She paused again. "You should know he also shaved her head."

"What?" I started to cry in earnest. "Why?"

"There's no reason for a man like that to do what he does. But—"
She paused and I thought it was odd, and my body thought it was even

weirder because my heart squeezed really hard and I couldn't quite catch my breath. "Did you know she was pregnant?"

My brain ran the scenes backward over the summer. I could answer honestly, "No."

"Okay, then you need to let her tell you."

"I really need to come see her."

"No, that's not a good idea. But I'll see if I can get you a phone call. Her dad is not letting any of us get in there."

"How did you know he beat her up?"

"She ran away to my house to get away from him." And I heard something in her voice that was very, very rare—a dark, wild emotion, filled with nuances I didn't quite get. Fury. Despair. "I got her to the hospital."

"Amma! She's my best friend in the whole world. I have to see her."

"I know, Phoebe. And I know there's been a lot on your plate this year, but you have to trust me. There will be a time you can be more help to her than you can now. If you write some letters, I'll get them to her one way or another."

"And a phone call! Please!"

"I'll see what I can do, sweetheart. Now, let your dad give you some TLC and remember that you are a very strong person. You're going to get through this season of darkness."

"But will Suze?"

She hesitated. "I'm going to do everything in my power to make sure she does."

"Good," I said, and hung up the phone. My dad was there, hugging me, and I wished that Suze had just one person in her life like him.

But I guessed she did. Amma. And maybe me, if I was strong enough. I leaned into my dad and wept, worrying about her, and then I had an idea. "Dad, can I make another phone call? I want to call Joel."

"Is that her boyfriend?"

For a long moment, I thought about it. And that was the first time I knew that they loved each other. I squished the knowledge down into a tiny knot of bitter jealousy. Choosing denial, I said, "Just her friend, but I want to make sure he knows what's going on."

I dialed the number I had for him, but it came back with an electronic voice. "The number you have dialed has been disconnected."

But I saw him one more time.

CURRENT DAY

Chapter Twenty
Suze

Joel and I sleep tangled like kittens, both Yul Brynner and Maui finding their way onto the big bed with us at some point.

When I wake up, milky light is coming through the windows. Joel's arm is flung around my waist, and his thighs shape themselves to the back of mine. I can feel the soft exhale of his breath against my neck, whispery and warm. My hand is curled around his, and Yul Brynner is purring on my pillow, and I don't move a single muscle because I never want to leave this moment.

I breathe it in. Now. This. Joel. My body sore from making love all night, both of us greedy and going back to the well until we were shaking with weariness. We both fell, laughing, to the pillows in the end. "I remember a day," he said.

"Oh, me too." I brushed hair from his face. "Once upon a time when we were young."

"I could never go back, be seventeen again. Could you?"

"No way. It was awful."

He leaned in and kissed me, very gently. "You're even more beautiful now."

"That's a lie, but thank you."

"No, it's not." He brushed my crow's-feet, the lines showing up around my chin that surprised me. "You have depth and wisdom now."

"Well," I said, "I don't know about you having more depth and wisdom, but you are still absurdly hot."

He laughed and pulled me to his shoulder and we crashed, both of us exhausted.

Now I can smell him, his hair and his skin, the faint lingering notes of aftershave he wore for me. I can feel him. I can hear his breath, a slight snore.

That stops. His hand tightens around my breast, and I feel his lips on my shoulder. "Good morning."

"Do you want some coffee?"

"Are you having tea? I can try some tea."

"No way, dude." I turn to face him. "I'm going to make you some amazing coffee and we can drink it out on the deck looking at the ocean, just like we always said we would."

He smiles. "Did you ever think for one single minute that you would actually live in this house?"

"I didn't even have a context for imagining it."

"What can I do?"

"Cook me breakfast?"

He laughs. "I can make toast."

We get up and slip into clothes, and carry blankets out with us to the deck, wrapping ourselves together as we watch the seabirds look for breakfast. Neither of us speaks, but I feel the wondering beneath our silence. "So, do you have a girlfriend?" I ask, lightly, tapping his toe with mine.

"No," he says. "I haven't had for a long time. You?"

"No girlfriend or boyfriend."

"Girlfriend? Did you have girlfriends?"

I lift my shoulders. "Sometimes." I sip my oolong, thick with milk. "Dmitri was the main person in my life. He was a good guy."

"The director, right?"

"Yeah."

He's quiet for a while. "Did you want kids?"

An ancient pain runs up my midsection. "No. That was a pretty brutal experience."

He bends and kisses my shoulder. "It was. I'm so sorry."

"Don't be. Neither of us had any power. What could we do?"

"I know." He hugs me and kisses my head. "But still."

"Anyway."

"Anyway," he echoes. "I'm going into Seaside to find some electronics and I'll be back later to install them."

"An alarm?"

"And a Ring camera, maybe cameras for some other spots around the house, too. You really need better security."

"I have great security at the LA house, and look what it got me. I never needed it here."

"Why didn't you bring a bodyguard with you?"

I sigh. "I mean, it gets old, having people in your house all the time. Like, all the time. I'm kind of a loner. I like to be alone."

"Funny career choice, then."

"Fair enough. I think you can be both an introvert and an extrovert at the same time. Be a loner and also like people. You can be more than one thing."

He studies my face for a moment, which gives me a chance to do the same to his. His mouth is wide and turns down slightly at the corners, and his neck shows the years of sun exposure. It makes my midsection pinch ever so slightly, that I have missed all the years between the long-ago days and now. "That's true." He takes my hand across the table. "I am so glad this happened. And I'm really sure it was a terrible idea."

A sting of tears makes me blink. "Are you sorry?"

"No, no, no!" He brings my hand to his mouth. "No, that's not what I meant."

"What, then?"

Instead of answering, he stands and draws me up so he can press me into his chest. I can hear his heart beating and his arms are fierce and tender. "It feels like six minutes have gone by since those days. It feels the same." His voice is low. "And I also know that we live in really different worlds."

It's true. There's really no way around it. "I know."

"What will you do today?"

I look at the water. "Maybe go back over some scripts my agent sent."

It's subtle, but I feel him move ever so slightly away from me. "Huh. That must be kind of fun."

"Maybe. Depends." I sigh. "I'm not going back to the series. I'm tired of the long hours and the early calls and . . . all of it."

He watches me carefully with those big dark eyes, and I remember again how well he could listen. "It's a pretty big show, though, right?"

"Yeah. And really, I just don't care."

For long moments, he drinks his coffee and stares at the sea. "Not to overstep, but sometimes not caring can be a sign of depression."

"I've thought of that," I answer. "My therapist has suggested the same thing. But honestly, between the pandemic and the attack, I started thinking about what I want for the next stage of my life. It's not that."

"What do you want?"

I shake my head slowly. "That's the question. I have absolutely no idea."

"You'll figure it out."

I smile. "I'm sure. Thank you." He drains his coffee and I ask, "Do you want another cup?"

"Much as I'd love to sit here with you, I really do have to get my day started."

"Okay." I walk him to the door and stand with my arms crossed as he gathers his coat. "You are coming back, right?"

He pauses. Stands in the middle of his redwood stillness and says, "I'm coming back."

THEN

THE TRACKS OF MY TEARS

Phoebe

Suze had been at the Magdalene Home for Unwed Mothers for nearly a month before I could convince my dad to drive me there. My mother had moved to LA as planned, leaving my dad and me to deal with the mess of her departure, including putting the house up for sale and figuring out where we were going to move. My parents had agreed to let me stay with my dad in Portland rather than going to LA with my mom. My dad had so much on his mind that I felt bad asking, but Suze called a bunch of times and it was strange and awkward. She was so furious with everyone that she was like the hero who turns into a villain. When I tried to make her feel better or cheer her up, she lashed out at me.

And I kept thinking of her having sex with Joel. Actual sex, with his naked body, his beautiful lips. If that was even true. But who else? I asked and she told me it was Victor. Who told me himself he was gay. At least that's what I thought he meant when he said he was a fairy.

It all made me feel sick to my stomach. I missed my mother more than I thought I would, but if I thought she'd warm up after the divorce, I was wrong. I cried at night sometimes, feeling like my entire world had been trashed, like some giant hand of fate had upended my box of toys and flung them all over the room.

And the one person I would have poured my heart out to had way bigger problems. A couple of times I tried to tell her how sad I was, and I could tell she thought I was an idiot.

But just because you don't have the worst problem in the world doesn't mean it isn't a real problem to you.

So I was reluctant to go see her. How could I make any of it better? Her dad, the fire, the beating. I was afraid to see her with her shaved head.

It was Amma who shamed me into it, appalled that I hadn't been there to support her. It made me mad, honestly. Suze had problems, but so did I! My parents were getting divorced and I was losing the only house I'd ever lived in, and nobody seemed to care!

Why did it always have to be about Suze?

The home was a long way across town, too far for me to be able to take a bus. My dad finally agreed to drive me there after he finished classes on a Thursday afternoon.

Rain fell hard that day, and the neighborhood was not the greatest. The house was a tall Victorian with a big porch that hadn't been painted in a long time. My dad peered at it. "This is where they sent her?" He swore under his breath.

"I guess. This is the address, right?"

"Yes." He smoothed his beard between his fingers. "Do you want me to go in with you?"

A part of me was really afraid of going up those steps, into that world, but I shook my head. "No."

"I'll come back in . . . what? An hour? An hour and a half?"

"Hour and a half. I haven't seen her in months."

"Take your time. I'll be right out here."

I dashed to the porch and up the steps, feeling like a girl in a gothic story. The screen door was extra wide and the door behind was open. I knocked, and a girl who looked younger than me appeared. She was enormously pregnant, her belly like a ball stuck on her body. "Yeah?"

"I'm here to visit Suze Ogden?"

"She know you're coming?"

"Yes."

She pushed the door open and I slid inside, dashing water off my hair. "She's in room seven. Two flights up on the right."

"Thanks."

The air smelled of cooking, and I could hear girls talking somewhere as I climbed. The first set of stairs was generous, but the second was narrower. Servant stairs, I thought, something I picked up from a book somewhere. The tight hallway I found confirmed that. The door of room seven was plain white. I took a breath, steeling myself, and knocked.

The door was yanked open—angrily, I thought—and a girl stood there. It took me a full breath to realize it was Suze. Her yards of hair had been shaved off, and only a soft blonde fuzz covered her scalp. She wore a smocked shirt that belled out over her pregnant belly, so shockingly weird that I didn't know what to look at first—head or tummy. She didn't help, just stared at me with the tiniest quiver of her lower lip. Her eyes burned like eerie marbles in her face, bright bright blue. I felt embarrassed for her. And sad. And awkward. And hurt. She'd excluded me from everything. She had sex and never told me! How could we really be friends?

I didn't know what to do or say or where to look. A roar filled my ears and I glanced over her shoulder to a window, where a thin curtain lifted in the breeze. "You're going to freeze to death," I said.

"Nah, I'm always hot." She stepped back. "Come on in."

I slid by her, turning sideways to slither by like a snake. The room was furnished with a single bed against the wall, a metal chest of drawers, and a desk with a gooseneck lamp. Over the surface were pencils and paper, drawings I couldn't make out. "You're drawing a lot."

"Your grandma sent me some art supplies."

"That's nice." I was standing in the middle of the room, waiting for some signal, some indication of what I should do. Like how did you act when somebody had been through something so big? My hands felt awkward beside my body so I tucked them in the back pockets of my jeans.

She ran a hand over her head, a soft blonde cap coming back, and I saw that there were tears in her eyes. "I'm sorry I look so weird," she said. "He shaved my head to punish me."

"You don't," I said, and did what felt like the only thing I could do—I hugged her. Her belly bumped into me hard, but I pushed my butt backward to make room and held her shoulders tight.

She sobbed silently, tears wetting my neck. "I hate him so much," she said. "Hate him."

"I know," I said, understanding that she meant her father. "I know. I brought you some books." I gave her the bag of paperbacks I'd collected. I had remembered that she'd wanted to read *The Drifters* because Joel liked it, so I got that one, and some other things I thought she would like.

She looked in the bag, and pulled out *The Drifters*. Tears filled her eyes and she dropped it back in the bag. "Thanks. I don't really have much to do."

"We should have my dad take us to Powell's."

"Hello?" she said, gesturing. "Jail."

I ducked my head. "Sorry."

We sat on the bed. An awkward silence rose, and I didn't know where to look. Her eyes burned like spotlights from her face. Her skin was broken out. "I wish I could see the church burned down."

"I should have taken a picture." I rubbed my hands on my thighs. "How are things here?"

She gave a short, awful laugh. "Terrible. Every girl here is somebody who is thrown away."

"No! You're not thrown away. It's only for a little while and you'll be out."

"I'm not going back to my dad's house," she said fiercely. "I'll never live with him again. Ever."

"Amma said he moved to some town in Texas." I touched her hand, but I privately thought there was no way around her dad taking ownership of her again. He'd put her in here, and he would come back and get her.

"Have you heard anything from Joel?" I asked. I thought of the letter tucked away in my drawer.

She stared at me hard. "Back to crushing on Joel?"

"No!" I sucked in a breath. "Also, that was really mean."

She looked away, but her mouth was still sullen. "Poor Phoebe. Life is so hard, isn't it? Your poor dear parents divorcing."

I blushed, painfully hard, and dug my fingernails into my palms. "Why are you being so horrible?"

"You're the one! I've been in this place for nearly a month and this is the first time you've been here."

"It's hard to get here! And you're kinda not easy right now."

"Gosh," she said sarcastically. "Sorry I'm not nice enough." She rolled her eyes. "You just don't get it, Phoebe. You're so spoiled!"

"That's not fair! My life is not perfect, either."

"Oh, right. I forgot." She bent her head into her hands, digging the heels of her palms into her eyes. The noise in her throat was filled with such frustration it might have come from a wild animal. "You think you get it, but you don't. You don't know what it's like to live with a parent who hates you. Who hurts you." Her spotlight eyes bored into me. "When he found out I was pregnant, he dragged me by my hair. He beat me with a belt until I couldn't even stand up. And then he shaved my head."

I whispered, "That's awful. He should go to jail for child abuse."

"Yep. He should. But he won't."

I knew that was true, too. It made me despair. All of it made me depressed—that she was stuck here, that she would have a baby she'd never see, that her father was such a bastard, that I couldn't help her, no matter how much I wanted to. I felt the wall between us acutely. "Why haven't you been writing in the diary?"

She closed her eyes. "I don't know what to say."

"Say whatever you want."

"No." She shook her head. "I can't write it down. I just can't."

We struggled through another half hour of the awkward visit, with me stepping wrong at every turn and her returning scathing comments that made me feel about two inches high.

"You were born under a lucky star, Phoebe," she said, when we were getting to the end. "Maybe try to enjoy it."

"So lucky," I echoed sarcastically. "My parents are divorcing. I'm such a geek that no guy is ever going to like me, and my best friend thinks I'm a total idiot." Tears sprang into my eyes.

"Stop crying!" she yelled. "You're driving me crazy."

"I don't know how to help you, Suze. I might be lucky, but I also didn't sleep with some guy and get pregnant."

"There it is, the truth," she said with bitterness. Her chin rose. "You can go now. Back to your pretty little life."

"Why didn't you tell me you were having sex?" I asked. "I'm your best friend. I would have told you."

"Oh, like when you lied about kissing Joel that time? Another time my dad was being an asshole?"

"That was years ago! I didn't even know you cared!"

"I didn't. But you didn't tell me the truth."

It wasn't an answer, but I'd had enough. "Fine." I grabbed my sweater and stormed out, my heart pounding all the way down the stairs. My dad was waiting, and didn't say a word when I slammed the door.

I didn't go back. I didn't speak to her again until she moved in with Amma and I was forced into proximity with her.

CURRENT DAY

Chapter Twenty-One
Phoebe

I'm fuming mad, crashing dishes around as I make lunch. I don't know who I'm angrier with—me or Suze. How could she have lied to me for so long? *So* long?

And why? It doesn't make sense. Why hide it? It makes me feel like our entire friendship is a lie.

Jasmine is upstairs playing Roblox on her iPad, time she earned by doing a bunch of chores in the house. I'm making tuna salad for lunch for me, grilled cheese for her. A knock sounds at the door, and I jump three feet before I realize it's Ben. I wave him in, so relieved.

"Hi," I say.

"You okay?"

I don't know if he means right now or last night, when I was so weird, but I answer for both. "I'm good. Just a lot going on."

He clears his throat and bends his head toward his phone. "Have you seen the news this morning?"

My body stiffens in fear. "What?"

He hands me the phone. On the screen is a news story.

JUNO GERHERT GUNNED DOWN

LNB claims responsibility

San Francisco—Singer Juno Gerhert, currently on tour
with her fourth platinum hit, was shot dead outside
a concert hall in San Francisco last night. She was 28
years old.

The domestic terrorist group the Leviathan Nationalist
Brotherhood has claimed responsibility, their fourth
such attack in eighteen months, all on women—
Nadine Truelove, the freshman senator for California;
Andrea Montague, a gay activist in Denver; Suze
Ogden, an outspoken actress who compared the LNB
to the Taliban; and now Gerhert, who had been de-
manding action against the LNB for over a year after
they stalked her after she released records on the
leader of the group, Jacob Cosgrove, showing ties to
white-supremacist groups. Of the four, only Ogden
survived.

My blood literally turns cold, slowing to sludge in my body. A
roaring fills my ears, and for a moment I don't click on the rest of the
story, trying to get my mind to capture what this means.

"Damn," I whisper. I hand back the phone.

"I thought you'd want to know."

Only Ogden survived. I think of the bloody squirrel on her porch.
The guy at the restaurant. The WHORE painted on her house. "I'll be
back in a minute," I say, and pick up my phone from the counter, carrying it upstairs to my bedroom, out of earshot. Right this minute, the
past doesn't matter. I dial Suze's number.

"Hey," I say when she answers. "Have you seen the news about
the LNB?"

"No." The word sounds hollow. "What happened?"

"They killed Juno Gerhert."

She makes a soughing noise and I imagine her sinking into a chair. "When?"

"Last night. Gunned her down outside a concert venue."

"Shit. That's bold."

"Yeah. Suze, do you want to come down here? I'm worried about you."

"Maybe later," she says. "I'm doing some writing, and Joel will be back to install a Ring camera in a little while. I've got Maui until then."

Joel. This is not the moment to reveal I know that she's been lying, and my feelings are so complex that I wouldn't even know where to begin. "You're the only one they didn't kill," I say, and it makes my chest hurt, like I'm going to have a heart attack any second. "That scares me to death."

She's silent for a long moment. "I know. Me too. But I need to do what I'm doing right now. I'll come down after Joel leaves."

I hang up, and for some reason, my mind coughs up an image of a velvet bodice Suze gave me for Christmas in ninth grade. She crafted it of dark-red velvet and edged the square neckline and the short sleeves with gold lace and hand-sewn pearls of alternating sizes, larger and smaller. She lined it with satin. "So you can be Juliet whenever you want," she said. When I wore it over a white dress, I felt like the most beautiful girl in the world, and even my mother loved it.

What difference does it make if she loved Joel forty years ago?

Except it matters that she's kept the secret for so very long. Why wouldn't she have said something when I saw her—

Oh my God. I sink down on the bed, haunted by the vision of her at the unwed mothers' home.

The sorrow—so many things hidden by both of us, so many things lost, so much I misunderstood—bends me right in half, and I cover my face with my hands, rocking myself back and forth as waves of regret and shame and a tangle of resentments and jealousies and ugliness slam me.

Oh, Suze, I'm so sorry.

When I'm feeling more settled, I take a breath and head back downstairs. To Ben. To Jasmine.

He's washing dishes, which touches me somehow, and looks up when I come down the stairs. "You okay?"

I shake my head. "She's the only one they didn't actually kill."

"I get that." He comes to stand beside me, and covers one of my hands with his own. "Where's Jasmine?"

I point toward the stairs.

"Good." He slides a hand under my hair and pulls me into a kiss. "Is that okay?"

I nod. "Very. I'm sorry I was weird last night. I just feel nervous about Jasmine."

He brushes a lock of hair from my face. "I get it. But you're allowed to have a life, too."

"Yes." Impulsively, I lift on my toes and kiss him back. "You can set the table."

"No!" Jasmine cries from the bottom of the stairs. "That's my job."

Ben doesn't move away as fast as I hope, and I slide around him, feeling embarrassed. Even more so when Jasmine says, "Did you guys kiss?"

"Yes," Ben pipes up. "Is that okay with you?"

"I don't care."

I finally notice that her fists are clenched and disengage from Ben. "Hey. What's up?"

"Did you know that we're going to be in England at *Christmas*time?" Her entire body is taut with emotion. "*Christmas!* Did you know?"

I squat so I'm closer to her level, and take her hand. "I figured you would be. It's fall now. Christmas isn't that far away."

"How can I have Christmas there? Huh?"

"Honey! Maybe it will be special. I'll come and help celebrate. How's that?"

"It's not that. Where will we put our Christmas tree? And we won't have Maui trying to eat the presents and I won't have any friends and it's going to be awful!" She bursts into tears and falls into my arms, sobbing with the heartbreak only a child can truly express.

I hug her, remembering how it felt when my parents didn't listen to me over their divorce and not even Amma had much to say because she was so busy taking care of Suze.

Whoa. Where did that come from? I think.

But Jasmine is what matters right now. I hold her tight, smelling her hair. "It's scary."

"Yes. And awful. And it makes me feel so, so, so lonely."

"I know." I stroke her hair. "Go ahead and let it out."

She simply leans into my embrace and sobs. Sobs and sobs and sobs. Behind me, I hear Ben doing something in the kitchen, but I keep my focus on Jasmine. After a while, she raises her head. I brush tears from her cheeks with my thumbs. "I wish I could make your life perfect," I say. "But I don't have that power. I can tell you that things work out."

She bows her head.

"Do you want some lunch?" I ask. "I made you a grilled cheese."

Her voice is small. Tragic. "Yes."

"I've got it ready right here," Ben says. "But I'm gonna need you to set the table."

"Okay." She wipes her face, then goes to the drawer and gets out napkins and place mats and carries them over, where she places them with exactness.

Ben has finished the tuna salad, and made sandwiches with lettuce and tomato and a little pile of chips on each plate. He's not waiting for applause or acknowledgment, just picks up a couple of plates and takes them to the table.

I pick up the glasses of water and follow him. When we've all settled, Jasmine says, "So, if you get married, will I have to call you Grandpa or can I still call you Ben?"

"Married!" I cry. My cheeks flame.

"Well, if that ever comes about," he says, winking at me, "you can keep calling me Ben."

She swings her feet under her chair. "Good. It would be different if you were already around when I was born, but it would be strange to get used to calling somebody new Grandpa at this stage."

I'm embarrassed and my laugh bursts out too loudly. "Because you are so old."

Her expression is miffed. "I'm not a baby."

"That is definitely true."

She picks through the dark chips to eat first. "I heard you talking to Suze. About the bad guys."

"You don't have to worry about it. They're a long way away."

"They beat her up really bad, though, right? And put her in the hospital?"

For a split second I wonder how to answer this in a way that's not even more traumatizing. "They did. But you see she's fine now."

"I don't think she's fine. I think she's really sad in her heart."

Ben takes a sip of water and raises his eyebrows my direction as if to ask permission. I give a faint nod. "You're a good observer, Jasmine," he says. "I think she's got a lot to think about, and sometimes you have to be a little bit unhappy to get to the next place in your life."

She looks away. "I never want to be unhappy."

"I know. Me either. Unfortunately, everybody is sometimes."

"But why?"

"Well, how would you know you were happy if you were never sad?"

Her look of recognition is so acute I have to stifle a chuckle. "I never thought of that!"

"It would all be the same and you wouldn't be able to appreciate anything."

She nods. "So Suze is unhappy so she can be happy in the end."

"Yes."

"Have you ever been really sad?" she asks.

"Yes." He puts his sandwich down and wipes his fingers. "Lots of times. But the worst one was when my wife died."

I frown, worried that this is way too much information, but Jasmine seems undaunted. "Was it a car accident?"

"No. She died of an illness you get in hot places."

"What disease?"

"Malaria."

"I've heard of that. There's also cholera, typhoid, and dengue fever." Which she pronounces *den-goo*.

"Where do you get this stuff?" I ask.

"YouTube."

I narrow my eyes. "You have a very curious mind, don't you?"

"Yes."

We eat for a while, listening to the '70s pop station I have playing on the speakers.

Very quietly, Jasmine says, "I'm not moving to London."

I let it go. Because of course she is. Just as I had to move when my parents divorced.

There are many things beyond our control, and the past years have brought that home more fully than any of us could have anticipated. I think of Dmitri, dying in a hospital alone, and Suze grieving him, and sitting by her bedside in LA after the attack, praying that she would live. I offered the universe all manner of things if they would save her—but the main one was that I would come clean. I still haven't done that.

I'm afraid she'll hate me forever.

THEN

SAVE YOUR TEARS

5/25/22
TO: theprivatesuze8912@gmail.com
FROM: phoebehudsonillustrator@gmail.com
SUBJECT: happy birthday week

Dear Suze,

It feels weird that we're not celebrating each other's birthdays this year. It's a momentous one, right? I hate that we're not talking right now. It feels lonely in the world without you. Jasmine has gone back to Portland for the summer and I miss her like a limb. It's hard not to get attached, but I am more able to be generous with her than I've ever been with anyone. It's easy to want the best for her and try to make it happen.

I was an asshole after my grandmother's funeral. Can you forgive me?

Love,
Phoebe

[UNSENT]

September 7, 2022
Dear Phoebe,

Weirdly, this is the anniversary of the day my dad tried to kill me. I mean, I don't know that he really wanted to kill me, but he mostly wanted me dead my whole life. I wish I'd told you everything that summer, but I just didn't know how.

I hate that we're locked in this awful space where we said awful things to each other at the funeral. I'm sorry.

[NEVER MAILED]

October 12, 2022
Dear Suze,

I miss you. I was so mad that it seemed like a good idea to cut you out of my life. But I don't really feel like me when we are not in communication. I just get more and more mean and small.

That doesn't mean I'm not mad. You hurt my feelings so much, and I don't know how to get over that. Do you really

[NEVER MAILED]

The day of the attack

Text string:

Phoebe: Suze, Suze! I'm so worried! I just saw the news. I'm flying to LA tonight.

Phoebe: I'm here. They won't let me see you or tell me anything about your condition, which I didn't even think about. They just think I'm a crazed fan.

Phoebe: I love you. I'm so sorry for everything.

Phoebe: It's been five days. I've rented a little studio apartment nearby and will stay until I can talk to you in person. I'm so scared for you.

CURRENT DAY

Chapter Twenty-Two
Suze

After Joel leaves, I skim through the scripts again but soon move away from them in frustration. Restless, I wander through the house picking things up and putting them down, looking for something I can't name. Maui tries to follow for a while, but at some point, he stops in the middle of the foyer with a huff and settles his head on his paws, watching me. I'm glad of his company, though, and bend over to scratch his ears. "You'll protect me, right?" I ask.

His eyebrows move in agreement.

I still haven't told Phoebe everything. About Joel. About the baby. About all of it. Now that Joel and I have reconnected, it's all the more urgent that I confess our history to Phoebe and try to explain why I've lied about it for so long. The idea fills me with dread, because things are really healing now.

But really, how did she not figure it out? Why didn't she ever ask me more about Victor, who I told her was the father?

How did I actually think those lies would work, anyway? Joel burned down my father's church! That's not exactly the act of a good friend.

Is it possible she *does* know? Isn't it more possible that she always has known?

I rub the spot between my eyebrows. How many times have we broken apart, come back together? At times I've hated her—namely, when I was banished to the Magdalene Home—and at times I was despairing over her choices, like when she married Derek and left her art lying in a forgotten pile at the side of her life.

A rumble of memory rises, the fight we had at the funeral. It poked me on the beach earlier, but in the space of quiet here now, it rolls itself out in spectacular detail.

We were sitting in the living room, big mugs of tea in our hands. Everyone else had gone to bed or gone home. A fire flickered in the fireplace. The mess of the wake was still scattered over the counters, the dining room table, the coffee table in front of us. I'd started to clean it up a little while before, but Phoebe said, "Leave it. We can tackle it all in the morning. Who cares?"

Exhausted, we sat curled on the two couches, watching the flames. Outside, rain fell, and it gave the room a damp chill. Beryl had been quite frail for two years, but to the end she kept her clear mind. The vacuum she left seemed impossible to fill, and it suddenly caught me in the gut.

I would never talk to her again.

A swell of grief roared through me, as impossible to halt as a train. Everything about the past three years, from the onset of the pandemic, then Dmitri's death, and now Beryl's, filled me to the brim. I heard a noise escape my throat that could only be called keening, and I bent over with it, rocking, letting it pour out, tears and pain and that piercing noise. I thought I should try to stop so I wouldn't wake anyone up, but it kept moving, rhythmic and towering, a wave of purest loss. I would never see her again. Never look into her eyes. Never hold her hand.

I was aware of Phoebe, but I didn't look at her. I just let it go, knowing she would understand, that her loss and mine were the ones that mattered. Finally, I got up and found a kitchen towel to sop up my tears and came back to sit down. "I can't even imagine the world without her. My heart is completely broken."

"Oh, of course," Phoebe said in a cold voice. "*You're* the one suffering, even though she was my grandmother."

I jerked my head up. "What? It's not a contest. And she wasn't my blood grandmother, but she was the only mother I really ever had."

"Really? So why weren't you here with me, taking care of her these past few years?"

I blinked in both astonishment and fury. "Are you really going there? You didn't *want* me here!"

"Because it's a three-ring circus with you, all the time, and I didn't think that would be good for her."

"I wouldn't have been in this house. I would have been in mine. I offered so many times." Some evil thing made me say, "And I notice you were quite happy to take whatever money you needed from me."

"There it is! The grand lady doling out her largesse!"

"You know that's not fair. Why are you always so fucking jealous?"

"Jealous?" She stood up, her face bright red. "You've always been the jealous one. You were jealous of the Portland house, jealous of my parents, and it wasn't enough to be jealous of my grandmother, you had to move in here to steal her."

"I didn't have to steal her. She loved me! And you know I had to come here to live. There was no other place to go." Her words were so sharp and painful that I instinctively struck back. I narrowed my eyes. "You've always been such a whiner! Poor Phoebe in her big house on the hill, with two parents and a grandmother and a fucking swimming pool."

"Material things are not the only things, Suze. You've never got that."

"It wasn't about the material part. It was about you having love and people who wanted the best for you. So what, your parents got divorced. Mine tried to kill me, in case you've forgotten, and at the worst time in my life, when I was only a few miles away from you in that horrible unwed mothers' home, you only came to see me one time. Once! Do you have any idea how awful that time was? How much I needed you? And you just deserted me."

"I did go see you. You were a bitch to me."

"Oh, sorry. I wasn't cheerful enough for you?"

She rolled her eyes. "There it is. You poor, poor thing. Poor Suze. You had such a terrible childhood. So what? You have everything. You got everything. You were born beautiful. You dazzled the whole world. You're as rich as a duchess and still you carry around that old story like it's some teddy bear."

"I do not!" Rage filled every corner of my body, my mind, every organ. My liver pulsed fury, and my veins ran hot. "At least I did something, took action, tried to make things happen, instead of rolling over to kiss a bloody jerk's ass. You just gave up. Beryl and I were both trying to get you to stay in art school and you flung all of it away with both fists. *Here, Derek; take this, Derek.* You gave all your power away to a man."

She slapped me. Hard. It stunned me for the blink of an eye, but my anger burst like a lake going over a dam, and I struck back, feeling a wild relief in the connection of my hand against her face. With a screech, she grabbed my hair. "You think you're the most important person in the world. I'm so sick of you!"

I was much taller and knocked her down, tears pouring from my eyes, feeling a hundred fights in which I had wanted to strike back. I held her arms, keeping her from hitting me. "I've loved you my whole life, you stupid bitch!" I screamed. "You want more, more, more—"

Her elbow connected with my cheekbone and eye. Stunned, I fell back. She stood up. Her face was red. "I don't love you. You take everything. Leave me alone."

She stormed away. I left in the morning, and didn't speak to her again until after the attack by the LNB. I woke up in the hospital to find her slumped in a chair, asleep. It touched me that she came, that she sat with me, but I didn't have the energy to deal with the fallout right then. When she awakened, I thanked her for coming and told her she could go home.

～

In the quiet of my living room, I take a sip of tea and run a fingernail along the seam of my jeans. I did have a lot of good luck—the lucky break of being born with the kind of face that was fashionable at the moment I came to the movies, the luck of that particular casting director being at the auditions on Broadway, the luck of a great script that fit me like Goldilocks's chair.

But I also worked hard. I didn't take the lucky breaks for granted. I looked for the people who could help me and listened to their advice. I did a lot of learning in public and there are definitely roles from those early days that make me wince now.

Phoebe kept saying that she wanted a big life as an artist, but what she really wanted was to be in love, have a boyfriend, and have sex, and be a part of a couple. Derek showed up and she dived in, headfirst. He was wildly good looking and talented, and in his own way, he loved her, when he wasn't gaslighting her.

Was it so wrong for her to want that life? Is it possible that both Beryl and I were wrong to try to talk her out of that marriage? By the end, she didn't like art school very much, and although the marriage ended, she found her career anyway.

You take everything, she'd cried. And she didn't even know about Joel. Was it true? Did I try to take things from a life I envied? I don't even know anymore.

We seem to always make our way back to each other, but is there a tipping point where our friendship breaks so completely that it can't be glued back together?

As if my thoughts called her, my phone screen flashes Phoebe's face. For a moment, I'm not entirely sure I'll answer. My emotions and my memories are so tangled I hardly know what to think.

But habits die hard. The news hits me in the middle of the chest like a fist. Juno was such a light, alive with a burning that came through her voice and her songs. She couldn't have been thirty. Phoebe gives me the details, and images blast through my protective layers, the blow to my head, the fall, the kicks. I close my eyes. Take a breath. If they'd chosen to shoot, I would now be dead, and the first thing that makes me think of is Joel, that I would not have had a chance to be with him one more time. She urges me to come down but I need to do what I'm doing.

I hang up.

I think of Nadine Truelove. Juno Gerhert.

I think of my father and the fact that the LNB failed to kill me. It comes to me that I've been looking at all this the wrong way. My father tried to break me and he failed. The LNB tried to kill me and they failed.

What will I do with that gift?

In a rush of emotion, I bend my head over the page. And begin.

I'm still here.

The only way through the morass of thoughts is writing. I've never lost the diary habit. I call it journaling now.

I pick up a blank Moleskine, connect my phone to Bluetooth, and settle at the banquette overlooking the ocean. I write the date at the top of the page and pause, wondering how to address it. I think about Joel, about the feeling of him against me, the way I felt when I saw him standing on the porch after such a long time, as if the world had righted itself at last. How he smells just the same. Below the enchantment lurks a darkness I am not ready to face, the things I told Phoebe I need to be here to finally let go of.

Another flash of Joel, eyes closed as he kissed me, plays across the screen of my eyelids. His hands on my body. His laughter in the middle of the night when we found ourselves exhausted and shaking.

How was that possible, that someone could not be part of your life and then suddenly they were so huge, right in the middle of it? But I can't write about that right now.

Nor can I write about the LNB. I don't even want to. My heart yearns toward the light, toward something bigger.

I write:

Edwina sent me a bunch of scripts and I am bored by all of them. The women are all the same—over fifty, struggling with families or lonely after being widowed or with husbands who are sick. Why don't they move me? What am I looking for?

They have no agency, these women. They're acted upon, not making their lives their own. Which might actually be true, that many women feel that way, but—

What I want are stories about women who are doing all the same things a woman does at every other stage of her life. Setting goals, having adventures, learning new things, having sex with a man (or woman) she finds hot, discovering new things about herself. Maybe I should write my own movie, write a part I'd like to play.

Huh.

What might that be?

I pause and tap my pen against my lips.

Maybe she would be an adventurer. Maybe a biography about Georgia O'Keeffe, striding through her life, living it her way until she died at 98. I've always thought she must have had an affair with the young guy who came into her life so late, and maybe that could be a good topic. Why not?

Because people might judge her as being ridiculous, allowing herself to have big feelings for somebody who clearly took advantage of her.

Or did he? Maybe they used each other.

But maybe a different angle. Maybe her decision to start traveling at age 60, going to India when she was in her 70s. What would that have been like back then?

Or maybe I could just make somebody up. An adventurer in the 1930s who went to North Africa, who had an adventure and a love affair at age 65. (Omar Sharif! Too bad he's gone, but there must be a similar actor out there.)

That would be a fun part to play. And I'd want the sex on screen, no fading away. Normalize it.

When Joel returns, I'm still pouring my heart out on the page. Music plays on the speakers, and I don't even realize hours have gone by until he knocks. I look up in surprise, and clouds have moved in heavily over the Starfish Sisters. My arm is very tired. I've filled many pages.

When I open the door, he has a fierce expression. "What is it?" I ask.

"Deer entrails in your driveway." He points.

I shake my head. "Whoever is doing this is not LNB. They don't give warnings."

"Maybe," he says. "But that doesn't mean whoever this is isn't dangerous."

"Agreed. Let's call the sheriff and get the alarm updated and go from there."

"I think you should stay with Phoebe."

I shake my head. "It's going to get pretty awkward once she realizes we've been sleeping together."

"First of all, why would she know?"

I raise my chin. "Because she knows us. Both of us."

"And secondly, why would it matter?"

I sigh. "I've never told her the truth."

For a long moment, he simply gapes at me. "You're kidding me."

I shake my head. "I know. But she had a terrible crush on you and I didn't want to tell her that we were together, and then you were gone forever, and I was pretty sure I'd never see you again, so it didn't seem like it was worth the drama to tell her the truth."

He frowns. "Except that it was a really big part of your life. At least then."

"It was." And suddenly an entire bubble of repressed memory and emotion boils up and explodes in my chest. I make a sound, overcome by a kaleidoscope of memories—my father knocking me down, the feel of the razor against my head, the loneliness of the unwed mothers' home. In a pained whisper, I ask, "Why didn't you ever call me?"

His body goes still. Poised. "I didn't know where you were. No one told me. I sent you a letter so that you could write to me, and when I never heard from you, I assumed you didn't want to talk to me again."

"A letter? I never got a letter."

"I gave it to Phoebe. To give you."

I meet his eyes, my heart thudding much too hard. "She never gave it to me."

His hands fall on my shoulders. "Oh, Suze." He presses his head against mine. "Oh my God."

A car pulls into the driveway.

"Speak of the devil," I say. Phoebe pulls up in her Subaru, her elbow hanging out the window. I'm about to storm over to her window and scream something awful, but before I move, she cries, "Jasmine is missing. Help!"

And everything else is forgotten.

Chapter Twenty-Three
Phoebe

"Tell us everything," Suze says, and I spill it out as coherently as possible. Jasmine was so upset yesterday about the apartment and insisted that she wouldn't move, but I didn't take it seriously.

She said she would run away. But kids say that. I said it and I never did.

I didn't take her seriously. The knowledge lives like a boulder in my chest, heavy and dark, making everything hurt. We split into three groups—me and Ben with Maui, Suze and Joel, and two deputies who agree to search for her. Suze and Joel take the trail leading away from the house up into the forest, while Ben and I search the flower garden and then the beach. Joel and the deputies are at a disadvantage because they don't know her, but one has an eleven-year-old daughter, so he searches the places she might have gone. As I walk the rows of the fallow fields, calling her, look in the greenhouses and behind shrubs, I can't help thinking of all the things that could hurt her out here. Mountain lions, bears and elk, getting lost completely and having no idea how to find her way home. People. People are the most terrifying of all.

In three hours, we find no sign of her. Every nerve in my body is drawn so tight that my limbs barely operate. I move in a jerky way, my mind roaring, flashing horrific scenarios. I barely avoid a complete, sobbing breakdown, and only because that will not help find her.

Gathering at my house, we show our empty palms. I have to call Stephanie, and the sheriff sends out a bulletin to look for her.

I close myself in my room and dial Steph's number. It's already late in the UK, but this won't wait. My heart squeezes when she answers. "Hi, Mom," she says, not at all groggy. "Is everything okay?"

"No." I brace myself, and spill it out: "Jasmine has run away in protest."

"What? What do you mean?"

"She ran away. She left a note and said that she had no choice because we wouldn't listen to her."

"Run away? Where?"

"I don't know. We've been looking for her for hours and we haven't found her."

"Mom! Why didn't you call me right away? Oh my God!"

"I thought we would find her and you wouldn't have to worry." It sounds lame, but I mean it. "I've contacted the sheriff and we're going to go back out and keep looking, but I wanted you to know."

"You're sure she ran away and wasn't kidnapped?"

"She left a note." I read it aloud: "Dear Nana, nobody is listening to me. I do not want to move to London, so I am running away." My voice breaks. "Love, Jasmine." With a howl, I cry, "She kept telling me she didn't want to go, and I just kept telling her it would be all right!"

"Jesus." She sounds winded. "Mom, it's not your fault. I'll be on a plane as soon as I can get a flight."

"I'm sure we'll find her or she'll come back when she gets cold enough."

"She could get hurt out there! She could die! Someone could kidnap her with offers of a kitten!"

Now it's my turn to be steady. Even though my hands are shaking, I say, "This isn't Portland." A mountain lion prowls through my mind. Rattlesnakes. Cliffs. "She's making a statement. We'll find her."

"I'm still coming home. This is insanity. If she's so against it, I need to figure something else out."

"We'll find her."

"Hanging up now, Mom. Keep me posted."

We all eat sandwiches and gulp down some coffee and head back out. Ben forces me to sit down and take deep breaths, and then we go down to search the beach. I try not to imagine sneaker waves and riptides. We search the opposite area from where we searched earlier, a trail in the mountains riddled with cliffs, and I block visions of her falling to her death at the foot of one of those bluffs. Ben is solid and silent, and I'm grateful.

We search and call until darkness begins to fall. A frantic noise of terror grows in my brain, riddles my gut with nausea. Why didn't I listen? Why didn't I pay attention? Winded, I halt on the trail and bend over, hands on my knees, sobs tearing out of my chest. "I feel like I should have known she meant this," I gasp out. Tears spill down my face. "I can't bear it if something happens to her!"

Ben rests his palm on the middle of my back. "We'll find her, Phoebe. She's going to be okay."

I let some of the terror leak out in my tears, then settle and straighten.

"We have to go back," Ben says. "It will be dark soon."

I stand at the top of a bluff and yell, "Jasmine!" The word flies over the shallow valley and disappears, and my heart cracks in two. "If she . . ." I gasp. "I will literally die."

"Let's get back to the house," he says, and leads the way. I follow on feet that weigh a million pounds.

Jasmine!

Chapter Twenty-Four
Suze

I'm exhausted by everything—the emotional upheavals on every level, and Joel, and memories, and the terror that Jasmine might be hurt somewhere. I adore this child, and can't bear the idea of her alone in the dark. Or worse.

The search has been called off due to rain and darkness, and I was going to stay with Phoebe, sleep upstairs so she wouldn't be alone, but she said, "Just go home, Suze. I need to be alone."

"Phoebe, I don't think that's a good idea."

She gave me a murderous look, as if somehow this were my fault. "I want to be alone."

"Are you—"

"I can't, Suze! I can't talk."

Which made me think about that letter, the letter she never gave me, and I want to shake her, but I also want Jasmine home, safe and sound, and on some level, I know Phoebe is barely hanging on. In this moment, out of respect for my long love of her, I can give her some space.

Even if a hole is burning through my chest.

Ben shook his head, so Joel drove me back up the hill. "We'll keep calling, looking, okay? She's somewhere. We'll find her."

At home, lying in the dark, I find myself praying. An actual prayer, not the wordless things I sometimes send up out of habit, the pleas or the longing, or the apology, things I can't seem to get out of my system. Once upon a time, I liked praying. It soothed me.

So lying there on my back with Yul Brynner on my belly, purring, I pray, specifically to Jesus, the nice God, the one who loves children (all the children of the world). "You know where she is, Jesus. Please send extra angels to look out for her. Keep her warm and dry. Don't let anything hurt her. Show us where she is."

It gives me peace to hand it over, and I start to drift off.

Until I wake up suddenly.

I know where she might be.

The night she stayed over with me, we walked to the beach by going down through town to pick up snacks. On the way, we passed the church and the bus, the paint Phoebe and Victor applied faded to almost nothing.

Did anyone check it? I fling the covers off and yank clothes on over my pajamas. I don't have a car here, so I'll have to walk, and it's very dark. Pressing my lips together, I wonder if I should call Phoebe, but what if Jasmine isn't there and it just gets her hopes up?

I *should* call Joel to go with me, but as absurd as it is, I don't have his actual number. We haven't made that connection yet.

It isn't far, maybe two blocks down the hill, and then another two to the lot where the bus is. Maui is with me, and I have good boots and a flashlight. It's pouring down rain, which will keep everybody but me inside.

I don't have a leash for Maui, and I'm worried that he might take off after some little animal, so I tie a long scarf around his neck and he accepts it happily. "You're such a good dog. Maybe I need a dog."

His calm eyes agree with me. I have my phone in my pocket, an umbrella over both of us, and a flashlight in my leash hand.

It's *really* dark. The road is awash in mud and puddles that make a mess of my hems. Maui doesn't seem to mind, trotting out slightly ahead of me.

A sound behind me, cracking or a snap or something not quite right, makes me spin around, the flashlight creating an arc that catches on a figure, then swings by, and I try to swing back but my hands are shaking and I miss the first time, then center in on—

Joel.

"What are you doing?" I cry. "You almost gave me a heart attack!"

"What are *you* doing? I slept in the truck in case anyone bothered you."

"Joel!" It shatters me. I close my eyes. "I would have let you stay."

"It doesn't matter. What the hell are you doing?"

I grab his arm. The more the merrier. "I might know where Jasmine is. Also, you need to give me your number."

"Do you want to just drive? It would be a lot drier?"

I pause. "Yes. That would be much better."

∾

The old block is deeply creepy at night. I've never been out here except in the daytime. My old bedroom window is shattered, and the house is decrepit. "Why haven't they torn all that down?" I ask as we pull up.

"Turn off your lights so she doesn't know we're coming."

"What difference does it make?"

"I want to scare the shit out of her, that's what difference it makes."

We creep up to the bus. "What if she's not even here?" he asks.

"I can't think about that."

The door is broken and stands open. I tiptoe up the three stairs as quietly as possible, peeking over the edge of the half wall, holding my breath. *Please be here please be here please be here.*

A lump of blankets is pressed against the wall on one of the platforms. I tiptoe over and reach under. Just before I do, my LA mind kicks in and I'm afraid it might be a homeless person, but my hand closes around a small ankle.

She wakes up, yelling at the top of her lungs. "Go away! I'll hit you with a rock!" Then she sees me. "Suze! You scared me half to death!"

"I scared you?" I snatch off the blankets and grab her, hugging her grasshopper body to me, her hair in my face. Tears spring into my eyes at the smell of her, the safeness of her, the physical reality of her when I thought we might not—

I squeeze my eyes tight. "Holy shit, kid, you scared the hell out of us!"

"Nobody was listening to me," she says.

"Get your shoes on. Everybody is looking for you and your nana was half out of her mind worrying that a kidnapper had taken you or a moose gored you."

"I left her a note so she wouldn't worry!" She shoves her feet into the Crocs she wears constantly.

"Oh, is that right? A note! Well, I don't know why we were freaked out, then. Oh, wait." I grab her junk into a ball and point toward the door. "Because you're ten! You're not supposed to be out here by yourself."

She turns around and stands her ground, arms crossed over her chest. "Nobody was listening to me. I don't want to move to London. It's my life, too, and I should have a say in this."

Good for you, kid, I think. Tears well in my eyes. She has fire. She has moxie. She will need them both to live in a world that will try to devour her. I fall on my knees and hug her again, tears in my eyes. "Baby, I was so worried about you. I'm so glad you're safe."

As we climb in the car, I text Phoebe. I found Jasmine. Got her and heading to you.

🎭🎭🎭🎭🎭

Chapter Twenty-Five
Phoebe

I'm standing at the open front door getting splattered with rain when Joel's truck pulls up. Suze gets out and carries Jasmine to the door, running through the rain, and deposits her in my arms.

As her long arms and legs wrap around me, I burst into tears, and bury my face in her shoulder, so relieved, so grateful. "Jasmine, baby," I murmur, shaking, smelling her hair. I sink down on the couch, still holding tight, and I feel her hug me back.

"I'm sorry, Nana," she says. "I didn't mean to scare you."

"You did." I rock with her, and try to get my emotions under control. I lift my head, wipe my face. "Do not *ever* do that again. Do you hear me?"

She nods, chastened.

"You know how you worry about tsunamis and bombs that are never going to fall and all those other things?"

"Yeah." She twines her fingers through my hair.

"I worry about *you*. My whole job when I'm with you is to keep you safe and make sure nothing hurts you, do you get it?"

"Yes." Tears are spilling from her eyes, too. "I'm sorry."

"Go take a warm shower and get in my bed. I'll be up soon."

She nods, keeping herself small. Before she runs upstairs, she gives Suze a hug, too. I see that my friend's hair is unbrushed and she's not wearing a bra—she jumped out of bed to go find her.

When Jasmine goes upstairs, I say, "We need to call the sheriff."

"Already done," Joel says. He cocks a thumb toward the porch. "I'll wait outside."

He touches Suze on the shoulder and there's that spark, the lingering that catches my eye. "You can go," I say wearily.

"Are you okay?" she asks.

"No. I'm not." All the roaring emotions surge through my body, and I'm shaking from head to toe. I can barely breathe, overcome with both the aftermath of terror and the relief. I sink on the couch, bend my head to my hands, and weep. "Oh my God."

Suze sits down beside me, wraps her arms around my shoulders. "It's okay," she says. "She's safe. Everything is okay."

After the worst of the toxic fear spills from my body, I raise my head. "Where was she?"

"In the hippie bus. We talked about you painting it when she was with me."

A twist of panic reappears. I would never have thought of looking for her there. "What made you think of it?"

"I don't know. I was praying and—it popped into my mind."

A zing of fury blasts through my sinuses. "Oh, of course God answers *your* prayers and not mine." The bitterness is ridiculous and even I know it as it comes out, but I need to be angry and she's there.

"Phoebe," she says with reproach. "That's not what I meant. You know better than that."

All the terror I've been feeling transforms into a white-hot anger. "I don't know what I know. Clearly I've been a fucking idiot for forty years because you and Joel aren't just friends. You never were, were you? He was the father of your baby."

"Look," she says with quiet reason. "You have some things to answer for as well, but this is not the time for that discussion. You're upset, and very understandably. Let's talk about this tomorrow."

But there's a roaring in my ears and her reasonable tone is more than I can bear. "Stop trying to settle me. Tell me the truth."

For a long second, she stares at me. She swallows and straightens her shoulders. "Yes." She sighs. "I've been trying to figure out a way to tell you for ages."

"It's been a while, so why didn't you?"

"I don't know. It was weird that I kept the secret in the first place and I knew you would get mad, and I've been trying to find the right time, but you can be so . . . volatile."

"Maybe because people lie to me!" I step back. Cross my arms. "You need to go."

"Seriously? We're doing *this* again?" She narrows her eyes. "I'm not the only person who lied, though, am I?"

A frisson of guilt moves through my gut. "What are you talking about?"

"Joel gave you a letter for me, and you never gave it to me."

I bow my head. Nod.

"So I guess we're even. Sort of. But you must have known when you kept the letter that Joel and I were together, that he was the father of my baby, the baby, by the way, that I had to give up. Maybe if I'd known how to reach him, how to talk about—"

"Oh, you would have kept it. What? Gotten married at sixteen to another sixteen-year-old? That would probably have worked out better."

"Who knows?" Her voice takes on a dangerous darkness. "Who knows? Because everybody made choices for me. Not even my very best friend was there for me in that moment."

Acute, wild guilt scalds my heart, and my anger pours away. "You're right," I cry. "I'm so sorry."

"Do you have any idea what you cost me? I counted on you, loved you so much, and all you ever do is undermine me and—" She breaks off. "You're exhausting, Phoebe," she says. "It's completely impossible to please you."

"That's not entirely fair. You know I try to take care of you."

"No. You hold me to this ridiculous standard, but not yourself and not anybody else. I have been in your corner since we were twelve, and you're only in mine when it's convenient."

"That's bullshit!" I cry. "I'm always here for you. Who sat in your hospital room for weeks? Who takes care of the house you love so much—a house I had planned to buy myself, actually, until you swooped in and stole it out from under me." I wish I could take the words back the minute they're out of my mouth, but they've already spilled. "Never mind—"

"You never told me that." Tears well up in her aquamarine eyes, making them even more ridiculously beautiful. "Why didn't you just say something? I thought I was doing the right thing!"

"I'm sorry. I don't know where that came from."

Her voice is raw with exhaustion. "I can't do this."

She slams the door, and as if the sound has broken me, I bend over, barely able to breathe. The aftermath of terror, the sorrow over not listening to Jasmine, the mistakes I've made for so many years, the terrible cost for my beloved, beloved friend.

I collapse on the floor and cover my face. Shame burns through me. "Oh, Amma, I am so sorry."

~

Jasmine is sleeping next to me when I wake up. It's an overcast morning, so I have no idea what time it is, but it doesn't matter. I turn in to her body without touching her and inhale the scent of her hair. Her cheek is as smooth as an egg, pale and faintly touched with pink. Her lashes spill in an arch below her eyelids. Her mouth is wide and full, and will one day be very pretty.

It's so hard to love people, knowing they might die, knowing they might not always be there for a million reasons. I have always worried about people being taken from me, long before they were. I worried about my grandmother, and she lived to be ninety-four. I worried about my dad, and he did end up dying too young, of a random soft tissue cancer when he was only fifty-one. Younger than I am now. I was a nervous wreck as Stephanie's mother, terrified she'd slip through some safety protocol I'd failed to set and be grievously injured or killed.

Somehow, she survived.

I turn over and stare at the ceiling, thinking of the fight with Suze. There's something I have to do.

Quietly, I get up and open one of the low drawers in my dresser. It holds diaries and letters from those days when we were young. The collection can still send up tiny puffs of stationery perfume, a scent I would recognize apart from any other stimulus. It swerves right past my rational brain, and my limbic system offers me a vision of opening the mailbox and finding a letter or package from Suze. How it lit up my day!

I pull out a handful of letters, pierced by our youthful handwriting, and open one at random. Seventh grade, classes, Suze excited about meeting Joel. I remember how jealous I was, that she had a friend and I didn't. It was the way I always reacted to everything she did.

Why was I like that? It seems so small and mean spirited now. I genuinely loved her and wanted to keep her for myself. I didn't want her to have Joel or my grandmother or Mary. I wanted her all to myself—her beautiful eyes and her kind nature and her curious mind.

At the very bottom of the letters, I find the one with Joel's handwriting on the front. It's sealed because I never opened it. On the front, it says, *Suze*. As I hold it in my hands, shame burns through me, shame and a resolution to finally put this right.

From downstairs, I hear a voice. "Hello?"

It's Stephanie. I texted her as soon as Jasmine showed up, but she was already on a plane. I go to the bedroom door and call, "Up here."

After a big reunion, with tears and then some coffee and pancakes, Stephanie and Jasmine sit on the couch. I've built a fire to offset the cold wet of the day. "Jasmine," Stephanie says, "you can never ever scare us like that again, do you understand me? It was very dangerous for you and terrifying for us."

She nods, her gray eyes serious. "I'm sorry."

"That said"—she sighs—"I'll let them know I'm not moving. I thought it might be fun for us, and that we could explore Europe, and you'd learn a lot of new stuff, but I didn't let you have any say in the matter."

The grandmother balance is knowing when to speak and when to be quiet. "Stephanie, you're the mother. You have been glowing since you arrived in London." I look at Jasmine, small and thin beside her mother.

She looks troubled. "Nana!"

Stephanie picks up Jasmine's hand. "We can talk it through, how about that? See if we can come to a compromise. I have been really happy there, and I think you would be, too. Can we at least try it for a little while?"

Jasmine falls into her mother's chest. "I want you happy."

"Let's see what we can figure out, okay?" Steph strokes her daughter's head, kisses her forehead. Such love. It pierces me.

I will miss them both so much.

Stephanie looks ready to fall over. "Why don't you both go take a nap?" I suggest. "I have some things I need to do."

"Can I sleep with you, Mommy?"

"Oh, yes, please," Steph says, and they head upstairs.

Chapter Twenty-Six
Suze

Joel has already left for work when I awaken. We both fell into bed and into sleep upon our return, exhausted by the day. I couldn't bear to deal with one more thing, and he seemed to sense that, pulling me into his body, a bulwark against the world.

I left Maui with Jasmine, so it's only me and Yul Brynner padding into the kitchen. Thick fog lies on the ocean, obscuring the Starfish Sisters and my view of Phoebe's studio. It's cozy somehow.

A rock of sadness sits in the middle of my chest. Is our friendship no longer sustainable? Have so many things gone wrong between us that there's no way to move forward?

Friendships end. I know that. But she's not really just my friend. She's my sister, the only person in my life who's been with me through everything, ups and downs.

But how can I encompass this betrayal? She hid Joel's letter from me. Because of that single action, Joel and I never had a single moment of agency over our fate or the fate of our daughter.

And all this time, I had convinced myself that she didn't know that Joel and I had fallen in love. If she didn't know, why hide the letter?

I rub the spot between my eyes. What a tangled, idiotic mess!

~

As if my thoughts have called her, she knocks in our special way, three short, one more. With some trepidation, I head for the door and open it.

She's bundled up in a thick pink sweater. The color makes the most of her dark hair. "I need to talk to you about something," she says. "Can I come in?"

I stand back, wave her in. I am feeling so angry and uncertain that I don't want to encourage anything normal. Not this time.

"It won't take that long." She has something in her hands, an envelope, and a howl of warning sounds in my heart. She pulls it between her fingers, once, then again. "This is the letter Joel left for you, before he went to juvie."

The sight of his teenage handwriting on the envelope sears me. "I can't believe you kept it. All this time."

"I honestly didn't realize that you—that he . . . the baby." She shakes her head.

"You know, Phoebe, all these years I kept that secret—even if it was stupid—because I wanted to *protect* you. And all this time, you did the opposite. Your secret was selfish. You also knew more than you're admitting."

"I know," she says. "There's nothing I can say to make this right." She swallows. "I am so sorry. Sorry that you had to go through all those losses alone, that I was such a fucking jealous idiot—" She slaps a tear off her face. "I didn't open it."

I touch my name written in blue ink. Can I bear to read what's in here?

Can I bear not to? I slip my finger under the flap and pull out the yellow notebook paper inside.

> Dear Suze,
>   I am so sorry for all the pain you are going through.
> Please remember that there is somebody in this world that

loves you no matter what. I don't know what's going to happen to me, but I wanted you to have my dad's address. He
said he wouldn't throw anything away from you. Considering
all the pain I've caused you, you probably never want to see
me again, and I understand that, but just in case, this is it:
Bill Minough
2586 Elliot Avenue
Seattle, WA 98109
I love you with all my heart. I am so sorry for my
part in all of this.
Love,
Joel

A howl burns through me. Without looking at her, I say, "You
need to go."

She doesn't say another word. I close the door behind her and
stagger into the living room, where I sink down on the couch, thinking
of the long, long, long lonely months in the Magdalene Home. I was
cut off from everyone but Beryl, who sent me care packages every week
with a cheerful letter and candy, home-baked goods, and art supplies.
Tablets, sketchbooks, pencils, pens, paints, brushes, charcoals. I filled
them up, an act of sorrow and defiance, and still have them somewhere.

I have the diaries I kept, too, plus many others I've written over the
years. Although Phoebe and I started the habit together, the practice stuck
with me. They're stored in a closet in the guest bedroom, stowed away in a
fireproof safe. It wasn't to keep them safe for the ages, only for myself, so I
could go back and touch the days of my life whenever I needed to. A day
written about is a day somehow saved from oblivion. Only those journals
saved me, writing and writing and writing about my pain. In some deep
way, I became the person I needed through that practice.

I run a thumb over Joel's young handwriting on the page and think
of how lost he must have been, too, sent away for an act of rage that

did, actually, save me. When the church burned down, my father was enraged, but he and Karen never came back to Blue Cove. When I declared my intention to emancipate myself, he barely fought me. I think he knew he'd met his match in Beryl.

Acting on some impulse I don't take the time to analyze, I pull on a thick jacket and a rain hat, tie on my shoes, and head down the hill. It's drizzling, and the wet air dampens my face and makes my hair curl. I barely notice.

The ruins of the church are hard to make out, but I know where it was and can pace it off easily. I wade through the weeds and wildflowers, my jeans getting wet, until I find a concrete pad that must have been the front steps.

As if the steps are there, I walk forward, through the place the front doors would have been, into the sanctuary. In my mind, I build it back in place, the pews and the windows with the midcentury geometric stained glass, the charmless walls. I build the altar and the pulpit where my father reigned in his good wool suits, his ties always demure stripes, his blond hair brushed back from that chiseled face. I hear him exhorting us sinners to get down on our knees. I allow myself to feel the terror when he saw my belly in the kitchen of this very building. How I ran. How he caught me. And literally nearly beat me to death. He bruised my liver and my kidneys and I couldn't see out of my left eye for nearly two months. It was a miracle that the baby survived, apparently whole and healthy.

I turn in a circle. How was it that they never charged him for child abuse? Was it like "domestic abuse," best left for families to manage on their own? After all, I was pregnant and had shamed the preacher.

I will never know. What should have been and what is are often two different things.

Rain begins to fall slightly more exuberantly, and I turn one more time, imagining Joel in this space, spilling gasoline or lighter fluid or whatever accelerant he used, and setting the whole thing on fire. He was extremely thorough. Beryl told me later that it burned down almost before the fire trucks could arrive.

A fierce sense of love fills me.

To that broken boy, I whisper, "Thank you."

To that broken girl, I say, "You're okay."

I'm still here.

Chapter Twenty-Seven
Phoebe

I retreat to my studio, dive into color to ease my heart, so I don't have to think. Not about anything. About Jasmine and Stephanie moving or keeping that letter hidden from Suze all these years—her face crumpling as she read the words, words she didn't share. About the responsibility I bear for her losses. So many losses.

On my tray, I mix a half dozen pinks, palest rose to deep saturated peachy pink, and aimlessly smear them on a primed board. I've turned Pandora to Amma's favorites, a playlist from the '60s and '70s that never fails to ease my heart, and as I paint, I sing along to *Tap Root Manuscript* by Neil Diamond, the "Childsong" she loved. We captured a phrase from the children's singing and used liquid embroidery pens to write it on pillowcases, and I can hear only one bar and be transported—

Amma.

If I could have anything in the world, I would ask to sit with her again for ten minutes. Sit with her and hold her hand and spill out my troubles. The vision brings tears to my eyes, and I rest my hands on the table, peering at her favorite chair as if she will appear. I see her at about seventy, when her hands had begun to be a little gnarled. She wore colorful blouses that always seemed to have a spot of paint on them somewhere. She loved berry lipstick and never wore any other makeup.

Her cheeks and chin and even her forearms were deeply wrinkled as time went by.

Standing there in her special room, I allow the sense of her to take over. I'm so hungry for her, for her wisdom, her cackling laugh. She smelled of apples and oil paint. She loved Joel and believed he was the best artist of the three of us, even though she tried to pretend she didn't. I see her bending over his work, pointing out some small thing.

I see her standing on the beach on a cloudy day, wind blowing her long hair, her eyes closed, hands raised in praise and love. To God, to nature, to all the things so much bigger than us. She believed in the holiness of things. She believed in nature. She believed in art and creativity and being kind.

She was unfailingly kind. It's a quality that's been lost in the modern world. But without her genuine kindness, her love, Suze would have had nowhere to go.

And I, her granddaughter, who loved her as if she had created the earth and everything in it, became the opposite of everything she was. I have become tight and small and guarded and mean. How did I keep that letter for so many years? How much pain did that single act cause in the lives of two people I loved?

How does love act that way?

I bend over, feeling that failure in my every cell. It surges and burns, and breaks the stiffness in my spine. Something inside me, bound tight and hard as a package tied with string, tears open. Dark matter spills from it, and dark thoughts, and mean words.

"Amma!" I cry, and give in to my grief. I sink to the floor and wail. "I'm so sorry!"

I cry for so long that my eyes are grainy and my face burns with salt. When I'm done, I can only take myself to the fainting couch and sleep, feeling something dark and heavy dissolving.

In my imagination, Amma strokes my hair. *I love you, child, just as you are.*

Just as you are.

"Phoebe," says a voice. Ben's voice. I'm sleeping so deeply that my brain spins a dream out of the single word, and we're off on an adventure, rambling around Europe together. Maybe even the pyramids. I'd love to see the pyramids. How would that influence my work?

My brain registers his warm hand on my arm, and with a sense of swimming back to earth from another planet, I struggle to open my eyes. It's dark with only moonlight or cloud light coming through the window. It falls on his face, a face that's become so important to me even if I didn't want it to. "Hi," I manage. "What time is it?"

"Nearly seven. You've been here all day. Stephanie sent me down here to see if you want dinner."

I test my stomach and realize it is dead empty. "That might be good." Rolling to a sitting position, I brush my hair out of my face. "I was really sleeping."

He sits next to me, brushes a lock of hair behind my ear. "You were. You needed it."

A swift longing moves through me, for this to come to something, to be something. I'm lonely and I have been for a long time. I want a partner, as we all do. Maybe it's really okay to *want* things. Want this. "I'm really glad to see you."

"Me too." He lifts my hand and kisses the palm, and a shiver moves through me.

If I'm going to be a better version of me, I have to start here. "You know that I'm hoping for something real here. I really like you."

"I really like you, too," he says.

My throat feels raw from crying. "I did something terrible, a long time ago."

"Did you?"

"I was in love with Joel. He was always in love with Suze."

He nods. "They were the couple everybody envied in school."

I look at him, my vision of the world shifting to accommodate this version of life, a version I would never have seen, obviously. "Really?"

"Oh yeah."

"I wasn't in school with all of you, so I never saw that."

He smiles gently. "I'm sorry you had a crush on him. That must have sucked."

"It did." I brush a fingertip over his broad thumbnail. "Realizing that they were a thing back then makes me feel even worse." I take a breath. "Because he gave me a letter for her, and I never gave it to her. I only did it this morning."

He says lightly, "Better late than never, huh?"

"I'm so ashamed of myself." I bend into his shoulder, and he strokes my hair. "It had real consequences, and I can never make it right."

"We've all done terrible things, Phoebe. Sometimes you just have to live with them."

I take a breath and straighten. "I guess. But I'd like to make amends somehow if I can."

"It's cold in here," he says. "Let's go get some dinner, shall we?"

"Yes. Let's do that."

Then he kisses me. It's gentle at first, and then it isn't. "Would you want to go to London for a while?" I ask. "Maybe we could explore a little."

"I might like that."

"Good," I murmur, standing up on my toes. Kiss him again.

"Hey," he says, taking my hand. He's looking over my shoulder. "There's something going on at Suze's place."

A cold squeeze steals the air from my lungs as I follow his gaze and see flashing lights. Police lights or maybe ambulance. Emergency lights, red and blue. My heart squeezes so hard I'm afraid it's going to explode. "Oh my God."

Chapter Twenty-Eight
Suze

I'm soaked by the time I get back to the house. I lock the door behind me and disrobe in the foyer, shivering, then dash through the kitchen into the master bath, where I turn the shower on hot. It's a glorious shower, with a rain head and all the bells and whistles. A window of glass brick allows a row of plants to grow in the humid light.

As I shampoo my hair, I wonder what to do about Phoebe. At first, her withholding the letter infuriated me, but I know it wasn't the current-day Phoebe who did it. And yet, some of what I said was true—she's riddled with little jealousies and her expectations are purely exhausting. We can't keep having fights like this, fights that erupt over nothing and turn bitter within moments. How do we fix it? And if we can't, how can I walk away?

When I'm dried and dressed in warm clothes, I pad into the kitchen, texting Joel. Will I see you tonight?

Nothing comes back immediately. Vaguely hungry, vaguely restless, I peer into the fridge. A fridge that has not been magically restocked by someone who knows my tastes and knows what I want in there. I'm going to have to figure out how to do my own shopping, or maybe I can find someone to help with some of these tasks. Do I really have to cook? Although I liked cooking during the pandemic, I'm not interested in cooking everyday meals. If I have someone to do the shopping and maybe make a few meals every week, I can probably do the rest.

I shake my head, laughing. So spoiled. But so what? I earned it, and it employs others and I'm not going to start feeling guilty just because I'm not living in the hothouse of Hollywood. I choose an apple—

And an arm grabs me around the neck, pulling me down.

My body responds before my mind registers what's happening, and my mind only wants to roar a loud white-noise warning. *Danger danger danger danger*—

Instinctively, I swing my elbow backward, feeling the bone connect with ribs, and a grunt escapes, then a roar.

"You think you're so smart, don't you?" he growls, and swings my body down sideways, knocking me off-center so I go down hard on one knee. I bend into the fall, pulling his weight with me, and manage to slip out of his grip. My heart is racing, but my mind is suddenly crystal clear. *Stay aware. Stay alive.*

I shove him and run for the door, but he grabs my hair and yanks me down.

My hair.

As I feel my body falling, weightless, about to crash, something in me breaks open. The girl I was, the one who had to suffer the brutal attacks of a man she couldn't fight back, lands and leaps almost in one gesture, and instead of running away, I whirl to face him. Him, the man from the restaurant, shorter than me, pale and bleary eyed. He smells of sweat and gasoline and his fingernails are grimy.

I bend and hurtle forward, aiming to ram my shoulder into his midsection. Instead, my right shoulder connects with his chin, and I hear a crack before he grabs me and we fall, hard, on the wooden floor. I feel my shoulder slam the table in the foyer, but I scramble to keep him on the floor, trying to elude his hands. He suddenly uses a wrestling move, and before I know what happened, I'm pinned beneath him, his eyes mean and small. He starts to yank at my waistband, greed wetting his lips. "Big movie star," he sneers. "Still a dumbass fucking girl."

With a singular cry, I bring my hands up between his arms, flinging his sideways, and as he's knocked off-balance I scramble diagonally, kicking him when he tries to grab my ankle. My body sends the table to the floor along with the candlestick lamp. Feeling his hands grasping my thighs, I grab the lamp and bring it down on his head with every bit of strength in my body. When he's still grabbing my body, I swing it again, harder.

He goes still. I scramble from beneath him and he doesn't move. Blood pours out from a gash across the top of his skull. It is possible he is dead.

Limping, I head into the kitchen, one eye on him. I grab the phone and dash through the back door, running down the stairs and all the way to the beach, where I feel safe enough to stop and call 911. When they're on their way, I call Joel, who promises to be there in five minutes.

For a moment, my thumb hovers over Phoebe's number, but I don't click on it. Instead, I stand in the rain in the dark, shivering.

Long ago, when I was in the mall with Phoebe, I saw that rainbow tennis bracelet and wondered what kind of wife would be awarded such a beautiful prize. It turned out that wife was me, my own gift to myself.

My gift to myself is survival, over and over. I hear Gloria Gaynor in my mind, singing, and it makes me laugh, ever so slightly hysterically. It the darkness, I'm proud of myself. And I'm grateful to Beryl, because without her, I might have survived, but I wouldn't have thrived.

On the hill, the lights in the studio are blazing, and my heart reaches for Phoebe, even if that relationship is something I need to let go of. I don't know if the relationship is broken beyond repair, or if we can find a way to build something from the ruins.

Joel comes down the stairs with a heavy blanket. He wraps me in it, and we go back up the stairs to meet emergency services. The man lies in a pool of his own blood, and in the back of my mind I wonder if it's going to leave a bad stain that will remind me of this forever, but the thought is so callous, I'm slightly shocked.

"Is he dead?" I ask the EMT.

"Nah," he says. "Way to knock him out, though. He'll have a nasty headache when he comes to."

"Badass," Joel says, trying to lighten the mood.

I give him a wan smile.

"Let's get a look at that cut," the other EMT says. "Can you come in the kitchen and let me take a look? It's dark in here."

"Cut?" I echo, but follow orders.

When I sit down, she blots my forehead. "You need stitches. Are you comfortable with me doing it, or do you maybe want to call a plastic surgeon?"

"A plastic surgeon? In Blue Cove?" I laugh.

She shrugs. "I'm guessing you care more about this than most people."

"Sorry. You're very sensitive, thank you. Can I see it?"

She holds up her phone on selfie camera mode and I see a jagged gash along my hairline. It has soaked the hair around it a pale pink and blood is still leaking out of it. "Wow. I don't remember getting this."

"Adrenaline."

"Go ahead and sew it up," I say. "It will never show."

As she deadens the area around the cut, Joel prowls through the house, opening closets and looking in cupboards. I wince at the needle but, in three minutes, can't feel anything. The guy is carted off to a hospital somewhere, and she's still stitching. "This is going to be a cool scar, isn't it?"

"Yeah," she agrees with a little laugh. "You earned it."

In my hand, my phone rings. I tilt the screen to where I can see the caller, and of course it's Phoebe, because she can probably see the lights from the studio. I let it go to voice mail.

It rings again. "Joel!" I call. "Can you answer this, please?"

He takes the phone. "She's okay. Long story, but she's fine and they have the guy who has been terrorizing her." He listens. "No, don't come up right now. I'll have her call you when she can."

He hangs up. "Good?"

"Yeah," I say. "Great."

And I actually mean it. I don't have to talk to her until I'm ready. If I ever get ready. This is my decision and I don't have to rush it.

Chapter Twenty-Nine
Phoebe

Suze has not answered a text or phone call for nearly a week. I found out from Ben that the same guy who'd been harassing her, starting at the Pig 'N Pancake, had broken in and Suze kicked his ass, basically.

I see her on the deck while I'm painting. I see her walking on the beach, sometimes with Joel. She came to see Jasmine off when she decided to return to England with Stephanie, but didn't even look at me.

Which is fair. Although, really, she must know how hard it is for me to let Jasmine go early. Before I could express as much to Ben, I realize that I've put my own agenda at the center of the friendship again, and it's time to let Suze do that.

If we even have a friendship left.

When a week stretches to two, then three, my heart is breaking so much that I know I have to make the first move. I have to try to somehow make amends. I know I can't fix the past, but I have to try to be present with what I've done. Rather than call, I scour the town for a box of stationery, and find only the most basic pale blue, meant for old ladies. Which, technically, I suppose we have become. It has that distinctive rose-lavender-flower scent, and that's enough for me.

Sitting at the studio table with classical music playing, I take out a sheaf of paper and begin to write.

Dear Suze,

I have spent so much time thinking about our friendship in the past few weeks, about my bad behavior and the ways I've let you down, and if things were reversed, I don't know if I could forgive you.

But I miss you so much it's like someone has chopped off my left arm. I think I can manage okay without it, and then I need to drain the pasta, and it's obvious that I really do need that arm.

I miss you.

I'm sorry. I'm sorry for hiding the letter. I'm sorry for always being so jealous and hostile. I'm sorry that I fought with you at our grandmother's funeral. It was my fault. I don't know why I got so mad.

That's a lie. I wanted to keep Amma to myself. I didn't want to admit that she loved you every single bit as much as she loved me. I wanted to keep you to myself, too, and not share you with Amma, or my dad, or Joel, and even worse, the entire world. The whole world knows you and that made me protective and jealous. Like, they don't know you. Not like I do. They don't know that you love sauerkraut even though it's the worst food in the world. They don't know that your favorite shirt is a sloppy T-shirt from the '90s. They don't know all the things you've had to get through in your life, your horrible father, the loss of your baby and Joel.

If I think of your shaved head, even now, I will cry.

I am so sorry I wasn't there for you when you needed me—so many times, but mainly when you were alone in that awful unwed mothers' home and I only went to see you one time. I don't know what I was thinking, and it actually doesn't matter. I let you down when you needed me most. I can't fix that, but I can tell you I know it was wrong, and I am so sorry. I hope I can make it up to you someday.

I'm most sorry for keeping the letter, and for all the ramifications of that. There is no possible way to make up for it, but I want you to know that I'm going to spend my life trying if you'll let me.

I don't know if our friendship is broken completely. If you feel like you can't be friends with me anymore, I will understand. This is all on me. I will never blame you for one second.

But if you think you can eventually forgive me, I will be down at the Starfish Sisters at 10 am on Tuesday the 12th, no matter what the weather. If you want to work on this, meet me there.

No matter what happens, Suze, know that I love you. You're one of the best people I know, loving and supportive and good. So much like Amma. She would be so proud of you. I'm proud of you.

I love you, I love you, I love you.
Your sister,
Phoebe

Chapter Thirty

Suze

Predictably, it's raining on the morning of the twelfth, but I don my wet-weather gear like the true Oregonian I am and head down the steps to the beach. I can see Phoebe down by the rocks, wearing red boots and a hooded rain jacket. She's peering into the tide pools, and as I come down, I see her stick a finger into the water. I know her touch is gentle. She's only moving something around, not bothering nature.

I thought long and hard about her letter. I didn't rush. I talked to Beryl in my mind, and Joel in real life, and we all came to the same conclusion—that Phoebe needs me. I also need her. My life would be so much thinner without her.

As I approach, she straightens. "Hi," she says.

"Hi. Anything interesting?"

"Yeah." Her face lights up. "A purple sea star. He's big."

I bend in to look, feeling water splatter against my hood. The sea star truly is enormous, a foot across and chunky. "Wow."

We stand at the same moment. She waits, and I'm grateful, because I need to choose my words. "Phoebe," I say, hands in my pockets. "I was so mad at you over the letter you hid that I didn't trust myself to have a conversation, but I've worked through it now. It was a terrible thing you did."

She bows her head. "I know. I'm so sorry."

"It was wrong of me to hide my relationship with Joel, too, and I'm sorry for that."

"I was complicit. I never admitted it to myself, but I did know you two were in love. It was so obvious sometimes."

I incline my head. "It was? What do you mean?"

"I'm not sure." She looks toward the top of the sea stacks, back to me. "Like you moved in tandem, as if you knew what the other person would do. It started at the beginning."

I nod. Close my eyes and think of all that was lost and all that came about because it was lost. "I wouldn't have had my career if I'd kept my baby. I would have had another life, maybe even a really good one, but I wouldn't be the me I am now, and that would be a loss, too."

"It would be," she agrees.

"I really don't want to live in a world without you, Phoebe."

"Really?"

I look at her, open my arms. "You are my person. You always have been."

She flings herself into my hug, and it's a tight, tight embrace. I feel the years, the months, the days, the hours rush through us, Phoebe at twelve and twenty and forty-five, myself at the same ages. I see us eating, and laughing, and shopping for our birthdays, and writing letters and notes and diaries. I see fights and making up and cooking some more.

"I love you," I say.

"I love you more," she says.

"You're right," I say, and we both laugh.

"It's freezing out here," she says at last.

"Want some tea? I have some fresh oolong."

"Absolutely."

NOW

F*cking Perfect

Chapter Thirty-One
Suze

A light snow is falling beyond the windows of the bedroom I've taken over as my office. A desk, built to match the Wright-era furnishings in the house, is tucked under a wide window overlooking the same view as the kitchen and the bedroom, endless ocean and rocks, and I had an open grid built just outside so that my seagull can join me while I work—he and his many friends. I don't feed them, but they're curious and like to watch me work anyway.

After the dearth of good scripts through the fall, I decided to form a production company of my own, teaming with four other industry women to find scripts centered on women over fifty. Once we started looking for original material, there was a lot of it—and we're also optioning several books. I am writing a script, too. I don't know if it's anything at all yet, but it feels good to stretch my creative muscles in a new way.

The man who attacked me was an LNB wannabe. He's awaiting trial, and I have no doubt he'll serve some time. I am still on the LNB lists and that won't go away, but Joel has installed major security features around the house, including cameras and motion sensors and an alarm system worthy of museums. It's what we can do. Living can be dangerous, but I refuse to hide from it.

Joel comes to the door. "You ready?"

"Yes." I add three words to the sentence, save, and shut down the program. Joel waits. He doesn't live with me, but things are easy, and sexy, and good, and I suspect it won't be long until he does. We'd be fools to turn our backs on such a dramatic second chance. He looks particularly good in a red shirt and jeans, his hair shiny and pulled away from his face. "You're looking fine."

He smooths a hand down his shirtfront. "Good?"

"Very."

We drive to Astoria, a beautiful small town at the mouth of the Columbia River. Neither of us speaks much, and it's okay—we're both reliving memories and dreaming of the future. It's a soft winter day, sometimes snowing a little higher up, sometimes drizzling below. The idea had been to go to a park, but it's too cold and instead we're meeting at a shopping mall.

I take a breath. Joel takes my hand and squeezes it. My heart is pounding, but with anticipation. "Let's do it," he says.

We walk to the food court and stand by a window, looking around anxiously.

A woman who has been sitting at a table stands. She has the darkest black hair, cut in a short, modern style that frames a face that could have been molded from Joel's. She's taller than average, and lanky, as we both are. She waves tentatively, and takes the hands of two children, about eight and nine.

"She's so beautiful," I breathe, and Joel squeezes my fingers. We move toward her.

"Veronica?" I ask as we reach her.

Her eyes are filled with tears that suddenly spill down her father's face. "When you said Suze, I didn't know you'd be Suze *Ogden*. You're famous," she says. "I hope you didn't think—"

"Never," I breathe, and, impulsively, lean in to hug her, tears streaming down my face, too. I smell her hair—she smells of apples, and I can feel the tiny weight of her baby self in my arms and all the years in between, both there and not there. A piece of me I didn't even know was missing falls into place.

After a long moment, I let her go, and pull Joel in. "Is it all right if I hug you, too?" she asks.

"Yes," he says, and he takes her into his embrace, his eyes closed. I think of him burning down the church, of the letter he wrote that never was delivered. I think of her face when she was so tiny and at least I had that.

After a moment, he releases her and clears his throat. "It's good to meet you."

"Yes." She, too, is emotional, and we are strangers but not strangers and it's both intensely beautiful and awkward. "These are my children, Alexa and Renee."

I'm struggling to keep my face composed to avoid letting tears fall, but it's very hard. I can't even speak.

"I've been hoping for a DNA match for years and years," she said. "I'm so glad you did the test."

I'm still unable to speak. She has my eyes, the same particular aquamarine, in Joel's angular face, and so does one of her children. "You're so beautiful," I say.

The children endure it for a long moment, and then they point to the center jungle gym. "Can we go play now?"

We laugh and sit down and begin the business of getting to know each other.

Acknowledgments

Sometimes, a book changes your life. In 2021, my husband and I took a long car trip up the coast of Oregon, and there is no way to express how deeply I fell in love with that wild, rocky, lonely, beautiful place. I found myself returning every few months, writing this book, looking at the waves and the seagulls and the skies, walking the beaches endlessly.

Thanks to the Waves Motel in Cannon Beach, where I wrote a *lot* of pages, and made friends with a giant seagull who banged on the window to get my attention. I did not feed him, but he came back anyway. A lot.

Thanks to the Haystack Rock Awareness Program in Cannon Beach (for a happy treat, follow them on Instagram at https://www.instagram.com/haystackrockawareness), particularly Lisa Habeker, who listened patiently to all my questions and waded with me through the tide pools to tell me all about the creatures that live there, and roost in the rocks, and create their own worlds. I fell in love with sea stars and puffins thanks to you, with all the magical, strange worlds along the edge of the sea.

Thank you to my wonderful team at Lake Union, particularly my editor Alicia Clancy, and all the hardworking people in marketing and PR who do so much heavy lifting on behalf of my books, especially Ashley Vanicek. Thank you to Shasti O'Leary Soudant for my beautiful covers. Thanks, always and forever, to my badass agent, Meg Ruley, who has been holding down the corners of my career for more years than I would say aloud. Your laugh is one of my favorite things.

And always, thank you to Neal, who walks dogs and does dishes and soothes me when I'm tangled up in my own head. I'm so glad I found you.

Oh, and dear reader, I moved to the Oregon coast, to a house with windows like Suze's, overlooking a moody, rocky beach. Sometimes, a book leads a writer home.

About the Author

Photo © 2009 Blue Fox Photography

Barbara O'Neal is the *Washington Post, Wall Street Journal, USA Today*, and Amazon Charts bestselling author of more than a dozen novels of women's fiction, including the #1 Amazon Charts bestseller *When We Believed in Mermaids* and *This Place of Wonder*. Her award-winning books have been published in over two dozen countries. She lives on the Oregon coast with her husband, a British endurance athlete who vows he'll never lose his accent. To learn more about Barbara and her work, visit her online at www.barbaraoneal.com.